THE MASCOT

ANA SHAY

ISBN 9798737978150

To all the mascots out there, I see you.

Especially you, Blooper!

Chapter 1

CALI

"No. No. No! There is no way I'm doing this!" Tresses of blonde hair fall from my perfect top bun because I'm shaking my head so vigorously. A cool, calm, and composed marketing intern was the impression I was trying to make this morning. But, yeah, that went down the toilet fast.

Okay, any of the employees watching this scenario may think I'm being overly dramatic, but they aren't the ones being asked to do this. I am.

And there's no way in hell I'm doing it. Mary can beg me until the cows come home, but I refuse to be brought into this humiliating and degrading task. I may be a life-long Fish fan but in the words of the almighty Meatloaf. I would do anything for love, but I won't do that.

"Come on, Cali. You know I wouldn't ask if it wasn't important." My best friend, or should I say *ex*-best friend, Mary, whines next to me. She may have helped me score this internship with an awesome recommendation, but that doesn't mean she can hold it against me for the rest of the year.

I shake my head, laughing bitterly to myself. In a way, it's kind of funny. I never thought this day would come, the day my love for the

Carolina Catfish would be tested to such an extreme. But, alas, it seems I have finally found the limits of my love for the team in the form of a neoprene costume.

Her head tilts as her eyes plead with me. She looks ridiculous, standing there with a mascot head the size of her torso chained to her side, like a child clutching at their favorite toy. I wet my lips, ready to say no again and tell her there is absolutely no way I'm going to do this. That is until she pulls out her secret weapon. The same one she's used against me since we were kids, and it's always worked.

With her eyes glossed over, she pops her bottom lip out, letting it tremble in time with her chin. I can see her eyes brimming, ready to shed those big, fat, wet droplets. Tears are my biggest weakness, and she knows that. They make me so uncomfortable; I swear I start breaking out in hives and give in to anything she wants so that she'll stop.

A single fat tear escapes her left eye, dripping down her cheek like the sweat soaking through my blouse. One. Two. More tears start flowing. If I'm not careful, she might even do that gross snot inhale.

Man, she's good. She's fully prepared to go into full meltdown mode in front of the entire marketing department – and my new work colleagues – just to get her way.

Sighing, I look toward the sea of desks, trying to find another answer. One that doesn't involve me before Mary unleashes enough tears to fill the bottom of Niagara Falls. Everyone is too worried about opening night to notice our fishy dilemma.

My pulse rises as I check my watch. 6:20. Damn. We're nearly out of time. Catty the Catfish needs to be out there in front of the fans in thirty minutes. With slumped shoulders, I drag my eyes back to her, begging, pleading, and hoping she'll take pity on me. "Isn't there someone else that can do it?" I whisper. Mary drops her eyes, still holding the headpiece, and takes in a long inhale. Her hapless demeanor is slowly breaking my resolve.

"I wish I could say there was, but I don't think there is. The costume was made to fit Tim; he's 6 foot 3." Her eyes flitter up and down my form. "You're the only person even close enough to his size in the marketing department."

Damn Tim and his obsessive-compulsive need for Funyuns.

Of all the days in the year, Tim just *had* to pick today to celebrate the start of the season with Funyuns before work. But, unfortunately, that ogre of a man was so focused on the Funyuns calling his name at the end of the aisle that he didn't bother reading the '*Wet Floor*' sign sitting on the tiles. He was already running late, so thought it would be a great idea to run down the snack aisle toward his one true love. The joke now firmly sits with me because he ended up slipping on his butt and breaking his leg.

The store felt so bad; they gave him a year's supply of Funyuns. So, while he is out, eating his obscene supply of corn snacks, Mary and I are left fretting about who will take the Mascot helm for the next eight weeks.

What kind of Major League Baseball team doesn't have a backup mascot plan?

The Carolina Catfish, apparently.

Well, I should correct that. *I* didn't think we had a plan. Mary always had one, it seems, and she's looking right at it. My stomach pits out as another tear drops down her cheek.

Of course, being a tall girl has always come with a string of disadvantages, but I've always been able to overcome them through extensive therapy.

However, no amount of sessions with Dr. Keppler could prepare me for this moment. No, there's no way I could imagine explaining this scenario to him without him having me committed on the spot for incoherent rambling.

Dr. Keppler, my best friend wants me to dress up as a giant, baseball-loving human catfish hybrid and dance around the stadium in front of our 40,000 strong home crowd.

It's crazy, ridiculous, and the worst thing you could ever ask of a tall girl.

"Please, please, please!" Mary drops the mascot head and falls to her knees, begging me. As if she isn't short enough, she thinks this begging helps her case, but all it does is remind me that I'm a giant amongst men in the marketing department. 5 foot 11 isn't *that* tall. The average height for a baseball pitcher is 6 foot 2; there's got to be one in the bullpen that could wear the costume just for today. In fact, I've got a perfect idea; they could alternate according to the pitching rotation. There's always a few pitchers with nothing better to do than sit in the dugout, chewing gum. So why not take that day of rest and do something meaningful for the team? Perfect plan! Although, with only an hour before Catty the Catfish makes his first appearance, I won't have time to write up the rotation.

Out of the corner of my eye, I notice Larry, the maintenance man, changing a lightbulb for one of the desk lamps.

A wide grin pulls across my face as the lamp lights up in time to the idea in my head. Then, dragging Mary from the floor, I whisper. "Couldn't we ask Larry to do it?" She follows my eyes, her brain working with the same thought. Yes, this could work. He's always loved the fish and declares that he would do anything for them daily. The other week, he was wearing nothing but a fin on his head – with pants, of course. He'd totally love wearing the new mascot outfit. It would be something he could tell his friends about in that catfish mancave he made in his basement.

Mary says nothing, still contemplating Larry as an option.

My palms rub together, and I have trouble holding back my maniacal grin.

Have I just gotten out of this?

"Larry doesn't know the dance routine," she whispers, and my shoulders collapse in defeat. "You're the only one that knows the choreography. It's Catty's first appearance, so it's important we get it right and show off his personality."

Life stops for a moment, and my mind drifts back to when I was eight, begging my mom to let me take those Justin Bieber dance lessons. Imagine if she had said no and forced me to go to that advanced tie-dye class instead. My entire life trajectory could have been different. I wouldn't be standing here contemplating shoving a fish head over my shoulders, that's for sure.

Catty's head lolls on the floor, its big googly eyes watching me with intent. Staring. Silently begging me to put him on. Well, at least he's better than last year's fisherman design.

"Come on; it will be fun." The lilt in Mary's voice and the curve of her lip does little to make her statement sound convincing. Fun? If it's so much *fun,* why don't we have a queue of people lining up for the job? Even Carl with the wondering eye in IT, wouldn't be convinced if he could hear her. And that guy would do anything for her. My laptop breaks down on the daily, and all I get is a snarky email telling me to lodge a ticket. Mary loses her charger, and he's up here in a shot with five brand new chargers in his hands.

Back and forth. Back and forth.

Catty's head lolls back and forth like a ticking time bomb.

Why did I believe all those college lecturers when they told me I'm built for marketing?

'*Go into marketing,*' they said.

'*You get to work on great brands and bring your personality into them,*' they said.

Sure, they were right for the most part. I've spent the first few months here helping to redesign Catty. I even got to create this awesome dance routine that will undoubtedly become his signature move.

So far, I've loved my job, and working for my favorite team has been a dream come true. Born and raised in Charlotte, I've grown up with the Carolina Catfish on my door, and I've loved every hit I've ever watched in their stadium, lovingly nicknamed 'The Tank.' But, dressing up as a fish with no pants on, in front of our sold-out homestand… That's not exactly what I've dreamed of.

"We can't back out now. We've spent thousands on this rebrand, and upper management will kill us. Scratch that. They won't kill us. We'll just be fired on the spot. Imagine how badly Josh would take it if we didn't find a solution."

My eyes drift to Josh's office. I can clearly see him yelling down the phone as he screws up bundles of papers in his fists. He's hated me since the first day I showed up here, and this would be his perfect excuse to get rid of me.

My stomach drops, my heart beats so fast I can hear it against my ears.

She's right. We don't have any other options.

I close my eyes, sighing out an exasperated breath. I guess I have to give into my destiny. "I'm going to have to do this, aren't I?" I ask, my eyes still closed, my body still. It's a strange sensation when you let all control go.

Let go. Be present.

My mom's words radiate throughout my body as the silence between Mary and me grows, making me question all of my life choices.

Mary waits a good few minutes for it all to sink in. Then, when I've finally accepted there is no other option than me dressing up as our mascot, I snatch the head from the floor. I swear, for the tiniest of moments, I hear the head yelp in excitement. Yeah, I'm losing it. "Fine, I'll do it." I swivel on my heel, pointing my perfectly manicured finger down at her. Still on her knees, she's making me look like Aaron Judge standing next to José Altuve at second base. "But just this once," I emphasize. "You have to promise me you'll find a solution for the next game."

She bites her bottom lip, giving me those damn puppy dog eyes again. "You know I can't promise that, Cali. The next game is tomorrow, remember?"

My eyes widen as I throw my head back dramatically and swipe my face. Groaning, I let the full realization of what I've signed up for wash over me. "I'm going to have to do this for at least the next four nights, aren't I?"

When I drop my hand, Mary smiles at me sympathetically and nods slowly. Could the world just open up and suck me into its hellish depths now? That would make all of this disappear and be marginally less embarrassing than what I'm about to do.

"Fine," I yell dramatically, stomping off in the direction of the bathrooms. Then, with the giant fish head in hand, I grumble over my shoulder, "where's my mini baseball cap?!"

Googly eyes, whiskered nose, and giant bobbing mouth.

Catty's head rests on the bathroom vanity, staring at me with the intensity of a man in love. Those big eyes cut through me and are a reminder of how Carl looks at Mary. Desperate and longing.

The shimmering blue of the costume glints under the harsh bathroom light and forces me to look at myself in the mirror. I hate to admit it, but Mary has a point. This costume is huge, and no one else on the team would have been able to pull this off. Hell, I barely pull it off myself.

Turning to the side, I pat down the slightly protruding belly, surprised at how roomy the costume is. I could stuff a sandwich in here, and no one would know. But, strangely, as Catty's head stares at me and I look at myself in the mirror, I start to feel something. It's a strong emotion that radiates through my chest.

It feels a lot like pride. Pride that I wouldn't admit I had outside this room.

"Oh my God!" Mary squeals as she opens the door. Scurrying in, she jumps to her tiptoes and grabs my shoulders, forcing me to look at myself in the mirror. "Take a good look at yourself, Cali," she says as the gray speckles in the furry fabric shine like a wet fish. "It's like this costume was made for you." Her eyes dart up and down in awe of my outfit. She looks prouder than my mom did when I somehow managed to bag Gary Finnegan as my Freshman Formal date. It was my first dance, and he was captain of the mathletes with one of those big head braces. She was just happy he was 6 foot 5, so I could wear heels and not look like a giraffe because she was certain I'd forever be destined to a life of sensible shoes and hunching.

"The fans are going to love this!" She's dancing in the small space she has now, and I'd join her in that excitement if I didn't have this deep, thick sense of dread in the pit of my stomach.

I'm not exactly the most graceful person in the world, and the last time I performed on stage starts to replay in my mind. I was eleven and was supposed to be the Sugar Plum Fairy for my ballet class. It was the year before my growth spurt and the last time I ever truly felt like I fitted in. I bumbled around the stage but took the wrong step, losing my balance. That one moment started a crescendo of disasters. I fell into the kid playing the tree, who knocked over the cardboard castle backdrop and ripped it in two. The entire ballet class was hiding behind that backdrop and were revealed to the audience.

The laughter and sniggers of the parents still haunts me to this day.

Ever since that moment, I've preferred choreographing for fun and have desperately tried to stay out of the limelight.

"The players will love it too." Mary squeezes my arms, trying to reassure me. Every squeeze only serves as a reminder that Tate Sorenson will see me in this.

The Tate Sorenson.

The best thing that has ever happened to The Carolina Catfish. The five-time golden glove winner is the only reason we even get talked about on sports networks. The consistent and reliable franchise player.

He's not so bad on the eyes either. Those who know me might say I have the teeniest, tiniest crush on our team's shortstop.

Okay, that's a lie.

It's a full-blown obsession, and it's the first time since putting this stupid outfit on that I'm happy in the knowledge that at least he can't see my face in this. Me dressed as an overweight man-fish isn't exactly the first impression I want to make.

"You're going to kill it. I can feel it." Mary grins, and I give her a hesitant smile back. I try to clench my fists together to ease some of the tension building inside, but the fin-like hands make that impossible.

Scrunching my eyebrows together instead, I don't think too long about my next words. "Let's just get this over with," I grunt, shoving the giant head over my face and letting Mary escort me down to the field. I will have to get used to the limited view I have out of this thing.

"You'll do great." Mary clutches my fin tightly, probably ensuring I don't bolt and leave the stadium. When we get to the Bullpen doors, she wraps my fins around our new blue ATV. "Are you ready for this?" She asks.

Throwing one leg over the seat, I take a deep breath. "Ready as I'll ever be," I say through the fish head.

The organ music starts to blare around the stadium, my body tenses at its implication. That's my cue.

Gripping the ATV as much as I can with these fins on, I take a deep breath.

Here goes nothing.

CHAPTER 2

TATE

Breathing in, a sense of comfort drifts over me as I look over the field. The grass is dewy, and as I stand there in my brand new jersey, spinning one of my brand new bats in my hand, only one thing comes to mind.

Home.

That's where I am, and after a season without playing October baseball, I'm happy to be back on my very own field of dreams. There's a slight bite in the cool April air; perfect spring baseball weather.

I scan the field, watching the rest of my team warm up until they land on the thick, springy grass between second and third base. My spot. I can't wait to wear it down.

It's been six years and four hundred games since I joined the Carolina Catfish, and I couldn't ask for a better team. Five Golden Gloves and two Silver Sluggers later, I still have so much more to accomplish with The Fish. I owe it to them after they took such a big chance on me. I was drafted into my home team, the Houston Knights, when I was nineteen. I'd been coasting along in their Minor League system for the better part of two years, never finding my groove, and then I caught a ball wrong, suffering a season-ending wrist injury. I thought my dreams of being a Major Leaguer were over and felt defeated when I heard they were planning on packaging me out in a trade deal.

I was disappointed and demoralized. What Major League Team would want a mediocre, injured shortstop? I was ready to retire and thought I was destined to be a mechanic like my dad. But then the Carolina Catfish happened.

Stepping onto the blue catfish logo stained onto the grass next to Homeplate, I look around at the stands. The only reason I'm here is that the GM saw something in me when no one else did. He called me personally, telling me he was taking on all these other players just to get me. Told me I better prove my worth and work.

Work I did.

I will never forget the risk he took and the opportunity the team gave me. After a year of rehab and training with their Triple-A team, the Minnows, I became the starting shortstop for the Carolina Catfish. I've been delivering MVP caliber seasons ever since. Being the fan-favorite and Fish for life, there's only one thing missing in my career – apart from that world series win, of course. I believe my sister put it best. I'm always the bridesmaid, never the bride. Over the last five years, I've come second or third in the MVP race. Never quite good enough to win, but always in the running.

"Hey, Steady," Grayson, our ace pitcher, grins as he slaps me on the shoulder. I hate that nickname. Being a quick, safe pair of hands with a good throw may make me the perfect shortstop, but it's not exactly the sexiest trait in baseball.

"Watch me strike you out," Grayson barks out confidently, hopping onto the mound like an excited kangaroo. Then, shivering, he makes some weird warm-up noise that sounds a lot like a strangled cat. I've said it before; I'll say it again, pitchers are weird.

Standing on the plate, I nod to our catcher, Marc, who rolls his eyes at Grayson's antics. I fly the bat over my shoulder, widening my stance to get into position. Grayson narrows his eyes, staring me down. He gives nothing away with his glare as he and Marc decide the pitch. As he lifts his leg, his left eyebrow twitches, and I immediately know he's throwing a fastball.

As the ball leaves his hand, I let the motion of my swing take over my body, putting all my weight into my left leg.

Clunk.

The bat strikes the ball precisely where I wanted it to, sending it straight to the back of the yard where one of our outfielders, Tommy, catches it with ease.

Unfazed by my hit, Grayson watches the ball with a smile stretched across his face. Then, he sets up for his next throw, staring me down. As the ball heads my way, I tip my toes, throwing my crotch back because the ball barely misses my pelvis. "Watch it, Gray," I yell, throwing my bat on the ground, annoyed that he pitched so close to the crown jewels for practice.

He shrugs, unbothered. "Atlanta loves to pitch you on the inside. I'm just testing your reflexes." He's not wrong. Out of the twenty times I've been hit by a pitch, Atlanta is accountable for twelve of them. To say they have a vendetta against me would be an understatement. They've hated me ever since I caught a hit, making them lose a chance in the playoffs a few years ago.

Grayson sets up, and as he throws the ball, his eyebrow twitches again. Another fastball is coming, and I'm going to hit it. *Clunk.* It happens again, only this time; it's too far back for Tommy. I watch my near homer bounce off the back wall. It's a double, at least. I hop over to second base, taking my time to admire the hit. At 6 foot 6, my body isn't built for speed, but my stride makes up for it. I'm on the second base before Tommy has the chance to compose himself and throw the ball back.

This right here is precisely why I'm batted fourth. I'm the clean-up guy, the one you can rely on to get the players with more flair home. Hence the stupid nickname, Steady. Unfortunately, the more reliable I've become, the less opportunity I get to show my stuff. As a result, I've been the most walked player in the National League for the last four years, which sucks, and seriously affects my MVP nominations.

Today marks the first day of my new ten-year contract with the Fish. I was the big free agent of the year, and although I got a lot of offers from other teams, the Fish still managed to offer me the best bucks. I neglected to tell them that I'd pretty much decided to take whatever they offered because of loyalty to the team. I still wanted them to bid competitively, of course. But, I certainly didn't expect the highest contract offer to come from them. I couldn't be happier, knowing I'd retire a bottom feeder.

It's crazy to think I've been playing baseball professionally for eight years, and I'm not even halfway through my guaranteed playing career – barring any major injury, of course.

Standing on second base, I watch Grayson gear up for another pitch, but before he can throw, a loud honk gets my attention.

"Ladies and gentlemen," the deep baritone voice of the announcer calls through the speakers as the organ player plays '*Under the Sea*.' "It's the moment you've all been waiting for." The words roll off his tongue as the crowd cheer. "Would you like to meet the most anticipated, newest Mascot of the Carolina Catfish?" I'm glad they've finally changed him. The last one was a fisherman, and his googly eyes freaked me the hell out. Every time I had to appear with him, I couldn't look him in the face, too concerned he was judging me with his haughty gaze.

"Allow me to introduce you to… Catty the Catfish." The audience cheer, and confetti spurts from the outfield, trickling onto the dewy grass. I startle when the Bullpen opens with a bang, and a Catfish themed ATV comes bounding out. I had no idea we even had one of those. Glancing around the field, the other players look just as confused.

That's when I see Catty for the first time; the most magnificent man-fish I've ever seen. I saw drawings of him before the season started, but nothing could prepare me for the dance moves he flips out on one fin while driving with the other. It's a dangerous combination that I'm not sure Catty is pulling off. The vehicle goes all over the place, and Catty looks unbalanced perched on top.

"Sorenson, it's time," Grayson calls, waving me toward the dugout. I jog off the field while volunteers run onto the grass with t-shirt guns, shooting the freebies out to the crowd. Then, standing next to the dugout, I drape my bat across my arms, stretching my shoulders while talking to a few of the players in the dugout, paying no attention to the raucous going on behind me.

'Tate. Tate. Tate.' The crowd chants my name, drawing my attention to the spectators. Strange, we haven't started the game, so why are they cheering me on?

"Sorenson. Get out of the way!" Coach Rantz yells from the side of the field, and it takes me a second to register the panic in his voice. A second too long. The deafening noise of a revved-up engine hits me before I have time to think, and just like that, everything starts to move in slow motion.

A rush of cool air whips across my face as the ATV misses me by inches, sliding straight into the dugout wall. The players inside the dugout, back up, shocked at the bang. I blow out a long breath.

That was a close call.

I spoke too soon. Pain ricochets through my back, and I feel a hard blow as I fall to the floor, bouncing on my chin and whacking my jaw.

Silence.

The entire crowd has been shocked into silence from whatever is pinning me to the ground. Lying face down, eating dust, I try to get up, but the weight on top of me is too heavy. I strain my neck to see what's blocking my movement, and it's then I see Catty's lifeless form draped across me, lying over my torso like some kind of dead fish. "Are you okay?" I kick my leg, watching his fin move, but he doesn't acknowledge me. Shit. Have I actually killed our mascot on opening day?

That would put a serious downer on the season.

The low hum of *Under the Sea* still plays as the crowd watches on. I start to hear more movement in the dugout, but from the sounds of it, the ATV is blocking their exit.

After a few minutes, I make my move. "Catty, are you okay?" I ask, worried that he actually *is* dead. It's been a good five minutes, and he hasn't moved. A dead mascot wouldn't be the best start to a season.

To my relief, I feel Catty moving above me, his muscles freezing in shock. I watch as he slowly raises his mascot head and turns to look directly at me. I'm nose to nose with the whiskered and opened mouthed fish. Damn it. The new googly eyes creep me out just as much as the old ones. He stares at me, his mouth flapping ever so slightly, then he slowly turns his giant head to the crowd, then back to me.

In an instant, he jolts as though he's been struck by lightning and starts moving his hips. I thought he'd jump off me, but the undulations feel more like he's humping my leg than anything else. Catty's full weight bounces against my thigh in a rhythmic thump.

Thump. Thump. Thump.

He's still humping when my teammates filter out, laughing at the scene before them. Then, grabbing my arms, Austin and Grayson finally manage to slither me out from underneath the mascot and the crowd rejoice, thinking it's all part of the show.

"You okay, man?" Austin asks, dusting down my jersey. Blood drips from my chin, and there's a dull ache in my leg, but I won't admit that out loud because I don't want to be taken off the roster.

Security surrounds Catty, who's still lying on the floor, floundering or convulsing; I'm not sure which. Maybe he's trying to look like a fish out of water, or perhaps he's really injured himself in the fall. Either way, I know it's going to take a long physiotherapy session to get my leg back in shape after that lump landed on me.

Moving away from my teammates, I stand above Catty, offering him my hand, but the medical staff pushes me out of the way, asking all kinds of questions, and starts to strap a bandage on my chin. All the while, I watch as Catty slowly gets up, waving at the crowd as he's dragged out of the stadium to a mixture of taunts and cheers.

I shake my head and widen my eyes, wondering if this was some kind of concussion-filled dream, but when Phil, one of the team doctors, pushes down on my chin, I know it's not.

"Tate, how many fingers am I holding up."

"Two," I say quickly, staring at his slender digits. He whispers something to another doctor and makes his way to the GM and Coaches standing in the dugout.

Coach points his thumb behind his shoulder. "Take a seat, Tate; you're out for the game. We're going to bat Kyle in your place instead."

"I'm fine, Coach," I say, pointing back to the area where Catty was dragged off too. "Catty got it worse than me. I'm fine to play."

He stares at me with thin lips and a curved brow. "Your chin is bleeding, son."

"Because of the awkward landing from being mauled by a manfish." I rub my bandaged chin, ignoring the pain. "See, it's all superficial. Right, Phil?" Phil makes some kind of incoherent mumble that I think is in my favor. He's a huge Fish fan; I'm sure he doesn't want to lose my bat for the opening game.

The Coaches look unconvinced, but after a lengthy discussion, they finally agree to play me, warning me that they'll take me off if I show any signs of wavering. Smiling smugly in the dugout, I wait to be called up and wonder if Catty will make another appearance tonight. He looked pretty beaten up, but surely they have a replacement just in case things like this happen.

"Tate. You're on deck." Coach Pits calls, and I give him a smile after grabbing my bat and making my way toward the Catfish logo etched in the sand to stretch.

I may have back pain and a bloodied chin, but life couldn't get any better than this.

By the time the game starts, the only evidence of the incident are the clips playing during the commercial break and my bloodied chin. The fans don't care; they're just happy to watch a good ball game. I didn't regret playing either because, on the first pitch, I hit the first homer of the season – a grand slam if you want to get precise. So yeah, that should get my MVP campaign off to a good start.

CHAPTER 3

CALI

"So, let me get this straight," Phil, the doctor on call, laughs while he inspects my arm. It's red, purple and puffy, but doesn't feel as bad as my bruised ego. I wish I could say Phil was surprised when he saw me limping into his office draped around a couple of security guards; he wasn't. "Your fin hand slipped and lost control of the ATV, and your giant foot was too big to press down the break effectively. So, you ended up heading straight for Sorenson?" He shakes his head in disbelief, still chuckling at my pain.

I'm not surprised he's asking questions. Normally, I come down here because I've whacked my head on the desk trying to get a pen, or I've tripped over my own feet and rolled my ankle walking down the stairs. Driving an ATV into the dugout while dressed as a fish isn't my usual MO. "I knew you were obsessed with the guy, but I didn't think you were the black widow type. If you wanted his autograph, you could have just asked me," he shrugs.

Shocked, I stare back at Phil. "I am *not* obsessed with him." He cocks an eyebrow, staring at me with a blank expression. I know he's silently referring to the Tate Sorenson calendar I have on my desk – the one I had to make myself because he doesn't have an official calendar. I remember the surprised look on the Head of Merchandising's face when I showed it to him on my first day, hoping that would convince him there was a demand for it. Instead, he very politely declined my proposal.

Obsession was a bit of a strong word, though. I would say it's more a healthy adoration for the best player ever to grace our team. "It was an accident, I swear!" He gently wraps my limp arm in a bandage. It's official; I look and feel like the dying fish I have become. "Turns out driving an ATV with a giant fish head on is harder than you'd expect." I pout, doing my best not to wince at the pain. Trepidation fills my chest, knowing that I'm going to have to do this all over again tomorrow night.

"But why did you hump his leg towards the end?" He asks casually, keeping his eyes focused on the bandage even though the edges of his lips are curling up in a smile.

"How did you know about that?" My mouth drops open like a blubbering fish, my left eye twitching in a way that is impossible to stop.

He meets my eyes with a slanted mouth. "Not going to lie. The entire medical staff has been talking about it in our group chat all afternoon." His suppressed chuckle comes out as a snort as he takes his phone out of his pocket, showing me all of the memes they've been sharing.

I gasp, looking at my fish-clad body, gyrating on Tate's leg in stiff gif images. It couldn't have been that bad, could it?!

"Also, doubt you've noticed, but Chally Sports have had it on replay before every commercial break."

My heart stops, my face pales. This must be what it's like to feel death at your door because I am most certainly dying of embarrassment right now.

Sighing, I curse myself. I knew I'd live to regret this decision. It's even worse than the time I thought I'd look cute perming and dying my own hair. I'd watched all of Brad Mondo's videos, hoping I'd make him proud. Long story short, I looked like Carrot Top for months.

I can't look Phil in the eyes, knowing that he and the rest of the world have been watching my most embarrassing moment on replay all afternoon. My mind drifts to all those blooper reels Chally Sports do at the end of the season. This moment will be like Conor McGregor and 50 Cent throwing out their first pitches, a disaster that everyone laughs at when they need something to talk about.

I will never live down going viral as a fish.

Defeated, I silently watch Phil twirl the fabric around my wrist, and after a few minutes, quietly add, "it wasn't supposed to look like I was humping his leg. When I fell on top of him, I think I was in the first wave of a concussion and panicked. I thought for sure Josh would fire me, and I did the only thing that my confused brain could think of to make it better. So, I pretended like it was supposed to happen." He nods encouragingly. "I thought if I started wiggling like a fish out of water, it might make the scenario look more intentional." Shaking my head, I still can't believe my fuzzy brain thought that was appropriate.

Tate's gruff growls while I unintentionally violated him played on repeat in my mind, and I couldn't stand it.

"Only you, Cali." His eyebrows cross as he ties the bandage. "How many times have I told you to take things slow before?"

"I know, I know. The stupid fish head made it tough to see the brake pad, and I couldn't grasp the handle because I was essentially wearing mittens. All in all, it was a terrible idea. I promise I will never drive an ATV while dressed as a fish again." Thankfully, after that performance, I think the opportunity may have sailed.

Snorting, he says, "That's good to hear." He checks over my wrist one final time before looking up with a smile. "Well, it looks like you've slightly sprained your wrist. You'll be fine in a couple of days, as long as you don't put any more pressure on it."

I hop off the table, surprised I didn't hurt my leg more. I may have had Tate break my fall, but he isn't exactly a soft landing. What with being pure muscle and all. "Thanks, P." I give him a small smile, and my face reddens, thinking back to lying on top of Tate and how good it felt. Even dressed as a fish, I could feel the thickness of his thighs. The same thighs I've watched for years when he does that wide batter's stance.

When I was dragged off, I tried to pass it off as no big deal by waving to the fans. Inside, I was dying from sheer embarrassment. If the security guards hadn't lifted me off, I'm not sure my legs would have been able to do the job.

The laughter and shame I felt after I nearly killed our best player was too much. Out of all the players in the world, why did it have to be Tate Sorenson that I hit? His perfectly sculpted body was the perfect landing. I could hardly breathe because my chest was tightening with excitement. Even through the thick layers of fabric, I could still smell him, then when he talked, I nearly melted. Hearing his deep husky voice ask me if I was okay made me like him even more (Sidenote: I didn't know that was possible). I nearly killed him, and the first thing he did was ask if *I* was okay. At least it made me feel good about my choice of players to idolize. If I'd have hit Grayson Hawk, I'm sure I would have been sued. He's got a lawyer left, right, and center waiting to deal with all his mishaps.

Biting my nails, I say, "Hey Phil." He looks up from the chart, giving me a small smile. "Can we keep the fact that I was Catty today between us?" From what I understand, only Phil, Mary, and Josh knew it was me in the suit. Everyone else thinks it was Tim. If people found out it was me in there, I'd never live it down. Hell, with all the Tate Sorenson memorabilia on my desk, they'd think I'd done it on purpose.

Phil nods, glancing back down at the medical notes. That's what I like about him; he doesn't ask too many questions.

Sitting there, twiddling my thumbs, I turn my head to see Catty's face staring at me. Only this time, he isn't trying to convince me to wear him; he's taunting me, laughing at my misfortune.

"Hi-Ya!" I karate chop Catty's head, sending it flying to the ground.

Now, I just need to get out of the silky threads and be done with him. I pull at the neckline of the neoprene costume, annoyed that I received no warning on neoprene's breathability. So much sweat is pouring from my body, I'm worried I'll dehydrate. "Is there a lost and found box in here by any chance? I can't go outside looking like this."

He smirks, looking down at my costume. *Damn you, Phil!* I know I look ridiculous; I don't need reminding. His head tilts to the side. "Yeah, there's a bunch of stuff in there." He points to a box in the corner with overflowing clothes and flicks his wrist to check the time. "Ah, the game wrapped up ten minutes ago; I'm late for the player checkup. Is it okay if I leave you in here to get ready? You know the way out." He smiles.

Waving him off, I barely give him a second glance, already making my way to the spare clothing items. "No problem. Thanks for the help. I promise next time I see you, it will be with donuts." He laughs, shutting the door behind him, leaving me alone with the Catty head.

Peering into the box, I wade through the vast amount of clothing, trying to find something that isn't too small. Another annoyance of having long legs is that only men's pants will work in this scenario. Otherwise, I look like the worst early 2000's trend ever, gauchos. I tried it once, thinking I'd look hot. Spoiler alert: I didn't.

Grabbing a pair of gray sweatpants, I hold them against my costume-covered body and assume they'd fit. Then, I snatch the first t-shirt I can find and throw them on the bench. I only need these clothes to get to my locker. With any luck, no one will see me in these rags either. Fewer witnesses, fewer questions.

Dropping the top of the suit, I thread my hands through the suspenders holding up the protruding belly, and continue rolling the costume off. At least the air conditioning in here is making it a little easier.

Sweat soaks through the little tank and shorts I'm wearing, and anyone seeing me for the first time would think I just got out of the shower. Taking off my tank, I use it to soak up as much of the sweat as I can, thankful that I have a stick of deodorant waiting for me upstairs.

How do other mascots keep cool?

I'll have to look it up when I've got the time.

Throwing the shirt on and rolling the sweatpants up to my waist, I'm ready to go upstairs and forget about this whole Catfish fiasco. Humping Tate Sorenson wasn't exactly how I planned my day to go, and now I'm late for my brother Penn's game.

As I pat down the shirt, the door starts to creak open. "Phil," I whine. "Please, no more comments. I'm already a fragile mess. I can't take any more of your taunting. This is all you had that would fit," I say, resigned to the fact that I must look like a drowned rat. With closed eyes, I turn around, bracing myself for his sniggers.

Except, nothing came.

I nearly jump out of my skin when someone clears their throat. Someone's voice who's way too deep to be Phil's.

Opening my eyes, I gasp.

I must still be concussed. This can't be happening. Can it?

Caramel and Heat.

Familiar butterscotch eyes narrow, watching my every move. Admittedly, the only reason they're familiar is that they're usually staring back at me from the paper they're printed on, but that's just semantics.

Glistening like poured honey, his eyes take me in, making me catch my breath. Is it hot in here, or has he just swallowed up all the air in the room? The corner of his lips lift as he watches me.

Why wasn't the world swallowing me whole yet?

Standing in front of me, watching me more intently than anyone I've ever met, is the man I unintentionally humped just a few hours ago. My cheeks flare as Tate Sorenson stands before me, wearing a dirty uniform and smelling like grass and leather.

It's the sexiest thing I've ever seen.

Images of stripping him down and licking that musky scent off him run through my mind, and I have to bite my lip to keep it to myself.

He scratches the back of his head, giving me the once over. My spine straightens, hoping he didn't notice my ogling. But, judging by his crooked smile, he knew exactly what I was doing. "Hi," he drawls out, more of a question than a statement.

I can't help it; I close my eyes because, for some insane reason, I'm worried he'll recognize me as the humper. Giant googly eyes and a wide mouth may have covered my face, but you can never be too sure. I'm pretty sure I was already concussed when I landed on top of him, so anything could have happened after that.

He silently stands there, waiting for me to talk. I breathe quicker because it feels like his presence is swallowing me whole. I open one eye to find him still staring at me, watching my every movement. "I'm sorry, I didn't mean to bother you." He points his thumb over his shoulder. "Phil told me this room was free." *Of course, he did.* Not content with embarrassing me in front of the entire medical staff, he has to bring the humpee to see me, too. I'm going to kill him. "I can go and find another room if I'm disturbing you." His thick southern accent has me in a trance, and I can feel my toes curling in my socks. It's such a turn-on; and way better in person than in all those countless interviews I've watched of him.

I want to talk, but my tongue is fat and my brain feels like thousands of fireworks are exploding in my mind. I flail my arms, desperately trying to talk, but nothing comes out.

Is this what it feels like to be starstruck?

I thread my hands through my sweaty blonde hair and start pulling, hoping that the pain will help me focus on anything except the jockstrap resting between his thighs. I couldn't help but notice it when he walked into the room.

That thing was ginormous.

My lips part, but still no words come out. That's when Tate rests a hand on my shoulder. I swear I nearly wet my panties. He's touching me. He's *choosing* to touch me, unlike this afternoon when I forced myself on him.

"Are you okay?" He asks, concern etched across his face, seemingly unfazed that I'm acting like a skittish kitten. My eyes dart everywhere except Tate's gorgeous face. Is he always this concerned about everybody else?

Nodding like one of the five Tate bobbleheads I have sitting on my desk, I finally muster up the courage to say something. I clear my throat. "Don't worry," I squeak, so high-pitched that I'm sure only dogs hear it. "This room is free. I was just leaving." I take a step, attempting to scurry out of the room and away from Tate. I need air. Unfortunately, when I take a step, Tate follows and uses his wide frame to block the exit.

Staring at his grassy cleats, I take my time, dragging my eyes up. I stare a little longer than necessary at his incredibly thick thighs and the fact that I can't see a boxer line. Even in bright white pants, there's no telltale sign of undergarments. Come to think of it, I've never seen a ballplayer with a visible panty line.

My eyes widen.

Is that because they don't wear underwear? Is Tate's jockstrap the only thing separating us?

I squeeze my eyes shut, doing my best to rid myself of naked Tate thoughts. Only; images of that calendar I made come to mind. I hold my breath and flick my eyes straight to his face. I know if I let them roam his chest, I'd get so hot, I'd probably faint.

Nope. That didn't work.

Even with that white bloodied bandage on his chin, it's still as chiseled and delicious as I remember. My stomach rolls and I thank the heavens he's not looking into my eyes; otherwise, I think my knees might give out.

His golden eyes are focused on my wrist, and he points to my hand. "Did you catch a ball today?"

My brows furrow, and I tilt my head in confusion. It takes me a few seconds to figure out what he means, and I lift my wrist, rubbing it with my other hand. "Oh no. I'm not a fan. I work here." I was still so flustered talking to him, but at least I was finally getting some words out. That's something.

When he looks at me with a crooked grin, all the air escapes my lungs again, and I have to remind myself to take another breath. He cocks his eyebrow, studying my face like he's cramming for a test on it tomorrow. "You do? How come I've never seen you here before?"

He takes a step toward me. I take one back. He raises his arm, and his hand comes out as though he's about to touch me, so I back away further. My brain is already having a hard enough time trying to process the fact that he's standing in front of me; if he touches me, I might just explode.

The cool metal bench connects with the back of my thighs, and I drop my hands to it. There's nowhere for me to go.

I swear the room has shrunk since Phil left it.

"I'm back office," I sputter, not sure where to look. He narrows his eyes, waiting for more. "I work in the marketing department, so I watch the game from the office on the shopping mall side of the stadium. So we don't get much time by the field." Unless you're dressing as a mascot, of course.

My fingers dance on the metal, and my feet shift from side to side as I watch him taking me in. He parts his lips, wetting them slightly with his little pink tongue. My stomach flips, and I swear I might hurl.

He chuckles; it's low and sexy like I'd always imagined it to be. "Does that mean I have you to thank for the Catty incident today?"

Wide-eyed, I mumble inaudibly under my breath, trying to think of something coherent to say. "I made up the dance, but Catty was dragged off before he could do it." I pipe out, not ready to tell him I was his fishy humper. His hand comes up between us, and he scratches his short blonde stubbled chin. *I want to bite it to feel the roughness across my tongue.* I can feel myself sweating, and I need to get out of here before doing something I regret.

"I'm sorry to cut this short, but I need to get out of here. My boss is going to kill me if I'm not back soon." I manage to catch him off guard and snake around him before he can stop me.

I'm home free!

Just as I start walking, his large hand wraps around my good wrist, spinning me on my heel, so I'm facing him. This time we were close. So close that it's the first time I realize just how tall he is. I have to crane my neck back to look into his gorgeous hazel eyes.

"You can't leave just yet." He husks out. "After all, you know my name, but I don't know yours." He offers me a small smile. I swear all my insides are melting.

"How do you know I know your name?" I'm curious, considering Mary talked me out of getting a Tate Sorenson tattoo on my neck last year; nothing else would tell him I'm his superfan.

He plucks at the fabric of my shirt as his eyes roam over my shoulder. "You're wearing my shirt." I can feel my face burning, and I have to stop myself from going on a tirade about how I'm only wearing this because of the stupid ATV incident since that would out me as the girl behind the fish. Imagine what he'd think if he knew it was me humping his leg? He'd think I'm obsessed with him… Or I guess more so than I actually am. Either way, I can't afford a restraining order on my record.

I pull the shirt away from my body to see for myself. *Damn.* It's his shirt from last year's players' weekend. The back has 'Tater Tot' scrawled over it, a nickname I believe he hates because his very public ex-fiancee gave it to him, but his teammates found it hilarious. I wave off his comment. "Ah, this old thing? It's actually my brother's shirt." I lie, hoping it will be enough of an explanation for him to let me out of this room. I still don't think I've taken a full breath since he walked in.

"My name suits you," he says, a smirk growing across his face. For years I've wondered what it would be like if I ever met Tate Sorenson. I'd always imagined I'd look my best and be able to eloquently thank him for all he's done for the Fish. Then, I'd finally invite him to watch my brother pitch. I'd prepared myself for any kind of scenario, except this one, because in none of my planning did I expect him to look at me like I'm a fresh Philly Cheesesteak (his favorite, by the way).

"Thanks." I flip my damp hair, ignoring his blatant attempt at flirting because, if I'm being honest, my head might explode if I think too hard on it. Why on earth would Tate want anything to do with me? He's a chiseled, charitable, amazing ballplayer. I'm a lanky, clumsy intern who could be classed as a stalker in some states. "Good luck with your game tomorrow night." I grab the door, thinking I'm out this time, but it won't open.

Tate gently places his palm on the door right above my head, stopping me yet again. I stare blankly at the wood grain, too afraid to turn and meet his gaze.

"Can I at least get your name, or are you going to make me follow you back to your desk?" He growls out playfully. Why did the tone of his voice make me think he wanted to bend me over said desk and spank me for being so naughty? I wonder if all that memorabilia I have with his face on it would make him think differently.

I turn, keeping my body as close to the wood as I can. "California," I mutter, lying my back against the door. He tilts his head in confusion. I get that a lot. I breathe in and close my eyes as I say, "my name is California. Cali for short."

He doesn't say anything, and I assume it's because he's stunned into silence. But, yeah, I get it; it's weird to be named after a state.

"Is it because you're from California?" He asks, trying to put the pieces together himself because I'm not helping.

"No, I'm from Charlotte." I can't believe I'm standing here about to explain the origins of my name to my all-time favorite player. "My parents named me California because they said my hair was so blonde and eyes so blue when I was born it reminded them of the beaches where they met in California." His gaze tracks my long strands as I wistfully continue. "My brother is Pennsylvania, Penn for short because his hair and eyes reminded them of the autumn leaves when they got engaged." I do my best to make it sound as though naming your kid after a state is a perfectly normal thing to do.

"I love it," he breathes out, looking down at me. His arm is still towering overhead, caging me in. "It suits you." He smiles, baring his perfectly straight teeth as his free arm pushes a piece of hair off my shoulder.

My hair.

It's a greasy mess after being stuck in that fish head all day, and oh my gosh, how did I forget I'm not wearing a bra under this jersey?

"Thanks, I think." Folding my arms over my chest, I let out a hesitant chuckle and bend down under his arm. This time when I go to open the door, he doesn't stop me. "It was nice meeting you, Tate," I call from over my shoulder because I'm already skipping out of there as fast as I can.

After turning the corner, I lay my back against the concrete wall, greedily sucking in the breath I was denied in Tate's presence. I swear my brain fried a little just having his eyes on me. Shaking out my hands, I jump on the spot, trying to get myself together before going back into the office. I need to get my story straight; otherwise, Josh will eat me alive.

Walking into the quiet office, Chally Sports is on, and no surprise, the humping incident is on repeat. I scrub my hand across my face on a moan. I open one eye, clearly a glutton for punishment as I watch the clip.

The crowd gasp, I can hear Tate grunt from the fall, and there I am. A catfish-human hybrid rigidly lying on top of him while he looks at my lifeless body, confused.

"Cali, it's about time you showed up." I try to keep my shoulders from falling. Then, my boss and the head of marketing, Josh, comes waltzing out of his office with his lips straight. With clenched fists and hard steps, I know I'm in trouble. Josh has hated me ever since I stepped foot in this place, and I have no idea why.

Humping the best shortstop in baseball wasn't exactly going to help.

I spin on my heel with the fakest smile I can muster. After such a long day, all I want to do is go home and hide under my covers.

Lifting my arm, I flash him my bandaged wrist. "Sorry, Josh. I hurt myself after the whole Catty incident. I had to get checked out by Phil. Luckily, I'll live." I try to giggle, making a joke of the whole thing, but the way he frowns at me, I know I've made the wrong move.

I'm in deep shit.

My stomach pits out.

"My office, now." He points without another word and turns around, stalking back the way he came. I stand there silently, watching him. Why did it feel like someone just hollowed me out like a pumpkin?

Trudging over, I take my time, trying to come up with an explanation as to why I humped Tate, but I come up empty. I lost control of the ATV. It's all my fault. I'm the reason opening day was a shambles, and I have to take responsibility for it. Even if it means losing my job, I can only hope Mary will be able to keep hers.

As I walk into Josh's office, I can see that the stadium lights are still on and the groundskeepers are cleaning up for tomorrow's game. Josh has one of the best views of the entire stadium here, but he never uses it. He doesn't openly admit it, but he's not the biggest fan of baseball. I can tell. When the games are on, he never tries to sneak a subtle look to see who's batting or what the score is. Sometimes I wonder if he even knows the rules of the game. But that's not important for his job.

I watch the groundskeepers sweeping up confetti for a second, trying to get a grip on my beating heart.

This is it. I'm going to get fired from my first job. My *dream* job.

"Take a seat." Josh gestures to the brown leather chair facing his mahogany desk. I slowly slump into it, a weary smile across my face.

"Do you want to explain to me why you were videoed humping one of our best players?" His tone is so serious, even though his statement is ridiculous.

"It was an accident. I lost control of the ATV, and then when I landed on Tate, I thought flopping off him would make it more realistic, and the fans would find it funny."

He says nothing, and I awkwardly chuckle with a snort, hoping he'll see the funny side. With straight lips and narrowed eyes, he stares at me.

"So, nearly killing one of our best players wasn't enough. You thought you needed to make him and the team the laughingstock of Major League Baseball?" He's acting like I did this on purpose, like I wanted to be dressed as a giant fish. Like it was my actual job to dress up like him, and I wasn't doing the department a favor by wearing it.

"That's not -"

"Save it, California," he says my name slowly, dripping with spite. "I've got a call with upper management tomorrow, and I'm going to have to explain this and how you were acting on your own volition because my department isn't going to take responsibility for your supercilious behavior. Imagine if you had injured Tate. His contract is 25 million dollars a year. Who do you expect to pay that if you took him out for the season? You?"

"Well, no of -"

"Did I say I wanted you to speak?" His booming voice shakes the pictures on his desk and startles me into submission. I just nod my head, too afraid to respond. "Consider this your first warning Collins," he sneers. "If you do one more thing to embarrass our team, you're out."

There's a pregnant pause between us as I wait for him to say something. When he doesn't, I bite my bottom lip. "I'm sorry, Josh. I'll make sure it won't happen again."

"Be clear; if you do anything to embarrass us tomorrow on the field, I will personally escort you out." *Tomorrow?* My shoulders slump. My body deflates. There it is. The only reason he's not firing me is that I'm the only one who can wear the suit. Lord knows he can't fit in it; he's only 5 ft 2. "Get out of my office." He doesn't have to ask me twice. After grabbing my files, I jump out of the chair, racing towards my desk to pick up everything I need before heading home. It's already late; everyone's gone home except for me. I'm fifteen minutes too late for the fast train, which means it's going to take an extra thirty minutes to get home. Ignoring Josh's grumbles, I gather my things and hurry out of the office without looking back.

Opening the door to my tiny apartment, I drop my jacket over my chair and sigh. The entire journey home, Josh's words replayed in my head. *I'm an embarrassment to the team. He'll fire me the minute he gets the chance. I'm only keeping my job because I'm useful.*

Sniffling, I wipe my eyes. The minute Tim's healthy, I'm screwed. He's going to come and take his job back, and I'm just going to be the creepy Tate humper.

Chucking my shoes off, I grab my phone and lay back on my bed, shifting my back to avoid the broken spring. It's the first time in hours since I've checked my phone; too embarrassed about the incident.

Scrolling through, I see a few messages from my mom about Friday night dinner and another from Mary asking if I'm okay. There's nothing else. Surely that means my secret is still safe.

I open up a browser and search the incident. Hundreds of articles have already been written about it, more memes than I've ever seen show up, and #Cattyhumper is trending. Everyone is talking and making fun of The Carolina Catfish because of me.

My eyes start burning with unshed tears. Maybe I should save everyone the hassle and just quit now. Not only have I embarrassed myself, but I've embarrassed my department, the Fish, and worst of all, I've made Tate look like a clown.

Throwing my phone on the floor, I roll over, letting the pillow soak up my tears and muffle my cries as I try to calm down. This is my dream job. I will never find anything I'm more passionate about, and I've just ruined all of it over one stupid mistake.

Chapter 4

TATE

I smile, waving at the desks of people as they watch me walk into the office. The one I didn't know existed until Larry kindly showed me this afternoon. The low hum of computers and artificial lights were a stark contrast to the stadium below – the only office I care to know.

How do people work in places like this? Sure, the windows are large, but the half roof of the stadium blocks any kind of natural light filtering in. Everything over here feels so dark and corporate.

"Great game, Tate." A guy wearing a Carolina Catfish tie waves, and I smile, mouthing a small thank you. It was a great game. I scored two homers and registered three RBIs. We're 2 – 0 for the season, which is always a nice way to start.

Normally it takes me a few weeks to warm up after Spring Training, but when our new field reporter Sienna asked me what had gotten into me, I couldn't answer. Well, that's a lie. I could, but it would have sounded nuts.

A girl.

It's not an answer I like to put out there easily. What with the fiasco of a relationship I had with Sam over the last couple of years. No, when Sam cheated on me, I decided I would keep matters of my heart private. No more public declarations of love until I'm certain they're the one.

But this new girl.

Cali.

Geez, she sure did light a fire up my ass.

Indigo eyes, mussed hair that looked like I'd been running my hands through it, and perky tits under *my* jersey. Walking into the first aid room yesterday was like walking into my teenage fantasy.

I knew she felt something too because her mouth gaped opened and her pouty lips quivered as she took me in. It almost looked like we'd been caught doing something naughty, and that was her reaction. But, I swear, just thinking about all those possibilities gives me a semi, one that would be mighty uncomfortable to get with a jockstrap on.

Last night, even though my chin was bleeding and my back was throbbing, all the pain melted away when I thought about her. *California. California.* I played with her name, enjoying the way it sounded rolling off my tongue. How is it that she's everything I ever dreamed of, but nothing that I thought I wanted? Because I was stupid enough to think that a girl like Sam would make me happy.

Cali's different. She's stunning, a baseball lover, and with one single look, she managed to make me feel like I could whack any pitch out of the park. I never had those feelings for Sam, even when we started dating when I was with the Houston Knights. She was pretty enough, seemed to like me, and I was dumb and naive.

When Cali tossed a piece of her sandy blonde hair over her shoulder, and I got a whiff of her coconut shampoo, I knew I wanted her. Bad. And if her longer than necessary stares at my thighs were anything to go by, I'm sure she's interested too. She's probably just intimidated by the fact that I'm a ballplayer or something.

I've got to admit; I was surprised when she refused to give me her number. Most of the time, women are shoving napkins with their numbers in my pockets, but not California. She couldn't get away from me fast enough. But, yesterday did help me learn something about myself. I like the chase, and I'll chase California's peachy ass as long as she'll let me.

Just as my lips start to tingle thinking about Cali, a blaze of auburn rushes past me. I tap her arm as she hurries by, stopping her in her wake. "Excuse me," I say with my politest southern accent, offering the petite woman my best smile. "Sorry to bother you, but I'm looking for someone, and I'm hoping you can help me find her."

She blinks, staring at me for a minute, and looks as dumbfounded as the rest of the employees. I know I don't normally come up here since I always do as I'm asked, but it shouldn't be that shocking to see players up here, surely? Grayson tells me he spends half his life talking with the PR department. The little redhead shakes her head, looks down to the floor, and then gives me a composed smile. "Hi, Tate. Sorry about that. I just wasn't expecting you, so I got a little confused for a second." She holds her hand out, and I accept it on a shake. "My name is Mary, and I'm more than happy to help you. Who are you looking for? Josh?"

When our hands disconnect, she motions her finger for me to follow her as though finding this Josh guy is a forgone conclusion. "No, actually. I'm looking for a woman. Unfortunately, I don't know her last name, but her first name is California. Cali for short."

That makes Mary stop and spin back around to look at me. "Sorry, did you say you're looking for Cali?" She sputters it out, almost incoherently, because she seems surprised. I nod, raising a brow. "Cali Collins?"

I shrug. "I don't know her last name, but I assume there can't be many California's that work here." Then Mary smirks. It's the same smirk Phil gave me when he told me that the first aid room was free.

"No, you're right. There's only one." Then, turning on her heel, she walks with an extra strut to her step. "Come on. She's just in the bathroom, but I'll show you to her desk. You can wait there. I'm sure she'd *love* that."

"Thanks, Mary." My mind goes back to California and those baggy gray sweatpants hanging off her narrow hips yesterday. She's a tall girl, tall enough for me to easily thread my hands through her hair and pull her in for a kiss. I lick my lips because that's something I'd very much like to do, preferably while her long, toned legs are wrapped around my waist.

Man, I have it bad. Five minutes with this girl, and she's got my head spinning. When I see her, I've got to keep my cool.

"So, this is her desk." There's a hint of amusement in Mary's voice as she holds her arms out, presenting the area.

What's so funny?

I round the cubicle and immediately stop in my tracks when I take in Cali's desk. A wry smile creeps across my lips. I'm guessing *this* is what Mary found so funny. An army of my bobbleheads stare me down, nodding lightly to an inaudible tune. Right above them sits a calendar that I most certainly did not sign off with Merchandizing. Not that I'm complaining about the photo. I'm wearing a towel around my waist, staring at the camera. Number 5 stickers, my number, is stuck across the top of her monitor with a hat from Sam's now-defunct clothing line draped over a pin on her cubicle wall. That was a stupid venture that Sam convinced me to do, only because she wanted to model the clothes.

Sam's not important right now. What is important is that Cali lied to me yesterday when she said she didn't know who I was. She's my biggest fan.

And that's hot as hell.

"Hey, Mary. I think we need to figure out some ventilation options for neoprene." Her familiar voice is like a melody, and I grin as I turn to look at my potential stalker. Her hair is up in a messy bun as she pats down her pencil skirt, looking flustered. Damn. She's hotter than I remembered. She hasn't looked up yet, which is a good thing because it's giving me ample time to look down her blouse, which seems to be straining at the seams.

Office fantasy, anyone?

I clear my throat, which makes her jump, and when she looks up, I give her a small wave. It takes her a few seconds to register me standing at her desk, and her eyes immediately drop to the multitude of mini Tate's sitting next to me.

"Tate, uh, what are you doing here?" With her brow pinched,

she tries to subtly stand in front of the bobbleheads, but that only succeeds in bringing her closer to me.

I take a tiny step closer, knowing she's left herself little option to get away. "Hey, Cali." My eyes take her in. I wonder if she'd consider a job as my PA? That way, I could see her in something like this every day. "It's good to see you again."

She laughs hesitantly, adjusting her hair as she dances on her feet. My girl is nervous. "I just wanted to check how your wrist was doing after yesterday." I bring my hand forward toward her delicately wrapped wrist, but she snatches it away before we can connect and starts to rub it instinctively.

"Yesterday?!" Mary squeals loudly. I almost forgot she was there. She looks between us, then trains her eyes on Cali, waiting for an explanation. Cali's cheeks flare as she looks anywhere but Mary. So she didn't mention our encounter yesterday. Interesting. I don't know whether to be excited that she wanted to keep me a secret or annoyed that she thinks she can forget me so easily. Not that I'm going to let the latter happen.

"Yeah," Cali drawls out, picking at the fabric of her bandage, so she doesn't have to make eye contact with her friend. "I bumped into Tate after the game after I got my wrist wrapped." Guilt pours from her voice. What's my girl got to feel guilty about?

"And you didn't tell me?" Still shocked, Mary's almost vibrating with annoyance.

"Shhh. Can we just save this for another time?" She turns back to me, ignoring Mary's glare. "Thank you, Tate." She pauses. "For coming and checking on me, but as you can see, I'm fine." She raises her wrist like it's a world series ring and smiles tightly. Between the two of these women, I feel like I've walked in on something I shouldn't have. That's when I take a look around and notice that the whole office is watching us.

I'm used to it. Hell, I've got over a million people a night watching me analyze a pitch well enough to hit it, but maybe Cali isn't. Maybe she doesn't like the attention and that's the reason why she ran away from me so quickly yesterday.

"Now, I should let you go. You probably want to shower." She seems breathless and still a little skittish as her eyes dart from my cleats to my dirty uniform. Yeah, I didn't change before coming up here today. Couldn't help myself. The way Cali stared at my crotch yesterday made me want to wear this to bed.

"Yeah, about that –"

"Tate, sorry to interrupt." Some dudebro sasses behind me, acting as though we know each other. He ignores my scowl and pats me on the shoulder while offering a smug smirk to Cali. Not that she noticed. She's too busy studying her heels. Her jet black, six-inch heels. How did I miss those babies when I walked in? They're adding all kinds of depth to my PA fantasy over here.

"I'm Josh," the guy continues like I'm listening or that I care. All I'm focused on are the mile-long legs in front of me. "And I just wanted to apologize for your run-in with our mascot yesterday," he says, giving Cali another stern look as she shuffles to her chair. "I trust Catty was better behaved today?"

"Yeah," I say, dragging my attention to him. Only realizing then that I have to look down to see him. Way down. Is everyone in this department short except for Cali? "Catty was great today. The crowd loves him, and he's got some fantastic dance moves." I emphasize the last part of my sentence, hoping Cali is listening. I want her to be impressed that I remembered she's the one that choreographed it. My head may have been full of some fantasy haze yesterday, but I was hanging off her every word like a lovestruck teenager. Josh snorts. It's gross and full of snot and phlegm and makes me feel a little queasy.

He smiles at me eagerly, and all I want to do is swat him away like an annoying gnat.

Cali pretends to ignore the conversation, tapping away on her keyboard while diligently staring at the screen. I know she's listening, though, because every time I start to talk, her fingers slow, and she leans back ever so slightly.

"I'm also sorry for all the press attention yesterday." Josh adjusts his tie, smoothing the fabric down as he speaks.

"Isn't that what you guys want?" Cali's tap, tap, tapping slows again, and I smirk at her lack of subtlety.

'Hump day,' as Chally Sports calls it, was all over the sports news last night, and every outlet wanted to interview me. My post-game interview wasn't enough. They wanted to see me reconcile with Catty. My publicist was ecstatic with all the positive publicity, so I plan on hamming it up a little in my next interview. I may be the face of the Catfish franchise, but that hasn't stopped criticism over my choice of girlfriend. Fans were insistent Sam was using me, and being the dutiful boyfriend I was, I stuck up for her. But, boy, did I feel like a chump when photos of her cheating on me with some NFL Tight End came out. Rival fans loved to troll me after that.

Josh jitters, his teeth grinding together. "Well, yes. We did get a large boost in followers, but we would have preferred it not to be at the expense of our best and most loved player." I roll my eyes because this guy is a serious suck up.

I wave him off, focusing on the back of Cali's head. "Ah, I couldn't care less about social media. I don't have it." My publicist advised I remove it once the trolling started to affect my sister. I turn back to this guy who's grinning crookedly. I need to get out of this conversation.

"Jared." I grab his hand, shaking it assertively. It's clammy and rough all at the same time.

"It's Josh." He corrects me as though I care. The only thing I care about right now is the tall, lithe, blonde thing sitting beside me, and this guy is getting in the way.

"Right, Josh. Thanks for checking, but I'm fine. Now, would you mind if I had a chat with Cali?" I ask purposely. At this point, I don't care if he knows my intentions. I just want to be able to talk to her again.

He looks between Cali and me. *Why does everyone seem so shocked I want to talk to her?* She's hot as hell. "Right. Of course. Of course.

Sorry. Good luck with the game tomorrow." Finally getting the hint, he slowly walks off, leaving Cali typing at a snail's pace, staring at the screen like it holds all the answers to life.

Her typing slows with each passing step I make towards her. I really don't think she could get any slower, but somehow, she does.

I quietly rest my thighs on the desk beside her keyboard, watching as her eyes home in on my right ass cheek, which has taken refuge against the wood. Her eyes drag up, getting wider as she goes. Okay, I had a suspicion yesterday that she had a thing for my uniform; this reaction confirms it.

I adjust one of the buttons on my jersey while her eyes creep to my hands. A very tiny, low yelp escapes her lips. I smirk, thinking of all the ways I want to torture her in my uniform.

I need to get her number first, though.

"Hey, Cali," I drawl out, slowly watching her chew at her bottom lip. I smile once her eyes finally connect with mine.

"He-hey," she stutters back.

I slowly take in her cubicle, making a point to look at her Tate bobbleheads, her number five stickers, and her bespoke calendar. "Thought you said you didn't know who I was?" I quirk my eyebrow in a mocking question.

Her back straightens, and she seemingly gains a little more confidence. "I never denied knowing who you were. I just thought it was presumptuous of you to *assume* that I knew who you were."

Fiesty. The way she's teasing me makes my lip twitch. "Well, is it presumptuous to assume that you might have a slight obsession with me?" I hold back my laughter when her jaw drops in shock.

She brings her lips together and closes her eyes, taking her time to respond. "Just because I think you're the best player the Carolina Catfish has ever had does not mean I'm obsessed with you." She sounds reasonable; if only she could see the game ball with my signature on it rolling behind her. Then she'd realize how unreasonable she looked.

"No. You're right." Cali takes a sharp breath when I raise my hand, pointing behind her shoulder. “But the homemade Tate Sorenson calendar does.” Some players would see this and run for the hills. I mean, clearly, she’s obsessed with me. I should be worried she’s another cleat chaser like Sam, but weirdly I’m not. I guess because if she was really after the clout of being with a ballplayer, she wouldn’t have run away yesterday. Even now, she’s doing everything she can to get me to leave her alone.

Leaning in closer, I whisper, “now, I do have a question. Am I in a towel every month?”

She drops her head sharply, focusing on her fingers. “No. It’s only for April,” she mumbles. “Because of April Showers.” I smirk. So she likes a good pun.

Nodding my head, I smile. "Ah, that makes sense." I pick up one of her bobbleheads, or, should I say, one of *my* bobbleheads, whacking the top of its helmet. Cali’s eye shudders. That’s a tell if I ever saw one. The one I hit dates back from when I first joined the franchise, so I’m guessing she collects these things, and she’s worried I’ll break it. I’ve got dozens of these in my storage container that I’d willingly give her if it meant she’d let me take her out. "So, as you know, I'm going to Philadelphia tonight for our first away game." She watches me diligently as I gently place the bobblehead down.

"Yeah."

I look down at her, losing my train of thought when I notice her button-up shirt is gaping, and the slightest hint of cleavage is popping out in the form of a white lacey bra. My jaw flexes. This girl is torture in an office skirt. Forcing myself to look back into her eyes, I say, "I'll be lonely on the bus..."

She scoffs, folding her arms. "It can’t be that lonely. You've got the entire 40-man roster with you." Backing away, I bite my bottom lip, hiding a smile. Why is she so intent on busting my balls? Why am I so intent on her busting them?

She wants this. The fact that my face is plastered everywhere tells me as much. I’ve come all the way up here just to talk to her, still in my uniform, and she’s still turning me down left, right and center.

Doesn't she appreciate all the effort I made in trying to find her?

"Why talk to them when I can talk to you?" I figure I'll try a more direct approach since I'm skirting around the subject too much. I lean in closer. Her eyes dart across my chest, and I notice her shoulders rising as she takes a sharp intake of breath. She's trying to pretend I don't affect her, but those rosy cheeks give her game away.

"And how exactly do you plan to talk to me?" She asks with a hint of humor in her voice but tips her chin up. She's still trying to keep up the façade, either that or she caught me peeking down her shirt?

I casually shrug my shoulder, enjoying the banter. "You're going to give me your number." I flash her a large smile, and she shakes her head, chuckling. It's the first time I've seen her crack.

"You're not getting my number, Tate," she quips, turning back to the computer, trying to ignore my giant frame covering half of it. During our conversation, I had slowly moved closer to her so much that I'm now practically sitting on her keyboard.

She grabs her phone beside the mouse, playing nonchalance until she freezes her thumb. I look down at the screen, wondering what has got her so flustered. Then, I bark out a laugh. Right there, on her home screen, is a picture of me holding my bat suggestively.

Just as I'm about to tease her, we're both startled by a booming voice. "Cali. I need to speak to you right now." That dudebro, Josh, yells and Cali's face immediately falls.

What an ass.

He can clearly see she's busy. With me, specifically. Cali jumps out with a skittish animal look sprawled across her face again. I swear I heard her let out a small whimper.

"I've got to go," she says, scrambling out of the cubicle, leaving me watching her cute ass as she leaves. Well, that went well. She doesn't look back, focusing all her attention on Josh, who watches her the whole way.

With her head hung low, she walks into his office and Josh slams the door shut behind her. The other employees are stunned, watching the scene unfold. What the hell did Cali do to garner a reaction like that?

I roll my body back towards her desk. I guess that means no number for me then. I glance across her workstation, grabbing the Catfish post-it notes and the baseball pen she has lying next to her mouse pad. I quickly scrawl my number down, asking her to call me, and stick the note onto the center of her home screen.

This isn't the end between us, far from it.

CHAPTER 5

CALI

"Can I get a Venti Iced Caramel Cloud Macchiato, please?" I ask the barista as I stand in line at the coffee shop. If there was ever a day I needed a morning fix to think straight, it's today. My eyes are dry, and my lids are puffy because I cried myself to sleep last night again. I was already on thin ice because of the Catty incident but fraternizing with Tate seemed to send Josh over the edge.

My fingers tap against my bag, thinking about all the things I could do today to make Josh hate me less. "Oh, can I also get a tall, flat white too, please?" Getting him a coffee might help. But then my eyes widen, a *tall* flat white? What if he thinks I'm making fun of his height. "Actually," I pipe up, and the barista gives me a chirpy smile. "Can I go for a grande instead?" She nods, writing my name on the cup. Surely, grande is better than tall? Who am I kidding? Getting Josh to look at me with anything other than discontent will be an uphill battle. One coffee isn't going to make a difference. At least it's a start, and I'm determined to prove to him that I belong here.

Chewing on my bottom lip, I let the pain stop me from crying. It's pathetic, really, that someone can make me feel like this. By the time Josh finished yelling at me, everyone else had gone home, and I had to spend another three hours of work before I could leave. The only thing that made me smile was seeing Tate's bright yellow note stuck on my screen.

I still can't get my head around the notion that Tate waltzed into the office just to see me and then asked for my number in front of everyone. I tried to do my best to act professionally since the entire office was watching, but every time he looked at me, my whole body shivered. Then, when he leaned in, I swear my panties started melting. I suppose I should be thankful in a way that Josh interrupted us because it was at that point that my defenses were crumbling, and I was starting to get a little flirty with him. Flirting with the players isn't exactly going to ingratiate me with Josh either.

"Can I have a vanilla sweet cream cold brew, please?" Mary saddles up next to me, offering me a small smile as she elbows my side. "Hey, hun. How you doing?" She asks. Her smile is a little forced, and I know it's because she doesn't want to come out and outright ask what happened with Josh.

"I'm okay," I say, moving further up the line. "Working late the last few nights has been a little hard."

She hums under her breath, and there's a moment of silence before she starts. "So, when were you going to tell me about Tate?" She coos, her eyes twinkling with interest.

"There's nothing to tell." I shrug, feeling slightly awkward and bashful about the whole thing. "I bumped into him in one of the first aid rooms after I accidently made him an internet sensation on Tuesday. That's it." I keep it vague, hoping that answer will satiate her curiosity.

When Mary lets out a loud snort, I know I haven't given my friend enough of an explanation. "Clearly, that's not *just* it." She cocks an eyebrow, her eyes taking in my messy hair and rumpled clothes, judging my answer. "He came up to the office still in cleats just to find you. I don't know how you kept it as cool as you did when he was at your desk. I swear I nearly tripped seeing the sweat dripping down his shirt, mixing in with all that mud and grass." She waves her hands around her chest, laughing lightly. A pang of something shoots through my spine. *Jealousy?* Surely not. Tate and I have only just talked. I haven't even given him my number, and it's not like anything could happen between us anyway.

"He gave me his number," I blurt, almost territorially.

Squealing, she jumps up and down, pulling at my sweater like a little kid who just discovered *Frozen* for the first time. "It was so obvious he was into you. The way he looked at you made me feel uncomfortable," she babbles. "You guys are a perfect match. Not just because you're both giants, but you're obsessed with him, and he's clearly obsessed with you. Bet he wants a bit of that California sunshine."

"Cali," the barista calls, giving me no time to address the blush staining my cheeks and deny Mary's assumption. After grabbing our drinks, her last statement plays in my mind.

Tate's obsessed with me.

I want to laugh because nothing about his behavior screams obsession. But, no. That label is just for me.

"The fact that he still gave you his number after seeing your desk says everything."

"You mean because I'm his biggest fan?"

"No, because your desk has 'killer Tate stalker' written all over it," she giggles.

I sigh, taking a sip of my coffee. "I think that's actually part of my appeal. When I first met him, I was wearing a Sorenson Jersey. Not out of choice. I just grabbed whatever I could from the lost and found box." Shrugging, I glance at Mary's amused reaction. "Maybe he thinks I'm an easy lay. You know because I'm his biggest fan." That thought had run through my mind several times. My favorite player could view me as the ultimate conquest. Like I was a game. But, when I thought back to how strongly he came on to me, he certainly made me feel like he was ready to win.

I take a slow swig of coffee, hoping the shot of caffeine will cover the pang of sadness in the pit of my stomach. The only thing I do know outside of Tate's incredible stats and butterscotch eyes is that he dated a very hot girl named Sam. She was one of those Instagram girls that you weren't quite sure what they looked like in real life because they used so many filters on their posts. I know that they had a very messy breakup, but I didn't look too much into it since I was studying for my finals at the time.

"Please. We both know that's not true. Your whole aura gives off ballbuster, not easy fangirl." She rolls her eyes, taking a sip of her drink. "That's why people rarely ask you out. Before you say anything. No, it's not because of your height. It's because you've got this permanent wall around you, and it makes you look a lot like hard work."

I narrow my eyes, studying her in disbelief. I can almost guarantee it's definitely my height. I've had guys ask me out before and then rescinded the offer after I stood up. I know my place. "I don't know. His last girlfriend is absolutely nothing like me."

"So?"

"So… why would he be interested in me for anything other than a conquest?" It's not something I necessarily want to believe in, but I feel safer thinking that than getting my hopes up on a guy that's so far out of my league.

I shouldn't be fraternizing with him anyway. Josh gave me a not-so-subtle warning about it yesterday.

As we push the doors to the office open, she gives me a broad smile. "Why don't you go out with him and find out? It might do you some good. It has been a while since you dated." She just had to go there, didn't she? She just had to remind me of Dan – the intellectual (his own description) – that I dated in college. He hated sports, especially baseball. The only good thing about him was his height. He was six foot two and made me feel short. Five months in a relationship, and that's the only good thing I can say about him.

"Even if I wanted to date him, and that's a big *if,* it's not like I could. It's against policy to date a player," I whisper, still feeling the eyes of the office on me.

"Against policy? Who told you that?" She asks, laughing.

I watch her walk past me, around my cubicle to hers opposite. "Josh. I'm already on thin ice when it comes to him. I'm not about to do anything else that would give him an excuse to fire me."

Mary places her coffee on the counter and stares straight at me, looking in disbelief. "Okay, there's all kinds of things wrong with your last statement. Firstly, let's be clear, nowhere in your contract does it stipulate that fraternizing with the players is off-limits. If it were, half this office would already be fired. Secondly, he can't fire you. Without you dressing up as Catty and me writing his responses, we wouldn't have amassed over half a million followers over our socials. No other mascot has been able to do that. Not even Atlanta's Armadillo could do it, and they won the World Series last year. So he literally can't fire you; you're Catty."

"Don't remind me," I grumble, falling into my desk chair with a flop. It's obvious that my height is the only reason he's keeping me around, and I'm on countdown. I close my eyes, wondering if I'll get jail time if I convince Tim to run down another slippery aisle once his leg is healed? I close my eyes, sighing out an exasperated breath. God, I must be desperate to work for the Catfish if I'm trying to think of ways to *stay* Catty.

"Josh is only salty because he's got some weird obsession with you."

Okay, that makes my eyes bulge out. "Yeah, he hates me," I state, still not sure what exactly I did wrong in the first place. Maybe I showed up a little too enthusiastically on the first day with my box of Tate memorabilia, but surely, you'd want someone who loves the Fish working for you?

"He wishes," she snorts, rounding back around my desk and sitting on it as she leans in. "I think it's a different reason entirely." She bites her bottom lip, looks around the office, and then leans in further. "I think he's got a tall girl fantasy," she whispers, giving me the once over. I wait for the punchline, but that seems to be it.

My brows knit together, and my lips part in utter shock. That's when she cackles. "Think about it. Haven't you seen the way his eyes are always drawn down to your pencil skirts and long legs? When you stand up, he's the perfect height for… you know."

Sucking in a deep breath, I will myself not to throw up on Mary's shoes. I got them for her as a birthday present, and I don't want to replace them. "Glad, I skipped breakfast this morning." My flesh crawls at the mere thought of Josh's face anywhere near my lady bits. "That image will be burned in my brain forevermore."

Mary jumps off the desk and says, "sorry," with a pop. That smirk on her face didn't make her look very sorry. "But now that I've cleared that up and you're free to do whatever you want with Tate, are you going to go for it?"

Sounds like a dream, right?

Baseball player and their biggest fan getting it on.

Yeah, that's definitely a dream.

One that will never happen to me.

"No," I quip, pushing her out of the way, and turning on my computer.

"Cali, do you listen to yourself?" She twirls my chair so I'm facing her. "Your celebrity crush wants to get to know you, and you're just going to brush him off for no good reason."

"I have a good reason."

"What is it then?" She cocks an eyebrow, waiting. Then, when I don't say anything, she continues. "Is it because you're chicken?"

"I'm not chicken," I state calmly. I'm not. Last night I thought a lot about Tate while staring at his number on that post-it note. "Have you ever idolized someone so much that you're worried if you got to know them, it would ruin the image of them?" Mary shakes her head. "What if Tate turns out to be this crazy lothario who uses me to get off and then drops me like the hot potato I had for lunch yesterday?"

She huffs out a laugh. "This is Tate Sorenson we're talking about, right? The guy that's so nice that even other teams love him? The guy whose only misstep in life was dating that bitch? Apart from that, he spends his weekends visiting sick children at hospitals and training the local little league team. We've never had to clean up one of his messes. Unlike Grayson Hawk." She shakes her head. "That guy is such a PR nightmare. Last year before you joined, we tried to impose a twitter ban on him by stipulating it in his contract. That didn't work. He just doesn't care."

Shrugging it off, Tate may be near perfect, but that doesn't mean I should go there. No matter how hard his muscles are. "They're away for a week now; he'll probably forget I exist once he finds a fan in another city. I can feel the corner of my mouth trembling, so I take another swig of my coffee and hate the bitter taste sitting in my mouth. I need to be realistic. Tate is too hot not to draw attention to himself.

Mary watches me silently as though she can hear my inner battle, and one side of her lip turns up. "We'll see about that." She jumps off my desk and walks back to hers. Before sitting down, she says, "Oh, by the way. I did look into the marketing budget to see if we could hire a tall guy to play Catty, but Josh refused to sign it off. He said since you'd managed to amass us such a following, you had to keep doing it." Amusement mixed with trepidation laces her voice, and I feel a dark void growing in my chest. I'm just a joke to Josh.

Groaning, I rub my hand over my face. "I hate this," I mumble, more to myself than anyone else.

"Come on. It's not that bad. Your dance moves are fantastic, and the kids love it. Speaking of, we need to take a few photos of Catty around the ballpark today. Do you mind donning the fish for a few hours?" She lifts her eyebrows in question.

"I don't have a choice, do I?" She shakes her head. Great.

I'm damned if I do, damned if I don't.

The tapping of my feet echoes across the hard concrete floor until I get to the corporate side of the stadium. Then, flashing my pass, I push through the barriers and rush to my desk.

My colleagues watch me shuffle in, and I adjust my shirt and skirt. Yes, I know I look like a wreck, but I've been running around the stadium dressed as a fish for the last couple of hours, for crying out loud. My hair is allowed to be a little messy.

I stupidly thought bringing my phone into Catty's costume

would be a good idea, but once I was in there, and all I could see was the flashing light of my emails, I knew it was a mistake. Josh knew I was with Mary taking photos, yet he continued to send me urgent emails the entire time. That's why I find myself looking like such a wreck. I sweated through that costume but had no time to shower because Josh had me on countdown.

Stopping in my tracks, I inhale sharply.

What the....

Flowers. A sprawling bouquet rests on my desk next to my computer, completely covering my Tate calendar. Blossoming white peonies and blue hydrangeas greet my tired and aching body with a relaxing floral scent. I look around the office, surprised that eyes are still on me, and that's when I realize why I'm drawing all the attention. They all want to know who the heck bought the intern flowers.

I shuffle closer to the bouquet, noticing an ivory note attached to the side. I sit down, hiding my face from all the prying eyes before I pluck the card from the side and open it.

Cali,

Not sure you got my note the other day.

Here's my number again, just in case.

Looking forward to hearing from you.

Tate.

Blink. Blink. Reread. Blink.

Now, if only my heart would stop fluttering at the digits printed underneath his name. At least that's easier to read than his messy handwriting.

Tate sent me flowers *and* gave me his number again. He hasn't forgotten about me. Maybe he did like me... What if I gave him a shot? Mary said there's nothing wrong with hanging out with him, and there's no denying I like him. He must like me too.

"Cali!" I jump when his familiar angry voice calls my name. I swear he has no other setting. My eyes pop up, and I see Josh standing at his door, his shoulders heaving. The whole office is looking at me again, but this time for a completely different reason. "Get. In. Here. Now." His words are enunciated through clenched teeth as though it hurt him to say them.

My stomach rumbles with fear and trepidation.

What have I done now?

Blood pumps through my body faster than I think it ever has before, and as I stand up, I worry I might faint. But I don't have time for that. Taking in an invisible breath, I hold my head up high, trying to remain positive as I walk to his room.

I've done nothing wrong.

I've worked my butt off all day and am just about to start the work he asked for.

He has no reason to be annoyed with me. I've done nothing wrong.

"Nice flowers," he hisses as I walk past him, and I close my eyes, hoping this meeting will end soon so I can get my work done.

Three hours. Josh lectured me for *three hours*. I could have finished all the work he asked me to do and be home within those three hours, but Josh just had to make a point.

Apparently, accepting a gift breaks some kind of accounting protocol in the marketing department, and since he views Tate's flowers as such, I'm in trouble. Of course, I didn't bother mentioning that I've seen other people receive flowers because he seemed hell-bent on making me feel like crap for it. He did a pretty good job of it too.

As I walk out of his office, making sure I hear the click as I shut the door, I notice everyone is already gone. Probably at home, eating dinner with their family while I have to stay here and finish that mountain of work Josh left for me.

When I get to my cubicle, I stuff the beautiful flowers under my desk, not wanting to trigger any more of Josh's anger as he leaves for the night.

As I start checking my emails, the petals of the flowers tickle at my legs, making me smile. Tate sent me those, which was a small relief from thinking about my boss, who hates me and thinks I'm terrible at everything.

I'm going to prove him wrong.

No matter what it takes.

CHAPTER 6

TATE

I scuff my cleats against the hard floor as I sit in the dugout, listening intently to the screeching noise. It's something I've always done before each game to mentally prepare myself.

Scorchin' Sorenson.

That's Chally Sports' new nickname for me because I'm playing so hot right now. In the last three games, I've batted in a combined 15 runs – the highest in the league so far – and it's where I want to stay. They're already mentioning my name in MVP conversations, but I do my best to ignore them. It happens every year, and I haven't won yet.

My psychologist thinks it's because the pressure tampers down my hot streak, and I end up colder than an ice cube, barely scraping in a performance after the all-star break. So this year, I'm trying a different tact. I'm ignoring all the talk and just focusing on the game.

The crowd jeer at Catty, who's decided to annoy the Washington team as they warm up. More specifically, their best player, Kyle Haward. Kyle's a good guy; I've always liked playing against him, and he seems to enjoy hamming it up for the fans.

Catty follows behind him, flipping his fins in the air as he holds a pen in one hand and a board in another. Kyle raises his hands, reluctant to sign an autograph, but Catty is persistent, bouncing up and down like a kangaroo until Kyle finally agrees to sign the bottom corner of the board.

Catty snatches the board away, taking no time to admire the signature. Instead, he unfolds the board, revealing a giant check addressed to Catty.

That's when I bark out a laugh.

Three hundred and thirty million dollars. The exact amount Washington paid for Kyle's multi-year contract during the off-season. Catty dances across the yard while Kyle chases after him – albeit leisurely since he doesn't want to sprain an ankle before the game – and I'm surprised at Catty's speed. Maybe I should talk to Coach Allport about Catty pinch-running for us sometime.

My mind drifts.

Did Cali come up with that stunt? I know she choreographed his dances, so I wonder if her talents extended to the jokes.

Why can't I get that girl out of my head?

Every time I think about her blue eyes, it feels like she's captured me, and I'm drifting faster into the deep without a life jacket during high tide. She didn't fall at my feet when I asked her out. She hasn't called, even though I've given her my number twice. She's done everything in her power to let me know that she's not interested in me, yet I'm still not letting go.

Not just yet.

Third times a charm, after all.

Sure, I was arrogant enough to think that maybe the first post-it note flew off her phone before she saw it (unlikely in a temperature-controlled office, but stranger things have happened). So, I thought it would be a good idea to make sure she got it again, just in case. When I saw the peonies and hydrangeas, I couldn't help but think of her. Summertime by the beach. I had to get them for her, which gave me the perfect excuse to write my number down again. Just in case.

I waited all night for a message from her, thinking she was probably busy working with that idiot boss of hers - there was something I didn't like about that guy, but I couldn't quite put my finger on it. Either way, I thought by the time she got home, she'd take a chance and send me a text. Hell, I would have settled for a gif or a meme at this point. But she didn't bother with either. I knew she got the flowers this time because the delivery driver took a picture of it on her desk, surrounded by all my memorabilia.

Maybe I was playing it wrong? I'd ask Grayson for advice, but he's not exactly gracious when it comes to women. I haven't dated someone that wasn't Sam in a while, and Cali was most definitely not her. Cali wouldn't be impressed with a flashy necklace or a dinner out. Still, I thought she might like me showing her a little attention and flowers.

It's like someone dropped her into my life as a joke. The hottest girl -my biggest fan- yet she wanted nothing to do with me. I've never looked at a woman and had so many questions running through my mind at once.

"Tate, you're on deck," the batboy calls, drawing me out of my Cali-filled haze. Right. I need to get in the game and out of my head. I take a few steps forward, clearing my mind and focusing on the task at hand. Winning this game. After, I can figure out a way to win Cali's heart.

By the end of the game, I'd broken three bats. Scorchin' Sorenson was still in the game, and now I knew exactly what was igniting the fire in my ass. Cali. If flowers and chasing didn't get her attention, maybe winning would. She is an obsessed Fish fan, after all.

"Good game," Marc, our catcher, clasps my shoulder. Not just good. Great. I ball up the towel in my hand, throw it in the laundry basket next to me, and mumble out a short thanks. Adrenaline pumps through my veins, spiking when I think about each hit I batted in.

"Hey, man," Grayson calls. "We're all going to dinner at Deena's in an hour. Do you want to come?" He nods towards the group of our already dressed teammates.

Waving him off, I rake a hand through my blonde hair. "Yeah, sure. I'll be ready soon." My initial plan was showering and then going back to the marketing department to see if Cali got my flowers because it would be rude not to check. However, since she'd been ignoring me, I figured maybe giving her a little time to miss me would work. We're home for the rest of the week; I'm sure I'd be able to come up with some plausible reason why I needed to go up there and bug her in the next few days.

After taking a shower and sticking some aftershave on, I grab my bag, striding out of the locker room.

I stop.

Am I seeing things?

Cali is standing in front of me, looking like the tall blonde goddess that she is. Tight pencil skirt, floaty blush blouse, spiked-heel tapping. She's a dream, fulfilling all kinds of secretary fantasies I didn't know I had. Yet, that outfit against the gray concrete walls feels inappropriate. Out of context almost and stirs all sorts of thoughts that might show through in my jeans soon.

Do those heels make her my height?

Is she wearing a garter under that skirt?

I wonder what it would feel like with her heels digging into my back?

And now I'm getting impossibly hard thinking about it.

The other players are leering, watching her as she stands there nervously. I would throat punch the lot of them if I didn't need them to win tomorrow's game. "You ready, Sorenson?" Max asks, standing with the players. He's the only one not staring at that peachy ass of hers.

Holding my finger up, I focus on Cali, striding towards her. "Give me a minute." With her pursed lips and crossed arms, I can feel the tension from here. She's ticked. I should probably stay away, but I can't stop myself. She's like a magnet, and I want to get spanked. Or burned… whatever happened when a couple of magnets got too close.

"Tate," she says sternly when I get close enough. Her shirt gapes at the front again. Damn those button-up blouses she insisted on wearing. It takes all my willpower not to look down and check the color of her bra. I like to think it's a deep blue to match the intensity of her eyes and the Carolina Catfish colors. She taps her toe in a slow, pissed-off melody. She really was the perfect height in those heels. I wouldn't get neck strain from kissing her, and I could easily grab her ass, haul her up and bang her against a wall.

I really was getting ahead of myself now.

"Cali?" I drawl out, making sure my thick accent is obvious as I smile back. "Did you lose my number again? Maybe I should get a sharpie and write it on your wrist. Or better yet, tattoo it there," I tease.

The apples of her cheeks and the tips of her ears turn red as she drops her head. "That's not why I'm here, Tate." I love how she says my name like it's all hers. She adjusts her shirt, only now realizing the hint of her bra was popping out. It was white, by the way. Disappointing for my little fantasy. An awkward laugh left her throat, and she ran a hand through her hair before glancing at me hesitantly. I loved that I made her nervous.

I quirk my brow. "Is it because you wanted me to take you out right now? I wasn't planning on it, but I know this perfect little Italian spot that has this private room."

She rests her hand on my chest, stopping me. The zing of exhilaration that runs through me from her touch is undeniable.

"You sent me flowers." She purses her lips in this cute way that makes me want to smash mine against hers. Strawberry ice cream. I'm betting that's what she tastes like. Looking over her shoulder, I notice the guys watching, smirking at my lack of game. Better than them looking at her rounded ass.

She jumps when I gently touch her elbow. Did she feel the same electricity as me? She watches the spot where my hand held her arm as if it were going to spawn new life. I tug her away from the guys because I want to have this conversation in private. Once I found a quiet corner, I leaned over her with a smile. "Did you like the flowers?" I ask like an over-eager teenager whose crush finally gave him the time of day.

She pauses, taking in my words. Then shakes her head, flailing her arms dramatically. She looks like one of those dancing balloons at the car wash. I hold off laughing because I don't think she'll appreciate the resemblance, and I am still trying to date this girl after all.

She shakes her head, her hand still on my chest as she stares at them for a beat. Her fingers flex, scratching across my white t-shirt like she's testing how it would feel underneath my button-up. *Perfect. Hot. Horny.* Are all the words running through my mind to describe this moment. "That's not the point," she whispers. *So that's a yes; she did like them.* "The point is you can't send me those anymore." Remorse runs thick in her voice. Why is she fighting this so hard? I can't be the only one feeling the attraction between us. I've never felt instantly connected to someone, and I want to figure out what it is about her that keeps drawing me in.

Tilting my head, I study her face, noticing she has this cute little birthmark under her eye, and her full lips have this pretty little bow on the top. "Why not? I thought you deserved them. The blue in the hydrangeas reminded me of your eyes."

A small smile plays on her lips. See, she melts at my compliments. She likes this. She likes me. Her expression is quickly covered with a hard line to the lips. "You *can't* send me those," she stresses, as though she's confirming it to herself as well.

"I'm hearing a lot of things I *can't* do but still no reason *why*?"

She looks around, leaning in so only I can hear. "You're getting me in trouble,"

Trouble? Pinching my eyebrows. "Why?"

"I can't receive gifts to the office."

I smile smugly. "I've got an easy fix for that; you could give me your number, and then I won't have to send anything here."

She shakes her head again, freezing because she notices her hands are still relaxed on my chest. I throw my head back when she flexes her fingers slightly, her nails scratching my chest in the most torturous way. Finally, she snatches her hand away like my chest is hot coal. “Look, you need to stop. Nothing can happen between us.” Her voice is stern again, like she’s trying to convince herself more than me.

Did she forget that I’m an athlete and competition is in my blood?

“I’m not interested in you.” It stumbles out of her mouth, and she looks almost as surprised as I felt. I wait for her to look me in the eyes, but she doesn’t. Instead, she just chews on her bottom lip like it’s a chocolate bar.

Before I can apologize for coming on too strong and telling her I’ll back off (for now), she’s gone, leaving me with just the click of her heels in the distance.

Slowly turning around, I trudge toward my team, trying to figure out what just happened. By the time I get to my teammates, my dejected and confused face has pretty much told them everything they needed to know.

I just got rejected but the hottest girl I’ve ever seen.

Grayson blew out a long breath after some awkward silence. “Tate, I told you not to let anyone see your dick in the daylight.” Everyone immediately starts laughing, cutting the tension, and I give a weak, pitiful smile, still trying to process everything that just happened.

Cali rejected me. She doesn’t want me, which might be a problem since all I want is a date with her.

Grayson shakes his head, walking beside me. "This is why I stay away from relationships. They get in the way, take up too much mental capacity, and pull your head out of the game. Can't win with them."

As much as I hate to admit it, maybe he’s right. In two short minutes, Cali had my balls shriveling into nothing when she told me to back off.

“Thank goodness you aren’t married,” Mike interjects. “You’d be a terrible husband.”

"Exactly why I'm not," Grayson chuckles. “One woman doesn’t

deserve this." But then, he showcases himself. "They *all* do."

There's a unison of groans at Grayson's remark. "Come on, guys. I could really use a cheesesteak tonight," I say, looking forward to the one woman who's never disappointed me.

Deena and her restaurant.

CHAPTER 7

CALI

Sweat trickles down both sides of my cheeks, but I can't do anything to get rid of it because Catty's stupid head is in the way. How do all those characters at Disney world keep up the charade in the Florida heat? Honestly, I'm considering just wearing a bikini under this next time. I'm already drenched in sweat; my clothes are ruined, the thirty-year-old washing machine in the basement of my apartment will be of no use on these kinds of stains. At least a bikini is supposed to be wet. Cleaning that would be a cinch, and I'd save a fortune on my laundry bills.

It'd been a long game, and I could have sworn Josh was punishing me when he extended the length of time I would be in the costume this morning. The first few times I was Catty, I only came out for the warm-ups and a couple of the innings in the middle. It gave me a little time to cool down and have a break. But Catty's popularity had grown exponentially since the beginning of the season a month ago, and Josh has now essentially forced me to go out for the entire nine innings.

Nine innings!

That's over three hours in a giant neoprene costume that doesn't breathe. It's a long-ass time. Today, one-half of those innings has taken over forty minutes. I swear Josh wanted me to faint so I'd quit.

It's now the bottom of the ninth, and I walk out of the stadium, too tired to stay and watch the last few at bats. Instead, I relax down on the sofa next to the locker room, still in my costume. Then, just as I'm about to take the catfish head off, I decide better of it. The idea of Tate seeing me like this would be horrific. Although that probably doesn't matter anymore. He's backed off. Just like I asked him to. No more surprise office visits or beautiful gifts waiting for me. It's as though all of that was a figment of my imagination.

And it still didn't stop Josh from being an ass toward me.

It'd been two whole weeks, and Josh is working me harder than ever, forcing me to do longer shifts as Catty and more marketing work after. The longer shift wasn't helping my mood and certainly didn't help me forget about Tate. I'd never admit it out loud, but I kind of miss him. We didn't date; I made sure to cut it off before we had that chance but I can't deny that I did like the attention. Okay, okay, I *loved* the attention, mainly because it was from him.

Tate Sorenson.

My dream man who's so far out of reach because I had to pick between my dream job and my dream man. Mary might say it doesn't break the rules, but Josh has different ideas, and I'd rather not give him more reason to hate me. And if I have to pick between Tate and my internship, I have to pick my job, right?

Yes.

I keep reminding myself that experience is essential. A job is more stable and reliable than a man. You get out what you put in. With a job, you know where you stand. With Tate, I risk my job, future career, and reputation. What if all he wants is a one-night stand? To bed his biggest fan. Giving up everything for a quick lay would suck and I'm not prepared to risk it.

The players filter into the hall, looking downcast because I guess they didn't manage to get the lead off Boston tonight. It's their first loss this year, so I'm sure they're taking it harder than usual. Resting my head back on the wall, I wait for the team to make their way into the locker room so I can leave and head home. The hairs on the back of my neck rise. From the corner of my eye, I can see Tate trudging down the hall.

Even with my limited view from the mask, I can tell he's perfection in those pants. "Catty," he says, pointing at me. I move my big head around and point at myself as a question since I can't speak. "Yes, I'm talking to you." Then, walking over to me, determination burns behind his eyes, he scowls, "you've been ignoring me." Sweat rolls down my temple as he stares into my googly eyes with intent. Can he see behind the mesh and see me? "Ever since that ATV incident, you're acting like I don't exist."

Lowering my head, I give a slight nod. There are two reasons I haven't been so forthcoming with him. Firstly, I don't want to embarrass him again. Making him the laughingstock of the MLB isn't something I want to make a habit of. The second reason is that I can fully admit that I melted whenever Tate was in the vicinity. I'm already a hot mess in this costume, and I'm afraid I'll become a puddle of my own sweat if I spend too much time around him.

"I thoroughly enjoyed our mock romp." He winks, or at least I think he winks; it's hard to tell through the mesh. He might just have a tick. Sitting down next to me, he leans back, lolling his head toward me. "Just so you know, I like to be part of the jokes. If you want to use me again. I'm right here."

I didn't know what to do. Should I take the head off and reveal it's me? Would he encourage the mock humping more then? No, wait, that's not a good idea. I'm hot and drenched in my own sweat. Even though I'm not planning on sleeping with Tate, there's still no way I want him to see me like this. So instead, I nod vigorously, giving him a thumbs up with my fin, or at least, I think it looks like a thumbs up.

He blows out a long breath, and now I'm fretting, wondering how long he's going to stay sitting there, swallowing up the air with his mere presence. I might suffocate in this thing if it's too long.

"Catty," he says more seriously this time. I turn the gigantic fish head in his direction to see him more clearly. He looks wearily in my direction, the googly eyes of the costume staring him down. "Have you ever had a crush on a girl?" My shoulders tense.

He knows it's me. Crap.

Raising his hand, he pats me on the shoulder, but it was more of a whack with his strength. I held back a cough of pain. "Ah, sorry, man. I know it's tough for you to find someone considering you're, you know, half fish, half man and all," he chuckles. The sound warms me from the inside. As if I wasn't hot enough in this thing. Playing with the bill of his cap, he tilts his head, thinking. "Maybe we could set you up with the Miami mascot. He's half fish too." He looks over for approval, and I shake my head quickly. "No?" Tate purses his lips. "You're right to be cautious. That pointy nose could be lethal. How would you even kiss?" He asks as though I can answer, or it's a plausible scenario. I shrug dramatically. "Maybe we need to go outside of baseball to find you a love match. I'll look into it." He leans forward, knotting his hands together as he thinks about Catty's next dating move. He looks more determined than I've ever seen him. It's then I realize Tate probably needs a hobby or some friends outside Baseball.

"I met someone." Is what I think he says, but I'm having a little trouble hearing him since he's speaking so quietly. Taking his cap off completely this time, he runs a hand through his sweat-soaked hair. "There's this girl." He starts, and my heart beats faster.

Is it me he's talking about?

"I haven't liked someone in a long time." He pauses, toying with his lips. "But there's something about her, and it's not just that she can probably reel off my stats without batting her eyelashes, although that *is* a turn-on." Then, pointing at me, he smiles. "Take note of that, Catty. If you find someone who knows everything about you, it will rock your world." He stares at me, waiting for a response, so I just nod diligently. He's not wrong; I could roll his stats off in my sleep. Just say a year, and I can tell you how many homers and his batting average in a second. I was kind of hoping I wasn't that obvious in front of Tate. But then again, he did see my desk.

"What's crazy, though. As much as she loves me as a player, she wants absolutely nothing to do with me as a guy." He scoffs at his own words. "I think it's because she's worried about losing her job. I don't want to push just in case she doesn't like me, and she's trying to let me down gently."

He rests his elbows on his thighs, revealing that broad, muscular back of his, and I can't stop my finned hand from reaching out and patting it. "Thanks, Catty," he pouts his bottom lip out on a huff. It's the cutest thing I've ever seen him do, and I've seen him do a lot. "I think it might be her boss. The guy is a tiny asshole, and I think he's trying to convince her she can't date players or something." I dramatically shrug my shoulders again because it's the only thing I can do. "But that's not true. I checked with one of the assistant coaches, and he told me it's fine." A cold shiver runs down my spine thinking about the fact that he looked into it for me. Surely, he would only do that if he *really* liked me. I don't think he'd put that much effort in for a quick lay. "But then do I run the risk of trying again with her? What if she really isn't interested, and I'm the one who needs to take the hint?" He contemplates, leaning back against the wall. Out of all the things to happen today, I did not expect to be consoling Tate as a giant fish over his inability to figure me out.

He scrubs his big paw over his face, looking up to the ceiling, letting out a saddened laugh. "I think I've got this infatuation with her, which is funny, right? Because she's my biggest fan. The stalker becomes the stalkee."

He waits for me to answer. I don't know what to do. "Tate? We need you to sign some stuff," an assistant with a mic says, walking down the hallway.

"Sure, Darren. I'll be there in a second." Tate smiled.

He clasps my knee, sending zings of electricity up my spine. I hate that I love how it feels and that it makes my panties a little damp. As if I needed the extra wetness down there. "Thanks for the chat, Catty. While I'm on my away trip, I'll let you know if I find a mascot to match your exacting standards." He stands, sauntering down the hallway without looking back. I'm left sitting there, gobsmacked and slightly lovestruck.

When I open the door to my measly apartment, the first things I see are the bright blue hydrangeas and white peonies peeking back at me in greeting. It's been two weeks since I got them, and they still look fresh as the day Tate bought them for me. I sigh, pulling my greasy, sweaty hair out of the ponytail, and walk towards the kitchenette. I throw my jacket over my tiny dining table and drop my bag onto the bed. Too much happened today to think straight, and I needed a shower before fully processing that conversation with Tate.

I groan as my aching body slogs to the bathroom, ready to wash the long day off me. The hot water soothes my sore muscles as I do my best to massage the knots out. The extra thirty-five pounds of weight from the costume didn't go unnoticed when dancing, and my muscles are screaming at me. Combine that with a straining headache from Josh, and you've got the recipe for an overly tired intern.

I still can't believe he stayed late just to yell at me about the fact I tripped up the stadium steps while standing next to a child. It's not like I did it on purpose. Someone spilled their Coke, and I couldn't see it under the mask.

If that wasn't enough, he then left me three budget spreadsheets to finish before I could leave the office. Tate's right. The guy's an asshole, and I swear I could poop gold, and he'd still find an issue with the nugget size. I just wish his treatment didn't affect me so much. That it didn't slowly chip away at my confidence one day at a time. But it did.

I don't know how long I stand in the shower, but it's long enough that my skin raisins to the point where I look like a crinkled chip. Dehydrated but still salty.

Wrapping myself in my Carolina Catfish bathrobe, I sit on my bed while mindlessly fiddling with my phone. Tate's face pops up on the screen every time I accidently turn the screen on, and I smile softly, thinking about all the things he said to me this afternoon.

Well, to Catty, not to me. I doubt he would have been that honest if he knew I was the real Catty crusader.

As I brush the knots out of my hair, a bright blue piece of paper catches my eye. Tate's messy handwriting is scrawled across it, and I can barely make out his number. Thankfully, the note from the flowers sits just underneath it with the same number printed in ink. Playing with my lips, I contemplate programming it into my phone. After everything Tate said today, I do kind of feel bad about how quickly I brushed him off, especially since it did nothing to change Josh's treatment toward me.

The flower's scent clings in the air, and a pang of guilt washes over me. Even if nothing comes of it, I really should say thank you to Tate. I start to reason with myself. It's rude of me not to thank him at all but instead embarrass him in front of his teammates. If I left it, and he didn't contact me again, I'd never get that opportunity. So, I should definitely text him to at least say thank you.

Sitting up, I grab the paper and type Tate's number in. My thumbs start typing, and I shoot off a text before I can talk myself out of it.

Cali: Hi Tate. Great game today. I'm sorry I was so rude last week. I just wanted to say a belated thank you for the flowers. They're beautiful and make my apartment smell amazing.

I cringe at how pathetic the message sounds. When the blue ticks appear, my heart beats faster, and I start to feel anxious. It's official. Tate's read the message. I gave him my number and opened the communication channel between us.

Tate: Hey. So, I don't have this number saved, but the only person I've sent flowers to except my mom in the last month is Cali. Is it you? Oh wait, I guess it could be Grayson, but I already have his number, and he thanked me for them yesterday. 😉

I laugh at his stupid joke, the pressure in my chest slowly dissipating because he's not making it awkward or giving me a hard time. I let a little squeal escape my lips because I'm alone in my apartment, and Tate's just confirmed I'm the only one he's sending flowers to; ergo, I'm the only one he's thinking about.

Cali: I don't want to know what you and Grayson get up to behind closed doors. Yes, it's Cali.

Tate: Are you sure? It would probably blow your baseball-loving mind.

Cali: I'm sure. Let me be the one to create my own fantasies.

Tate: Fantasies, huh? More like FANtasies.

Cali: Stop!

Tate: You started it. Although, after seeing your makeshift work calendar, I'm frightened about what your fantasies might entail. Maybe you can tell me about them sometime.

I giggle at his flirty messages and gnaw at my bottom lip, wondering what to say back. I want to say something cute, maybe even a little flirty too, but I've never really sent anything like that before. So finally, after five minutes of thinking, I quickly type something, not wanting him to think I'm ignoring him.

Cali*:* Maybe one day I'll let you in on the secret.

Tate: A guy can dream

My body heats when I think about all the things I'd do to Tate if we were ever left alone in the first aid room again. Of course, they aren't decent, but I think he'd be game.

Tate: Can I ask you something?

That last message piques my interest.

Cali: Sure.

Tate: Why did you decide to message me now? I gave you my number weeks ago, and then you brutally turned me down in front of my entire team. It's something my ego will never forget.

My body slumps. If I explained everything that was going on in my head, it would be a long rambling message. One that would make no sense. I also felt a little sheepish that I was so concerned about losing my job. I still am. Josh seems worse when I'm happy, but it's not against the rules. Both Tate and Mary confirmed as much.

Cali: Sorry about that. I shouldn't have come in so hot. My mind was all over the place.

Tate: Work stressing you out?

Cali: Yeah, I guess. I thought if you weren't in the picture, things would be easier.

Tate: Were they?

Cali: No.

Tate: I'm sorry.

Cali: Not your fault.

Tate: So, California, is this your way of letting me know you're on for a date?

It takes me seven attempts to write the message before I'm happy enough to reply. I don't want to come off too strong or eager, but equally, I want him to know I'm interested.

Cali: Take from that what you will, but we can at least be friends.

Tate: I'm holding onto the fact that you said *at least*. :)

Wetness pools against my cheek, waking me up. My neck is strained, I'm still in my bathrobe, and I'm clutching my phone tightly. Dampening down my messy hair, I look around the room, trying to remember what happened last night.

Tate and I texted for hours, talking about our weeks. He's so funny and charming and… normal. It felt like I was talking to a friend I've known for years, not a multimillionaire ballplayer.

It's so easy to get lost in Tate. He's always eager to ask questions and find out more about me. It's almost like he can't get enough of me, and I can't get enough of him.

Opening my phone, I go to my messages and gasp in surprise. There, sitting in my messages, is a picture of Tate's tanned, bare chest as he holds onto the edge of his boxers.

How the hell did I fall asleep after that?

I quickly swipe up through the messages, only to realize that I'd stopped replying at around three am, and he continued to send me messages to see if I would wake up. Finally, after I didn't respond to the picture, he left a simple goodnight text with a kiss.

Scrolling back to the photo, I zoom in, taking in every crevice and ridge on his beautiful chest. It's definitely his, I've seen that little mole on his nipple before, and even though I'm half asleep, I'm starting to feel slightly aroused. That never happens. I hate to admit it to myself, but I want Tate badly.

The little clock at the top of the screen reminds me that I'm already running late, and Josh will yell at me if I don't get him another coffee from the coffee shop again. I bought him that drink one time as a nice gesture, but he assumed it was my new normal.

Sighing, I head to the bathroom to get ready for the day. At least Tate's bare chest is filling my mind instead of Josh today.

CHAPTER 8

TATE

"Strike Two."

"Argh," I grunt, whacking the bat in annoyance, fully expecting it to split from the impact. When it doesn't, I straighten up, cracking my neck, trying to get my shit together. I glare at the umpire, annoyed at how generous he's been with the strike zone today. Too generous. If I'm not careful, I will get my third strikeout of the day. Something that won't be good for maintaining my MVP caliber stats. It doesn't matter that we have one hundred and twenty games left; I need to maintain them if I want to be considered again this year.

The New York Knaves pitcher, Adam Jeffries, stares me down, hoping to psych me out. Too bad I've played him enough to know his tells. His nose twitches, and in a split second, he throws a fastball. I lift my front leg, winding the bat back to swing with enough momentum to knock that ball out of the park. The next few seconds are like slow motion as I watch the ball slowly sink. There's no way I'm going to hit it, but I can't stop my body. It's already in full swing.

"Strike Three."

I hear the leather of the catcher's mitt against the ball as the umpire waves his arms. *Well, crap.* Adam smiles smugly on the mound, gripping the ball in his hand. Someone must have told him about his tell. Walking back to the dugout, I kick the wood, feeling defeated. Where's Catty when I need him? He high-fived Austin in the fourth inning, and the guy scored a three-run homer straight after. I need some of that luck.

"Tate deserves better!" The shrill voice of a fan cut through the noise, making me jump. It's not often that I can hear the chants, but the woman is close enough to hear her clear diction. It's well known that the Catfish are the most dedicated fans in the league. It's something I like to take advantage of when we're at home games. I look up to the crowd, fully intending to wave at the fan and maybe sign something.

I lose my breath when I spot her.

Cali is standing right above the dugout, looking like she's about to murder the umpire as she threatens him with a foam fin. She'd look utterly menacing if she weren't so cute. It takes her a minute to notice me watching her, but when she does, she gives me a bright smile and waves enthusiastically, her blonde hair shining in the dusky light.

I haven't been able to get my mind off her since she sent me that text a few weeks ago. We text daily now. It's nothing major; we just talk about our days, and she usually gives me pointers and tips for my game if she finds time to watch, which doesn't sound like often. We get along, and it's all been very plutonic so far. I've been trying to figure out a way to broach taking our relationship to the next level, but she always seems so tired when we message.

Patience is key with a girl like her, and that's something I've got an abundance of. I already know she's not interested in my fancy car or big apartment. She just likes talking to me. Tate Sorenson, the guy. Not the brand which Sam seemed most drawn to. It made me like her even more. So much so that I had to remind myself to cool it. Relax and pace myself.

Not trying to sound like an asshole, but I didn't have to work for it in High School. Girls would ask me out. When I got to the Minors, and things started falling apart, I felt lost. I was a thousand miles away from my family, and the guys weren't exactly friendly. Sam was persistent, always waiting for me after the game and always asking for an autograph until she finally asked for my number. I liked that she had a determined and tenacious attitude to begin with. I thought it meant that we were well suited. Little did I know the insidious nature our relationship would take. She was like a leech, not bothering me much until she was hungry. Then she started sucking the life out of me. That's when I knew I had to get rid of her.

Cali's the exact opposite to her in every way.

Younger. Full of life - not herself. Loves that I play ball but doesn't care about the fame. In fact, I'm pretty confident that was the thing that's putting her off the most about me. Even though she has enough bobbleheads of me to fill our 40-man roster, she's still making me chase her. She's making me work for it, and I love it.

As I raise my hand to wave back, some dude plops down beside her, handing her a Catfish shaped hotdog, which she takes eagerly. They're perfectly matched. What with her fin hand and his whiskered baseball hat, they look like the perfect little couple. Clenching my jaw, I watch as the guy follows Cali's gaze and lands on me. His eyes brighten just like hers, and he waves just as enthusiastically before pulling Cali into a side hug.

What.

The.

Fuck.

My lip curls, and I have to stop myself from snarling. Rage courses through my bones, and adrenaline takes over. *Is that her boyfriend?* Clenching and unclenching my fists, I hope the little pain there is enough to erase some of my anger. I wish I were going up to bat now so that I could smash that shit straight out of the park.

"Sorenson! Get in the dugout." Coach Snider yells. Without waving back to the hat-wearing woman stealer, I stalk down the steps, through the dugout to the locker room, and pace. No one dares to come near me, giving me a little time to compose myself. After that lousy at bat, all that relief and excitement I felt from seeing her was completely trampled on by that dude she was hugging.

Why am I letting myself get so worked up?

Granted, we've only been talking a few weeks, and that was just through text. I have no claim on her, and we aren't anywhere near dating. It's just that after a few of our flirtier messages, I thought we both knew where this was going. I thought she wanted us to get to know each other first. She's never once mentioned another guy before. There was no ring on her finger the first and second time I met her – I checked. I thought she was a free agent, ready for me to acquire.

What if *he's* the reason she hasn't jumped at the chance to go on a date with me? What if I've read the whole situation wrong, and she's only humoring me because she wants to be friends with a famous ballplayer. Maybe her only interest in me is watching me break wood on the plate and not in bed.

Kill me now if that's the case because I want her. I've had too many fantasies about her at this point for it not to happen.

"Dude, what the hell has gotten into you? You need to calm down." Max, one of the pitchers, follows me in. "You've struck out three times; it's not a big deal. You'll get up to bat at least two more times this game. You've got this."

I force my gaze down, embarrassed that I let a girl affect my focus, something that has never happened before. Not even when I was a 16-year-old virgin. I shake my head, ridding myself of thoughts of Cali. "You're right. I just gotta get my head back in the game."

When I eventually connect eyes with him, he smiles. "Good, because we're top of the inning. Let's go."

He's right. I need to focus on what's important. This game. This team. This win. That girl can wait. I grab my lucky glove, punch into the leather, and jog back out onto the field.

With all my energy and vigor, I slide into Homeplate. My toe tips the base just as I feel Trey's tag brush my leg.

"Safe!" The umpire calls. I know they're going to challenge it. It's a close call, and if I get it, Marc's just scored his first walk-off.

Standing next to the base, I scuff my shoes against the dirt with my hands on my hips, waiting for the verdict. The crowd boo, and I can distinctly hear the shrill cry of Cali. I will myself not to look over and keep my focus. That's what I've been doing since the sixth inning, and it seemed to be working. In the seventh, I focused all of my anger and rage on a pitch and whacked the ball so hard I stood there for a minute, admiring as the pummeled ball flew straight out of the park. I scored two runs on that homer, tying the game.

When the umpire slices his hands, yelling 'safe' again, the crowd's cheer is deafening. The rest of the team rush out onto the field, grabbing me with a hug.

Grayson drenches me in cold water, still celebrating the win. From the way we're celebrating, you'd think we'd won the World Series instead of sweeping a series with our division rivals.

Bending forward, I gather up my wet hair and flick it at my teammates as I stand up. This win feels good, and I want to celebrate with the crowd. Sauntering over to the cheers, I raise my hands, hyping the fans up. Although I admit, it feels good scoring like that in front of Cali and her boyfriend. I'm not sure what point I was trying to make, but I knew I had proved something.

I shouldn't look above the dugout. I should focus on all the fans chanting my name. Not on the hot girl cozying up to her boyfriend.

I shouldn't focus on her.

I shouldn't.

But I do.

Cali's drawing away from a hug with that guy as I look over, and when she meets my eyes, she smiles that gorgeous smile again. It's like somehow she knows I did all of this for her. Her fist waves in the air as she screams and jumps up, her boyfriend failing miserably at calming her down. Something about how embarrassed he is by her makes me want to go to the batting cages and whack a few balls.

Stepping into the dugout, I grab a drink and stroll into the locker room. Getting that win is great except for that festering pissed off feeling radiating through my bones. How do I broach the boyfriend subject with her without sounding pathetically eager? Although, if I'm honest, I've sounded pathetically eager the whole time. This is no different. What's wrong with me? I'm the star of the Carolina Catfish, yet here I am, on my knees begging for a date from a girl who has a boyfriend.

Teammates whack my back, congratulating me, but the victory feels hollow somehow. I just wanted to go home and clear my brain. Skipping the shower, I grab my bag, waving goodbye to the guys as I leave. I twirl the keys in my hand, ready to get the day over with. When I open the door, Cali is standing there. Fin in hand with a smile on her face.

"Tate," she breathes out like I've just given her the best orgasm of her life. I focus on her face, hoping she'll focus on mine too - not on the uncomfortable strain in my pants.

She jumps into me, taking me by surprise when she clasps her arms around my neck. My whole body freezes, unsure of what the hell is happening. It's the first time she's actually touching me, and she's acting like we're… friends? The sports drink in the dugout must have been spiked because I'm delusional. Her boyfriend shuffles over, standing behind her with his hands stuffed in his pockets, awkwardly rocking from side to side.

Cali ignores him, focusing solely on me. "You played great tonight. That homer in the eighth was incredible." Unrequited lust laced her words. I can hear it, and I'm beyond confused as the guy looks on with an awkward smile.

Flicking my gaze at her boyfriend, I look back down at her. Screw it. I can't help myself. I want her. I drop my hand to her hip, liking the way her body feels pressed against mine.

She squeals a little when I press my fingers into her skin, and she leans back slightly to ask, "what got into you?"

A smile curves across my lips. I want to flirt and ask her the same question - hoping her answer is me - but I don't. He looks all kinds of nervous and young enough to need a car seat. I'm not fazed; I'll win this.

How old is Cali anyway? I've been guessing around twenty-two or twenty-three since she's interning, but this guy looks a lot younger than that. I drop my hands, suddenly worried she's not legal. "Cali, what are you doing here?"

She stiffens, taking a step away from me. Yeah, I'm being rude, but I need to keep my ego intact and make sure I'm not trying to date a minor. Although, if she came down here just to show off to her boyfriend that she knows me, I'd be humiliated. That would be almost as bad as when Sam posted a picture of her 'cheating' on me online. We'd broken up a month before but hadn't informed the press. She took that as her chance to create her own narrative and embarrass me in front of the entire state.

Cali bit her bottom lip, looking between her boyfriend and me. "I, uh," she hesitates. "I just wanted to introduce you to my brother, Penn." She takes another step back, but I instinctively stop her, my whole body relaxing.

Her brother.

Of course, he's her brother. The only guy she ever talks about in our messages.

Penn shuffles forward with a little pink in his cheeks and an awkward smile. How did I not see it before? They have the same mouth and button nose. "Hi, Mr. Sorenson. It's nice to meet you." He speaks formally with an air of nervousness. Well, now I feel like a dick and a moron.

I wave at her brother, smiling at him. *Her brother, you idiot!* "Please. Call me Tate. It's great to meet you, Penn." I hold my hand out, and he accepts, shaking it earnestly.

The tension leaves the air, and I notice Cali's body relax as she leans in close to me. "I don't know if you remember, but Penn is a starting pitcher at The Charlotte High Hyenas." Of course, I did. I've read her messages hundreds of times, searching for a deeper meaning like I'm some kind of teenage girl hoping my crush notices me. "He's their Ace," she says proudly while Penn's cheeks flush at the recognition. "He wants to go pro after college."

"Oh yeah? Maybe you can pitch to me sometime," I offer.

Penn raises his arm, scratching the back of his neck. "Maybe in a couple of years. I don't think I'm good enough for that just yet."

Cali makes this sweet whimpering noise after hearing her brother. "That's not true, Penn. You're awesome." She rushes over, pulling at his arm, adoration clear in her eyes. It's how I want her to look at me.

"It's all about the attitude with pitchers," I explain. "Maybe I could introduce you to Grayson Hawk sometime? He's got an attitude the size of North Carolina. I'm sure he could teach you a few things." Penn studders a little as his mouth parts, and his eyes widen. He looks at Cali, giving her a large smile, and then turns to me.

"I would love that, Sir." He shakes his head, muttering under his breath. "I mean, Tate."

Leaning close to Cali, I wonder how much she's told Penn about me. Has she mentioned that I'm trying to date her? "It's not a problem. Just let Cali know when you're free, and I can arrange it sometime." I can feel Cali's smile beaming at me, and all that tense anger I felt before has slowly disappeared.

Penn grins earnestly. "We're going out for dinner if you want to join? Ouch! What was that for?" He asks, rubbing his belly because Cali just tried to elbow him subtly. Too bad her pink ears give away her embarrassment.

"Ignore him. I know you're busy, and you'll be traveling tomorrow, so you don't have time for dinner with us." Her whole body is vibrating with awkwardness as she squirms on the spot.

Still rubbing his stomach, Penn grimaces. "I thought you said you were friends?" Interesting definition of me. We won't be *friends* for long if I have my way.

"Where are you going?" I ask Penn, ignoring the surprised look from Cali.

Penn straightens up, running a hand through his dark, red hair. "It's this place just around the corner we always go to after watching a game. Have you ever been to *Deena's*?"

I snort out a laugh. "I love *Deena's*. I'm surprised I haven't seen you there before." Wrapping my arm around Cali's shoulder, I look between them. "Let me just change out of my uniform, and I'll meet you out here." I point to the floor, directing my conversation to Penn since I don't trust Cali from bolting.

"uh, oh-kay," she stumbles out anxiously, tripping over her own feet when I back away from her.

Now I've just got to dress as fast as I can so I can spend as much time with my girl as possible.

"I'm stuffed," Cali proclaims, throwing her napkin on the table as she relaxes back into her seat. Looking at her empty plate, I'm impressed. She managed to eat two tacos, a bean burrito, and an enchilada. My gaze drifts down when she starts to rub her belly. I really shouldn't find the move erotic, but I've come to the conclusion, Cali could burp the alphabet, and I'd still be horny.

"Glad you've finished. Now, will you let *me* finish?" Penn quips, turning his attention back to me. "As I was saying before I was rudely interrupted." He glares pointedly at her. "Cali's been obsessed with ballplayers all her life. Her first crush was Jerry Walker and then Brian Liddle. I also remember a Brady Combs phase too." Penn throws his head back when I hear a loud bang under the table. I'm guessing Cali gave his leg a little whack.

My eyebrows shoot up, and my lips curve into a smile. "So, what you're telling me is, Cali's had a crush on every shortstop the Fish has had to offer since she was born?" He nods, and I scoff, feeling a lot less flattered that she picked me to obsess over. I fold my arms, resting them against the table. "Good to know she's got a type." And that I'm the Fish's shortstop for the next ten years. I lift my glass, taking a long drink of my cold water. Cali watches my throat with interest as I swallow. Her lips get smaller and smaller, but her gaze gets hotter and hotter. I pulled the glass from my lips, hiding my smirk. "Tell me something, though." I directed my question to Penn. "Does she have a bobblehead collection of the rest of them?"

Pann cackles, throwing his head back. "Nope, that's all you." I love how bashful she is, and I gently tap my shoe against hers. We've spent the last three hours just talking and laughing together. "The bobblehead thing all started when she got a freebie of you for attending one of the first home games a few years ago." Cali smacks her hand across her face, groaning as she slides down into her chair. "I think you scored a homer that day and won. The next game she went to, you were having a real stinker, so when the Catfish lost, she assumed that having a bobblehead was good luck. So she bought a bobblehead the next time she went to a game and you scored a walk off homer. That solidified it. From then on, she bought a new one every time she thought you'd have a tough game ahead." I tilt my head and watch her. She moves from side to side, looking anywhere but me.

Cali quickly shuffles, pushing Penn out of the way. "On that note, I need to go to the bathroom." She scurries out of the booth without another glance. My eyes track her every move. I fully planned to watch her ass in those tight jeans but got distracted by the name on the back of her jersey instead. *Walker.* "Interesting choice," I mutter under my breath as I turn back to the table.

Penn laughs. "She always wears her Walker jersey whenever she watches a game on Saturday. She never wears a current player's jersey at home just in case she jinxes them."

I raise my eyebrow in surprise. "Your sister seems very superstitious."

"And you aren't? Isn't it true that you wear an old raggedy t-shirt under your jersey every game because the great Hank Arnold gave it to you?" He catches me off guard with that question. I've only ever mentioned that in one obscure interview a few years ago. No one has ever asked me about it. Should I be all that surprised, though? His sister is my biggest fan and seemingly knows everything about me.

I shrug. "Good point." Glancing over my shoulder, I make sure the coast is clear before leaning over the table to ask, "what's the deal with Cali?" After today's miscommunication, I figure I might as well bite the bullet and ask.

Penn's eyebrows cross. "What do you mean?"

"Does she have a boyfriend?" I ask the question flat out because I refuse to be blindsided again. Of course, I could wait and ask Cali myself, but I figure I'll get a straighter answer from Penn.

He holds back a smile. "I knew she was lying when she told me you were just good friends." He rolls his eyes, "Cali told me she was working with you."

I squint, thinking about it. "Interesting take on the situation."

"I knew it." He laughs, shaking his head. "No, she doesn't have a boyfriend." Penn clarifies, and I let out the breath I didn't know I was holding in. "She's never had one that I know of." My mind nearly explodes. Cali is one of the hottest girls I've ever met. How are guys not lining up to take her out? "Oh wait, I think mom mentioned there was a guy when she was in college, but she's never brought one home." My ears prickle at that interesting tidbit. But, of course, I'll take that with a grain of salt. I doubt Cali often talks about guys with her family and her baby brother, but it's good to know she hasn't liked a guy enough to bring him home.

"Cali loves you, though," Penn emphasizes. That, in itself, could be part of my issue. She could be in love with the Tate Sorenson, who wins games for her favorite team. Maybe she's afraid she won't like the real me once she gets to know me. Maybe she doesn't *want* to get to know me like that.

"Sorry, what did I miss?" Cali hurries back into her seat, smoothing her hair down. God, do I want to run my hands through those blonde strands. To grasp a few clumps of it and kiss her senseless. You know, everyday thoughts.

Penn clears his throat. "Tate was just about to tell me how you two met." Her mouth gapes open, and she looks like a gulping fish waiting for me to respond. The waitress walks over, dropping off the bill into the center. I grab it before either Penn or Cali can. As if I would let them pay.

I throw a fifty down, staring at Cali, lifting my brow in a silent invitation for her to answer. "We met when I went down to see the medic for this." She raises her wrist, showing a smaller bandage in Carolina blue fabric then gestures toward me. "Tate was there for his post-game checkup."

"Interesting place to pick up women," Penn mumbles, but I hear it and bark out a laugh. It's not like I haven't made my intentions clear with Cali. I know I've got no chill when it comes to her. I own that shit.

"How did you hurt your wrist again?" Penn asks. It's a good question because I've asked a few times and I don't remember her telling me. She usually changes the subject instead. When I asked Phil, he said something about her being clumsy but was notably vague about her wrist injury.

Cali's eyes narrow, looking between us hesitantly before grabbing her phone. "Oh, look. Is that the time? Mom and Dad are going to kill me if I keep you out late on a school night, Penny," she says through clenched teeth, squeezing his shoulder extra tight.

Penn rolls his shoulder out of her hold. "Firstly, don't call me Penny. I'm not ten." He adjusts his jersey, sitting up straighter. "Secondly, I'm eighteen. Mom free birded me months ago. I can come and go as I please. Thirdly, it's Saturday, and I'm the one driving your ass home." He shakes his head, snickering.

"I'll drive her." The offer came out of my mouth before I thought it through. I wanted to see where she lived. What made her, well, her. But mostly, I didn't want the night to end. It felt too soon.

Cali doesn't say anything; she just has this surprised look on her face. She doesn't outright reject it, though, so that's a good sign.

"Thanks, Tate," Penn says smugly with mock surprise. I'm guessing that was his plan all along, and he was doing me a solid. I'll send some free tickets to his team as a thank you. "That makes my life easier. Her apartment is a good thirty minutes out of my way."

Cali gulps as she watches me high-five her brother. She's

accepted the ride home, and I can't wait to get her alone.

She's all mine now.

Chapter 9

CALI

"My apartment is just here." I point at the tall building ahead, worried that he's judging my slightly sketchy neighborhood. Okay, very sketchy neighborhood. "You can drop me off out front." Tate's quiet, ignoring my request when he flips the indicator up and turns into the graffiti covered parking lot. Not the type of place you'd typically see a brand-new red mustang. Nerves creep through my stomach, wondering what thoughts must be running through his head about where I live. It's run down, old, and the main reason I want him to leave me out front is that I'm not sure his car is safe down here. The security camera hasn't worked since I moved in six months ago; if it ever worked at all.

Tate parks up, and before I have a chance to think of a way to get him to leave, he's already on my side of the car, opening the door for me with that million-dollar smile of his. Why did he have to be so gorgeous? "Thanks for coming tonight," I say, taking his hand, totally ignoring the tingly feeling in my heart as he helps me out. Lord knows I need the support; these seats are deep, and my legs are long. I'd look like a gangly spider on its back trying to get out without a helping hand.

Standing outside in the darkened parking lot, my brain stops working for a second when I hear the car door shut and feel Tate's presence all around me.

There's a comfortable silence between us as Tate stares down at me. I feel his gaze taking me in hungrily, and I don't know where to look.

This wasn't a date; I know that because my brother was there, but it sure feels like one when Tate places his palms on either side of my shoulders. When he leans in, I can smell the sweet scent of strawberry bubblegum on his breath – his favorite on game day.

I take a greedy inhale, feeling giddy that I'm close enough to smell it.

"The pleasure is all mine, Cali." And there he goes again, making my knees feel like jelly. The way he says my name makes me tingle all over. My chest starts rising and falling rapidly when he drops his head, so his mouth is next to my ear. His breath tickles under the collar of my jersey, and I can feel my skin pebbling, anticipating his touch. "Thanks for inviting me," he coos, and I close my eyes, breathing in his cologne. Woody, grassy, and all man.

He backs away, letting his butterscotch eyes travel the length of my body until they return to my face. Then, biting on his bottom lip, I'm reminded of my makeshift calendar in the office. It's the same smile as July's photo. I picked it because I loved the intensity burning in his eyes. Never in my wildest dreams did I think he would ever direct that smile at me. "Can we count this as our first date?" *Did he know I was thinking the same thing?* The corner of his mouth lifts, his eyes sparkling with mischief. It feels like he's pleading for me to legitimize this.

Legitimize him.

Resting my hands on his chest, I shake my head, pushing him back. "That was not a date, Tate. I don't go on dates with my brother there." When I try to take my hand away, he grabs it, placing it just above his heart. Of course, I leave out the fact that I don't really go on dates, period. I don't want him to think I'm a lonely beaver or anything. But, wait, maybe that's the wrong choice of animal.

The cold night air sends a shiver down my spine, and when Tate notices, he gently places his hand on my back. Warmth pools in my belly as I watch a smile grow on his lips. "Guess I'll just have to take you out when I'm back from my road trip then." His confident words make me involuntarily purr as I watch his head drop down. We shouldn't be doing this. There's a chance if Josh finds out, I could get fired. Tate's lips are inches away from mine, and I should stop it.

But I don't. Because as much as I love working for the Catfish, I love being chased by Tate more. Besides, there's this nagging thought in the back of my mind. Mary and Tate checked; there's nothing wrong with me wanting to date Tate. He's free game and is making it very hard not to like him. Spending the entire dinner asking my brother about his team and treating him like one of his friends didn't help my resolve either. It all felt so easy sitting there with him and made it hard to resist.

Tate gently brushes his lips against mine, barely kissing me but igniting every single nerve in my body. I close my eyes, enjoying the feeling running through my chest, straight down to my toes. Anticipation builds as I wait for him to press harder and kiss me like he means it, but he doesn't. Instead, he's intent on grazing his lips across mine, not kissing me fully but teasing me relentlessly.

Just as his body presses against mine and I finally think he's going to take me out of my misery, he backs away. Cold air splashes across my wet lips as reality settles in. Eyes shut, feeling a little too wanton from just a kiss, I invertedly groan in protest. That kiss can't be finished just yet. If I'm going to break the rules, I want more than just the gentle brush of his lips.

Tate shakes his head as though he's trying to stop himself, but when he sees my reaction, his gaze drops to my lips. "Screw it," he wisps out, threading his hand through my hair, guiding me towards him. I can feel his fingers tighten their hold as his lips claim mine with force.

Controlling the clinch, he pulls me closer, resting one of his hands on my hip, keeping me firmly in place. His kiss is soft, hard, intense, and soothing all at once. It fills me with a deep-seated need to be closer to him. As his fingers thread through my hair, I realize

I've never been kissed. Not like this. Not with nearly as much passion and vigor as he shows. His tongue swipes across my bottom lip, and I open for him.

I'm hungry. Insatiable, even. I want more of him, and I'll worry about the consequences later.

With my back against his car, Tate's jeans rub against my thigh as he moves his body against mine. Even through all the layers, I can feel his hardness against my leg, and I find it hard to believe I'm the one making him feel like that. "You're so hot," he says in between kisses and thrusts his body into me one more time just to emphasize the point. My head lolls back, resting on the roof of the car as he kisses down my neck. It's delicious and naughty being outside in a parking lot while getting ravaged by the hottest guy I've ever laid eyes on. Tate had a way of making me feel adventurous, sexy even with just a single glance.

I jump when a horn honks on the other side of the lot, combined with a flash of what I presume is a passing headlight. My hands clutch at Tate's muscular shoulders. He looks up at me, concerned and confused. "Are you okay?" Brows furrowed, he waits for an answer, and the cold air hits me like a bucket of ice water. Dampening the mood and bringing me back to reality. We were dry-humping in a parking lot. We shouldn't be doing this because we're not horny teenagers, but also, anyone could take a picture and sell it to the highest bidder. It would be all over the news, which wouldn't look great for the Carolina Catfish or us. I shouldn't be doing this. For my job's sake. For my sanity's sake. But as I turn back and see his full lips, all I can think about is how much I want to do it again. And again.

He leans back in, ready for round two, but my palms meet his lips before he can get too close. His eyes widen as he takes in my attempt at a stony face. "I should be heading to my apartment." I feel his lips curling into a smile under my touch. "Alone." I clarify, and his body slumps ever so slightly. To call my apartment humble would be exaggerating, and even though Tate didn't bat an eyelid at the parking lot, I'm not sure I could say the same for the rest of my place. The walls are so thin; I can tell when Mr. Bricks, my next-door neighbor, flushes the toilet, which is a monumental mood killer. Not that I'd ever set a mood in there before.

I force myself away from him because if I had a choice, I'd let him touch me for hours. Since this wasn't a date, though, I really shouldn't be inviting a guy up to my apartment. Instead, he stands back, watching

Do I really want to do this?

Do I really want to end it now?

My perfect guy is standing in front of me, begging me with his eyes to bring him upstairs, and I'm hesitating because of an unpaid job. One that forced me to work overtime because of my mascot commitment and that I only got because my best friend begged for me. The job was my dream, though, and although it wasn't paying now, it could happen in the future. "Are you really going to leave me like this?" He laughs, arms in the air as he watches me click the elevator button.

I nod, watching my feet, and suppress a giggle. "Oh no, I know why you don't want me up there," he says confidently, making me whip my head back up. "You're worried I'll see all your Tate Sorenson memorabilia?" He barks out a laugh. Flashes of my room come to mind. My framed Tate Sorenson jersey from his 40/40 season, the five trading cards sitting on my desk with his face on them, the make-shift calendar of Tate in little more than a towel (I created a more risqué one for my home collection). He can't see all that. He'll think I'm obsessed with him. Well, I guess I kind of am, but he'll assume that's the only reason I've been talking to him. A bat chaser I am not. Or, I guess, not on purpose.

"No, It's not that," I lie. "You've got to be up early for your trip to Milwaukee tomorrow." I know that because I have a calendar on my desk with all their games marked and pretty much have their schedule memorized at this point.

He shrugs a shoulder, scratching the stubble on his chin. I turn around, needing some respite from his too gorgeous face. "I'll be on the bus with a bunch of smelly guys all day. I won't miss anything if I sleep through it." The elevator dings open, yet my feet were planted firmly in place. I don't want this night to end. As I look into the metal interior, I hear footsteps coming up behind me. I know who it is without looking. His hand touches my hip again, immediately scorching me. "Can I come up, Cali?" His voice thick with intensity and want.

"Your car. You can't leave it out here." It's my final defense before throwing caution to the wind and ignoring all instincts about my job. It was also the truth; I didn't want to be the reason he had no tires when he came back down.

"I don't care too much about my car right now," he purrs into my ear, and I pause. No man has ever been so forthright about wanting me. It's a turn on that I can't deny, and it's screwing with my head and my decisions. He lifts his hands off me, raising them to his sides as I glance over my shoulder to look at him. "But if you don't want me to come up. That's fine. I *will* take you on that date, though." His feet back away, but I don't feel the sense of relief I was hoping for. It's more like an ache of sadness. I don't want him to go. I want him to fight for me. Instead, he watches my reaction as he walks backward.

I don't want this to end.

It's now or never.

He stands at his car, hand on the handle, still watching. He's leaving it up to me, and I'm the most indecisive person I know.

Raising my head to the ceiling, I swipe my face, already thinking about the decision's consequences and not caring. "If you come up, you have to promise to give me a few minutes to sort out my apartment before you come in," I speak to the ground because I can't handle the look on his smug face. I brush over the fact that I've never invited anyone up to my apartment, let alone a guy that I like. Who also just so happens to be a multi-millionaire.

He lifts his hands to his heart. "I promise." A wry smile plays on his lips, and it makes him look gorgeous. He jogs over, tucking me under his arm, and grins. I just wish his smugness wasn't so attractive. "What's your floor number?"

"Six," I say, nuzzling closer into his chest, inhaling his scent. This thick thumb presses the button, and my heart clenches.

Well, here goes nothing.

Chapter 10

TATE

Standing outside Cali's apartment, I lean against the door, waiting to be invited in. She's on the other side, rushing around; I assume cleaning. Every now and again, I hear the occasional grunt with a swear word mixed in. Objects drop loudly, and I wonder if she's a hoarder. Maybe just a baseball hoarder. The thought goes out of my head when I could've sworn I heard some symbols clanging. I laugh to myself when I hear another curse word leave her mouth. It's adorable.

I gently rasp my knuckles against the door. "Everything okay in there?" I ask quietly, noting the neighbor's door is close, and I don't want to disturb them.

The noise stops for just a second. "Everything's fine," she pipes back, but there's just the slightest strain in her voice. Why is she so afraid of me seeing all her baseball stuff? All that fiery passion she has for The Fish is hot, and her dedication to the team is commendable, especially to the team shortstop. She's not the average fan. She's not the average girl. I already know that.

I gently rest my forehead on her door, closing my eyes and thinking back to the parking lot when her hands clasped my shoulders, and I was rocking my hips against her. I would have taken her then and there if there wasn't a risk of the police being called for indecent exposure. I don't know what will happen between us tonight, but I have this aching need to be closer to her. The fact that she invited me up gives me some confidence that she might be feeling the same way.

When I open my eyes, I notice a piece of thick green paint peeling off the door. I pick at it, wondering if I have time in the next month to come back and re-paint it as a surprise for her. I'll paint it Catfish Blue. She'll love it. Maybe I could even find her a little catfish door knocker. Shaking my head, I laugh at my own desperation. One kiss, and this girl's already got me tied in knots, planning surprise maintenance on her house. With my ear pressed against the door, I can hear her shuffling towards it, so I take a step back. She sighs as the doorknob turns and the door opens.

As she opens the door, her intoxicating coconut scent invades the hallway. Biting her lip, she looks more nervous than the first day we met. I raise my brow, smiling encouragingly. "Can I come in?" I ask softly as she looks behind me. Her eyes were a little skittish and wild, something I liked.

Stepping out of the way, she looks anywhere but me as I breeze past her.

And then I stop almost instantly.

My smile falters because I nearly walk straight onto her bed after taking two steps into her room. Okay, now I feel like I'm intruding. As comfortable as her white bedsheets look, I don't think that's where we should be starting. There's a little kitchenette just off to the side, and a door leading to what I assume is the bathroom. The whole place is clean, fresh, and beautifully decorated, but the room is… small. Smaller than the third guest bedroom in my apartment. No wonder she was so hesitant to bring me up. She probably thought the only thing I wanted to do was get her into bed. In all honesty, I just wanted to spend more time with her. We'd talked a lot through text, but it was just that. Text messages. I wanted to talk and really get to know her without her brother as a chaperone.

The clean white lines decorating her apartment evoke a coastal vibe, exactly what I expect from Cali. I imagined she'd do a beach style house if she had the space. Did the marketing department not pay her enough to get a better place closer to the stadium? Not that I'd tell her since she already seemed a little hesitant to let me come up, but this is far out on the wrong side of town.

"I know what you're thinking," she starts, moving around me and into her kitchenette. "It's small. I don't often let people up here, and I think it feels smaller with someone of your height and width in here too." Her eyes flitter across my shoulders, inspecting me. "But you asked." She shrugs, turning towards her fridge. "Would you like a drink?" She asks, and I watch her perky butt as she bends further into the refrigerator. "I have water, coke, orange juice, and cranberry juice." I barely listen to the options because all I can hear is the nervousness crackling off her voice. I feel like an ass. Maybe I shouldn't have pushed her to invite me up.

As she talks, I rub my thighs, glancing around the room. Where should I sit? There's no room for a sofa in here, and there's one chair tucked under her makeshift dining table. "I'd love a water." She grabs a couple of bottles and shuts the door with her butt, walking back over to me with a crooked smile. "Please, take a seat." She gestures with her head towards the bed. Now, it feels really awkward. Yes, I know I invited myself up, and maybe there was a small part of me that was hoping I'd get into her bed, but this just feels forced. I edge my body down to the mattress, resting my ass as close to the end as I can. My knees nearly hit the wall.

"Penn mentioned your parents live locally?" I ask as she hands me a drink and perch a comfortable distance away from her. The place is far from downtown and even further away from the stadium. So why on earth did she pick it?

"Yeah, they live about ten minutes away from the stadium." I stop myself from asking the obvious question. "They wanted me to live with them after college, but after four years of independence, I couldn't imagine anything worse. I like being on my own… and not smelling of incense all the time." She takes a long swig of her drink, and I watch the long drag of her delicate throat as she swallows. Perfect silky skin resides there. I want to know how it feels against my lips.

I lean back, noting the springs on the bed are piercing at my butt. There were times in my life that I was sad I missed out on the student lifestyle, but as I look around this small, damp apartment with a piece of metal stabbing into my thigh, I know this isn't one of them. Why would you go to college, spend so much money, only to end up with this? How was she able to function in the morning with a shredded back. Maybe while I'm here painting her door, I'll get a new mattress too. One with memory foam. I would get it solely for her sleeping purposes, of course. "Is that why you didn't pick something closer to the stadium? Because it was too close to your parents?"

Barely making eye contact, she snorts, playing with the cap on her water bottle. "No, it's not that. I can't afford to live any closer." She pauses, her eyes darting up to meet mine, and then flutter back down to the bottle cap she's fiddling with. Her cheeks and neck are a little rosy. "My internship with the Catfish is unpaid," she mumbles and shrugs with no amount of sadness or remorse in her voice. My stomach immediately drops. She worked four years on a degree to work at a job unpaid. How does that even happen? When I graduated from high school, I went straight to the minors. I wasn't paid much, but the accommodation was sorted during the season, and I could go home when I wasn't playing. I had it easy compared to her. Now, I'm earning well over 25 million a year, and she's not getting a cent by the same corporation.

"Interns don't get paid?" I sound dumb, and, in a way, I am. It's not like I went to college or ever intended on working in a back-office career. I have no idea how they function or what you have to go through to get them. Apparently, it's worse than playing in AAA and more like a hobby.

She shakes her head, tucking a blonde strand behind her ear as she squeezes the bottle tight. I did my best not to think about what her hands would feel like doing that around me, but she was making that hard - literally. "Nope. Marketing internships are popular because there aren't a lot of them in Charlotte. The Catfish program is one of the most sought-after. I think they had over three thousand applications this year for ten spots." My eyebrows raise in surprise. "I may have had a little help from my friend, Mary. You met her the other day, the small girl." I note her name for future reference as Cali turns toward me, her cheeks ruddy as she slowly drags her eyes up. "They usually have ten interns. This is the first year they've had eleven." The implication is hanging there, but she wasn't going to explicitly say it. She's only there because Mary helped her. No wonder she's so afraid of losing her job by taking a chance on me. She has such little confidence in her abilities. That ass of a boss knows that and is praying on it. I knew that guy was an idiot the minute I met him.

I tilt my head, squinting as I watch her expression, desperate to understand her. I wanted to take residence in her head, so I could figure out what she was thinking. "You don't do it for the money, though, do you? You love the Catfish more than any person I've ever met."

"Yeah, I mean, not many people can say they're in their dream job fresh out of college. But I am. Now all I need is a salary to match." She giggles, lightening the mood in the room entirely. I wanted to ask her how she was paying for this place, but it was too personal, and frankly, all commonsense left my mind when her mouth connected with that water bottle she was toying with. Her lips wrapped around the opening like they would if she were sucking my -. "I'll get there eventually," she says with a stilted smile after finishing her sip and wiping her mouth.

"Uh huh." I drawl out, not listening because all I can think about is how much I've been missing out on the Californian beaches all these years. It's like I've been dehydrated, and now I'm ready to drown in the sea. Her half-lidded gaze flits between my lips and eyes, the dazed expression telling me everything I need to know. She's thinking the same thing I am. My body is vibrating, itching to touch her, but waiting for her to make the first move. I forced myself up here. She has to initiate it because she has to want it as much as me.

I glance around the room, looking for storage, and run my tongue across my teeth when I find none. "So, where did you hide all the Tate Sorenson memorabilia?" I ask with a chuckle. She catches me off guard, grazing her palm against my stubbled chin, guiding me to look at her as she turns, edging us closer. I stay quiet, worried that I will scare her away like some kind of feral cat if I make another noise. She leans in, her lips touching mine tentatively. My cock immediately stirs, but I hope she doesn't notice. She pecks hesitant kisses across my mouth, scratching my stubble as she goes along. I languish in her touch, letting her explore me however she wants, waiting patiently for her to deepen the kiss.

Her body relaxes, and even though we're connected at the lips, she keeps herself at a safe distance from me. It's as though she thinks she might lose all self-control if we touch.

She drops another kiss to the corner of my mouth, watching as my lips quirk at the touch. Then, with eyes wide open, I watch her press her mouth across mine. She slides her hands past my shoulders, her nails scratching as they make their way to the nape of my neck. When she deepens the kiss, she grapples with my hair and forces my mouth to part.

She pushes her tongue into my mouth as her body curves against mine, silently begging me to touch her. As much as I feel like she wants me to take the lead, I don't move my hands from the safety of her comforter because I want her to choose to take this further. If all I get from her tonight is a hot make-out session, then I can live with that. But, her regretting us taking it too far is not an option.

Cali's kisses come fast and light, and I can start to feel the hesitation in her touch. She may have initiated this, but her inexperience is showing. She's floundering, unsure of if she wants to keep going. I can't deny how much I like this girl, but I'm not about to push my luck by goading her on.

Gently, I place my palm against her cheek, backing away. Deep, heady intensity is all I see when she opens her eyes. I smile when her brows cross in confusion, and she places her soft hand over mine. "Cali, I think we should stop," I whisper. It feels like I sucked all the light out of the room with that suggestion. She drops her gaze, gnawing on her bottom lip. "I just don't want to make you feel uncomfortable," I say, rubbing my thumb across her bottom lip, freeing it from her teeth because watching her was making me feel a little lightheaded.

She flutters her eyes shut at my touch, humming softly as she leans into my palm. "I'm not uncomfortable." Her voice sounds like a satisfied kitten who has just had a bowl of warm milk. "I like you." She opens her eyes and looks straight at me. "I *really* like you." I can feel my heart beating as adrenaline courses through my veins. She's been tiptoeing around the subject for a week now, and although we just kissed, I like that she verbally confirmed she's on the same page as me. God, I'm pathetic. I'm like a love-struck teenager around her. If Grayson could hear my thoughts, he'd ask who took my balls hostage. Cali, that's who. "It's just I'm worried we're moving too fast. I don't want you to think I do this all the time. We haven't even been on a date yet," she exasperates as her hands flail by her thighs.

I flick her lip, staring into her indigo eyes, and chuckle. "Are we back to a first date again? You know I would have taken you on multiple dates by now if you'd have let me. I don't want you to think I do this all the time either. I tend to steer away from women." Sam's indiscretions stung more than I'd care to admit because I don't want Cali thinking I'm still hung up on her. "Especially during the season," I pause. "There's something about you though, that keeps pulling me in. I'm more than happy to wait for you." She gives me a small smile and silently nods, pushing away from me. Cali adjusts her hair, refusing to look past her knees. For some reason, it feels like I've offended her. "Would you still let me take you out on a date?" I place the tip of my finger under her chin, so she has to look at me.

"Yeah," She drawls out almost deliriously.

"Great. Then when I'm back. That's what we'll do." Dropping my hand from her face, I stand, thinking of all the places I want to take her. "There's this Italian bistro I love. I could take you there. Or even to the baseball hall of fame. Have you been?" She shakes her head; her lips pursed, and she seems muted as I stand by the door, ready to leave. This girl is excellent at giving me mixed signals. "Are you okay?" I thought this was what she wanted?

She keeps fiddling with her hands, refusing to look up. "I'm fine," she quips. I stare her down, waiting for the honest answer. She finally looks at me with a wave when she realizes I'm not leaving. "I was just kind of hoping you would stay here a little longer." She has this tiny, sexy, but timid smile on her face. "I was kind of enjoying kissing you," she mutters as her toes tip up and down. Her nervousness to admit that is cute as hell.

I walk all of two steps from her door, straight back to where she sits. She swallows, watching my approach with surprised, wide eyes. Instead of joining her, I kneel in front of her. Still watching me with intrigue, I keep my gaze trained on hers as I grasp her thighs, open her legs and shuffle forward to settle in between. She feels warm, strong, and inviting – exactly as I imagined. We are face to face and hip to hip in this position; our bodies melded together perfectly. Tickling down her arm, I wrap my hand around her wrists and guide them to the back of my neck, knotting her hands behind my shoulders. Her body relaxes as I place my hands on her hips, watching her reaction. Her skin goosebumps as I swipe my thumb under her shirt, stroking the soft velvety skin. Any hesitation she had about touching me should be gone by now, but I want to make sure she's comfortable.

I lean in and press our lips together, kissing her deeply, just like I wanted to the first time I saw her. She groans, opening her mouth so my tongue can explore and taste her. She surprises me when she nips at my bottom lip, pushing for entry. The longer we kiss, the more comfortable she becomes. Her breathing labors as she arches her back into me. Her breasts graze against my chest, and my fingers tense, wanting to touch them so badly. I drop my hands down to her thighs, trying to keep it respectable while our kissing grows heavier.

As her confidence builds, her hands travel down my shoulders to my biceps, squeezing me, and she gently rocks her hips against my groin. It's the sweetest form of torture I've ever been involved in. Her moan spurs me on, and I take the chance to move my hands higher up her thighs towards the apex of her jeans. Little breathy moans escape as she presses her hips into me, feeling my hard dick against her as she starts to rub. That's all the invitation I needed. She yelps when I grab her by the ass, forcing her to wrap her legs around my waist, and I pull her closer.

Cali giggles as she tilts her head back, giving me access to the smooth skin across the nape of her neck. She hums when I rub my mouth against it, scratching her with my stubble. Her body rocks against me while I play with the ends of her blonde hair as I leave a trail of kisses down her neck.

I don't know how we got from dinner with her brother to this point, but I'm not about to stop it. She pulls at the top of my hair, forcing me closer to her hot skin. It's like she can't get enough of me. I love it. I haven't had a make-out session this hot since high school. Usually, the kissing stage is passed over, and we get down to business, but I think this pace with Cali because I want to feel every inch of her body, every ounce of her soul seeping into mine.

Cali arches her back, and it's only when I follow her down that I realize she's practically lying on the bed. Still grinding into me, my boner Is now so impossibly hard that I'm worried it might break. She's driving me wild, and I still haven't seen her naked. Oh, how I want that.

Her moans grow louder as my mouth trails down the buttons of her shirt to her chest. The tiniest amount of cleavage pokes out of her shirt, and using my nose, I unbutton the top button so I can gently kiss the valley between her breasts, smoothing my lips against the soft skin there.

Cali is starting to get loud, moaning in unabashed pleasure. It's almost as if she forgot she has paper-thin walls. I can only hope she's this loud watching the game, so that's what her neighbors think she's doing. Cop calls for a loud make-out session in a slightly sketchy neighborhood wouldn't look great in the news.

When her back finally reaches the comforter, she grabs my collar, hauling me down with her. Lying on top of her, she tightens her legs around my waist, and the first thing I think about is her concerns about moving too fast. "Maybe we should stop?" I say reluctantly between kisses. I don't want to stop, but I need to check. She pulls my mouth to hers, ignoring my question. I pull our lips apart, leaning back on my arms to give her space.

Cali breathes heavily below me, and I brush a few strands of hair out of her face while I wait for her to answer. It feels like an eternity until she finally shakes her head. "No. I want to keep going." She grabs my hand, moves it up to her chest, and spawls my fingers out, so I'm holding her breast. She watches as I squeeze her flesh, feeling the soft weight. I round my thumb, doing my best to find her nipple under all the fabric so I can play with it. My cock is so hard; I swear I'm hornier than when I was fifteen and touched a boob for the first time.

I back up onto my knees, slowly unbuttoning her jersey, and bite my lip. I want her so bad. Her lips part in surprise as she watches me expose more of her smooth, tanned skin. "I've never been happier to take a jersey off," I exasperate. She looks at me, chewing her bottom lip. "The only name I want to see on your back from now on is mine." I grind out, flinging the jersey to some dark recess of the room. I don't care where; the important thing is that *Walker* is no longer on her.

My eyes greedily take in the blue, lace fabric covering her perfectly proportioned tits, happy that my fantasies are coming true. I snicker at my thoughts, playing with the little blue bow in the valley between her breasts. "You coordinated your underwear with the jersey?" She smiles sheepishly, and I shake my head. "God, you make me so hard." Bending down, I kiss her dusky nipples through the sheer fabric. She gasps, arching her back to my mouth when I gently bite down. Her moans are asking for more, and who am I to deny such a request? I toy with her nipple, nibbling it until my tongue traces under the fabric and connects with her deliciously smooth skin. She tastes like honey and strawberries, just like I'd imagined.

Now that we've gone this far, there's no way I want to leave. Moving across her chest, I languish her other breast with the same amount of love and attention. Her breath gets shorter, her body getting needier underneath me. The friction of her jeans has been giving me enough gratification up to this point. But, now that I've felt her soft skin, I want to feel more.

My hand roams freely as I gently skate my hands across her toned stomach as she moves against my touch. When I get to the waistband of her jeans, I trace my fingers over the buttons, down the zipper, slowly torturing her. When I clutch her center through the stiff fabric, she gives me another one of those sexy, breathy moans. With each moan she lets out, I'm getting harder and harder thinking about the noises she'd make if my mouth were on her pussy. Bet she'd taste like strawberries down there too.

I move my hand in time to her hips, applying pressure to her clit as I climb back up and kiss her hard. She digs her nails into my back, and the pain shoots down my spine. Delicious pain that I know I'll be wearing for days as a reminder of the best night of my life.

When she breaks our kiss to lay back down on the bed, I move to her collarbone, placing small kisses there. Her fingers flex against my shoulder, and she pushes me down.

Down past her breasts.

Down past her belly button.

Straight to the button of her jeans. When I look up to question her, she's too lost in pleasure to focus, but her fingers squeeze me a little tighter, urging me to continue.

Slowly, I pop open her jeans, the blue of her panties peek underneath, and I work my way back up her body, playing with her nipples again and kissing her hard on the mouth, letting our tongues mingle.

I slink my hand down her body, letting it slip underneath her jeans. She spreads her legs eagerly, watching, anticipating my next move. Dragging my palm over the center of her thong, I feel her warm heat. My cock twitches. I lightly press my fingers down, drawing slow circles across her mound. Dampness seeps through with every little stroke.

She clutches the bedsheet so tight, her knuckles turn white, and I love that I'm the one doing this to her. "Tate," she begs. Pushing her panties aside, I stroke her slit.

"You're so wet." I grin into her neck, swiping my tongue across the skin there. Then I gently dip a finger inside her wet, warm pussy. "You feel so good," I mutter, focusing on licking and kissing every inch of her body.

Cali can't speak; the only thing leaving her lips are these hot, breathy mewls. It makes me want to know what she'll sound like when I make her come. "Your tits are incredible," I say, worshipping her body.

She gasps in surprise when I add a second finger, moving in and out of her slowly, while my thumb toys with her clit. I was expecting more erratic breathing, but Cali goes quiet.

"Is everything okay?" I stop what I'm doing, worried she'll suddenly regret this.

She can't look at me. She bites her bottom lip, scrunching her eyes closed in pleasure. "Keep. Going. Please," she strains, clasping my wrist and rocking against my hand, trying to get more movement.

Instead of granting her wish, I draw my fingers out of her and stand. It's torture for the both of us, but it will be worth it. "Tate," she moans in displeasure, looking up at me. But, apparently, she can't wait because she stuffs her own hand inside her panties and starts to touch herself.

I swear all the blood in my body went straight to my cock.

Growling, I grab the waist of her damn jeans because they're getting in the way of my view. Then, gruffly pulling her jeans off, my palms skate up her legs as I watch her fingers work her clit in a circular motion while she calls out my name. I'm torn; I wanted to watch her come like this, but then again, *I* wanted to be the one doing it.

Her hips rock, her body arching as she gets closer. I push her fingers along with her panties aside and start playing with her without constraint. She's shaking, so close that she loses all ability to speak. With her eyes squeezed shut, I decide to surprise her. With two fingers slowly moving inside her, I swipe my tongue across her clit.

She cries out, gripping the sheets, and when her body starts to clench around my fingers, I stop holding back. Burying my face between her legs, I press my tongue thickly against her clit, and roll it against me. That's all it takes for an orgasm to wash over her.

I watch every inch of her body as she slowly comes down from her high, slowing my fingers down and flicking her clit gently. Her breathing slows, and her eyes close as a small smile draws across her face.

She's perfection.

And I want to do it again.

So I do.

I start so gently with the occasional flick of my tongue and move my fingers so she doesn't know what's coming until it's too late. She was hot and bothered again within minutes. Licking at her clit, I devour every inch of her delectable pussy. She can't stop me now. Not that she would. She's close again, and I'm competitive. I want that second orgasm.

"Tate. I'm. I'm." She can't finish the sentence because the orgasm takes over. Her whole body clenches around my fingers again, and I watch every movement of her body and do my best to commit it to memory. Then, when her breathing slows, and she's in the gentle post-orgasmic haze, I slowly crawl up on top of her and place a gentle kiss on her cheek. Then, I lay down next to her, staring at the ceiling.

That was epic.

I was still hard as stone, but I didn't care because Cali tasted like strawberry champagne, and I wanted to get hammered all over again.

Her haze didn't last long, and she surprises me when she flings a leg over my waist and bends down to kiss my neck, returning the favor. She nips at my earlobe and whispers, "that was the best thing that has ever happened to me." I don't know whether I should feel proud of myself or sorry for her because I know I can do better than that.

"Babe, that was only the start." My voice was shaky because she was currently grinding her bare pussy against my jeans, making me curse the man who made denim so thick.

Cali giggles, throwing her head back like she's drunk on my touch. "I know." She trails kisses down my neck, and the more she moves, the less control I have over my hips jerking against her. I want to feel her on me. Her hands. Lips. Whatever she'll give me because I know I won't last long after thoroughly eating her out. Her tits bounce above me as she dry humps me into oblivion. I haven't done this since I was a teenager, but watching her scream my name and pleasure herself on my jeans against my dick is more than enough to get me excited. I hold her hips in place, showing her what spot to hit.

"If you don't stop soon, I'm going to come," I tell her, hoping she'd think I was joking, but all I get in return is a challenge-accepting smirk. She rocks her hips faster and grinds down harder, so I can feel every inch of her. I roll my head back, grunting loudly.

What the hell is this girl doing to me?

It's too much.

Excitement courses through my veins when she unzips my jeans, pushing them down just enough so she can sit on top of my boxers. Directly on my cock. I repeat, directly on my thick, straining, so close to coming cock. There's only a tiny scrap of fabric in our way as she starts to ride me.

She's going to do it, isn't she?

She's going to make me come in my boxers, and I'm going to let her.

Cali is a visual feast. She's naked, moving her body like a wave on top of me, and is getting off while she rides me hard. Her head dips back while she moans in pleasure. Watching her get her rocks off made me harder than that steel bat the team had me try once. Grimacing, I say, "Cali, I'm going to come." Her body works faster, grinding against the length of me with reckless abandon. I close my eyes, grasping her hips, trying to slow her down so I can savor the moment. But she won't stop. I'm edging closer and closer to the precipice.

Then it happens.

My hips slow to a few sharp jerks, and I grunt as pleasure fills my body.

Then, the room goes silent.

The only noise filling it is our heavy breathing. I scrub my hands across my face, needing a minute to get it together. I can't look at her out of sheer embarrassment. I'm a 27-year-old MVP-caliber baseball player, and I willingly just let the girl of my dreams watch as I squirt my load into my pants.

She bends down, lying her chest on top of me, and sighs as she clutches my sides. Lying there, I marinate in my own come, feeling gross but judging by the small smile on her face, she doesn't seem to mind. This wasn't how I thought the night would end.

I run my fingers across her bare back, only now noticing that I'm still fully dressed. "That was amazing," I husk out. "But is there any way I can use your bathroom?" I need to clean up before the come soaks through to my jeans.

Cali's body shoots up, and she grasps her boobs, moving off me at a pace only seen when I'm running for a base. Her eyes immediately drop to my jeans, specifically the area where you can clearly see my wet black boxers. I'm thankful my jeans are currently covering up the crime she just committed. "Uh yeah, sure, sure. Sorry," she says sheepishly. "I just wanted to return the favor."

I grasp her hand, focusing her attention on me. "Cali, that was one of the most intense moments of my life. My dream girl just dry-humped the shit out of me. Thank you." She gave me a small smile, still dubious. "However, if I don't clean up now, it's going to soak through, and I'd rather not have to drive home pantless."

An amused grin plays across her face. "I think I can help you out." She jumps up off the bed, and my dick twitches, watching her perfectly peachy ass as she walks to the dresser. I don't know where it finds the stamina to want to go again, but I ignored it for now. She pulls out a pair of boxers, throwing them my way. "I wear these to bed. They're clean and a men's large, so they should hopefully fit you," she says, putting an old t-shirt on. I'm missing her naked form already; only her tanned upper thighs are now visible. It made me realize that even in a potato sack, she'd still look hot.

I lift the boxers up and growl when I see my face staring back at me. Of course, she has Catfish Baseball boxers. "Are you telling me you sleep with my face on your pussy at night?"

She bites her bottom lip, her cheeks flushing. "No," she quips. "More like on my ass. That's the back." Is this girl for real? It's like she takes pleasure in making me horny.

I glance at her, my cock ready for another round, but I need to cool my jets. I don't want her to think I'm a 27-year-old virgin. I say coolly, "next time you want my face on your ass, just ask me." Her face reddens while she dances on her toes, making the hem of her shirt ride up. My gaze moves to the dancing fabric, hoping I'd see more. When she sees me looking, she pulls the shirt down. Even after everything she let me do to her, she's still acting shy about her perfect pussy.

Tucking a rogue blonde hair behind her ear, she smiles as if that would change the mess on top of her head. I'd run my hands through it so thoroughly; she's going to need a lot of conditioner to get the knots out. "Did you want to stay the night? I understand if you don't. I mean, I can't guarantee your car will be there in the morning, but I kind of thought that after everything that happened, you might want to stay," she says fast and meekly. When I don't respond, she starts again. "And I'll stop now. I'm just rambling." Her hands are flailing everywhere as she speaks.

Could she get any cuter? Nope. Not even if she tried.

"There is nothing more I'd want to do than spend the night with you while wearing your Tate Sorenson boxers, but I can't." I watch the hope disappear in her eyes. "I've got to be at the stadium tomorrow at 6 am, and all my bags for the road trip are in my apartment."

She shakes her head almost violently. "Of course. It was stupid of me to offer."

I stand up and encase her in a hug. It takes her a few seconds to relax into it. "No, it wasn't." I place a kiss on the top of her head. "Next time, I'll stay over."

"Next time?" She backs away so she can look at my face.

"Yeah, next time," I confirm, and she smiles less nervously this time.

Relaxing her head against my chest, she says, "I'd like that."

I kiss her forehead lightly, enjoying the new intimacy we now share. "Great, and don't forget that awesome date I'm going to take you on too."

"I can't wait." She hums into my chest.

It takes me another five minutes before I finally garner enough courage to leave, and by the time I get home, I've already thought of a thousand different dates for Cali. None of which are good enough for a girl as perfect as her.

CHAPTER 11

CALI

I wipe away the sweat from my brow, rushing back into the school before it's too late. Thank goodness Mary didn't make me wear this stupid costume the whole day like Josh did. A few hours with children clawing at me in a classroom is more than enough after the last few shifts.

Don't get me wrong. I love the excitement of greeting the little kids, but even with the makeshift air conditioning I installed in the form of a hand fan, it was still too hot to wear anything other than underwear underneath… which felt a little pervy considering I'm hanging out with kids all day. It's weird and makes me feel like one of those Furry people I saw in a documentary once. While Mary was conducting a quiz on the Catfish, I slithered away to change out of it since some pitchers were planning on showing up later.

I stamp down the Catty costume until it fits into Mary's trunk and adjusts the Sorenson jersey I was asked to wear. Okay, I wasn't specifically asked to wear Tate's jersey, but after his declaration that I was to never wear another man's name, I felt it would be rude to consider it. He also proceeded to send me four variations of this year's jersey the next day. Since he ripped my *Walker* one, I had no other choice.

Pulling at the buttons of the jersey, I pat down the fabric and then pull my hair into a high ponytail as I walk back to the school. "Crap!" I curse, annoyed that I left my phone in the Catty costume because I wanted to take the time walking back to see if Tate had messaged me. I have no idea what he's up to today, but since it's his first day back after a long two-week road trip, I'm kind of hoping he wanted to see me. Heat rushes to my face as I shuffle down the hall, thinking about the last time I saw him. Half-naked and riding his boxer-clad crotch into orgasmic bliss. I must have looked so desperate and depraved that night. Although I was slightly embarrassed when we said our goodbyes, he didn't seem to mind.

Since that night, he's been texting me almost every night and attempting to initiate some dirty talk that I've been too afraid to follow through on. I'm not a prude, but it's not like I'm the queen of sex either. Before Tate, I'd only ever had a few sexual encounters that ended up in fumbled disappointment. Tate is the exact opposite of that. Just the way he looks at me turns me on. It's like I'm the sexiest woman he's ever seen. I've never really felt sexy before, and I'm certainly not the type of girl to go around letting anyone's hands down my panties, but here I was letting Tate do it like he belonged down there.

Something about it felt right, and it wasn't just the fact that I didn't know orgasms could feel so good before then. I think it was just how comfortable he made me feel. He didn't judge my apartment even though I know he lives in one of those swanky high rises by the stadium. He didn't judge me when I told him I was doing my job unpaid, and most importantly, whenever he talked to me, it felt like I was the only person in the room he cared to listen to. He wanted me; he was making it perfectly clear.

Opening the double doors to the school, I make my way down the hall back to the library. Still hot from the suit, baby hairs stick to the side of my face, and I swipe them back as I walk with an added skip in my step, still thinking about Tate.

When I get into the library, I shuffle my way to Mary, who is speaking to one of the teachers. "They're just so good with the kids," the teacher coos, pushing her glasses further up the bridge of her nose. My brows crease in surprise. *Are the pitchers already here?* I was supposed to escort them in.

I play with my fingers, looking at Mary to gauge her reaction. She doesn't look particularly pissed off. Usually, when she's ticked, there's a big, blue, bulging vein in her forehead. It's not there. Glancing across the room, the children sit cross-legged on the floor, diligently watching Max, Grayson, Austin…

I catch my breath.

And Tate…

Ball cap, low-slung pants, and a tight jersey to die for. My baseball fantasy is standing right in front of me, smiling at the kids.

What the hell is he doing here?

He wasn't on the roster today. Mike was supposed to be here. Not him.

Our eyes meet.

A smirk grows across his face. He's looking sexy as sin while he leans against the librarian's desk, one foot in front of the other. Casually nonchalant is the perfect description of him. His honey gaze gets hotter as he watches me squirm, completely ignoring Grayson and Max explaining the different types of pitches. I don't know why they're bothering, as if any of these five-year-olds understand. I've been watching baseball my entire life, and I still can't figure them out.

My body warms when Tate's smile broadens. I feel warmer than I did in the Catty suit an hour ago. I spin on my heel, turning away quickly because I'm desperate not to draw attention or let anyone else in on our secret. No one knows we had dinner together or that I humped him into near oblivion, and I wanted to keep it that way. For now, at least.

Tate knows I want to take it slow since I don't want my colleagues to think I'm sleeping with him just to get a leg up in the office. Not that it would have that effect. Knowing Josh, he'd probably make it worse. Either way, I want to keep it quiet, at least for now, and Tate seems perfectly okay with that.

"Thank you for allowing the guys to come today," Mary says to the teacher. "The guys love doing this kind of thing. And they hardly ever have time during the season, so I'm glad we managed to get them here."

"How did you get Tate here?" The bespeckled teacher asks in hushed tones, giving him the once over. He's in jeans today, a rare sight, and he fills them nicely. Her lips curve as she keeps her eyes trained on him. I resist the urge to look back and see Tate's reaction. I can't be too obvious, even if I wanted to throat throttle her for looking at him. "He's such a superstar. I thought he'd be busy." It came out as more of a purr than an actual sentence, as though she was trying to seduce Tate through Mary. Gross. My heart beat faster again. There was a serious possibility I was going to have a heart attack if I didn't harness this rage into some useful energy.

Mary shrugs. "You know, he wasn't supposed to be here, but he said he loved the cause so wanted to make an appearance."

The teacher nods, her predatory gaze still firmly focused on Tate. "Is he single now?" She asks without a nervous bone in her body. "I read that he broke up with his girlfriend, but there was something about a reconciliation in the news the other day." My ears prick because she kept closer tabs on him than I did. I didn't know there was anything about a reconciliation with Sam in the news, and he's my favorite player. But then again, I never actually planned on dating him either. That was kind of thrown out of left field.

Mary looks between me and Teach with unease. She knows Tate brought me flowers and asked me how, but that's it. "I don't know. We try to stay out of gossip." She looks at me for confirmation, but I stay closed lipped, not wanting to give anything away. Teach purses hers, still hungrily focused on Tate. When I quickly flick my gaze over, I grin because he hasn't noticed her at all. He's still watching me.

"Would you be able to slip him my number?" *Really?!* Did she really think that was appropriate? At a Kindergarten meet and greet?

Gah, why couldn't she be interested in Grayson? Of course, she wouldn't be, though, because anyone with more than half a brain cell knows to stay clear of that guy if you want an actual relationship. He explains his three rules for women in every interview he gives, as though we don't already know he's a *'pump'n'dump'* kind of guy. His words, not mine. But why couldn't she be interested in Max instead? He's a nice respectable young man, and most importantly, he's *not* Tate. The same Tate whose fingers were sailing on the California beaches a couple of weeks ago.

Did I really just compare my vagina to an ocean? What has gotten into me?

The teacher slips Mary a piece of paper, who in turn awkwardly stuffs the paper in her pocket. The ultimate betrayal that she didn't know she was committing. "Of course." Mary fake smiles, looking anywhere but the teacher.

"Excuse me, miss," A little girl with blonde hair pulls at my jersey. *Right.* I need to act like a normal adult today. I kneel, smiling at her. "Where did Catty go?" She was loud enough that the whole room turned to listen. There were a few mutterings from other kids who suddenly just noticed his absence too. My eyes ping to Mary; I can't go back in that costume. Not now that Tate's here. He'd know I'm the Catty Crusader; ergo, he'd know I'm his humper.

Mary smiles, encouraging me to answer. "Uh, Catty had to go back to the river because he can't breathe without water." I wince when the room fills with gasps from the children. Stupid. Stupid thing to say to a bunch of five-year-olds. Smooth isn't exactly a trait of mine, and that only intensifies when I'm around kids. Or some hot teacher is trying to make a move on Tate. My Tate.

"Catty died?" The little girl's lip quivers through bleary eyes. Sweat prickles at the top of my hairline, and I scan the room, feeling hot glares from the children as they anticipate my answer.

When one of the children's frowns turns into a screech, I nearly jump out of my skin. Why am I so awkward? "No. No. He's not dead. He just had to leave; otherwise, he *would* have died." *Oh, God.* Why can't I stop talking?! That did not make it better. The wails of children fill the room, and I can feel myself breaking out in hives. I've screwed up again. When Josh finds out about this, I'm going to be fired.

A loud, commanding voice booms out. "Hey, kids, don't worry, Catty's just having a nap in my car. I've got a fish tank in there," Tate says with a warm and encouraging smile. I grin back, thankful that he diverted the attention away from me. "He's had a long week visiting other children just like you and needs his rest." My shoulders relax when the children stop wailing, and Austin gets their attention by juggling some baseballs.

"How about we let Grayson and Max finish their explanation of the Slurve," Tate says once there are no sniffles in sight. He speaks with such confidence; it's no wonder he's considered one of the most stable members of the team. Everything about him makes people feel calm.

Max and Grayson take over, and children start to giggle again. Thank goodness. I can still feel Tate's gaze on me, probably waiting for me to mouth 'thank you,' but I know if I look over, I'll turn into a pile of goo. I look at the window, then at the door, then at the scuffed floor – anywhere but him. Because if I look at him, I might give it all away, and somehow everyone in the room will know that I rode him like my own personal horse the other week.

"Cali," Mary whispers to get my attention, and I'm thankful for the distraction. My mind was riding off into the great unknown there for a minute. "Can you get the gifts for the kids? We left them in my car." She gestures to the keys dangling in my hand that I'd forgotten I was holding.

I nod frantically with tight lips, hiding any emotion. As far as Mary is concerned, I turned Tate down, and she thinks the hot teacher has a chance. As much as I hate to admit it, I need her to keep thinking that way.

"Uh huh. Sure," I say, almost deliriously. When I leave the building, I suck in air hastily. So many thoughts are running through my brain, I can't get my head straight. The hot, humid air does little to settle my stomach, and I bend forward, resting my hands on my thighs to take in more gulps of air. I give myself a few minutes and adjust my shirt as I walk to Mary's car. The bright red of Tate's

Cherry Mustang catches my eye. How the hell did I miss that before?

As I walk back from Mary's car, I balance a large box of caps, jerseys, balls, and mitts in my hands as I make my way back inside and mentally prepare myself for more questions from the kids, so I didn't embarrass myself further. My sneakers squeak across the quiet hall; I'm concentrating so hard, I hardly notice the creaking door opening beside me. An arm wraps around my waist while a hand captures my mouth.

My body vibrates in fear, and the box falls to the floor of what seems to be the supply closet. My capture's hand squeezes tighter when I try to scream for help in the darkness. My life flashes before me, and my biggest regret plays over and over again in a taunting fashion - my mother convincing me that a zoot suit would look good at a friend's sweet sixteen.

The door slams shut, and the box jiggles on the concrete floor. I raise my hands, ready to take on my attacker with some Judo I learned from *Kung Fu Panda.* Wait, it was Judo, right? I bring my hand up to Judo chop my assailant's ass, but before I can bring the heat, he takes my hand and waffles our fingers together. "Hey, Cali," Tate's deep voice whispers in my ear. There's a hint of humor in his voice as his hand presses my butt into his crotch. "It's been too long." He nuzzles his nose into my hair, and I stand there, trying not to melt every time we touch.

"It's only been a few days." A giggle escapes my lips when he nips at the sensitive spot behind my ear and turns me in his arms.

I close my eyes, imagining staying in this supply closet forever and never leaving. Close up, I can see wisps of his week-old stubble, and I immediately want to brush my lips across it. God, the stubble, muscles, and chiseled features had me. He's such a man.

"A few days?" He scoffs, his eyebrows lifting in surprise. "Try fourteen."

I roll my eyes, trying not to show that my heart skips a beat, knowing that it wasn't just me counting down the days. *Take that, Teach.* "Is that why you pulled me in here?" I ask, not fully expecting an answer because Tate's hands are sliding under my jersey, skating across the exposed skin of my hips as he kisses my collarbone.

"Partly," he mumbles with amusement. "I'm only here because Gray mentioned that he was coming, and a few marketing people would be here. I was hoping it was you."

I back away from him, looking down at his perfectly shaped, rosy lips. "Wait a minute. You only came here on the off-chance I *might* be the one escorting them." He grins, nodding. "It's your only day off for the next week."

"You know my schedule already?" He teases, pushing me against the shelves, his hands sneak behind me, and he pulls my hair out of the ponytail. His eyes track my hair as it floats down my shoulders. He gives me no time to worry about how sweaty I look because he threads his hands through my hair and kisses me with such urgency, I lose my breath. His tongue demands entry, and for a second, I let him take over all my thoughts.

Tate's smell, Tate's taste, Tate's touch. I'm all in.

Until I'm not.

"We shouldn't be in here. We'll get in trouble," I mutter as his mouth trails down to my chin, biting gently at my skin. The words are meaningless because I want this so bad that I let my hips grind into him, knowing I can't get fired.

"Oh yeah?" His hands grasp mine, bringing them over and above my head as he continues to trail kisses down my neck. "Are we being naughty, Cali?" He drawls out with heady want thick in his tone. "Are you being a bad girl?" He teases, and my body melts at his words. How is it with just a few questions, he can make me feel like a naughty school girl late for church? Something about Tate, though, turns me the hell on. Even through the thick denim of both of our jeans, I can feel his hardness pressing against me. I guess that's why I feel sexy with him because he isn't ashamed to show me just how much he wants me.

Stifling a groan, I push him off. "We have to stop. We're in a school, Tate." Getting caught would definitely put the nail in the coffin for my job. Josh's stupid rictus grin comes to mind, and I hold back my anger.

Tate's hands relax against the shelves, encasing me in as he takes long, slow breaths, trying to compose himself. I did that to him. Me. His eyes drop to my lips with a smirk. "I can't help it. I was disappointed because I thought you weren't coming and then you walked into the room, looking all kinds of hot and flustered. I loved watching you squirm. Then when you walked out, my mind went blank for a second. All I could focus on was the fact that you were wearing *my* jersey and your cute little ass in those pants. I wanted you." His big paws clasp my butt cheeks, drawing me closer in. "It's like you're trying to tease me."

I can feel the heat of his gaze without having to look. His fingers dig into my ass, and he takes my lack of response the way he should – as permission to continue. Lifting me off the ground, he draws my legs around his waist and nibbles at my ear.

Throwing my head back to one of the supply closet shelves, a hot sensation works its way into my stomach, and just as he starts to nibble at the sensitive skin under my ear, I squeak. "They're going to notice we're gone soon. We need to get back out there to give away this stuff." He answers with the slightest swipe of his tongue.

Shivers run through my spine, but I know we can't do this.

Reluctantly, I unwrap my legs from around his toned stomach and push him back in the process. "You know I'm right," I say sternly. I'm the one who's got to be strong here. It's my job on the line, not his. If we get found out, I would just be another byline on articles about Tate.

"Mhm. I know. It doesn't make you any less tempting, though." Why does he have to be so charming? I want to throw all my resolve out the window and keep going, but then I think about all the kids waiting for us and getting caught. Because if we keep going, it's not going to end with just kissing. "Since it's my only night off this week, will you let me take you out on that date?"

I bite my bottom lip, feeling nervous. Who cares that I nearly just let him ravish me in a closet? He still makes me flustered.

"What's wrong?" He asks, bending his knees so he can look me in the eyes. It's pathetic how much I love that he has to bend down to look at me. It makes me feel small and somewhat fragile. "Are you getting cold feet?" His brows cross, disappointment clearly laced across his face.

Shaking my head, I try to look back at him with a little more confidence. "No, it's not that. It's just if people see us together; I could get in trouble." I admit. It's something we've talked about, so he shouldn't be surprised. Hell, he told me the other day that his publicist was asked about the mystery blonde he went to *Deena's* with. He passed it off as meeting friends since Penn was there, but that's already too close for comfort. I'm not so sure Tate can be as discreet this time. Especially with how openly affectionate he likes to be towards me.

Tate stays silent, probably contemplating whether to argue with me or not. He might be used to his private life being splashed in the news for everyone's consumption, but I'm not. "If you're worried about people seeing us together, how about you come to my apartment? No one will know you're there, and it's completely private. I've got round-the-clock security preventing that kind of thing."

My mouth parts, but no words come out because I don't know what to say. He wants me to go to his apartment. His apartment?! That has all kinds of implications that I'm not sure I'm ready for. Sure, he came to my apartment last time, but that was different. It wasn't planned, and the term date wasn't used to describe what happened.

"I'll make you dinner and arrange for a car to pick you up. You won't have to worry about anything." He smiles eagerly, anticipating for me to return it.

Bending down, I grab the box from the floor and pick it up. Tate opens the door, still waiting for my response as I walk out. I'm too busy scouring the hallway to make sure no one sees us to answer.

"Can I take your silence as a yes?" He asks, taking the box from me once we're out of the room and strolling back to the library.

"I guess," I say hesitantly. That's when he stops and turns so he can watch me. It feels like he can read me like I'm a book sometimes.

"Come on, Cali, let me show you a good time." His smile is lopsided and awkward, a side I'd never seen from Tate. In all the promotional pictures, he's usually giving the camera a smoldering look, and it feels like this smile is only for me.

My hand rests on the library door as he waits for my answer. Then he winks, making my body ignite with warmth. "Okay, fine."

"Be ready at seven." Tate grins just as the door pushes open. I swing out of the way, tripping over my feet because I nearly get whacked in the face.

Mary pokes her head out, her eyebrow raises as she looks between the two of us. *Subtle.* "Is that the merch?" Her eyes drop to the box in Tate's hands, and I nod. "Come on." She opens the door wide enough to let us in. "The kids are getting antsy."

As he walks past, Mary glances at me with a questioning glare. I know what she's trying to ask, but I'm not about to answer in front of everyone. So I ignore it and follow Tate instead.

Mary's fingers drum against the steering wheel, waiting for the light to turn green. It's deathly silent in the car, and I firmly watch the road even though I can barely see out of the windscreen since I'm holding Catty's head. "When were you going to tell me that there's something going on between you and Tate?" She asks in a slow, calming voice.

I pretend to fumble around with Catty's head, jiggling one of the eyes, so it's difficult to answer straight away. "I don't know what you mean," I say, playing dumb.

She huffs out a breath on a laugh. "You're not going to play those games with me, Cali." She fans her fingers on the steering wheel, clutching down tightly. "Did you forget that I know your tells? Your left eye is twitching, which I know for a fact means your hiding something."

I whip my head to the window, trying to hide my eyes. "There's nothing going on between us." I try to sound as convincing as possible but the little squeak at the end of my sentence doesn't help.

"And now your leg is jumping. Another lie." She laughs but lets me sit in my own embarrassment for a minute. "Also, Tate threw Miss. Sprinkle's number in the trash before looking at it, so…" My breath hitches a little at that.

I jump when Mary gasps, stopping the car short. "Jes-us, Mary." I clutch onto Catty's head for dear life, watching the pedestrians walk in front of the car.

"Don't you dare try and change the subject," she yells. "Something's already happened, hasn't it?" She's bouncing in her seat now, embarrassing the hell out of me. I chew on my bottom lip, knowing that my eye is well and truly twitching. "That's the same face you pulled when you saw Gary Finnegan's wiener the first time." A smile curves on her lips. "You've seen Tate's wood, haven't you?!"

My face burns in embarrassment. "No," I say, holding my left eye straight because that statement is true. *Technically.* Technically, I only rubbed myself against it. He changed in the bathroom before I could see anything.

"Something happened that you aren't telling me about." She glances back to the road after eyeing me suspiciously. We aren't far from the stadium now, maybe five minutes, and I'm looking forward to some respite from the interrogation. "I'm your best friend," She pouts, "and you haven't told me."

"You're also my boss."

She rolls her eyes as she parks the car. "Pu-lease. I'm your boss on paper. Josh is the one that looks after both of us anyway. Besides, our friendship is thicker than that." She relaxes her arm on the side of the steering wheel while smiling brightly at me. "As your boss, I don't care either way what you and Tate do as long as you keep doing your job well and enjoy it. As your *friend,* though, I have a thousand questions, and I deserve answers."

I relax my head back on the seat, closing my eyes. I will tell her. Eventually. "Can I tell you how it's going in a couple of weeks? I don't want to jinx anything."

She laughs with a bitter edge. "Sure. You must really like him if you're not willing to tell me about him." I purse my lips; my silence is enough of an answer for her. Just as she turns the car off, she turns and looks at me. "Cali, in all seriousness, if you need any bat handling advice, let me know," she cackles, skipping back into the stadium and leaving me to carry the heavy and awkward Catty costume into the stadium on my own. Good thing my arms are used to it at this point.

Chapter 12

TATE

Rubbing my hands on my thighs, the rough material of my black slacks doesn't feel right under my palms. I'm more of a gym shorts kind of guy, but tonight I wanted to make a good impression on Cali. I thought she might like to see me in my uniform again, but then I started thinking about all those 'intellectuals' she probably hung out with at college and knew I needed to make an effort if I wanted to win her over. I run a hand through my hair and adjust my belt before stalking over to the bathroom mirror to check I don't have anything in my teeth.

Exhaling a breath, I glance at my watch, checking the time. Fred, my driver, told me he'd arrived at her apartment about thirty minutes ago, which means she should be here any minute.

The oven beeps, and I hurry out of the bathroom, grabbing a hand towel and swiping my sweaty palms across the fabric to calm me down. I open the oven, checking on my homemade lasagna. My mom would be pissed if she thought I'd burned it since it's the only recipe I've ever been able to commit to memory.

Sweet Italian sauce drifts in the air, and I place the hand towel next to the white peonies I bought for Cali. When I see that the lasagna is doing just fine, I put some garlic bread in the oven too.

The doorbell buzzes, and that's how I know Cali is here. A light knock on the door makes me jump, and I take one final look across the apartment to check it's clean before walking to the door.

I can't breathe.

Mussed hair, black dress, and lips to die for.

Cali is still the most gorgeous girl I've ever seen.

She adjusts her form-fitting dress, tugging it down her slender thighs before smiling awkwardly. "Uh, hi," she spouts with a nervous chuckle. She swallows when her eyes flit to my black button-down shirt and slacks. "You look nice."

I shake my head, trying to get my mind to focus on anything but ripping that dress off her. Shifting to the side, I make room for her to walk in. "Sorry, I had trouble talking for a second because you took my breath away." As she walks past me, I grab her hand, pulling her in for a hug while my foot shuts the door with a bang.

Cali jumps at the noise and places her hands on my chest. "I bet you say that to all the girls. That's why you were voted Baseball's Most Eligible Bachelor." Her fingers tease at one of the buttons of my dressy shirt. "Even that teacher gave you her number." I smirk because as much as she tries to sound unbothered, her twitching eye says something completely different.

When she finally tips her head up to look at me, I kiss her with the same passion I did in the supply closet earlier. I've never shied away from things I want, and she's no exception.

"I didn't want her. No other woman has taken my breath away quite like you," I whisper against her lips.

She laughs, pushing past me with a sigh. "I wish I believed that." Her black heels clink as she walks further into the room. Then she stops, almost comically on the spot. "Wow, Tate. You could fit the floor of my apartment block in this one room." She spins on her heel, smiling in awe as she looks around.

Laughing at her quietly, I pad into the kitchen, taking the garlic bread out of the oven. By the time I've finished, Cali is leaning against my marbled countertop, looking around the kitchen. And more importantly, looking like she belongs there. "Dinner will be ready in ten minutes," I say as I adjust the timer.

"I can't wait," she coos, and I force myself to look at her face, not the hint of red popping out from her slightly draping dress as she leans forward. Imagining what's under there will drive me insane.

"Why don't you take this," I offer her a glass of champagne. "And wait in the living room? I can put the game on while you wait."

"Which one?"

"Atlanta is playing Milwaukee tonight. I thought you'd want to watch our division rivals?"

She chokes out a laugh. "I'll watch it to give you time to make dinner, but let's get one thing clear, I only watch the Catfish." She grasps the glass and makes herself comfortable on my grey sofa. Yeah, I could definitely get used to this.

"What if I got traded? Then the number one Tate Sorenson fan would never watch me again?" I laugh after turning the tv on and busy myself in the kitchen. I can see her shoulders rise in a shrug from here.

"Meh, it wouldn't be the worst thing. We'd get a new shortstop, and now that I work in the marketing department, I wouldn't have to buy the bobbleheads. I'd get them for free as a perk."

I drop everything and hop over to the sofa, grab her wrists and push her onto the couch. She lets out a cute, breathy squeal. "You better take that back," I chuckle, kissing her neck with teasing pecks.

She giggles, trying her hardest to escape, but it's no use. I'm too big. "Like that's going to happen. You've signed a ten-year deal. No one is going to buy you out of that thing. You'll be an old man by then."

"Are you ticklish? It's almost like you want to get tickled." I take it further, nibbling her neck and letting the stubble scratch across her delicate skin. She tastes like salted caramel tonight. Her body stiffens underneath me, and I pull back, ready to tickle her senseless.

"Stop. Okay, okay. I'm sorry. I take it all back. The only baseball player I'll ever adore is you. Your face is the last one to ever grace my panties." She speaks through exaggerated breaths, trying to regain her composure. I ignore how the word 'adore' makes me feel like a God.

Before I can take it further, the kitchen timer beeps, and I place a quick, gentle peck on her cheeks. "Dinner's ready," I say, sitting up and holding my hand out for her.

Her slender hand slides into mine, and I lead her to my glass dining table, tucking her in when she takes a seat. As I walk back into the kitchen, I hear her mumble, "I'll make sure to hide my Jacob Miller panties next time you're over."

I stifle a laugh. There's no way she's a football fan. She's too obsessed with The Fish, and with the amount of games we have in baseball, she has no time for it.

Cali takes a seat while I get the lasagna, and she lets out a small moan when I place it on the table. That noise alone makes me want to throw all of the dishes out of the way and take her right now. But that would be a waste of good food, and I'm hungry. "This smells delicious. Did you really make this yourself?" Her eyes widen when I cut out a large piece for her.

"Yeah, my mom taught me," I explain. "She wanted to teach me more, but baseball's season is so long, I hardly get any time back home."

"Does she come out to watch the games?"

I nod, taking another swipe of my dinner. "Yeah, when she can. If there's a particularly big game on, I'll fly her, my dad, and sister out."

"Do you wish you played for a team closer to them?" She asks. I could barely concentrate because, with every bite, she'd give a satisfied moan. Her lips would purse together, and her eyes would shut, giving me the same look she did when she came all over my fingers.

I break a breadstick in two, forcing my brain to think of something other than my hand down her pants. "When I started out, I did play closer, but they came less then than they do now, and it's not because I was in the minor league. I think having to plan helps them to decide which games to come to. It's been nearly seven years since I lived in Texas." I shrug, chomping on a breadstick. "I'm used to it now, and I like my own space." That statement could never ring more true than when Sam came to my apartment for the first time and tried to 'accidentally' move in and left engagement ring photos everywhere. I leave that bit out because it might ruin the mood.

"Kind of like you." I point out.

She slows her chewing on a nod. "Yeah, but I think mine is more of an independence thing than yours."

"In what way?"

"Well, you could easily have a house in Texas and Carolina. You'd be able to fly on a private jet and be home in an hour. For me, I just want a little place to call my own that I know my little brother won't sneak into when I'm not around."

"Oh yeah?" I raise my brows. "Have you got a few things in your drawers that you don't want Penn to find?"

That makes her swivel her fork and focus on her food. "Maybe, or maybe I was tired of him messing with all my baseball memorabilia. I remember this one time I came home, and he'd left greasy thumb marks on my vintage Jerry Walker baseball card. I wanted to kill him."

I smile, watching her. "Why do you love Baseball so much?" She looks at me with surprise. "I know why *I* love it. The sound of the bat hitting the ball, the smell of the field, the feeling I get watching my ball leave the park. But what about you?"

She pouts her bottom lip out in contemplation. It's cute and hot at the same time. "I think the question should really be, what is there to hate about baseball?" Her smile emanates across her cheeks as she looks up wistfully. "It's everything. It's like a wholesome apple pie on a Sunday afternoon."

I lean back in my chair. "Ah yes, I love a good old afternoon delight. Don't you?" I run my tongue across my lips suggestively. She rolls her eyes, ignoring my innuendo, and gets back to eating the lasagna.

"Baseball reminds me of when I was a kid, and my dad would take me to a game to pass the time. Boy, did he regret it when I got older. I would cry when we'd leave, especially if the Catfish lost. That would be a bad day for my family."

I chuckle at the image of a little version of her pouting in the corner, wearing a fin on her head. Then stupid thoughts come to mind, like what it would feel like if that little version of her was my daughter. "Your love for baseball is almost as sexy as your legs." I wink when her head shoots up. Her brow furrows, and she chews her bottom lip anxiously. "What's wrong?"

She releases her lip. "Nothing really." She pauses, too embarrassed to meet my gaze. "It's just you're the only guy that's ever called me sexy, and I find it weird." My eyebrows rise in surprise, and even though the grimace on her face is currently not sexy, it doesn't bother me in the slightest. "I'd get called Green Giant a lot. Daddy Long Legs. Even Slender Man on occasion. But no one talks about me like you do." Her cheeks are on fire now, and when she hazards a look, she immediately pushes her gaze back down to her lap. "Or looks at me like you do, for that matter."

Stifling a laugh, I reach across the table to hold one of her fidgeting hands. "I'm just saying it like it is," I say. "But, if you don't like it, I can keep my thoughts to myself. Save for a few occasional slip-ups I know I'll have because I can't help it, Cali. I'm already filtering at least two-thirds of my dirty thoughts as it is. You're my type, and I can't stop thinking about the other night." I hum. "Your legs draped over my waist while you bounced on top of me nearly naked is a memory I never want to forget."

She laughs. If there was a noise I could bottle up and save for later, it would be her genuine laugh. So carefree and innocent. "I like it. It's just I never thought I'd hear someone like you saying stuff like that."

"Well, then you better get used to it because I'm not stopping." When she smiles, it's like watching the sunset on the beach; you have to stop and take notice.

God, I've got it bad for this girl.

We spend the rest of the dinner in deep conversation about the intricacies of Baseball's rules and potential trades next year. Usually, when I'm with a girl, they could care less about baseball, showing more interest in what fancy restaurant I'm taking them to. My mind drifts back to Sam and all the time I wasted with her. How stupid and naive I was to think she was actually interested in me. While I was focusing on baseball, she was focusing on my wallet. Thinking back on it now, she did me the biggest favor, cheating on me because it gave me an excuse to finally end it. Plus, it gave me the opportunity to meet Cali.

Cali's passion for the game is refreshing; I swear she knows more about the Catfish than I do. Watching her awkward beauty all night makes it hard to want to look at anything else. I guess once you've seen perfection, there's no point in looking away.

While cleaning up after dessert, I decide to tease her a little. "You know, Jacob's married, by the way." She stops loading the dishwasher, and her eyebrows cross in confusion. "Jacob Miller." I clarify, turning and leaning against the counter, resting my hands on either side of her. She still stares at me blankly, and I shrug. "If you're going to wear a guy's face on your ass, the guy should at least be single." I point out. "Ergo, those Jacob boxers you have should be thrown out."

She throws her head back in a cackle, placing one of her hands on my chest. "I can't believe you'd think I'd betray the Catfish like that. Rest assured, your face is the only one." She pauses, blushing. "On my ass, as you would put it."

I like the sound of that, so I give her a deep kiss. "I need to put this dish away." She holds up the white china, and I back away, only slightly, to let her organize the dishwasher. When she's done, I tip the machine closed and grasp her hand, leading her to the sofa.

As we relax down, I wrap an arm around her shoulder and then lift her legs, so they're draped over my knees. "The sofa's big enough for us to stretch out," she says with a hint of humor.

I twirl a few strands of her hair, pulling her close. Close enough that her lips are gently resting on top of mine. "What's the point of a large sofa when all I want is right here?" I kiss her as she giggles, backing away. Now she's the one teasing me. Growling, I try to capture her lips, but she's making it near impossible.

As she finally leans into the kiss, the commentator shouts, diverting Cali's attention to the TV. I'd hardly noticed or cared that the game was still on, too focused on the game Cali and I were playing right here. She watched as the Atlanta team celebrated a three-run homer in the eighth.

"Are you worried about playing them?" She asks while her hand lazily plays with mine.

"Who?"

She nods to the TV. "Atlanta. Now they've signed Zeke LeBeck, they've filled their biggest gap at third base, *and* he's a heavy hitter." Zeke was in the dugout, high-fiving everyone as he took his seat.

I wave off her concern. "Nah, I'm not afraid this year. Zeke's wife is pregnant with twins, and last time I talked to him, he was stressing about that because she's due towards the end of the season. His head isn't in the game this year. Next season though," I blow out a breath. "Yup, I'm nervous."

She looks at me with a brow cocked in mild amusement. "You talk to Zeke?"

I nod. "What else is there to do when you're standing on base for so long?"

"I don't know. I kind of thought everyone had rivalries and didn't talk to each other."

I laugh, waffling her hand in mine. "Sorry, babe. We all pretty much like each other. Except for the Parrots. No one likes the Parrots."

She nuzzles into my neck, and I, in turn, nuzzle into her hair, enjoying the coconut scent. "No one likes a team who gets their fans to squawk when they score. It's just annoying and distracting. I can barely watch the games when you play them."

"But you do, though, right? Because you're our most dedicated fan." I husk into her ear, swiping the shell with my tongue.

"Yup." She yawns, resting against my chest as we watch the game. Playing with her hair, I can't help but think about how very domestic this whole scenario is. My chest tightens as I kiss the top of her head in a silent promise that we will do this again. "I think this year is going to be your year." She says groggily. I know she's not far from falling asleep, and I should probably let Frank know so he can drive her home, but I'm enjoying her company too much to formally end it.

I scoff at her confidence. "Oh yeah, what makes you think that?"

"You're already leading the National League in RBI's and Homers." Even drowsy, she could speak eloquently about baseball. "The team is soaring at the moment. No one is going to be able to catch you."

"Mhm, I always start hot, though. My issue is maintaining it over the one hundred and sixty two games," I explain, wincing when I see Atlanta scoring another homer. Maybe I should be concerned.

When she burrows further into my chest, I lean back, giving her more space. "But you've changed your swing, and your average is higher than last year. I think you can do it."

I shake my head, hardly anyone noticed change in my swing it was so slight. Only Grayson, who I was pitching off during the off-season, has asked about it. "Your knowledge of the game is ridiculous."

"I could learn more. I still can't always identify a pitch." Her head falls further down my chest, and I'm letting it.

I snort. "If you could, you'd probably be the best player of all time." Her breathing slows. "Why did you pick marketing? Why not sit in the analytics department or try for a role with more direct involvement."

"Marketing *does* have direct involvement. I just want to get people as hyped up about the game as me. It's my passion, and I want to share it," she mumbles out the last part of that, hardly awake, and I don't have the heart to move her. "Even if it does mean dressing like a fish," she mumbles so quietly I barely hear it.

I leave one final kiss on the top of her head. "Well, I'm glad you shared your passion with The Fish." She doesn't respond, not that I expected her to, what with her heavy breathing.

By the end of the game, I glance down at Cali, who's still sleeping. I don't have the heart to wake her or to say goodnight. So, I don't. I gently wrap an arm under her knees and then lift her up.

I stand in the middle of my living room, looking between my bedroom and the guest bedroom. I should drop her off in the guest room, but I don't want her to freak out when she wakes up in a bed that isn't hers. I'm also selfish. I want her all to myself for as long as I can. Time during the season is precious, and I want to spend as much of it as possible with her. When I deposit her onto the bed and gently remove her shoes, she instantly curls up, snuggling into my pillows like they're swallowing her whole. A small smile dons her face as she adjusts her back into my memory foam mattress. I'm not surprised she looks so comfortable; that thousand-dollar mattress should be better than hers.

After stripping down to my boxers and brushing my teeth, I slip under the covers. At first, I wasn't sure how close I should get to Cali. It's a big bed; we could go the whole night without touching each other, but I don't want that. I want to wake up tangled in that strawberry coconut scent of hers.

When she adjusts herself against the sheets, I softly grasp her hips, bringing her closer to me. Her warm back is against my chest, and I let the soft smell of coconut from her hair help me drift off to sleep.

"Tate," Cali shrills, waking me up instantly. I look around the dark room, wondering what the hell happened. Cali is shuffling around with her rumpled black dress on, nearly tripping as she tries to shove her heels on. "I'm going to be late for work," she stresses, her breathing quickening.

I'm still in a sleepy haze and have to rub my eyes to focus on the girl in front of me. "I need to get home."

"What time is it?" I ask, my voice low as I try to find my phone on the bedside table.

"6 am," she cries as I throw the covers off. The cold morning air hits me, and I wanted to grab her and drag her back into the warmth with me, but I don't think she'd be happy about that. She stops fretting for just a second when she notices my bare chest. "Josh is going to kill me." She shakes her head and scurries out into the kitchen, not looking back.

I jump up, following her. "Cali, calm down. I can get Fred to pick you up in about five minutes." I grasp her hips, dragging her body to my chest, kissing her collarbone. "You can just take a shower here, and I'll buy you some clothes from the mall. It is attached to the stadium, after all," I offer.

She bounces out of my hold, grabbing her purse on the kitchen counter. "Stores don't open until nine, which would already render me late."

Nodding my head, I shoot off a text to Fred. "He'll be here soon, and he'll wait for you to get ready and drop you off at the stadium."

Her shoulders visibly relax when she takes in my words. "I'm sorry, it's just I really want to make a good impression, and Josh was already ticked off about the other day when I." She stops herself, eyes wide. "It doesn't matter. He's just hard to please."

"Josh sounds like a hardass." Especially considering she's free labor.

She nods. "I wouldn't say working with him is pleasant, but I will do everything I can to make it work. For The Fish."

I pour her a cup of coffee to go as my phone rings. "Fred's already here." The disappointment I feel with Cali leaving is new. It's like we never have enough time. She grins, wrapping her arms around my neck.

"Thank you for such an awesome night and delicious dinner." Pecking my lips one last time, she grabs the coffee from me and walks to the door.

As her hand plays with the handle, I ask, "When will I see you again?" Because I'm desperate to see her again.

She turns on her heel, a mischievous grin on her face. "Soon. Text me."

"Bye, Cali." I watch her ass as she walks out, already looking forward to the next time I'd see it.

CHAPTER 13

CALI

My fingers type furiously as I do my best to get this memo sent out. I can hear my phone buzzing in my bag, but I have no time to check it, adding to the ever-increasing anxiety swimming in my stomach. My eyes flick over to my laughing colleagues by the water cooler. Jealousy courses through me because I wish I had time for moments like that.

"Cali." His voice startles me, and the hairs on the back of my neck rise when I hear his footsteps stomping toward me. I'm just one paragraph away from finishing this. Why couldn't he come over in ten minutes? "Where's that note? I should have sent it to the director's twenty minutes ago." His snarling voice makes me want to fight back. To yell at him and explain that he only gave me the assignment twenty minutes ago and I'm not God. I can't just magically create a stupid memo that he could have written himself in half the time. But I don't because I can't screw up this opportunity.

I roll my chair, so I'm facing him. "I should have it for you in about five minutes," I say with my brightest and most unfazed smile. He will not beat me. He's just a sad, lonely guy who gets off on –

His angry rumbles interrupt my thoughts. "When I give you a task, Cali, I fully expect you to immerse yourself in it. Not socialize with your colleagues." My brows cross, and he tips his head to my screen. "You've been spending too much time on the office messenger system. That's why you haven't finished." I follow his gaze, noting the orange flashing on my menu bar. Mary was probably messaging me about work, but the fact that it was flashing meant that I must be talking to her, and I'm still in trouble.

"I'm sorry, Josh. I'll get this done for you now," I say sternly. What's the point in explaining anything to someone when you know they don't want to listen? He wants to make me the bad guy. I roll the chair back around, fingers poised to start typing when I feel his body lean over.

His mouth is close to the side of my head, and it takes all the willpower I have not to shiver with disgust or hurl. His breath smells like stale coffee. "If it's not in my inbox in the next five minutes. We're going to have a problem."

Sucking in my lips, I nod. I can't give him a verbal response because if I do, I might cry. I start typing; it's all nonsense, but the keyboard pater relaxes me, and when he leaves my side, it's like a dark cloud has been lifted.

For the last two weeks, Josh has been nothing but relentless with the work he's been piling on me. I've barely had time to brush my teeth, let alone do anything that isn't related to his workstreams. What's worse is, I still have to be Catty, and he critiques my every dance move or knee-jerk. I don't even get a thank you for working overtime, still unpaid.

I round off the memo, sending it straight to his inbox and relax back into my chair. "You okay, Cali?" Mary asks tentatively over the cubicle. When I lock eyes with hers, I feel fragile, like an umpire that just got whacked in the balls by a pitch. But I hold it together, choosing to bite my lip and relish in that pain instead.

"I'm good," I nod, checking the time on my screen. "How long have I got before I need to go out there?" I ask. It's really saying something when you view dancing around in a giant furry costume as your point of solace for the day.

She winces, rounding the cubicle and leans against my desk. "In ten minutes. Are you still okay to do it?" What does she want me to say? No. I hate it. This was supposed to be my dream job. Now, it's swiftly turning into my nightmare, and it's not like I'm even being paid for the privilege of embarrassing myself and working overtime almost every night.

"Yeah, I can do it." I drawl out. She rests her hand on mine and leans in.

"I've got a meeting with Josh's boss, Jonah, tomorrow, and I'm going to casually mention how great you're doing." A small smile brushes across my lips, more out of respect than anything else. "I'm going to find a way to get you on more of my projects and less of Josh's. He's using you like you're his PA, and that's not why they hired you." My breath hitches. It's not like she's much higher in the food chain than me, and Jonah would take notice, but at least she's trying.

The vibration of my phone is now reverberating through my foot. "You might want to check your phone before you go out there." A grin plays on her face. "It's been going off like crazy. Are you playing hard to get with Tate?" She asks quietly. It still wasn't openly known that I was seeing him.

I know she's dying for details and is holding back since I'm in near meltdown mode with work. I shake my head, checking my emails one last time. "No, I've had no time to think about anything *but* work."

She doesn't press me. "Okay, maybe we can go to dinner after?" She suggests. "My treat for saving my ass and dancing around like a fish for me." I nod as she gives me a shoulder squeeze. "Great, let's skip out after the seventh inning when you're finished. Catty's wearing a lobster outfit today." She huffs out a laugh. "I can't wait to see it."

Catty in costume. *Great.* The last time Catty was in a costume, we dressed him up as a painter, and I was painting Austin while he manned third base. The fans loved it, but when I got back to my desk, proud of myself, Josh was there waiting with a red, blotchy face. Apparently, he couldn't tell what I was drawing and that ticked him off. I wanted to ask him to try and paint while partially blindfolded, but once again, I kept my mouth shut.

"Tim's physiotherapy is going well," Mary says, trying to raise my spirits. Tim's been back a few weeks now, and he seems fit as a fiddle, albeit with a limp. There's no way he's ready to walk up and down the stands for hours, and I'm starting to think he'll be out the whole season.

"Great," I say sarcastically, grabbing my bag and head down to the locker rooms to change. I manage to get my phone out and see the multiple texts Tate left me. My heart drops; he keeps sending me memes because I'm so busy. I've suddenly become terrible at responding to him. When he finishes his games, I at least manage to send him a text, but most of my responses are one word, if that.

He probably thinks I hated his date, and I'm trying to brush him off. I kind of wish that was the case because it would be a lot easier to manage. The constant knot in my stomach and aching heart when I think about him is too much for my mind to handle. I feel like every part of my being is working overtime, and I'm still getting no satisfaction.

Stuffing my phone into my pocket, I trudge down the stairs, taking in a deep breath as I accept my fate. Lobster Catfish. Here I come.

I sit down at my desk, feeling refreshed and rejuvenated after my Catty stint. I've managed to find a private ladies' locker room, which has made working after mascoting a much more pleasant experience. Mary waves, grabbing her bag and making her way over. My stomach's growling and I can't wait to get some food.

Quickly, I check my emails to make sure there's nothing I missed before leaving for the day. My body sags when I see the two bright red messages at the top of my inbox. Both from Josh, and both urgent. Obviously. "You ready to go?" Mary asks, playing with her purse string.

I contemplate ignoring the messages and just throw caution to the wind, but before I can, his footsteps are already making their way to me. I always thought the Jaws theme tune was the scariest thing I'd ever heard. Nope. It's Josh's big fat footsteps across the carpeted floor. "Cali, did you get my emails." He leans into my cubicle, completely ignoring Mary, who's quivering next to me.

"Yup," I say with a pop of the 'p.' I'm being surly for the first time, and it's because both my mind and bones ache at this point. I need a break.

His sinister smile comes into view. "Then why aren't you working on them? I need these press releases ready for 7 am tomorrow," he demands, and my insides deflate like that day-old Catfish balloon I refused to get rid of when I was seven.

"She just got back from finishing a shift as Catty," Mary butts in. Josh's face slowly turns to look at her. He's not happy about the quip, but he can't do anything about it since she doesn't directly report to him anymore.

"That was ten minutes ago," he grinds out.

"I'll start it now," I say, too tired to argue.

He straightens up, adjusting his tie. "Good." He smiles at Mary as though he's won something. "I expect both press releases to be proofread by morning." Just like that, he's walking away from my cubicle, the Tate Sorenson bobblehead's tipping with every step he takes.

"Do you want some help?" Mary asks earnestly. "If we do it together, we might still have time for dinner."

Toying with the signed baseball rolling around on my desk, I turn away from her. "Thanks for offering, but I've got a feeling Josh will have a problem with that, and I'd rather not get you in trouble."

"Are you sure?"

"Mhmm."

"Okay, well, I'll be working for another 45 minutes if you want my help." She silently walks back to her desk, and I open the two PDFs Josh sent me. They're both more than 20 pages long.

Sighing, I know I'll be here a while. I stuff my earbuds in, hoping my music will make this a much less excruciating experience.

By the time I've finished proofreading, I look up from my desk, surprised that even Larry has gone home. *What time is it?* I gasp when I realize I've been sitting here for four hours. It's ten o'clock, the game finished over two hours ago and I'm the only one left.

I wipe my tired eyes, ready to get home and go to bed, annoyed that it will involve another 40-minute trip on the train. As I trudge to the station, I pull my phone out. Tate's left me a message.

Tate: Feeling shitty after the loss, do you want to come over?

I was so busy trying to proofread, I completely forgot about the game. I check the score and wince. It's bad. After looking down at my haggard expression reflecting off the phone screen, I decide as much as I want to see Tate, I need to sleep more.

Cali: Sorry about the loss. At least you can beat their butts tomorrow. I had to work late tonight so can't come over. Hopefully, we can meet soon.

I type it out and send it before I can think about it anymore. My brain is tired and needs a break. As I sit on the train, I close my eyes to get some shut-eye, making a mental note to myself to save up some more money to buy a new mattress. When the train is more comfortable than your bed, that's really saying something.

Chapter 14

TATE

With my elbows resting on my knees, I sit in the locker room while the rest of the players pass me by, patting me on the back. Things are looking up because we've finally broken our seven-game losing streak. I'm getting nervous, though, because Atlanta is gaining on us, and we can't lose to them now that we're halfway through the season. I batted in another three runs, which was all it took to win today and the series, but I still don't know how long I can keep this up for.

I want to celebrate the payback win with Cali tonight, but I'm still waiting for her to respond to one of the five messages I sent her today. Her text response has been lackluster, to say the least. If I didn't know how busy she was with work, I'd think she was avoiding me. I toy with my phone and check my screen one more time just in case I missed her message. Still nothing. I can't hide the disappointment because I wanted to surprise her with a rooftop dinner under the stars tonight. My next game isn't until tomorrow night, which means we'd get to spend the night together, and all I want is to spend some more time alone with her. Preferably naked, but I'll take fully dressed at this point.

Stopping myself from calling her, I place my phone on the bench next to me. She'll respond when she has a free minute. She always does, even if it's just a couple of words.

As the locker room door opens, cheers and chants echo throughout the room. Catty rushes through, looking tired with an extra limp in his gait. With all that extra work he did to hype up the crowd against Atlanta today, I'm not surprised he's worn out. A couple of times, I saw him sprinting up and down the seats, riling up the crowd when we were close to a run, and I winced. We have to do that during practice without a costume on, and it's tough. Wearing that must make it ten times worse.

Austin places a hand on Catty's chest, stopping him before he can slither away. "Hey, Catty," he says with that deep voice of his. "Do you remember the other night you painted me when I scored that three-run homer?" He asks earnestly. Catty nods. "Do you still have it? Some girls on Instagram are going crazy for it. They've asked me to send it to them signed." His cheeks pinken, knowing the whole locker room can hear his request. This is Austin's first year in the league and to say he's getting attention from the lady fans is an understatement. They seem to love his light green eyes and dark hair, or maybe it's the fact he's built like a linebacker and has thighs for days. I don't know. Either way, my title as team heartthrob has well and truly been taken. And that's fine by me. The fewer ladies chasing after me, the better. Cali has made some unsubtle remarks about the attention, and I'm happy for anything that makes it easier to get on her good side.

Grayson waltzes into the room with a towel slung around his waist, his tall frame dominating the space. "You want to be careful with those girls, Rookie." He holds the towel across his neck, heading to his locker. "You give them your signature, and they could use it on all kinds of things. Fake checks, leases on homes, paternity tests…"

Austin looks nervous for a second, and I roll my eyes, "Ignore him, Austin. Grayson's just bitter because he can't get a woman who isn't paid interested in him." Grayson is the last person Austin wants to take dating advice from. If you look up 'Dash and Go' in Urban Dictionary, his face is there, smiling smugly like a crocodile who just caught a chicken.

Grayson smirks. "Is that what you think I do? Pay women?" There's a silence that answers the question. He chuckles, "Believe me, I do not pay any woman to sleep with me. We have an arrangement, and they all leave perfectly satisfied."

"Ever the romantic," I deadpan.

"So, do you have it?" Austin asks Catty again, who has been standing there shifting on his feet while listening to our conversation. Catty bows his body, fin on his head, and shakes it remorsefully. "Ah, it's okay, Catty. Next time, could you save it for me?" Catty nods with the enthusiasm of a toddler. "Thanks, C," he says, patting the fish on the shoulder. *Do fish have shoulders?* That sounds like some crazy fact that Cali would know the answer to. I absentmindedly check my phone, annoyed when there's still no message from her.

"What's got you so tense, T?" Austin asks as he walks past me since I was cracking my neck without realizing it.

I grumble out a non-response, too annoyed to explain.

Grayson sits down next to me, drying his hair with the towel that's hung from his neck. "Our boy's just ticked that his little blonde plaything is ignoring him." My back straightens, and shoulders tense. "Do you think we didn't notice you sneaking out of the library trying to find her? Funny, when you came back holding the box of merchandise, she had this dazed look on her face." He barks out a laugh when he sees my menacing expression. "Save that for the other teams, T. I know you're soft like a mashed banana on the inside."

"What's her name?" Austin asks. He was already dressed, tying his shoelaces opposite me. I look around, surprised that Catty was able to sneak out of here without any of us noticing.

"Cali," I mumble, checking my phone one more time before leaning back against the locker and closing my eyes. *Why the hell hasn't she responded yet?* I know she's been busy and is slow to respond, but this is getting ridiculous. I'm busy too, but I still manage to find the time to text her. It's been three weeks since she spent the night at my house, and I'm parched. I need to see Cali to touch her, and taste her again.

"Be careful, T. Now that you've signed your big contract, a lot of women are going to come crawling out of the woodwork for some of Sorenson's sausage." I growl at Grayson, annoyed that he would question Cali's intentions. Especially since I'm the one that's been doing all the chasing. Cali seems to be barely bothered by the fact that I'm her favorite player.

He raises his arms in defense. "Hey, we all know what happened with Sam." My head starts spinning at the memory. Why did he have to bring her up? It's been a year since that fiasco, and I'm still dealing with the fallout. I should have dumped Sam the minute I got my first golden glove, and the media started showing interest, but I kept her around because I thought it would be easier than breaking up. You know, less drama. How wrong I was. It only served to fit her narrative when we broke it off. She's been all over those cheap rag mags telling any reporter that will listen that I broke off our engagement, and she had to run into the arms of Theo Leitch, a hotshot football player I introduced her to while we were still dating. She can repeat that lie all she wants, but the reality is, I never proposed, and we broke up months before she allegedly cheated on me with Theo. At least, I think she did. We'd barely seen each other those last few months.

I shake my head, doing my best to rid my mind of the memory. Coach and the GM had to have words with me, and my sponsors were ticked after all those lies came out. I hated seeing my face all over the news like that. I got so much press attention that they wanted me to do the Body Issue again because everyone wanted a view of Tater's Tots. I declined, preferring that my stats were why the press were interested, not because Sam was touting out information about my Tots. It's another reason why I like Cali. She's nothing like Sam, and even though I'm coming on strong, she's still making me work. She's taking her time to decide if she actually likes me instead of jumping into bed with me because I'm rich. My money or clout in this organization hasn't been a factor for her at all. I'm sure she knows I could sort out her work arrangements, but she's never asked.

She's just a genuine, sweet girl who wants to work hard. How can there be anything wrong with that?

"Sam was a mistake," I ground out, gripping my phone harder, refusing to drudge up those details.

"See, Rookie." Grayson turns back to Austin, baring his teeth. "You need to learn from the old-timer. Women are trouble."

Austin nods along, and I've had enough. I get up, hauling my bag over my shoulder, and say my goodbyes. Walking out of the player's area, I decide to do a little pit stop before leaving for the day.

The stadium's back office is becoming a second home to me, which is funny because I didn't even know it existed until the beginning of this season. I walk past empty office spaces and relish in the quiet. Desks are only lit by the little lamps next to the computers; it's past seven, after all. Rounding the corner to her desk, I'm disappointed when she's not there. The Tate Sorenson bobbleheads stand to attention guarding her space. I salute them and notice her phone tucked behind the bobblehead of me dressed in the old Fisherman mascot costume, flashing away (the phone, not the bobblehead). Well, that explains why she's not responding. She doesn't have the thing on her.

I prop my head over the cubicle and look around. That idiot boss of Cali's is in his office, laughing about something on the phone, acting like he owns the place. His cackle reverberates through the office as he kicks his legs up onto his desk to relax. *What a dick.* I still can't believe they can't find a pot of money to pay her any kind of salary. Jack Luckson is the worst relief pitcher in the league, and we still manage to pay him one million a year. Yet, she gets nothing. She works more than I do and has nothing to show for it. I contemplate waiting for her because I want to take her home with me; maybe a takeout would make her feel better, but then her boss comes out of his room.

"Mr. Sorenson," he says in that suck-up voice he used last time. *Great.* Cali's going to be pissed. She's wanted to keep what's going on between us private, and here I am accidently announcing it to her boss by rummaging through her desk.

"I just came up here to borrow a pen." I grab the first one I can find on her desk. No surprise, it has a giant smiley-faced baseball on the end. "See ya." No way do I want to get into a conversation with that douche canoe.

As I walk out of the office, I decide that I will make it my mission to figure out a way to make this job better for her. Yeah, she says she's rewarded because she works for the Fish, but I want her to know just how vital she is to the team here too. Without the back office working as hard as they do, no fans would be here.

By the time I get home, it's already past nine. I figure Cali must have left her phone at work since I don't receive a response from her. After eating dinner on my own and brushing my teeth, my phone flashes, and I do my best not to skip over and check it excitedly. Taking my time, my heart settles when Cali's name pops up.

Cali: Hey Tate. I'm sorry I didn't respond sooner; I fell over and rolled my ankle. I'm such a klutz. Can we rain check on dinner? I really want to see you, but I'm feeling exhausted and in pain after today.

Tate: Don't worry about the dinner. Are you okay? Do you need me to come and pick you up? You shouldn't be walking on a twisted ankle.

Cali: Already home. Believe me, I've done worse than walking on it today! Promise me after your week of evening games; we'll meet up?

That last message brings a smile to my lips, happy with the confirmation she's not avoiding me. I would offer to go over and *help* her, but I don't want to come off too strong. Or, I should say, stronger than I already do.

Tate: Promise.

CHAPTER 15

CALI

When I open the door and walk into the room, my whole world stops. The music may be blaring and children are running in all directions, but the only thing I see is Tate.

Perfect.

Beautiful.

Tate.

His butterscotch eyes twinkle as he lifts a little girl up, smiling and talking to her parents. They must be talking about those two homers he scored today, one of which flew out of the ballpark and dinged a fan's car. He's leading the league in homers again this year, and I have no doubt he'll be MVP. If he isn't, then the voting's rigged. It's his year; we're all just living through it.

As the little blonde girl burrows into his neck, looking bashful, he gives her a reassuring nod. She lifts her hand and whispers something in his ear. When she's finished, he leans back, looks her in the eyes, and laughs. I can hear his deep throaty chuckle from here, and I think my ovaries are bursting as I watch this display. Suddenly, another little boy pulls on his pant leg, drawing Tate's attention down. He's at ease, in his element, even when he's talking to kids.

Does Tate want kids?

I mean, I know eventually, he'll probably want children, but judging by the way he interacts with them, it makes him look like he'd be a great dad. It makes me wonder if he'd want them soon.

He's 27 now and was serious enough to have a fiancée last year. That must mean he's thinking about it. My eyes widen. What if he wants a whole team of kids before he's 30? How would my vagina cope? Worry clouds my mind. I'm only 23. There's no way I'm ready for children yet. I've only just started my career with the Fish. Not to mention the fact that we aren't officially dating. I need more time. But does he have it to give? He's ready to settle down; I'm hardly ready to settle on my hair color, let alone a man for life. The closest I've ever been to a fiancée is Ricardo at the Waffle Hut. Granted, he had a wife and two kids already, but I relied on that man daily for my waffle needs, and he always delivered. The only reason Tate and Sam broke up was that she cheated on him. If she hadn't, they might have kids right now, and I might still be pining over Ricardo.

All thoughts leave my mind when the little girl points to me with excitement, and he looks my way. My legs turn to jelly when that smile is directed towards me. I lift my arm to adjust my hair, stopped by the stupid giant fish head. Because that's right. Tate isn't smiling *at me*. He's smiling at Catty.

Crap!

Reality sets in. While I've been deliriously dreaming about Tate, kids have been tugging at my legs and calling my name. Get it together.

"Hey, Catty," Tate chirps, holding the little girl in his hands. "I'd like to introduce you to Phoebe. She's your biggest fan." Sweat trickles down my back in fear that somehow Tate might know I'm inside. I've still not had the balls to tell him I am, in fact, the girl behind the fish. Partly because he talked to Catty about a girl he liked, the one I can only assume is me, and partly because I saw the way he looked at me when I told him that my internship was unpaid. He's already questioning the hours I put in. Imagine if I told him the majority of my overtime is mainly because I prance around like a fish during home games and charity events.

I wave my fin dramatically, shaking off the chubby fingers holding onto my arms, and feel them immediately grab my jersey in their vice-like grip instead. Phoebe squeaks out a high-pitched giggle. "Catty helped me out today," Tate says. "We won all because of him." If my body could melt more in this hot suit, it would. *Get it together, Cali!* He's talking about Catty, *not* you. I bend back, pretending to laugh, and pat phoebe on the head. Tate's gaze flicks around the room. "Where are the rest of the mascots? Phoebe wanted to get a picture with all of them."

Double crap.

They were supposed to be right behind me. I spin on my heel just in case Tate can't see them. Although, side note, if he can whack a tiny ball coming at him at 80 mph, I'm sure he can see three people dressed in furry costumes. Unlike Tate, I have tunnel vision in this costume and can only see what's directly in front of me because the gills get in my way. When I establish they aren't in the room, I stomp out of the door, doing my best to hide my ankle injury because Tate texted me about it earlier, and I didn't want to leave any hints that it's me under here. I look down the hallway in both directions and immediately spot a crowd of children around the other mascots while their parents take pictures.

Every year, the mascots of all the major teams in Charlotte get together to celebrate the local kids in a Children's Day event. We invite all of Charlotte's underprivileged kids over to watch the game and have a dance party after. Even though today has been one of the worst days for working double-time with Josh and my Catty responsibilities, it's been one of the most rewarding too. The smiling faces and giggles of the kids have made it bearable.

During the game, we pulled pranks on the fans and players. Most notably, Chilly the Chinchilla asked Austin to marry him, who said yes, by the way. Then there was a moment when we were all sitting in the stands as inconspicuously as four mascots could and waited for the opportune moment to jump up, throw popcorn in the air, and start a dance party in the stands. The kids loved it even if we got a few grumbles from the parents, picking popcorn off their clothes.

Back to the scene in front of me, Mr. Purrfect has Barry the Crow in a headlock. Chilly, on the other hand, is posing with a couple of children and their parents. It all looks like chaos, and I have no idea how to get their attention. It's not like I could shout. Mascots talking ruins the effect for the kids. Kind of like them finding out Santa isn't real for the first time. I can't scare these kids. Not today. What's the universal mascot sign for 'get a move on'? I knew we should have agreed on some mascot sign language this morning.

Walking over to them, I wave my fins and dance in their direct eye line, assuming they have the same tunnel vision I do. They stop what they're doing, nod at me, and I point my fishy fin in the direction of the party. That's enough to get them to follow behind as children skip by my side.

My stomach bottoms out when I notice Tate still standing at the door, waiting for me to come back. *For Catty.* Phoebe claps while the other mascots enter, basking in the cheers from the other children. I motion them to follow me to the photography area before they have a chance to get sidetracked.

By the time I've prepared everyone for the photo with Phoebe, I've got Tate's arm draped around my shoulder and children hanging off every body part - except my whiskers - thankfully.

After a few quick flashes, Tate says, "thanks Catty." Dropping Phoebe off on the floor, watching her run back towards her parents, I fully expect him to follow behind, but instead, he turns and places a palm on my shoulder. The connection sends tingles down my spine, making my toes twinkle. It feels inappropriate to be aroused while I'm dressed as a fish and producing enough sweat for said fish to live in… but I kind of am.

"Catty." Tate's serious tone cuts through the noise. "I just wanted to say thanks for all the advice." Advice? I rack my brain trying to think about what the heck he's talking about. "You know, about the girl." I jump at that reference, looking deep into his eyes to check he's not making a joke because he knows it's me under here.

There's no amusement, just full-on sincerity. "Things are going well." He nods, almost deliriously happy. "She seems to be warming up to me." I find it interesting that he categorizes dry humping and allowing him to stick his hand down my pants as 'warming up.' I'd consider that pretty damn hot but each to their own.

A smirk draws across his face, and for a split second, I wonder if he knows what I'm thinking, but that's impossible. He has no idea I'm under here. I nod my big old fish head as my way to say you're welcome, because what else am I supposed to do?

There's a rumble of noise as the other players walk towards us. "Tate, we need you," Grayson grouses; his tall frame and surly attitude look out of place at the party.

"Yeah, I'll be two seconds." He replies, and I sigh a relieved breath, thinking I can go about my catfish business, but weirdly he's still watching me. "Hey Catty, can I ask you a favor?" I nod, wondering what the kids must think about Tate having such a serious conversation with the team Mascot. "Bottom of the seventh tomorrow. Could you possibly stand on top of the dugout?"

I don't ask questions; I just nod. His shoulders relax, and he slaps me on the back. "Great. Thanks so much. Alright, I'll see you tomorrow." He waves off, walking backward. I flap my fishy fin at him and get back to playing with the kids.

My back relaxes down onto the dirty subway seat. I'm tired, hot, and sweaty. Ready for a shower and bed, I don't bother staying in the office because I was in that Catty costume for over 12 hours. I wonder if that's a record. Do the people at Disneyland wear their costumes for that long? I can barely answer my own thoughts because my body and bones are so tired.

The party finished a couple of hours after the game, and once the players and kids were gone, Mary and I were left to clean up. I ignored her probing questions about Tate because, frankly, I haven't been able to see him, and I'm starting to get a little sad about it. I don't think Josh can work me harder, but he always seems to find a way. I've barely been able to see my bed, let alone think about Tate.

By the time we finished cleaning, it was already dark, and Mary forced me out of the office before Josh could see me. Hence why I left with no shower, and I'm now starting to regret it. I stink. I can literally smell myself, and it's disgusting. The only good thing that happened today is that I missed the after-work rush, so at least no one is sitting next to me on the train. They'd probably think I was trying to gas them.

When I take my phone out to check the time, I'm pleasantly surprised to find a text from Tate.

Tate: Are you working late again? I need to see you.

A chill runs down my spine through my damp clothes, reminding me that I soaked through them all today. I had a hard time putting my shoe on because my throbbing ankle was at least two times its average size now. I thought my rolled ankle would be fine in flats, but apparently not. I'm a wreck, and as much as I want Tate to kiss it and make it all better, I don't want him to see me like this.

Cali: Still at work, not sure when I'll finish. Might have to raincheck again. Sorry.

I lie. It's not like he will be waiting outside my apartment for me.

Tate: Playing hard to get… Two can play at that game.

My tired eyes re-read the message, confused, and then I look up to the top of the carriage where the signage is. Two more stops until I reach mine and I can get some sleep. I can't wait.

The phone buzzes in my hand, and I gasp so loudly, I wake up the homeless person sleeping on the other end of the carriage.

"Sorry," I mumble loud enough for him to hear. My eyes dart around, hoping no one thinks I'm looking at porn on my phone in public. When I'm certain no one is watching, I take another look, fully expecting it not to be there so I can laugh at my delirious mind making it all up.

My eyes bug out as my brain catches up to what's sitting on my screen. Tate's tanned, toned, hard, and slightly wet abs glare back at me tangled in his silky black sheets. I know they're his abs because I've lovingly studied them for years, and he has this mole under his left pec. It's right there, taunting me. That's not the part of the picture my brain is trying to get used to, though. Right at the bottom of the photo, his hand is stuffed down his baseball pants. Tate, lying in bed, topless with his baseball pants on, holding his dick. My face is hot as I think about the most inappropriate things.

I nearly pee my pants when my phone goes again, and a new message from Tate pops up. Do I have enough nerve to check it here? We're nearing my stop. I can wait until I get home. That would be the sensible thing to do. Another message comes through from him. I chew my bottom lip and look at the homeless man who's still sleeping. There's no one else here. Another buzz.

I can't take it. I open it up.

Tate: Thinking of California…
Tate: And her hot wet beaches.

He put a little beach emoji next to my name. Embarrassment flares through my body because even though these messages are just for me, no guy has ever been so forthright in letting me know how I make them feel. It makes me hot. Hotter than I'd like to admit. Even to myself. I push my thighs together and close my eyes when another text comes through. This is not the time to feel hot and bothered.

My body relaxes when my stop is called. I jump up, scurrying to the doors, and shove my phone in my bag. When I've showered and am ready for bed, I give my cellphone another glance.

Tate: Since you didn't respond, I've either offended you, or you're letting off steam, so to speak. I hope it's the latter. If it's the former, I'm sorry. I just wanted to see you.
Tate: Okay, I think I've definitely offended you. I'm sorry. Can we start over? I'm Tate, a tall, roguishly handsome baseball player that would like to take you out on a second date.
Tate: Wait, I just realized, if we're starting over, it would be the first date. So yet again, I'm back to a first date request.
Tate: [Groundhog picture]
Tate: You there?

Bubbles pop up. I know he's typing, but I want to get in there first and put him out of his misery.

Cali: Sorry, T, I'm here.
Tate: Thank fuck. I thought my abs scared you away.
Cali: Never. I've seen it all before.
Tate: Not all of it… Yet.

A small smile plays on my lips, and I'm reminded that although he's seen me naked, I've yet to see him out of his jeans in person. I can't wait. I sink further into my bed, my eyelids dropping because I'm so exhausted. Another buzz on my nightstand jolts me awake. There's no way I'm going to be able to maintain a fully functioning conversation in the next five minutes.

Tate: We've got a lunchtime game tomorrow. Will you let me take you out to dinner?
Cali: Sure. I can't wait, but I've got to sleep T. I'm exhausted. Night.

I quickly type out the last message, too tired to dwell on the shortness of the response. I'll explain it all tomorrow when my brain is functioning better. Within seconds, I'm fast asleep, dreaming of Tate's abs.

CHAPTER 16

CALI

"Cali, have you finished the marketing budget yet?" I hunch further into my desk, hiding my face as I roll my eyes. *No, because I'm too busy editing the website like you asked. Oh, and then there's that whole pretending to be a fish thing you make me do every day.*

Huffing out a breath, I plaster on a fake smile, jumping up to meet his gaze. Is it wrong to imagine your boss tarred and feathered? "Not yet; I will try and have it done for tomorrow morning," I say in my sickeningly sweet tone. I sink back down into my seat, thinking that's the end of our conversation until his head pops up over my cubicle.

"I need it for our meeting with Jonah at 9 am," he stresses. Of course, I can see how this is going to go down. I estimate the marketing budget; Josh takes it to Jonah, his boss, and claims he did it if Jonah loves it. If Jonah hates it, Josh can blame me even though he checked and signed it off himself. He is so infuriating.

"No problem, it will be in your inbox when you arrive in the office tomorrow, so you can check over it," I emphasize, almost passive-aggressively with a smile. "I'll have to work late to get it done, but it will be finished."

He tilts his head, squaring me up. "Well, you wouldn't have to stay late if you weren't out having fun most of the day."

My eyes widen, and I nearly choke on my own spit. Is he implying that I'm enjoying being Catty? Okay, so maybe it's not the worst thing in the world, and it sure as hell beats seeing his face, but it's still very much work for me. Why my other work isn't given to

Tim, I'll never know. He's still sitting around the office, nursing his injury, and getting paid while I'm doing double the load and getting none of the return. It sucks. Balls. Big hairy ones. "I only do what the team requests. No fun to be had here. It is a job, after all," I say sarcastically because I'm tired, and my resolve is cracking.

He snorts. "Make sure you have the work in my inbox by 7 am. If not, we'll have to have a discussion about your attitude and performance." He walks off, not even giving me a second glance. All the breath catches in my throat, and I don't move. That one act of rebellion might cost me my whole job.

I look back at the screen, ignoring anyone coming over to talk. Apparently, our conversation was loud enough that everyone heard it in the office. My eyes are stinging. Not just from tiredness but from holding back tears. Josh shouldn't get to me. He's an idiot. But I feel powerless and hopeless and stupid.

I keep my head down the rest of the day, ignoring Mary waving goodbye and all my colleagues' footsteps leaving for the day. I miss those days. When my evenings were empty, and I had the choice over all the fun things I wanted to do.

I squint, trying to make sense of the excel sheet in front of me. I've been staring at it for so long that the numbers are joining together and jumping around the page, making me worry I'm inputting the numbers incorrectly. I didn't realize just how much budget management was involved in Marketing, and I cursed myself because I knew I should have paid more attention in my stats class. I don't bother checking the time; I know it's late. The ceiling light is motion-sensitive, and around every ten minutes, I'm clouded in darkness. If I didn't wave my hand above my head every now and again, it would automatically turn off. I close my tired eyes wishing for my bed, which is saying something because my mattress has some serious unsightly spikes.

Typing in some numbers, I barely care if they're right at this point. I'm exhausted and sad. I want a break. I want my bed, and most importantly, I want to see Tate. Between us, we've had no time to see each other. He's either on the field or on a bus. And I'm either dressed as a fish or in the office. The last time I saw him, I woke up in his arms, fully dressed in his bed. It was magical, and I wanted to stay there, but I knew if I arrived even a minute late, Josh would count that as an insubordination attempt. *Dick.*

The closest I've gotten to a night off and seeing Tate was last night when I was dressed as a Fish with all the kids dancing around us. My back straightens, and I open my eyes wider, trying to muster up some more energy to finish this damn spreadsheet. That's why I'm here, and I'm doing this. It's for the Fish. I *love* the Fish. Josh can go stick a carrot up his ass for all I care. I'm not doing any of this for him.

I try my hardest to focus, but my head is pounding. I can't remember the last time I drank, and my whole body feels dehydrated. I lean my head back, covering my face with my palms to force my scratchy eyes shut. They're so dry; it's like scratching sandpaper across my irises. But I need a break, if only for a second.

"Cali," My lips curve, imagining his soothing voice helps ease the tension in my bones; his deep baritone fills my body, warming me up. "I thought I'd find you up here." His piney smell takes over my senses, and I'm back in his bedroom, his hungry eyes on me, and I'm ready. Ready for everything he has to offer.

Warm hands wrap around my shoulders, shocking me back into the room. My eyes burst open, only to be met with a familiar pair of hazel brown ones staring down at me. "Tate?" I jump, nearly falling out of my chair. *How the hell did this happen? Did my mind magic him up?*

A grin spreads across his face as he watches me try to regain control of my senses and surroundings. I stand up on jittery legs like a newborn baby calf and shove my chair to the side, hoping it hides the Tate Sorenson Bobbleheads on my desk... The collection may have grown since he was last here, and I'd rather he didn't notice. "Hey, Cali. I've missed you." He coos, and I nearly wet my panties. Is that normal? Maybe I need to mention it at my next OBGYN appointment.

"What are you doing here?" My voice is flustered, my hair sticking to my already hot and sweaty forehead. I look like a wreck, but I can only thank my lucky stars that I took a shower before coming back to my desk, so I at least smell okay. The Catfish t-shirt he's wearing stretches across his expansive chest, showing off all that work he does at the gym, and my fingers tingle, wanting to touch his corded arms.

He answers by stepping closer to me, crowding my space. I tiptoe backward, feeling the wood of the desk poking at my backside. He doesn't stop, and the only way I can gain some space and clarity is to perch my butt on the desk, squashing the keys of my keyboard. I really hope I have autosave on that excel sheet turned on.

Tate chuckles, watching me squirm when he places his hands on either side of my hips, leaning in and stealing all that space I just created. The smell of his body wash tickles my nose, and his proximity sent tingles straight to my core. I swear the things he does to me are unnatural. "I've been blowing up your phone for the last hour, Cali." He drawls out my name, so I can see his pink tongue poke out from between his lips. The same tongue that drove me wild when he kissed me the other night. I can barely focus, too deliriously lost in his presence. "We were supposed to go on a date tonight. Remember?"

I shake my head, doing my best to focus, and roll my eyes, trying to ease any tension from the room. *How did I forget?* "It's been a while since I've seen you," Tate continues. At least he doesn't think I'm purposely standing him up.

"It's not been *that* long," I quip. After all, it's only been a few hours since he had his arm around my shoulders after he batted in one of Austin's runs. I may have been dressed as a fish, but it still counted.

"It's been three weeks," he deadpans as his eyes flick down to my perfectly pressed pencil skirt. He groans, biting his lip and looking to the sky. "Did I ever tell you I've had a thing for secretaries since meeting you?" He's stealing all the air in the room, forcing me closer so I can share his. He drops his head back down, holding my gaze and leaning in.

We've barely said a few sentences to each other, but the whole room is so charged with energy, it's nearly vibrating. Something that only seems to happen when I'm in his presence. His mouth is close to mine, nearly touching, and I so desperately wanted to feel the softness of his lips. I've almost forgotten what they feel like in all my work haze. Goosebumps appear on my skin, anticipating his touch.

Ding! Ding!

"Crap!" My noisy computer brings me back to the room, and I push him back, my feet hitting the ground as I bend over to check the screen. *I cannot screw this up.* Luckily, it's just a save reminder, so I quickly shut the spreadsheet in fear of doing more damage if I leave it up. Tate kisses the exposed skin on the back of my neck while I type. *Damn.* It's like he knows exactly which buttons to press to turn me on. His hands spread across my hips, and I tilt my body back, leaning my head on his shoulder to give him better access to my neck. I reach my hand over to play with his still wet hair and close my eyes, enjoying the stolen moment, knowing it won't last for long.

"Come to mine for dinner tonight, Cali?" His voice is filled with heady intention as he whispers in my ear. A smile plays across my lips because I hoped *I* was on the menu. But then my eyes shoot open, and I remember that stupid spreadsheet needs to be done for 7 am. I bend my body forward, bumping Tate with my butt to push him back, and open the spreadsheet again, doing my best to focus while Tate radiates all his Baseball player hotness behind me.

"I can't tonight, I've got this big meeting in the morning, and my boss will kill me if I don't get this done."

"Mary won't care. You're working your ass off, and they don't even pay you for the pleasure," he retorts. "Do they even ask you to clock your hours so they know how much time of yours they're taking?" I ignore the question because the answer hurts. No. He seems to take my silence and position as an invitation. He sprawls his hands across my butt, gently stroking it and every now and again digging his fingers in.

"Mary wouldn't care, but Josh would," I stress, still staring at the numbers, and ignoring the throbbing sensation that's paving its way down my center. He waits patiently as I tap the keyboard and gently kisses my neck every now and again. With every touch, he knows he's closer to breaking my resolve. When I finish a row of numbers on the sheet, I relent and spin on my heel to face him.

He smiles broadly as his eyes flitter across my face. "Take a break. I'll get you dinner in the mall. You can come back here, finish up, and then when you're done, you can come to mine." I laugh because he has it all figured out, and the idea of food has my stomach growling, but I know if I leave this office, I will never come back.

I glance over at the spreadsheet calling my name. '*California. California.*' It's like I'm on that show, *The O.C.,* for all of ten seconds. "I really shouldn't. I really need to get this done."

His fingers bite into my hips; I have a hard time thinking when he does that. It's like he makes my brain fuzzy in all the right ways. "Come on, just a little break. With me." He enunciates the last part. God, why does he have to be so hot? And perfect. And everything I've ever wanted.

I'm tempted. So tempted. He holds my cheek in his palm, rubbing his calloused thumb against it, and watches as I bite my bottom lip, contemplating my fate, but he doesn't give me any more time. Instead, he roughly brings my face to his and presses our lips together. Hard. My tired body wakes at every touch and stroke of his tongue. My fingers try to grasp anything on the desk to maintain control.

The keyboard taps underneath me, and I know I'll regret this kiss later. For now, though, I'll let myself get lost. His hand spreads down to the base of my neck, tilting my head back to grant him easier access while his tongue dances across my lips. When I finally open up, it's like I've unleashed the tiger in him. He gruffly pulls my legs apart, nearly ripping my skirt as it bunches up the sides, so he can push himself against me. I back away from his lips, surprised I can feel his erection through his jeans. He rocks his hips against my center and looks up towards the ceiling. I follow his gaze, wondering what he's doing. "Are there security cameras in here?" He asks, still inspecting.

"Only at the entrance. Why?" His head whips back to me, a wolfish grin spread across his face, and he drops his hands to bunch my skirt up higher. He pushes it so high; I can feel the cold air dance across my skin as my black thong is on display.

"What are you doing?!" I hiss nervously, looking around just in case someone is still in the office. No one is here, I know that, but that doesn't mean I want to get in trouble for indecent exposure.

But without responding, he drops to his knees, kneeling between my thighs as he glances up at me. "I'm starving." He shrugs. "And just because you won't let me take you out doesn't mean I don't get to eat."

My hands grasp his shoulders. Little mewls of resistance come out but are no match to the man before me. When he wants something, he takes it, and right now, he wants me. "Tate, we can't do this," I whisper.

His hands toy with the edges of my panties; I swear I can feel his breath on my center. "Just relax. It won't take long; then you can get back to your stuffy spreadsheet fully satisfied," he says confidently.

My legs are already open, butt on the keyboard, panties wet from the way he's staring at me. This is going to happen, and I should just lean into it. It's not like I don't want it. I watch as his deft fingers take hold of the strings of my underwear, gliding them down my legs and off, only for him to quickly stuff them into the back pocket of his jeans.

With closed eyes, I fully expect his mouth to come down on me. My body tingles, waiting for the sensation, needing the release. He started this burning fire inside me; now, it's his job to put it out. Only he doesn't. Legs wide open, I can only feel the soft caress of his touch on my knees. When I look down, he's staring at my center, licking his lips. "Did I forget to tell you how good you tasted the first time?"

I moan, my hips shifting, trying to force his mouth closer. Just when I've nearly given up, his hands grip my knees, and he dips his face down to my slit. His tongue grazes over my clit with the lightest of touches. My whole body shivers with the anticipation of more. Flick. Flick. Flick. So soft, they were barely felt. It's like he wanted me to cry out his name for the whole stadium to hear.

His fingers draw slow circles across my knees as his mouth moves to the side, licking the outer lips of my pussy. He's driving me wild with his barely there touches. "You taste better than last time," he says, pressing his tongue down then flicking faster. My hips buck at the sudden shock of pleasure coursing through my body. I breathe out his name, leaning back onto the desk so I can watch him. I don't care that I'm sitting on the keyboard or that anyone can walk in now. All I care about is the man kneeling in front of me, making me feel alive.

His hands grip my knees, keeping me open as his tongue travels down the length of my slit, then back up to quickly flick my clit. I hum, barely able to put together a coherent sentence, happy that the desk was underneath me for stability because my legs had given out long ago.

He drapes my legs over his shoulders. As if he couldn't get any closer, he does. His lips kiss and suck at my clit; then his tongue takes over. Satisfied moans reverberate in his chest, and I'm so lost in the moment, I hardly notice when his fingers come to play. He dips two fingers into me, stroking me from the inside while he feasts on my clit. Sucking. Nipping. Licking.

It's everything.

I tangle my hands in his hair, moving my hips as he devours me. No one has ever eaten me out so thoroughly or showed that much enjoyment while doing it. My brain's malfunctioning with pleasure, clenching every few seconds. I'm on the edge, and he knows it.

He's persistent, never letting me catch a breath as his big paws grab at my ass to angle me just right. That's all it takes. "I'm coming."

Is all I get out before I convulse around his tongue, moaning out in pleasure.

My chest is heaving as my hands unclench from the papers on the desk that I screwed up. Tate is still between my legs, and my arousal is dripping all over my budget notes. Reality quickly starts to settle in.

The silence in the room is deafening.

What the hell just happened?

What the hell did I let him do?

I glance around the room again, worried that someone was here and watching, but the office is definitely empty. The only person in here is now standing up next to me with a satisfied smirk on his face. As I tip my head up, he closes my knees and drags my skirt back down, setting it in place. He gives me a little pat on my thighs at the end. It would have been like he was never here if I wasn't wet, horny, and pantyless. "That should help you concentrate." He holds my hands, leaning his forehead against mine.

He watches our fingers lace together; those soft, gentle touches are exactly what I needed after that frantic moment. "I want to see you, Cali," he stresses in a whisper. Guilt courses through my veins. I should have texted him before, but I was so lost in my own workload, I'd forgotten.

I look into his eyes, barely functioning after the fantastic orgasm he gave me. "I do too. Work's just been crazy," I sigh, closing my eyes and hoping I can think of a solution.

"What are you doing tomorrow night?" his voice is optimistic as his eager eyes bore into mine.

I chew on my bottom lip. "I might be working."

He squints and scrunches his nose in contemplation. "How about this. Tomorrow is Friday so you won't have to work on Saturday. My game is Saturday night which means I could spend the morning with you. Even if you have to work late tomorrow, come to mine after. I'll come to pick you up," he offers.

It sounds like a great idea. Only, I will have to work on Saturday too. When Catty calls, I've got to be there to answer. "It doesn't matter what time you work until. I'll be here waiting for you." He must have taken my silence as hesitation.

"I'd like that," I reply with a smile.

His smile matches mine, and for a split second, we laugh nervously, our foreheads still connected and hands still laced. "Good."

"Cali." Mary's whiny voice breaks through my sleep while she violently shakes my shoulders. I jump, grabbing the leathery sofa beneath me, trying to get my bearings.

"Where am I?" I ask, still half-asleep. A sharp pain radiates down my neck, and I feel like crap.

"You're in the office," she answers, looking at me concerned. "Did you sleep here last night?"

"Last night?"

"It's 7:15," she stresses, and that's when my brain starts to act, remembering what happened. After Tate left, I spent another few hours working on the budget, and I wanted to take a teeny tiny break before I checked over my work to send it off to Josh. When I sat down on the sofa, I thought I'd close my eyes for just a second. I'd get a quick cat nap, and then I'd be able to get up refreshed and start work again.

"Crap. I fell asleep," I shout, racing towards my laptop to send the email that's sitting on my screen. I have no time to check it now. I look up to his office; Josh isn't in yet. Thank God he wasn't the one to find me on the sofa. That would definitely be grounds for firing.

Rolling my chair, I sink down into the seat and quickly send off the attachment to Josh. I know I promised seven am, but since he's not here, it's fifteen minutes later than he expected, surely, he can give me a pass.

"Do you need some clothes?" Mary's voice surprises me, and I look down at my crumpled shirt and creased skirt. I still don't have any panties on, which currently stands as the only confirmation that Tate was here last night. If I were in my usual happy mood, I'd laugh at her suggestion. Anything she owns would make me look like a stripper because I'm just so much bigger than her. Right now, though, I'm too busy fretting about Josh's reaction to me.

"No. I've got some in my locker downstairs." I try to remember what I have left in there from the other day, hoping it's better than what I've got on. "Would you cover for me while I change?"

She waves me off. "Of course, take your time." Mary throws a small black bag my way. "There's some dry shampoo and make-up in there. You might want to fix your eyeliner." She points at my left eye as she ushers me out of the room.

When I get to my locker, I change into a fresh pair of underwear and put a pair of jeans on. Having no clean shirts left meant that I had to steal one from the lost and found. My outfit is considerably more casual than I'd usually go for, but at least it's Friday, and most of the office dress down for it.

Hurrying back to my desk, the first thing I notice is Mary running behind Josh as he paces his office. His face is red and blistering, and I swear if I look hard enough, I'll see steam coming from his ears. He's furious to the point of looking slightly unhinged. When his eyes meet mine, he stomps to the door, opens it, and points at me. "Cali. My office. Now." It's all he had to say. My heart deflates like a popped balloon. I guess he can't give me a pass. I trudge to his office with my head hung low, wholly demoralized.

I knew I shouldn't have taken that break with Tate.

Chapter 17

Tate

"So, are you going to tell me what's wrong?" I ask carefully. Cali sits next to me, staring at the bottom of her Chinese takeout box with her bottom lip jutted out in a pout. She's been at my apartment for a little over an hour, and the only noise she's made is a small grunt when Washington scored a grand slam off Atlanta. And she hates Atlanta. Normally, she'd be celebrating as though she was the one to hit it. She may not be that forthright with her feelings and emotions, but I'm pretty sure I can guess what's got her upset.

Work.

After playing three and a half hours of baseball and taking my sweet time in the shower, Cali still wasn't ready to leave the office for the day. So, I went down to the batting cages and whacked a few balls before taking another shower. Cali was ready five hours after the game finished, and when she came into the parking lot, all I heard were the pitter-patter of her heels and her sniffles. I didn't want to pressure her then to tell me what was wrong, figuring she'd probably just want a hug after a crappy day, so I held her tight. So tight that I could feel her whole body shake from her soft whimpers.

By the time we left the parking lot, the only question running through my mind was if work should really make you that unhappy?

Cali stabs her Kung Pow Chicken and pops it in her mouth to delay the answer. Her eyes were still a little bloodshot, but thankfully the color had started coming back to her face since she started eating. "Just overreacting over some stupid work stuff." There she goes trying to pass it off as nothing again. She's done it before when I've asked her about work.

I get it. When I've had a bad game, I don't want to sit around and analyze what I could have done better. *Chally Sports* does that for me, but when it's about Cali, I want to help. Does she not realize that I find it hard to breathe when her cheeks blotch and her nose reddens? It feels like someone's gutting out my stomach. I hate seeing her like this, and if there's anything I can do to stop it. I will.

"Is it to do with that idiot boss of yours?" The wideness of her eyes and poutiness of her lips tells me everything. She seems surprised that I know about him. As if I could forget about that cockblocking asswipe. "He seems like he's an ass," I say, taking a drink of my water, conscious that I have a game tomorrow and need to stay clean.

She nods, still nursing that chicken box like it's on its death bed. "I guess I thought I'd love my job," Her body slumps in exhaustion. Then she looks up at me, her light blue eyes almost navy. "I don't."

Tired of the distance between us. I grab her feet, pulling her, so her legs are resting over my lap. She drops the chicken onto the coffee table and leans into me, melting in my arms. A warm fuzzy feeling brews in my stomach, and I know what it is. Belonging. Cali belongs right here, with me. Not confident that declaration will go down the way I'd want it to, I keep it to myself and tuck a few errant blonde hairs behind her ear and kiss her forehead. "It will get better, I promise." Her head collapses onto my shoulder, and she draws her hand up my chest. I rub her back, feeling her breathing calm.

I still don't fully understand why her boss is such an idiot. Cali is obsessed with the team, and I can't think she's anything but conscientious. She wants to do a good job, even at the expense of her own health. It feels like Josh is punishing her for something. For what, I don't know. I do know one thing, though. I don't like him. "At least you've got all the Catty experience to use if you end up looking for another job," I offer, not sure what to say. I feel a little out of my depth when it comes to office jobs.

Her head jolts up; she looks at me like a deer caught in headlights. "You know about Catty?" She says, pulling out of my hold and sitting on the seat next to me.

I tilt my head. "Yeah?" My brows furrow when she doesn't say anything. "You mentioned you manage his social media accounts," I clarify, and she blows out a relieved breath. "Didn't you manage to grow it like 400% since the start of the season? That sounds like a pretty impressive stat to me."

She nods, leaning back to get her takeout box. I watch the curve of her ass as she does it."Yeah, I suppose all the hours racked up in the office will pay off." Her tone is brighter than it has been for a while.

"You missed Catty at the Children's event the other day. All the kids loved him." She stuffs her face with chicken, trying to smile as she chews. "He was doing this stupid one leg dance, and Austin got involved, calling it the limp fish," I chuckle, and she laughs, albeit somewhat forced along with me. It's almost like she didn't find the joke that funny. Then it dawns on me. "Oh shit. Did you choreograph that?" I'm an idiot.

"No. No." She answers quickly, waving my question off dismissively. "Just happy to hear that he's doing such a good job." She stands and walks over to my kitchen, grabbing a container of noodles, and comes sauntering back. When she plops down next to me, she swivels her legs and rests her feet on my lap. Her toes wiggle in a pair of my Catfish Baseball socks that go over her calves. She insisted on wearing them the minute she came into my apartment because her feet were aching from her heels. Who am I to turn down such a request?

I wrap one of her feet in my hand, and she winces. "Oh shit. I forgot to ask, how's your ankle? Should you be wearing heels if it still hurts?" Studying the foot, even with the sock on, I can tell it's big and swollen compared to the other one.

She nods frantically. "Yeah, much better, thanks. Phil showed me a few exercises to help it."

"You spend a lot of time downstairs with Phil." I cock a brow, trying to hide the jealousy in my voice. I can't help but be a little suspicious, it's where I met her, and the way she affectionately says his name has me wondering if something happened between them. Phil's a nice guy and a doctor, too.

"It's because I'm a klutz. Always falling or doing something stupid. Now that I'm doing more - " She pauses, connecting her eyes with mine for a second, looking skittish as per usual, before she tentatively continues. "Running around after Catty, I've got to be a little more careful." She finishes very slowly as though she's making it up as she goes along.

"You're doing a great job with Catty. I think he's fantastic. Granted, when he humped me that first time, I was petrified of his googly eyes, but now, he's my good luck charm." She offers me a small smile, seemingly more relaxed. I thought she might be happy with that statement, considering how much effort she puts into him.

"Your good luck charm?" She squeaks out, and I nod.

"Yeah, every time he's standing on top of the dugout, and I look over, I manage to get a hit. I think it's because of him." I pause, thinking about it. "Who is it under there, by the way?" Her eyes dart around the room. "I wanted to send him a fruit basket or something. Do fish eat fruit?" She whimpers, sinking further into the sofa.

"It's Tim," she squawks quickly. "I'll let him know. And he's a meat man. Because he's a man, and he's all meaty." I shake my head as she unconvincingly flexes her muscles. She's so weird sometimes, but I like it. I like it because I feel like a regular guy that she's dating, not a famous athlete who can get her on the news. Since we started dating a month ago, she's asked for nothing. Not even orgasms – although I do like bestowing them on her even when she hasn't asked.

"Great. Now, are you finished?" I gesture to the empty food boxes and take them from her hands. She leans back onto the sofa as I toss the boxes onto my coffee table. "All this fish talk has made me hungry," I say, growling into her neck. She giggles as I kiss the spot behind her ear. Her smooth skin is delicious, and the smell of her coconut shampoo makes me feel like I'm drugged and reminds me of her face when I ate her out last night. How I want to do it again. I can wait, though. I'm a patient man, after all. Anyone who plays baseball needs the patience of a saint and good bubblegum. Cali, however, has been testing my resolve. She doesn't even realize how crazy she drives me. When she doesn't protest my kisses and arches her neck, I drag my mouth down to the opening of her white shirt, kissing her clavicle.

I can feel the hum reverberating in her throat as she leans her head back, giving me greater access to her chest. The buttons across her shirt strain almost as badly as the erection in my pants. My fingers tighten around her hips, leaving a bruising touch. I want her, and judging by the way she wraps her legs around my waist, I know she wants me to.

Bringing my lips to hers, I kiss her gently before checking her legs are securely locked around me and pick us up, blindly walking us to the bedroom. "Where are we going?" She asks with a hint of humor in her voice, knowing full well what I wanted to do.

"I haven't been able to get you off my mind since last night." She flushes at the memory and brings her lips down to kiss me while I fumble into the bedroom, thankful she's light. I don't want to have to explain a back injury tomorrow.

She relaxes back as I drop her down onto the bed. The top buttons of her shirt are undone, with a hint of white lace poking out of them. Those jeans are doing little to hide her beautiful curves, and my socks she's wearing are just taunting me at this point. I lick my lips, trying to settle my heated skin. Watching this woman is going to give me a coronary, I swear.

I lock eyes with her, fully ready to pounce until she sits up, placing a hand on my chest. "Wait, we shouldn't do this," she says, and I try my best to hide the disappointment as I back away. "No. Wait." She shakes her head dramatically. "I didn't mean we shouldn't *do this.* I meant it shouldn't happen like this." She explains as if that made any more sense.

"How did you want it to happen?" I ask, confused.

Sitting up straight, she has to tilt her head up to look me in the eyes as she explains. "Well, you've seen me naked multiple times now..."

"Not true," I interrupt. "I've only seen you naked once. Yesterday, all I saw was your glorious pussy." I move in, ready to tackle the rest of the buttons on her shirt, but she swats my hands away.

"Either way. You've seen me naked. You know what that looks like."

"I've got it burned in my memory for the rest of my life." I point to my temple with a smirk.

She stands, giving her a few extra inches in height but nowhere near enough to match mine. "Well, I'd like the same memory engrained in my brain too. I want to see you naked." Her grin could light up Times Square during Christmas; it's so bright.

I breathe out a laugh. "Is that what this was? You just wanted to see me naked? Why didn't you say before? That's fine with me."

"STOP!" She yells just as I grab the hem of my t-shirt, fully ready to fulfill her request. I keep my hands in place. "Don't move. I want to be the one to do that."

Lifting my hands and arms, I chuckle. "Be my guest, Babe." I back up to give her more space.

It didn't take her long to edge towards me, toying with the hem of my shirt. She bites her bottom lip before looking up at me with excitement. Her slender hands slip under the fabric, tracing my abs before she can see them. It's almost like she's counting to make sure they're all present. When her fingers rest on my pecs, she scratches her nails down the front. My knees nearly give out at the tingling sensation making its way down my body.

When she finally rolls the piece of fabric off, she takes a moment to look at the golden skin of my chest. "It's even better than the pictures," she says in awe with a wide-ass grin on her face.

"Hopefully, you won't be disappointed with the rest." I urge her on; my cock is uncomfortably hard in my jeans now.

Smirking, she places a gentle kiss on my lips as she flicks the button of my jeans off. Then, she drops to her knees, watching as she unzips them. Jerking my hips forward, I force the fabric to fall to the floor, and she gasps in surprise. Bet she wasn't expecting me to be going commando under there.

So here I am, full of confidence, standing buck naked in front of her. My straining erection is staring straight at her pillowy lips, and she sits there, staring at it for a beat. "Well, no wonder you're a great batsman," she scoffs out. "You've had that piece of wood to manage your whole life."

I bark out a laugh, grasping onto the base of my cock, and start to move my hand up and down. Her eyes track my movement as her mouth unconsciously parts. "How long have you been waiting to say a pun like that?" I ask, watching her lick her lips as she stares at my dick.

"I never thought I'd get to say it," she breathes out, her eyes flicking up as her mouth gets closer to my skin. "I never thought I'd be here with you." She gives me no time to react to the statement. Instead, she shoves my hand out of the way, replacing it with hers. She opens her mouth wide, greedily taking in as much of me as she can.

I groan as the soft, wet feeling of her mouth takes over every part of my being. Her lips hold tight as she shoves me further down her throat until I hit the back. Damn, I don't think my legs can handle this deep throat. Light flicks of her tongue make my legs vibrate. If she keeps sucking me like this, I'm going to come so fast, I'll look like a teenager. This can't end yet, though.

"Cali," I grind my teeth, doing my best to ignore the build of tension at the base of my spine. I am so nearly about to burst in her mouth. She stops moving, looking up at me with my dick still firmly in her mouth. "I want to be inside you when I come."

Her blue eyes are intense, the side of her mouth curling up even with me blocking most of the view. As much as I wanted to come in her mouth, I wanted to feel her too. I've waited long enough. She backs away, moving on to the bed and slinking herself out of her pants and shirt.

There she is, draped over my bed in white lace, smeared lipstick, and baseball socks. My biggest wet dream smiling back at me with a certain kind of innocence only Cali possesses. I stare at her longer than necessary because I'm trying to commit every curve, every line, every goddamn mark to memory. Opening her legs, I kneel between them and place my hands on either side of her head. I lean down, kissing her thoroughly for the first time tonight, telling her all the things I'd like to do in a kiss instead of out loud. Her lips are soft, hungry, and ready for me to take this further.

Even though I've imagined this moment since I first saw her, nothing could have prepared me for this. With her back arched and hints of her perky pink nipples scratching against the fabric of her bra, I couldn't have asked for more.

Unfastening her bra, I make sure to lather both her breasts in equal attention, biting and nipping whenever I hear a satisfied moan from Cali. Her hips move against mine, and even though there's still a tiny piece of fabric keeping her from me, I can feel how wet I'm making her through her panties. "I can't keep waiting," she sputters out. That's all the encouragement I need.

Taking a condom from the bedside table, I slowly roll it down my shaft as Cali watches on hungrily. She pushes her panties down, baring her glistening pussy as she opens her legs. I'm torn. I want another taste, but I also want to be inside her.

Leaning back over her, I plant another kiss on her lips before positioning myself, so I'm just at the entrance of her slick heat. After locking her eyes, I push into her slowly. She's so tight; I have to hold back, worried I'll hurt her. She grasps my shoulders the further I push in. Squeezing my eyes, I try to remain calm, but the feeling of her body tightening around me is amazing. It's like I'm in heaven, and I don't want to leave. In fact, I'm thinking of all the ways I can stay in her while still playing ball. Maybe no one will notice the hot blonde attached to me.

Cali surprises me when she rolls me over, and pushes me onto my back, taking control of the situation. Her perfect tits bounce above me, and her hair is wild, just like her personality. A little hard to tame, but I'm willing to try. Lying on my back, I watch her take pleasure into her own hands, groaning out with an almost reckless abandon.

After all the foreplay, I know I'm close, but I don't want to come before she does. So I dip my hand down, playing with her clit, and nibble at her nipples while she cries out in pleasure. Her body is like an arcade game. I want to hit all the buttons and get the prize. Her head whips back in pleasure, and I can feel her clenching around me. Happy she's close; I thrust my hips up. Cali squeals at the unexpected hit of pleasure. I do it a few more times, disrupting her rhythm but getting her closer and closer to the edge.

Finally, her pussy squeezes my cock like a vice, and that's all it takes for me to lose control too. We come together, and as we slowly come down from our high, Cali lazily falls onto the bed beside me.

When I'm sure my legs won't fail me, I get up and get rid of the condom, only to come back and lie next to Cali, tucking her into my side. "That was…"

"Amazing. I know. It always is with me." I finish the sentence for her, laughing.

She swats me on the chest. "Yes, but you can't say that about yourself,"

I shrug with one arm behind my head and look up to the ceiling. This is perfect. "I wasn't saying it about myself. I was talking about you." I turn, studying her face. It's almost symmetrical, save for the little mole resting above her eyebrow. Her face still has hints of red lipstick, and her eyes puffy from where she'd been crying earlier. She's still the most beautiful girl I've ever seen. "You're perfect," I say.

She smiles meekly, chewing on her lip like she's stopping herself from saying something. "What?" I urge.

"It's nothing. I just had this thought." Her finger drags up and down my chest as I wait for her to carry on. "Have you ever come home without showering before? You know, still sweaty from the field?" She asks sheepishly.

I want to laugh, but the question is kind of hot. "No?" I say, watching her reaction as she closes her eyes – imagining me, I hope. "Did you want me to?"

"I mean, would you be all muddy with grass stains everywhere?"

"Depends on how hard I play. If I know I'm coming back to you, then yes, they'll be every type of baseball stain you could think of."

A smile grows on her lips, and her hands edge down to my hips. "I wouldn't say no to stripping you off and helping you shower after," she teases, leaning her body over mine and licking the bottom of my lip.

"You're a kinky one, aren't you?" I chuckle, excited to see where her hand is going to go.

"Coming from the man who ate me out on my desk. You have no idea how hard it's been to sit there and concentrate without thinking of you." And just like she wanted. I'm hard all over again.

"Oh yeah? Why don't you show me just how hard it's been for you?" I kiss her lips and roll on top of her, ready to show just how much I've been thinking about her too.

CHAPTER 18

TATE

"Tate. I don't know what to say." Jonah, the Office GM, looks at the check, astonished. "This is an extremely generous donation. One that we didn't need or ask for." With crossed brows, he scratches his beard, I'm guessing because he's trying to figure out why on earth I've decided to do this.

As I lean back on one of his office chairs, I crane my neck, looking out of the glass onto the office floor. All I see are cubicles, none of which are Cali's because she works on the other side of the building, but I can't help myself; I have to check. I have no chill when it comes to her. It's probably best that she doesn't see me up here with her bosses boss because she'd have my balls in a vice-like grip, asking me questions that I haven't quite figured out the answers to yet.

"When you walked into this office today, I was bracing myself for the worst, thinking you might have torn your ACL or broken your wrist. But then you surprise me with this." He holds the piece of paper up, still shocked. Yeah, I surprised myself too. The things I'm doing for a girl I've only had a few dates with are unreal and could potentially be classed as obsessive.

I shrug, looking back to Jonah. "It's not that big a deal." Because it's really not. That is less than a week's salary for me, and I give more to Charlotte's children's hospital once a quarter; I'll hardly notice it coming out of my bank account. But it will make a huge difference for the interns, and I want to make a point. The Carolina Catfish should respect everyone's contribution to the team. "I just believe that the hard work and dedication of our interns should be acknowledged. We aren't the best team in the MLB without their contribution, and I'd like to see them compensated for that. I'm hoping this will set a precedence moving forward."

"Just how much of the interns' work have you seen?" He pops a curious brow suspiciously. Have any players ever shown as much interest in the back-office staff as I have? No. I'm not donating it because I'm sleeping with Cali either, although that is a big incentive. It's just hearing the hours she's been working makes me feel like I have an unscratchable itch. When she mentioned in passing that she slept on the office sofa the other day, I nearly blew a gasket. I had to breathe in slowly while I gripped the steering wheel so tight, my knuckles went white. They should not be working someone that hard unpaid.

"Oh yeah, I've seen a lot of their work through the volunteering you've set up. I think it's having a good effect on the team's public image and also mine after that whole… fiasco last year." I go quiet for a beat because we both know what I'm referring to. Sam took a hit on my popularity; the nicest guy in baseball didn't seem all that nice for a little while. She'd tell bogus stories to the press about how horrible I was as a boyfriend and that I essentially forced her to cheat. It was a nightmare, and my publicist spent months trying to rehab my image. I sigh, already not looking forward to the conversation I'll need to have with Cali about it. Some grainy pictures of us making out in her parking lot have ended up online. So far, they aren't interesting enough to go up on anything other than those terrible gossip sites, but still, I know she's going to hate it. "The new mascot is also a great addition to the team this year," I say almost mechanically because I want to make sure Cali gets credit for that too. I rub the back of my neck, trying to remember what I had planned to say next because I didn't want to slip up. "I know it's not any of my business, but do you monitor their working hours?" I know. I know. I shouldn't get myself involved in this. But it's Cali, and not only do I want her to be paid enough to eat, but I also want her to be happy and to be able to afford a nice mattress (if I wasn't already planning on buying her one, that is). There may also be an added benefit in there for me. The less time she's at work, the more time she's in my bed. I've been spoiled over the last week because she's been at my house every night, and it's been bliss. The only thing breaking me out of said bliss is the fact that I'm now off for a two-week away game stint. I told her she could stay in my apartment while I was gone since it's closer to the stadium and has twenty-four-hour security, but she refused because she didn't want to take advantage of me. Doesn't she get it yet? That's all I want her to do. Trying to build a relationship during the season sucks, and I wish I'd met her in the winter before spring training started, so I could have actually built it up a little more. I like her so much. Too much to admit to her without sounding like the Belieber in this relationship.

Jonah grabs the baseball stress ball rolling across his desk, rocking back on his chair. "Nope. Should we?"

Okay, now I'm in the deep end, swimming without armbands, but I'm going to keep going. No point stopping now. "I guess I'm just a little confused because, after the game on Friday, I stuck around to practice in the cages." A disapproving noise came from his throat. No doubt annoyed that I wasn't resting my muscles after the game. "It was after nine when I left, and I noticed that one of the interns was still here." I leave out that I was specifically waiting for her because that's just semantics. "No one else was here at all," I emphasize. "I think she was getting the train home too, which seemed a little dangerous."

His eyes narrow, and there's a part of me that's relieved he seems oblivious. If Jonah was condoning that kind of behavior, I don't know what I'd do. "Really? Do you know which one?"

My back straightens; you could say I know which one quite well. In fact, I could tell him where every freckle on her body was. "I think she's one of the kids in the marketing team." I opt for a more straightforward, less graphic answer. "She's got blonde hair, tall. I saw her at one of the school events a couple of weeks ago."

He nods, pressing his lips together. "Okay, thanks for letting me know. I'll look into it."

"Thanks." I rub my knees, leaning back on the chair. "Alright, I guess I'm going to get some early morning practice in," I say, getting up and walking to the door. As I grasp the handle, I turn back, watching Jonah study the check. "By the way. Could we keep this donation between us? I'd rather the interns don't know about it because I want them to think they earned it. After all, they did."

"Sure, no problem." He smiles, looking at his computer screen.

"Thanks." I open the door, and as I shut it, I wave at a few of the employees watching me. I make a mental note to spend more time on this side of the stadium, so people aren't so confused when they see me up here, as I'll be coming up more often.

"Mr. Sorenson," a familiar whiney voice calls my name. My jaw tenses as I hear the man's voice who's been treating Cali like she's that last piece of bread in the loaf. You know the piece. The heel that always ends up all crusty and moldy by the time you get to it. No one wants to eat that slice.

I turn on my heel to come face to well; actually, I have to look down to see Josh's face because I'm so much taller than him. "Hi, James, is it?"

"Josh.," he corrects. I know. I'm just being a dick.

"Ah right, sorry. Josh, what can I do for you?" I ask while walking, slightly ignoring him. It's not how I usually talk to people, but karma's a bitch, and Josh is getting it dished today.

He scurries behind me. "I was just wondering if you would be able to sign this for me." I stop so suddenly; he walks into me. The pen stabs me in the back, and I'm suspicious about signing anything for him since he seemed like the type of guy to sell it on eBay for a jacked-up price. "It's for my nephew. He's your biggest fan."

I look between the pen and his face before snatching it out of his hand. I can't say no to a child. It's not the kids' fault he has this guy for an uncle. "What's his name?" I always ask because if I write a name, then it's harder for people to sell.

"Charlie." He hands over the ball, watching me eagerly as I sign it. Just as I'm about to hand it over, an idea pops into my head. Raising the ball, I dangle it just out of reach. "James."

"It's Josh."

"Right. Josh," I slur his name. "I'll give you this ball if you promise me one thing." His brows furrow in confusion, probably wondering what he has that I could possibly want. "Be nicer to your staff," I quip, leaning down so he can hear me clearly. "Something I learned in the minors is that you should be nice to everyone. You never know who the next superstar is going to be."

He snorts, his true colors showing through the façade. "I treat them just fine." James lifts his hand, trying to snatch the ball. He seems to have forgotten that I'm a pro athlete and at least a foot taller than him. I lift the ball even further out of his reach, and there's a moment I almost feel sorry for him. He jumps up, trying to claw the ball, but obviously still can't reach it. It's pathetic.

"You don't. I've seen the way you treat them, and it's shitty." With his hands still in the air, he looks at me in horror. I close my eyes before delivering the next part of this. It's something that I don't want to do, but I need to hammer the point home. "You know I've got a lot of clout here?" He doesn't respond. "If I hear you've even looked at one of your employees the wrong way, I might have to mention it to Jonah." I glance back to Jonah's office, who's already on the phone talking to someone else.

Josh stops and adjusts his Carolina Catfish tie. "Um, yes, of course, Mr. Sorenson." He was a compliant little thing when put under pressure. I knew he would be, the little gnat that he is. I drop the ball, and he catches it with both hands.

"Great." Spinning on my heel, I walk to the elevator without giving Josh a second glance.

I'll give him the two weeks while I'm away to change his ways. If

I find out Cali is being treated in any other way than perfect, well, I'll just have to get him fired. Simple. As the elevator doors shut, my phone vibrates in my pocket. Must be Cali. I haven't heard from her since I left her in my bed this morning to go work out.

My jaw flexes, and my body tenses when I see the name flashing on my screen. It's not Cali.

What the hell does Sam want?

The last I heard from her was a few months ago when her face was splashed across those magazines she was obsessed with. Something about her waiting for a ring from Theo. I'm sure there's some truth in it. After six months, she pushed me so hard to propose it was embarrassing. I played dumb, ignoring her 'subtle' hints around the apartment. After a few months, she became more obvious, leaving giant photos of expensive rings around. I still ignored them.

She probably planted that latest Theo story herself. She did something similar when trying to get a reality show picked up based on her. *The Real Housewives of Baseball* was her idea; no one greenlit it, obviously. Out of all the sports in the US, baseball players have the least interesting lives. Hotels and phone calls for most of the year. That's it. There was also the glaringly obvious point that she wasn't actually my fiancée or wife that she also had to contend with. Her persistence waned when she realized that she'd milked my cash cow for all it's worth. That's when the crappy boyfriend stories started, up until she moved on to Theo. Really, I should be sending him a thank you gift for getting her off my back.

I pressed ignore, shoving my phone back in my pocket. When the elevators close, I can feel a smirk growing on my face. Today's been a good day. I've just solved a bunch of Cali's problems in less than an hour.

Now all I need to do is deal with the fact our relationship could be exposed in the media at any moment.

CHAPTER 19

CALI

"Are you okay? You look kind of pale, and your left eye is twitching again," Mary whispers, sneaking into my cubicle and leaning against my desk. She flicks one of Tate's bobbleheads and laughs to herself as it shakes.

Keeping my eyes trained on my computer, I say, "I'm fine." I feel her hot glare on me, but I ignore it because I know I'll get upset. She huffs out a breath because she's my best friend and knows something's wrong.

Mary tilts her head, trying to get a better view of my face. "Cali. I know you better than you know yourself. What's up." Well, isn't that a loaded question? The answer is pretty pathetic too.

Instead of responding, I reach over and lob a few magazines her way. They aren't magazines I read, but someone left them on my desk this morning. Normally, I'd be fine and assume that somebody was asking me to read the stories, but not today. Today's magazines had my heart beating faster than a priest in a strip bar. Suffice to say. I nearly hurled into my trash can when I saw some of the pictures.

Mary inspects the covers, reading the headlines aloud. "Sam Vine will do anything to get Tate back." She throws that one to the sidc and looks to the next magazine. "Tate's rebound blonde," she muses on that one, studying the little blurry shot of Tate smiling at said blonde. "Is that you?" Gnawing at my lip, I nod. She raises her brows, flipping to the next one. "Tate's Revenge… Tate and Sam, back together?" She reads off a few more headlines, but I don't bother listening. I'd already memorized them. *Sam fighting for her man. When will Tate end this rebound? Sam & Tate, True Love! Tate goes back. Tate threatens Leitch. Leitch out of love.* They were all annoying, and all irked me in ways I couldn't describe. I should have been prepared for this since Tate warned me about the photos, but that was when they were just in the dark crevices of the internet. Now they're in magazines. Thank goodness they're only the back of my head and not my face because then the whole office would know. That's something I'm still not ready for.

But that gnawing feeling in my stomach wouldn't go away because even though the office knows it's not me, they think he's getting back with Sam. It's not true, I know that because he's too busy texting me, but those photos don't lie. And there are photos of them together. Hugging and smiling at each other. "Who left these on your desk?" She asks curiously.

"It wasn't you?" I was kind of hoping it was, considering she's the only one who's supposed to know about Tate and me. She shakes her head in confusion.

My eyes dart around the room, watching my colleagues' reactions. "Maybe it was one of the other PR guys. They're the ones that usually look after the tabloid stories after all," she says, trying to calm me down.

My hands tremble because not only am I worried about the headlines, but I'm also now concerned someone in the office knows about Tate and me. I tap the keyboard a little harder than necessary to release some of the pent-up energy.

Mary flicks through the pages of one of the magazines, reading a few paragraphs of the article. "This is all so ridiculous. It's just a bunch of made-up stories."

I lift my brow and stare at her. "His *ex-fiancée* wants him back," I emphasize, grabbing one of the magazines and flicking to the article. "Look. There's a picture of them together. *Hugging.* And then they're saying he's just seeing me to make her jealous." I was doing my best to be rational, reasonable even. But the idea that he's been seeing her behind my back kind of sucks.

I glare at the glossy paper, and Sam's gorgeous face smiles back. Her perfectly tanned and toned body is in the skimpiest bikini I've ever seen. I feel like a scruffy teenager compared to her, especially with my greased-up hair and sweaty back, which seems to be a permanent fixture these days. I didn't bother showering when I left the house today, knowing that I would be Catty later this morning and would have to shower after anyway.

When I was in college, I used to love Sam's posts on Instagram because she constantly posted pictures of Tate topless - a lot of those made my personal home calendar. But after a year, I unfollowed her when it became clear she was more obsessed with fame and followers and didn't have a clue about baseball. The photos slowly became less of Tate and more of her posing.

"Isn't she dating that hottie, Theo Leitch, now?" Mary asks, already flipping the page, reading a different article about some woman who's in love with a hamster completely ignoring my predicament.

"Clearly, you didn't you read the full article? She's thinking that maybe she made the wrong decision and has been trying to contact Tate because she thinks he's the guy she should really be with."

Mary snorts. "Maybe you should write these articles. You're good at making up crap." I stare at her, long and hard, but she doesn't meet my gaze. She places the magazine on the desk, smoothing down the edges before putting her hand over mine. "Come on, Cali. Over half the stuff is made up in here." She points at another headline. "This woman thinks she gave birth to a puppy." I want to laugh because she's probably right, but it's more the fact that *all* of them have the same story, and in each story, I'm the loser. The one he doesn't care about. No smoke without fire and all that. "Have you asked Tate?"

I play with my lips. "No. I only found out this morning."

She shrugs, looking nonchalant. "So, don't freak out. Speak to Tate first, *then* freak out if you need to."

I sigh, clicking out of my inbox. "You're probably right. I'm probably freaking out over nothing. Happens on days I've got to dress as a giant fish."

"That's most days then."

"Yup. Pretty much."

Lumbering into the locker room, I'm chafing everywhere and slightly disturbed with the amount of sweat my costume has absorbed. Do we get this thing dry cleaned? I hope so. Otherwise, it's not going to be pleasant when I have to wear this thing tomorrow. Maybe the stench will add to it, giving it a bit more fishy realism. Urgh, I don't want to think about this right now. All I want to do is get this damn costume off and take a nice cold shower.

As if it couldn't smell worse in my little mascot prison, the stench of the locker room penetrates its furry barriers. Admittedly, it's usually ripe in here straight after a game; but today is different. The 90-degree heat took us all by surprise because the stadium was like a magnifying glass, filtering in the heat. I nearly fainted on a child due to a lack of ventilation in my costume. Poor Mary had to rush me to the bathroom and soak my head under the faucet just to get me through the game.

The players, having just showered, walk around me, and I do my best to keep my focus on the exit. It's not like they walk around with their dongs out or anything. It's just last time I wasn't so vigilant and I may have accidently seen flashes of flesh I wasn't supposed to, and the high-pitched yelp nearly gave my identity away. They all still think it's Tim under here, and I'd like to keep it that way until I figure out how to tell Tate that I've been inadvertently spying on him the whole time. I should just do it. Rip it off like a band-aid, but I'm too much of a wimp.

A couple of the outfielder's high-five me as they walk past, singing in celebration. They've just cemented an 8-game winning streak with their win today, so it's no wonder they're in such a great mood. My heart flutters as Tate walks past me, giving me a wink. Even sweaty and dressed as a fish, Tate can somehow make me feel like I'm the only person in the room - or half-person, half-fish.

It's the first time I've seen him since he got back from his two-week away trip, and to say I missed him would be an understatement. We've been texting, but nothing is the same or as magical as when he's here, with that rare ability of his to suck up all the air in a room. Even when I'm annoyed at him about potentially seeing his ex, he still has a way of squeezing my heart.

As he sits down to untie his shoes, I find myself watching, wishing it was just us in here. Firstly, so I could ask him about all those Sam rumors, and secondly, so I could unwrap him like my favorite chocolate bar. Then I remember how much I stink and that although it might be sexy for all of two minutes, my stench might make Tate pass out. Plus, he might not be as accepting of Catty's advances as mine.

Grayson walks smugly in, giving me a heavy slap on the back as he goes. He barely has an ounce of sweat on him because he's been out of the game for the last three innings, throwing less than 90 pitches to get 21 outs. The guy is a freak of nature. That reminds me, I should pester Tate for that pitching session he would arrange for Penn.

"Tate," Grayson chuckles, leaning on the locker across from him. "What's all this stuff about you getting back with Sam?" The question makes me stop in my tracks. Insecurity flares through my veins, especially after all the articles I've read, and now even his friends are asking him about it. I might be the one he's texting the minute he's off the field or alone in his hotel room, but that's not enough for me. I need to know the answer.

Standing in between the door leading to the other changing rooms, I wait for his response. "Nothing," Tate grumbles. *Nothing. Is that it?* I wait for a few seconds longer, but that's it. What a crappy answer, and it's in no way good enough to settle my nerves. In fact, it sounds a lot more like a shitty answer to get Grayson off his back.

"Are you sure about that?" Grayson snorts, kicking Tate playfully while Tate rubs his face with a towel, doing his best to ignore his friend. "Looks like she wants another round after seeing your new side piece."

My shoulders tense, and that's when I realize I'm just standing there, watching the two of them with my big googly eyes. I look from side to side because I need to at least pretend I'm there for a reason other than eavesdropping. Grabbing a towel from a hook next to a locker, I start to wipe down my scaly body. I sweated so much during that game, I won't be surprised if it permeated through the fabric.

My eyes are focused solely on Tate, trying to gauge his reaction through my sweat-filled haze. The room might be air-conditioned, but that doesn't stop the sweat dripping from my brow, and since I can't wipe it off, it's dripping to my eyelashes. I know. Gross. I still need to sort out this whole internal fan situation when I have some time.

"It's not going to happen," he says with so much spite, I could definitely hear it through the muffled suit. Why did those five words make me so deliciously happy and treacherous at the same time?

Austin's bulky body comes into view, and he's just wearing a towel around his waist. My eyes widen because I know I shouldn't be looking, but he's got muscles for days. His arm flexes as he opens his locker and bends forward. "But what about the pretty marketing girl? I thought you were dating her?" He asks, and it makes me smile because Austin is such a sweetheart. Maybe Tate *has* talked about me. I know I'm not keen on my colleagues finding out, but it would be hard for Tate to hide it, considering he's with those guys twenty-four-seven. Pathetically, the fact that Austin knows about some marketing girl makes me deliriously happy.

Pulling his shoes off, Tate quips, "yup." Silence. *Yup?* That's it? I'm just a *Yup.* No 'She's so great I forgot Sam's name?'

Grayson grins, shaking his head. "Wait a minute. You're *still* dating her?" His surprise makes me want to smack him upside the head with my fishy fin. "I'm surprised she's not afraid of the wrath of Sam?"

Tate cracks his knuckles, then his neck, but he still says nothing. "Wasn't she supposed to be a pump'n'dump?"

My heart stills.

That's it.

My instincts about him were right all along. He's a lothario and just wanted to get me in bed. And he accomplished that mission in less than a month.

That's what doesn't make sense, though. He's had me countless times, and he's still trying to chase me. Am I just a means to an end until Sam comes groveling back to him? What if this latest gesture has finally convinced him, and he's trying to figure out a way to dump me that won't be too embarrassing?

I shake my head in frustration. I've tortured myself for too long listening to this. I need out of here. Dropping the towel to the floor, I walk quickly to the door. As I slither out, I regrettably hear Grayson say, "you should get back with Sam. You were a fool to let that hot piece of ass go."

I don't know if they noticed how hard I slam the door, but I vent my frustration with the loud slam and stalk to the ladies' locker room. Thankfully, it's usually empty on baseball game days, which means I can stand in the center of the room and scream. I drop to the seat, sitting in the quiet and let it consume my thoughts.

I reach for the zip, pull it down, and peel out of the now sticky fabric. It lands on the floor with a thump, and I quickly walk to the showers, hoping the cool water will give me some respite.

It doesn't work, though, unfortunately. As I showered and dressed, I kept replaying Grayson and Tate's conversation in my head over and over. There were no hints from Tate that I was anything more than a casual lay, which made me nervous. What if I was just a conquest for him? A way to get his mind off Sam for a little while. What if all those nice things he said and did were just so he could get in my pants? It's not like I made him wait long. Hell, I've put my entire job at risk letting him eat me out on my desk.

I close my eyes, holding back my tears. What a stupid thing to do. If we got caught, I would have been fired, my reputation would have been ruined, and my family would be so embarrassed. His reputation might get a little knock, but that's it. No slap on the wrist. Nothing.

Pushing all those thoughts out of my mind, I hurry up the stairs, fully expecting to have an inbox full of work that would be more than enough to distract me from my thoughts.

When I sit at my desk and look through my emails, I frown. There are hardly any emails, and none of them are urgent. My body deflates because if I've got nothing to finish tonight, then I have all the time in the world to think about Tate. I could even see him, not that it's something I want to do right now.

Just then, Tate's face flashes across my phone.

Tate: Miss you. Want to meet tonight?

My head is scrambling. I don't want to ignore him, but then again, I don't want to see him right now either. Not just yet. I need time to think, to get my head straight.

Cali: Can't tonight. I've got dinner plans with Mary.

I send it before I can regret it and start striding towards her desk. "Mary," I call, and she pops her head up like those meerkats do in that nature documentary I watched the other week. "Are you around for a bite to eat tonight?"

Her eyes dart from side to side. "What's the catch? You haven't been free for dinner since you started here," she asks with furrowed brows.

I shrug. "All the stuff in my inbox can wait until tomorrow."

"Um, okay. Let me just shut down my stuff, and we'll go."

"Great." I jump on my heels, heading back to my desk with a

smile on my face. One night down on my 'avoid Tate' mission. Only a few more days, and then he's back on the road for a week. That should give me plenty of time to figure everything out and see where the chips may fall with Sam.

CHAPTER 20

TATE

Swallowing the cold liquid, I thank the waitress when she drops the plate of ribs in front of me. "Thanks, Chrissy," Grayson says, smiling at the waitress. After a particularly rough away game against Atlanta, I didn't want to come out, but it's better than sitting in my hotel room and sulking about my performance.

The smell of the meat makes me feel marginally better. "I have a question," Austin says, chowing down on his steak. "Can I technically vote for myself in the all-star ballot?" He asks without a hint of sarcasm in his voice.

"Even if you voted for yourself every hour of every day, you still wouldn't reach the numbers to get on the team," Grayson says bluntly. "Sorry, Rookie, but I played six years in the league before they finally recognized my brilliance enough to vote me in."

I roll my eyes, pushing at Grayson's shoulder. "Ignore him, Austin. I didn't make the All-Stars until a few years ago. Even now, it's not guaranteed because it's who the fans vote for. I could be having the best year of my life, but if no one likes me, well, then it ain't happening." I leave out the fact that the PR team chooses which pony to back, and this year, it's Grayson and me. I've been hounded by them to get these negative stories about a love square (i.e., Me, Cali, Theo, and Sam) out of the papers to make room for some positive press. If I don't get on the All-Star team, we'll only have Grayson to represent us as the hosts for this year. The worst part about it is that it's not like our fans actually like Grayson. He's got a cocky attitude and a habit of ticking off other fanbases, which means he only gets votes from the team he plays on. He knows that, and like most things in this world, he doesn't care because he likes the infamy.

"Aww, are you worried all the furor about you and Sam is getting in the way of the fans voting for you?" Grayson chortles, his eyes tracking a waitress's ass as she walks by. He's blatant with his perusal, but he doesn't care.

My gaze flicks up to the screen, and the Carolina Jaguars are playing. As if I don't need further reminding of her tonight. "I already told you. I'm not interested in Sam. Was hardly interested in her when we were dating." Grayson opens his mouth to say something, but I already know what it's going to be. Thus, I already knew the answer. "*And* yes, if she showed up naked at your door, I wouldn't care. You could have her."

Grayson's smile stills for just a second. I think he was hoping to catch me out and prove that I still cared for the money-grubber. I don't. I haven't in a long time. It took Cali walking into my life to realize that I never cared about Sam, not in any way that mattered. I wouldn't donate part of my salary to her and ten other people just to make sure she got paid, that's for sure.

That reminds me. I need to follow up on if she's started to get paid because Cali hasn't mentioned anything to me. If I'm being honest, she hasn't mentioned much at all recently. In fact, since the day I donated it, she hasn't had time to see me. Still too busy with work.

"Oh, that's right. I forgot. You're in *love* with that marketing chick," he teases, unimpressed. The guy wouldn't know love if it punched him in the face and left a bruise the size of Texas.

"What does Cali think about all the articles?" Austin asks.

That's a good question. It's something I've been planning to bring up with her since the articles first started appearing in the news. Honestly, I thought the articles would die down after there were no pictures or responses from me, but as per usual, Sam's been persistent. She's been calling the media, feeding them lies about secret meetups we've been having and reusing old shots of us to create a narrative that works for her.

My agent keeps getting calls, asking to verify stories which he denies, of course, but it doesn't stop Sam from calling the press on herself. She's been doing bat shit crazy things like driving to my apartment block and staging shots of her walking out just to keep the momentum of the story going. That reminds me, I need to get them to change the damn gate code. She even staged some weird photos outside my bar, *Tate's Tavern,* where she was stroking her belly. The desperation on her part to make it look like there's some double play going on is unreal. Apparently, she's doing such a good job that I even got a threatening message from Theo the other day. The dimwit told me to back off his woman, and I was speechless because I couldn't believe he'd fallen for her antics.

The only good thing about all those staged shots is that the media has almost forgotten about the girl in the parking lot, which means Cai's dignity is somewhat safe for now.

"I'm sure she doesn't like it." It's my only response because as much as I would love to know how she feels about it, I don't.

Grayson whistles. "Trouble in paradise already? I told you women weren't worth it."

"Who hurt you?" Austin asks semi-seriously.

"No one. That's the beauty of not letting anyone close enough to care about what they do." He wraps his arm around Austin's shoulder. "Do you want to know the key to winning at baseball, A?" Austin nods fervently. "It's to focus on baseball and only baseball. Women are dispensable and should only be used to get your rocks off. That's it." He leans back, and I watch as Austin's ears and cheeks pinken. If this is the kind of world-changing advice Grayson has for the younger generation, maybe I should introduce Penn to Max instead. He's single, but at least he doesn't treat women like garbage. "Letting them get in your head during the most pivotal point in your career is not good."

"So, you're never planning on having kids?" I'm surprised

Austin is still engaging Grayson in this ridiculous conversation.

He lifts a shoulder. "Didn't say that. But right now. Definitely not. Women only want your cash. Cash you won't get if you don't play well enough to earn it."

I lean over the table to get Austin's attention. "Please ignore him. Grayson wouldn't know what feelings are if they were smacking him across the face. Besides, baseball is all about feeling and the love of the game. We aren't all robots like this jackass." I elbow Grayson in the ribs, and he grins. "Why are we even friends anyway?"

"Because you'd be bored without me," he says, his eyes flicking across the room, and the smallest hint of a smile pulls on the edges of his lips. "Now, if you excuse me, I've got a meeting with Atlanta tonight."

"Atlanta? That's her name, and she lives in Atlanta?" Austin's eyebrow quirks in amusement.

"No," I answer as Grayson's chair screeches across the floor. "That's *his* name for her because he doesn't bother with actual names."

Grayson tucks the chair in and bends forward, whispering, "I've got a different one in every city we visit. Imagine trying to remember all those names."

"Don't forget the game starts at eleven am tomorrow," I holler as he walks away, his shoulders a little more upright and his head a little higher.

"I'm not starting, remember?" He says casually over his shoulder as he confidently walks towards a girl who was dressed like I'd imagine my lawyer would if I got into some deep trouble. She barely registers his approach, too busy talking on her phone and staring at the laptop resting on the table. There's no predatory smile from her when he sits like his usual hookups. She almost looks annoyed that she has to entertain him for the rest of the night.

Austin watches Grayson in awe. "Ready to head upstairs?" I ask, wanting to get him away from the bad influences. He's only young, and lord knows we don't need another Grayson on the team.

"Uh huh." When we're in the elevator, I text Cali, asking if she has time to talk tonight. I wanted to talk to her, to hear that sweet melodic voice of hers. I wanted to ask her about her day and determine if Josh took my warnings seriously. It's been weeks since we'd been together, and even now, I can't get her off my mind.

The bubbles pop up, and I watch as she quickly types back, telling me that she's working late tonight. I roll my eyes. Clearly, nothing has changed, and she still isn't getting paid. I'll need to speak to Jonah when I get back after the game tomorrow.

CHAPTER 21

CALI

"Don't you think that bobblehead makes him look… I don't know, like a vampire?" I whisper to Mary as we sit in the boardroom as Josh presents the latest selection of bobbleheads for the last half of the season. So far, I'm not exactly impressed with the designs.

I feel like raising my hand and telling them that they've got Tate's features all wrong, but I don't know how they'd take it. Tate's perfect teeth are way too big for his head, and that golden tan of his looks whiter than a carton of milk. Granted, it's not as bad as the colossal butt they gave Austin. He may have well-developed quads, but his bobblehead is more akin to a rhino. Poor guy.

Mary tries her best to suppress a giggle, but a few people hear it, flicking their heads in our direction with disapproving glances. *Crap.* I hope Josh doesn't notice. He's only just started to lay off, and I don't want to get on his bad side again.

He flips to the next slide, and that's when Grayson's face appears. Pinching my lips together, I do everything I can to hold back the laughter. I blow out my cheeks, and my shoulders rise, but I manage to keep the giggles to myself.

Grayson's bobblehead is mid-throw with a giant ball leaving his hand. Unfortunately, the expression on his face makes it look like he's in a losing battle with the toilet. It's awkward to look at. He'll hate it if he takes any notice of this kind of thing.

I twiddle my pen, doing my best to concentrate on Josh. His monotonous voice is hard to listen to for an extended period, and this meeting has been running for the better part of an hour already. I take the opportunity to glance around the room, and it seems like I'm not the only one having trouble listening to him. One of the other intern's heads is tilted back, and his eyes are fluttering shut.

As Josh continues talking, there's a light knock on the door, reinvigorating the rest of the room. I nearly faint when I see the Head of Back Office, Jonah, pop his head inside the room. My heart beats faster, and I have to remind myself to breathe. I imagine for most people, this is the same feeling they'd get meeting their favorite celebrity. Jonah looks around, bares his teeth, and waves at everyone. It's like I've suddenly lost control of my body. I can't move because being in a room with such greatness is beyond comprehension. He is the man who has made the Fish marketing what it is today and why it's one of the most followed franchises in the league. What do you say when you meet such greatness?

"Hi, sorry, was I interrupting anything?" He asks Josh, who waves him off almost immediately with the widest, fakest smile I've ever seen

"No, sir. I was told you'd be coming in today." Josh speaks with more enthusiasm than I've ever heard in all the months I've worked here. "I can finish this in our meeting tomorrow. Would you like to take over?"

Jonah pushes himself further in, his presence swallowing the room with every step he takes. "That would be great," he says, adjusting his blue tie with the little Catfish logo on the point. I've seen Josh wear the same one on several occasions.

I grab Mary's thigh from under the table, squeezing to emphasize just how much I'm freaking out on the inside. She swats me off, giving me a heavy side-eye with a frown. Right. I need to cool it.

Jonah rubs his hands on the front of his pants, waving again.

"Hey guys, I'm not sure if you all know me." I snort because what a ridiculous thing to say to a group of marketing colleagues. Heads spin in my direction, but I keep my gaze focused on Jonah, knowing I'm turning red. "I'm head of operations, and I've got some great news for the interns." *Interns? As in me?* I hope he's not going to insist we play in the staff baseball tournament. Let's just say I played one game of softball my entire life, which ended in a hospital visit for two of the players, and I broke my ankle. I have never stepped foot on a field in a player's capacity since.

"Can the eleven interns we have this year stand up, just so I know who I'm talking to?" I make eye contact with a couple of the other interns before scraping my chair back and standing with pride. "I'm sorry I haven't had the time to meet you all, but I wanted to thank you for all the hard work and dedication you've put into this team. I've heard good things about you, and we're proud to have you on board working for the Fish."

We all mumbled a thank you, still not sure why he came all the way in here just to say that. "On that note. I would like to extend some good news. We've received a generous donation given to us specifically on your behalf. As of this month, we will be paying you for all of that hard work and dedication you've shown." He said with a grin. I wanted to jump up, scream and dance around the room, but I opted for a slight toe lift and a smile instead.

Is this actually happening?

Am I officially a paid employee of the Carolina Catfish?

I squeeze my hands together behind my back as employees clap and congratulate us. My smile turns into a grin, and Mary kicks me under the table, hinting for me to tone it down. I don't want to look like the Joker with a maniacal grin. It's hard to stop, though, because I'm an actual paid Catfish employee.

I sit down and can't stop my toes from tapping and my fingers from strumming through the rest of the meeting. For the first time since joining the company, I feel like a legitimate employee, and I can't wait to get back to my desk and work my butt off. The rest of the meeting went by in a blur, and by the time it ended, I was already thinking about buying something other than macaroni and cheese for dinner. I don't know how much they plan on paying me, but it might even be enough to afford an apartment closer to the stadium or even a car. Gah, I can't stop my mind from racing with possibilities.

"Congratulations, Cali," Mary says, stopping at my desk and braces me in a hug. "You deserve it. You've put in more time and hours than me this past year, so I'm glad they're finally acknowledging it." Her eyes are deep and blue as she proudly smiles at me.

"No, no. Thank you for helping me get this job." Is this what it feels like to accept an Oscar? With your stomach constantly flipping because it's brimming with excitement? I pull out of the hug, my smile still wide. Yeah, it's not going to leave my face for days.

"Are you going to tell Tate?" She asks, and as much as I didn't want to admit it to myself, that was pretty much the first thought that popped into my head after Jonah told us. My mom and dad would say congratulations, and Penn would think it's cool… But Tate… Tate would be proud.

A loud chortle interrupts my thoughts. "Tate already knows," Josh laughs sarcastically, trudging past us with a snarling lip.

"Sorry, Josh, but this is a private conversation," Mary says, and I want to gasp because I could never imagine speaking to him like that.

He raises his hands in defense. "If you wanted to have a private conversation, maybe you should have it in the bathroom next time. The office is like an echo chamber, and your voices are particularly loud." He rolls the 'l' of the loud, looking at me as he does it.

As he strides past, thinking nothing of Mary's brashness, a thought comes to mind. "Josh, wait," I call, and Mary's brows cross. He stops, turning back on his heel with a smug smile because he was just waiting for me to take the bait, apparently. "What do you mean Tate knows? Did they tell the players or something?"

A wicked smile spreads across his face as he shakes his head.

"No, but I was told that a player donated the money a few weeks ago. I thought about it and realized it must have been Tate." Hairs prickle at the base of my neck. "Considering he's been hanging around the marketing office like an unwanted fruit fly and the fact that I saw him walking into Jonah's office with a check the other week." He says the last part of his sentence so casually. "Bit too coincidental, don't you think?" He pauses, raking me in as the smirk on his face grows. "Must be nice having a player fight your battles for you." His face turns red, and I swear he growls ever so slightly before turning on his heel and walking away. He didn't say it, but the implication was there, hanging around like a bad smell. He knows I'm sleeping with Tate, and if he knows, then the whole office must have figured it out.

"Does Josh know about Tate and me?" I ask, nervously playing with my hands.

Mary scrunches her face. "No, of course not. He's just messing with you because he knows Tate came up to visit you that one time."

"And about the flowers…" I trail off, realizing just how obvious Tate has made it, even if it wasn't his intention. My eyes flitter around the room, looking at the other interns who are happily getting on with their work. If they found out their salary was donated by a guy I was sleeping with, I'd be mortified.

"You know it's not against the rules. There's nothing Josh can do." Mary shrugs, seemingly unbothered by Josh's aggression, probably because it wasn't aimed at her.

"Except make me feel like crap and embarrass me by telling everyone that Tate did it because he's sleeping with me."

"Firstly, he can't spread a rumor like that without getting in trouble, and secondly, he doesn't know if Tate donated the money; it's just speculation." Mary leans against the desk, watching my reaction while I think back to Josh's exact words. Tate donated the money. *Tate?*

"Come on, think about it. It doesn't make any sense. Why would Tate donate money?" Mary asks the very question that's been running through my brain since Josh planted it there.

"I told him I didn't get paid," I say despondently, trying to figure out what this all meant and why he would do it.

"So, if it's true, and that's a huge *if* because this is Josh we're talking about. Maybe Tate was being generous. He wanted you and the other interns paid for your work." She says brightly, clearly not as bothered about accepting money from someone you're sleeping with. Does this technically make me a hooker? A high-class one because I also helped others get paid. Are the other interns technically my pimp because of it?

"Tate went quiet when it came out that I wasn't paid. What if he did it because he was embarrassed for me?" I feel queasy at the thought and edge myself closer to my trash can, just in case I hurl.

She adamantly shakes her head. "No. That's not it. Tate's not like that."

Then it hits me like a ton of bricks. "You're right. He didn't do it because he felt sorry for me. He did it as a form of a payoff." Saying the words out loud made me feel filthy.

Her mouth gapes open, "What?" She barely stutters out and then furrows her brows. "Cali, you're way off base with that one."

"No. I'm not. Think about it. What if all those rumors *are* true and he is getting back together with Sam. It's not like the story has died down over the last few weeks. Maybe this is his way of saying, 'thanks for the memories' and keeping me silent." I fall into my seat. "I was only the girl he used to try and take his mind off Sam for a while. When he had the chance to get her back, he took it."

Mary kneels in front of me, forcing me to give her my full attention. "Woah, Cali. Stop. You've gone and invented this whole scenario in your head. Did you ever talk to Tate about the Sam thing?"

"No." I leave out that I've been avoiding him in fear that he just wants to officially break up with me. My little baseball-loving heart couldn't handle hating one of my favorite players. It's much easier to think I had some semblance of control over the situation and let it naturally fizzle out, so Tate had no choice but to go back to his ex than admit he was never that into me in the first place. There's no need for it to be confirmed that he used me for sex. This payment just adds insult to injury, though. "But I don't have to. It's obvious to everyone but me. Tate's best friend is Grayson, after all. The same guy who openly talks about sending contracts to women before he sleeps with them."

Mary clasps my shoulder. "I think it would be better to talk it out with him than making yourself crazy. The last time your eyes shifted this much, two girls ended up in hospital." Did she have to bring up the softball incident again?!

"I'll think about it," I say more to appease her than anything else. I spin on my chair, checking the time. The game was going to start in ten minutes. "I better go; I've got to get dressed as Catty." I really wasn't feeling it today, especially because one of the things we had planned involved Tate. "Penn's coming after the fourth inning, and we're going to watch the rest of the game together."

"Will you be done by then?"

I shrug. "Probably not, but he can wait for me."

"Do you want me to sit with him until you get back?" She asks, and I notice a little color in her cheeks.

I stand up. "Sure, whatever." She's known Penn as long as she's known me, so at least he'll have some company while I'm sweating my ass off dressed as a fish. After saying my goodbyes, I limp my way to the locker room, ready to face my fishy doom for the day.

I hurry to my seats, grumbling to myself with each passing step. As if I couldn't be in a worse mood with Tate after Josh revealed he paid for my salary, Tate had to go and annoy me while I was Catty too. What did he do? Well, he was nice to me, patting me on the back, hugging me, and dancing along with my routines. He even walked with me around the stadium to sign autographs for kids before the game. I wanted to push him over, maybe slap him in the face with a wet fish a few times, but every now and again, he'd flash that perfect smile of his making me forget how annoyed I was. My body always seemed to melt at the memories of being with him, and I hated that.

Penn's bright red hair flashes into view, and I take a moment to compose myself. Adjusting my blank Carolina Catfish t-shirt (because I refuse to wear 'Sorenson' on my back today), I walk through the empty plastic blue seats to Penn and Mary. Penn laughs at something Mary says, and he's focusing on her so intently, he doesn't notice me at first. "Hey, guys," I mutter, slumping into the empty seat next to Penn.

"Hey, sis." Penn greets me with a broad smile and an arm over my seat. "Mary was just telling me about how you were nearly decapitated last week." He barks out a laugh, and I shake my head in regret at the memory. Max got distracted by something, threw a wild pitch that not only whacked me but also hit one of the new reporters in the dugout. It was carnage; her nose was bleeding, glasses were broken, and she was still sporting a black eye. I'm surprised Penn hadn't seen it on the local news. Although I guess there was no one to report on it because he hit the woman that would have done it.

"You might want to look into a life insurance policy now that you're getting paid," Mary adds.

Penn shucks my shoulder with his fist. "Congrats, C. That's awesome news." Great. Now my brother knows about my unintentional hooker ways.

Mary stands up from her seat, wiping down her pencil skirt. "I better go. I've got some work to finish up." She looks between Penn and me anxiously. I thought she'd already finished that big focus group project she was working on, but I guess not.

"Are you sure? We were having such a good time. You should stay," Penn says with a smirk plastered across his face as he opens his arms out for her. I roll my eyes and groan at his forwardness.

Her eyes linger on his, and she reluctantly shakes her head. "I can't. I should go. I'll see you later, Cali. See you soon, Penn." Before I had time to say goodbye, she was already striding through the seats like a mouse. She didn't need to walk so fast; it's not like she was in anyone's way since it was a late afternoon weekday game.

When she's out of view, Penn slides further down his seat until his head rests on the back of it. He lets out a low groan before shoving his fist in his mouth and biting hard. I shove him in the shoulder, grunting in disgust. "She's my best friend, you sicko." Ever since we were kids, Penn's always had a crush on Mary. He's made no effort in hiding it, either. Quite frankly, it's disturbing, and I shouldn't have let it go on as long as it has.

"I can't help it. She's so hot."

Groaning, I scrub my face, annoyed at his persistence. I do not need this right now. "Please, stop. I cannot bear the thought of my best friend dating my brother. The same brother who hasn't graduated high school yet."

He scrunches my hair. "I graduate next month, and I turned eighteen in December. It would all be perfectly legal and fine."

"She's 23!"

He shrugs, completely unfazed. "I like an older woman. More experience," he winks mischievously. I can't take it anymore, so I stomp his foot. "Ow."

"If there is one thing in this world I do not want to talk about. It's your sex life. Which you shouldn't have. You should only be doing *that* when you're planning on giving me nieces and nephews, and I don't want any for a long time; thank you very much."

Penn snorts, lolling his head from side to side. "Okay, sis. I'm sure you and Tate just talk baseball when I'm not there to chaperone." My eyes bug out because I'm stunned into silence. Did he really just go there? "Why are we sitting all the way back here anyway?" He relaxes his foot on the seat in front. The closest fan is standing several rows below us. I could have gotten my regular tickets right above the dugout, considering I'm a season ticket holder (the only thing I'd ever splash out on), but I switched them today since I didn't want Tate to see me. "Normally, you want to be as close to the dugout as you can, so the umpire can hear you yelling the 'correct' calls."

Shrugging, I say, "I just wanted a change of scenery. Now that I work here, I think it's important to consider all the fan's perspectives. Not just the die-hard ones that sit front and center." My words come out so confidently, I nearly believe it.

"Uh oh. Trouble in paradise? What did Tate do?"

"There is no trouble. Like I said, I'm doing this for research."

"Yeah, right. You've spent years analyzing the most optimal seat. I'm surprised they don't have a plaque with your name on it; you buy it every year."

I shake my head just as the crowd starts screaming. Thank god, Austin just scored a two-run homer, forcing Penn's attention to the field and stops him from asking me more questions. It left me time to think about my next move with Tate.

Sadly, I come up with nothing.

CHAPTER 22

TATE

Knock.

Knock.

Knock.

I stand, shifting my weight between my toes, smelling the blue orchids that I specifically bought for Cali. Everything about them reminded me of her. From the sweet soothing scent, to the color of her ocean eyes and, of course, how well they match the Carolina Catfish home jersey. I haven't seen her in weeks, and I'm nearly bursting out of my baseball pants, hoping to surprise her.

A smile grows on my face when I hear her shuffling on the other side of the door. She opens it without looking up, too focused on the honey she's holding in her hand. "I'm sorry, Ms. Mckenna, I've run out of sugar, but I do have honey if you'd prefer?"

"I'll take whatever you're offering." She jumps when I chuckle. Her large indigo eyes stare back at me, dropping the honey jar in the process. Thank goodness it's just plastic.

Her mouth drops, then shuts, and she looks like a bubbling fish. No matter what ridiculous face she pulls, she's still the hottest girl I've ever laid eyes on. "Tate, what are you doing here?" She stutters, bending down quickly to grab the squeezy bear before clutching it to her chest and looking all kinds of flustered.

Scratching my stubbled chin, I lean back, glancing up and down the hallway. Then, happy that it's empty, I look back at my beautiful girl, who's too busy studying my gray shirt and jeans to notice the large smile on my face. "Any chance I could come in? I'd rather talk to you inside if that's okay?" I flick my eyes over her shoulder to her small apartment. She's got a bowl of food sitting on that little kitchen table of hers in front of an iPad that's playing a baseball game.

Is she going to move closer to the stadium now that she's getting paid? Jonah called to let me know that he'd finally announced it to the interns, who all seemed pleased, but she still hadn't mentioned it. Not that she'd messaged me much since. I've only received short answers to my texts because she's been so busy.

Her face is stony as she wraps the belt of her silky pink robe around her waist, securing it with a tight knot before resting her hands on her hips and blocking my entrance. "I'm kind of busy," she says with this sexy little angry tone in her voice.

I tilt my head, studying her facial expression; her lips are straight as a board, but her left eye is twitching ever so slightly. So she's lying, which therefore means she's avoiding me again. But, geez, what is it with Cali? Why does it always feel like whenever we've taken one step forward, we've actually taken another two steps back?

"Are you sure? Because I called Mary before venturing over, and she told me you didn't have any plans tonight." There goes her eye again. Was it a shitty move calling her friend before coming over? Maybe, but I wanted to surprise her.

Her gaze flicks down to the flowers in my hands, and I notice her body softening. She drops her hands, toying with her silk belt, and I'm thankful for the flowers in my hands. If they weren't busy, I'd be unraveling that fabric myself.

A low rumble emanates from her throat while she contemplates if she will let me in. The door creaks as she widens it, making room for me. I make a mental note to fix that when I come to paint it. She watches my every step as I walk in, almost like she was annoyed with herself for giving in to me. I swear Cali's the only woman to ever make me unsure about her feelings towards me.

Turning on my heel, I hand her the flowers. "I got these for you." She does her best to hide her soft smile and not smell them as she mumbles a quick thanks in response. Okay. I know when a woman is pissed at me, and Cali is definitely pissed. I just don't know why yet.

I point my thumb over my shoulder to the bed. "Is it okay if I take a seat?" I'm pushing my luck, asking to sit on her bed when she's annoyed with me. I know that. I was just kind of hoping it would make her tell me what was wrong. She nods, scooting past me to the kitchen. Since she doesn't have a vase, she gets a drinking glass from her cabinet and fills it with water, tucking the flowers safely inside. I crack my knuckles then my neck because I'm feeling nervous. "Haven't seen you in a while, Cali. How are you doing?" I thought I'd ease her in with my questions, still unsure how she would react.

"Oh, I'm great. Just dandy, actually." Each word is spiked with intent. I can almost feel my balls shriveling with every roll of her tongue.

"Something wrong?" I say lightly, wincing as I wait for the answer. I did it. I purposely poked the bear, and now I was waiting for the repercussions. She fluffs the orchids, humming a sweet tune, pretending there's nothing else on her mind.

"Nothing's wrong," she hums out. I wait. She'll tell me eventually. I'm not leaving her apartment until I know after all. "Oh, wait, there is one thing." There's a sarcastic edge to her tone as she looks up to the aging ceiling. "I found out I was getting paid for my internship yesterday," she says flatly, connecting her eyes with mine.

"That's fantastic!" I breathe out a heavy sigh of relief, thankful that she finally told me. I stand, fully ready to wrap her in a congratulatory hug, but when I take the few steps to get close enough to her, she plants her hand over my face, smooshing my features with her palm. "I didn't need to tell you that, though, did I, Tate?" My body freezes, and my mouth slants.

Shit. There it is. The reason why she's pissed. "*You* were the one who donated money so I could get paid, weren't you?"

I slump in her palm, her fingers still wrestling with my features as I fight the urge not to lick her hand. Her tight spun lips and crossed brows suggest that she wouldn't take too kindly to the jovial move.

"Ah-ha." Her hand finally frees my face, and she points her finger straight back at me. I go cross-eyed watching it. "I knew it was all too good to be true." She drops her head in shame, covering her face with her hand until she drops it. "It was all a payoff, wasn't it?" She yells as she stomps into the kitchen. I really hope her neighbors are as old as she made them out to be because I don't want them to hear this. "I'm not a hooker."

Silence. I swear the shrill of her voice still echoes around the room. Hooker? What the hell is she talking about?

Her shoulders are dramatically rising and falling, and her face is a little flustered. I know I shouldn't be, but I'm shocked and mildly amused by her outburst. "I literally have no idea what you're talking about."

Oh boy, was that the wrong thing to say. With her hands on her hips, she strides toward me, her nose on mine. "I was just an obsessed little fan to you, wasn't I?! You knew I'd be easy to get into bed because of all those damn bobbleheads I have of you."

She flails her arms in all directions, looking deranged and out of place in that silky little robe. I'll never admit it, but watching her body vibrate with anger is kind of hot. It was kind of turning me on. Maybe it's because I liked the idea that *I* was the one making her that bothered and crazy. "Woah, wait," I say, grabbing her arms before she knocks anything over and injures herself. Phil mentioned some of her past injuries to me the other day, and I swear the girl could find a way to hurt herself in a padded room. "What on earth are you talking about? I didn't pay you off."

She grunts, shrugging me off. "Likely story. I was just a fan you could get your rocks off with until your true love came back. Admit it."

Stifling a laugh, I watch her crazy eyes run wild with implication. She thinks she's caught me in some elaborate lie, but she's got it all wrong. I'm not that smart. Grabbing her again, I whisper against her ear, "is there a reason you think my life is like a low-budget Spanish novella with bad acting?" She struggles in my arms, but I don't let go. Instead, I just patiently wait for her to calm down, smelling the sweet coconut of her shampoo, thinking about the last time I touched her.

When she relaxes a little, I try again. "Cali," I drawl out her name, nice and slow because I know she likes the way her name sounds with my accent. "When I'm not out on the field playing ball, I'm either texting or thinking about you. I only donated that money because you deserved to be paid for all the hours you've been working. After I talked to Jonah about all the hard work you guys do, he agreed to find a way to pay for all the interns in the coming years."

She gasps, looking betrayed. "You told Jonah about *us*?"

"No, of course not. I talked about the interns in general." I fib since It's probably not the right time to mention that I specifically hinted at *her* workload. "Who even told you about my donation? It was supposed to be anonymous."

I felt her shoulders slump, and her resolve weaken a little. "Josh." It was a muffled response into my shirt.

"How the hell did he find out?" My mind returned to the day he asked me to sign the ball, and I lightly threatened him. Nothing serious, just enough to make him pee his pants a little. He was smarter than I'd given him credit for if he put all that together. Genuinely thought that the guy was an idiot.

"I don't know. Stop skirting the issue. You donated the money and made it look like a payoff. Did you think about how it would look if anyone else found out about the donation?"

"No one is going to find out about it."

"Josh did."

"Josh isn't going to say anything," I scoff. I'll make sure of that and pay him another visit tomorrow.

"But now he has something on me." She frowns, dropping her head as she backs away from me. "And I'm going to look pathetic when you end up back with your ex." That sentence is the biggest red flag I've ever heard fall out of her mouth. The fact that she thinks I'd even entertain the idea of a reunion with Sam makes me realize that we're on completely different pages.

I bring her back into my arms and tip her chin up with my finger, seeing the sadness in her eyes. "Cali, I still have no idea what you're talking about. You're the only girl I'm interested in." She reaches over to her kitchen counter and slaps a magazine across my chest. I hold onto it, looking down at the picture of Sam and me from over a year ago.

"You're right. I'm sorry you weren't just getting back with your ex. You were *proposing* to your ex-*fiancée*?!"

She walks past me, attempting to stomp off, but in her bathrobe and this tiny apartment, there's nowhere for her to go. So instead, she turns on her heel, dramatically lying back against the wall in a huff. As much as I like seeing how jealous she gets over a girl who literally makes my dick softer than cottage cheese, her bathrobe is riding high on those tanned thighs, and my fingers are itching to feel that silky smooth skin again. It's been nearly a month since we've been together. Now I know why. She's been making herself go crazy over these articles, and that payment just intensified it.

I stand directly in front of her. "First things first," I say, keeping my voice calm and low. "I haven't seen Sam in over a year. That would make it very difficult to propose, don't you think? Also, those pictures they're publishing are from when I dated her." I place my hands against the wall, caging her in between my arms and towering over her. She lets out a little whimper as she watches my arms flex. "Second thing, I was *dating* Sam. I never proposed to her. She just told the magazines I did in hopes it would inspire me. Believe me, she left enough hints. I ignored them, almost as much as I should have ignored her."

I take a chance and place my hand on her cheek, bringing her full attention to me. "Sam ceased to exist the minute I met you," I answer honestly. Something about this girl has got me hooked, and it made me realize just how little I cared for my ex. She starts chewing on her bottom lip, and my thumb drags across her cheek to pop it out. I'm desperate to kiss her. It's been so long since I felt my lips pressed against hers, and I wanted to taste her again. "I'm sorry that you thought I was cheating on you with Sam, but it's not true. Why would I want her when I have perfection right here." She pulls her lips together, pursing them in defiance. "I did not donate the money as a payoff to get rid of you because, frankly, I want to keep you around." She looks to the side, staring at the wall beside us. "I'm *not* sorry that I donated the money. You deserved that salary, and I'm glad I was able to do that and set a precedence for other interns moving forward."

Finally, she rolls her head back to look at me, and that's when I take the chance. I bring my lips to hers, catching her breath before she can argue with me again. She doesn't stop me but lets me tangle my fingers through her hair and nip at her bottom lip. So plump. So perfect. So mine.

She's slow to reciprocate, her brain still deciding if she's going to stay mad at me or not. When her body arches into mine, I know she's in a losing battle with herself. I help her along, twining our fingers together and raising them above her head.

Cali whimpers, and her sweet mouth finally opens for me. One sweep of my tongue makes her claw away from my hands and run her fingers through my hair, clamping down on the strands to force me closer. I move my lips down to her jaw and neck as she hisses out in pleasure. I can feel her pulse quickening under my lips, and as she knocks her head to the back wall, I know any resolve she has is gone. I tug at the belt of her bathrobe and lean back to watch it fall.

I nearly choke when I see what's revealed underneath. A skimpy Catfish tank top and little tiny boxer shorts.

I trail my fingers down the center of her white tank, her breasts heaving as I pass, and I stop once my fingers reach the waistband of her red boxers. Tickling the elastic by her naval, I listen to her quivering breath. "Now, these better be Tate Sorenson boxers, or we're going to have trouble," I tease. A devilish grin gleams back at me when I catch her eye.

"Mhmm, not so sure." She shakes her head, and I chuckle. She's warming up to me, and I can tell she's enjoying where I'm taking this. "Jacob Miller did just blow out the Florida Fox's in his football game last night."

Jacob Miller again?

All I see is red.

"Oh, you better be joking," I tell her. "You better *not* be wearing Jacob Miller pants right now." I grab her by the waist, lifting her and then throw her down on the bed. Giggling, she tries to swat me away, but I'm too nimble, tickling her as I turn her, so she's face down on the bed.

"No!" She squeals in mock protest when I flick her robe up. I stop immediately; all the adrenaline drains from my body because right there is my own face smiling back at me. Her butt crack swallows my nose, but I can see my teeth and eyes. Shaking my head, I rest my hand gently on her thigh, right at the hem of her boxers. "Sometimes I don't get you, Cali. You're angry with me, but you're still wearing me on your ass?" I still stare at my face on her delectable butt, letting my thumb stroke the skin just at the hem. I wanted to smack her for being such a bad girl, but that might have to wait.

Turning her head, she leans her cheek against the bedsheet with a shrug. "I may be angry, but you've got a big game against LA tomorrow. If I don't wear these, we might lose, and just because I'm annoyed at you doesn't mean I want that to happen." Logical. That's what I like about this girl. It's about the Catfish above everything else.

I squeeze the curve of her ass, and she, in turn, pops her backside up, bucking her hips in time with my hand. Everything about her is pure ecstasy, and I can feel myself getting hard just watching her. However, that erection was an almost permanent fixture around her at this point. "Would it be bad luck to take these off tonight?" I tickle my finger across the hem, moving down towards her center and gently brushing across it.

She was squeezing the life out of the sheets, hardly registering my question until my long fingers start to tickle under the edges. That's when her eyes pop open, and she rolls onto her back with a groan. Then, with a defeated look on her face, she whines, "We can't do anything. Not tonight, at least. I can't take these off."

She's lying below me now; her arm covers her face as though everything is too much for her. I watch her breath as I draw light circles across her upper thighs, tracing up until I reach the hem again. "We could always tuck them to the side," I suggest. "That way, you haven't taken them off." She props herself on her elbows, watching me while I let a finger slip under and gently graze at the top of her thigh, so close to her center.

It's like I've rendered her speechless for a few seconds, but alas, she doesn't stay under my spell for long. She shakes her head. "No. I'd have to change them if we did stuff, and that could be bad luck. I wore these three years ago before an LA game for the first time. Do you know what happened the next day?" My fingers stop moving, and she peeks from under her arm to watch my reaction.

Shaking my head, I do my best to keep my eyes focused on her instead of the little bit of pink skin I revealed with my fingers. "You won the game with a three-run homer in the eighth." She looks up at the ceiling wistfully. "It was awesome. You hit the ball so hard; it landed in the fishpond above the tank shop." I remember that day. It was one of my fondest memories in that park. I had no idea that it was one of Cali's too.

"I thought nothing of it at first. Thought I'd give it a go and wear them again the next time LA came to town. Well, do you know what happened in that game?" It seems she knows my batting history better than me. "You got home because the pitcher slipped and messed up his throw, putting us in a 5-point lead. A lead they weren't able to catch. Do you know what happened the *next* time?"

"Alright, alright. I get it. I get it. These are sacred boxers. My face cheeks must be on your ass cheeks and my nose in your crack before we play LA at home. Personally, I would suggest maybe the real thing might bring more luck..." She eyes me angrily for the suggestion. "Okay, maybe next time. We need to win this series against them anyway." That answer seems to satisfy her.

I move my hand away from her heat, knowing if I keep my fingers there too long, they will take matters into their own hands. I sit on the mattress next to her, adjusting my thighs so the springs aren't piercing my butt. "Are we good?" I ask with caution. We may have been just about to get naked, but that doesn't mean she's forgiven me.

There's a hesitant look on her face before she meekly replies, "I guess." My stomach lurches because that's not a good enough answer for me, and it makes me feel like a jerk. I've got to make this up to her and make sure no one else finds out that I was the one that donated the money.

I lay back beside her, looking into her eyes. "I meant what I said, Cali. I haven't spoken to Sam, and I'm only interested in you." She remains silent for a beat, letting my words sink in.

"You can sleep here tonight if you want," she says awkwardly with a grin.

I'm torn. As much as I wanted to spend more time with her, I didn't want to pressure her any more than I already had. That, and this mattress might poke holes in my back, causing an injury. Coach will kill me if I'm not okay for tomorrow's game.

I should go, but when her coconut shampoo wafts through the air, I know my answer. I'm staying. I want to be close to her, to assure her and reinforce that she's the only one I'm thinking about.

"I'd love to stay," I say, knowing I'll get an earache from Coach Allport in the morning and not caring one bit. Those lucky boxers have got to count for something, after all.

CHAPTER 23

CALI

"I don't think we can see each other anymore," I sputter out, my hand already bracing the car door handle as I speak, ready to jump out like someone planted an explosive in Tate's car. Instead of waiting for his response, I open the door, leaving Tate behind.

The fresh July air hits me the minute I'm out and even though my skin is cooling, the anger inside me is burning hot. I'm not even angry at Tate at this point. I'm angry at myself.

"What the fuck, Cali?" Tate yells, his booming voice bouncing off the walls, only to be toned down by the few empty cars scattered around the parking lot. My heels tap against the concrete as my eyes dart around the floor. I wonder if any hidden paparazzi are filming this for a good story. That would be a great plot twist. *Tate's side piece leaves him high and dry.*

My teeth clench against each other. He told me he hadn't spoken to Sam in over a year. He *told* me I was the only one he's been interested in since he first saw me, that Sam ceased to exist when he met me. I lapped it up like a kitten waiting for warm milk. *What a pile of crap!*

My hair covers my flushed face as I walk with my head bent down. I don't want to be identifiable if this *does* end up in the tabloids again. Imagine what my parents would think? What the rest of my colleagues think? What was *I* thinking? The minute he admitted to paying my salary, I should have kicked him out. That should have been enough of a red flag for me. But no, his stupid cologne made me dizzy, and when his corded arms wrapped around my body, I couldn't think straight.

I focus my thoughts on the clicking of my heels as I head towards the elevator, refusing to look back, knowing that I'll lose all my resolve again if I do. Those hot honey eyes of his poured into my soul and burned at my edges last night. And I stupidly forgave him. I could only thank the baseball gods that I had to wear Tate's panties all night. Otherwise, I would be regretting more than just offering him a place to sleep. What a mess *that* would have been.

Tate calls my name as his feet pound against the floor. I walk faster; the button to the stadium elevator is in sight, the amber glow pulling me in. My hand reaches out to press the button, but Tate's forearms wrap around my waist before I can protest. He drags me to a dark corner behind the elevator and places my back against the cold concrete. Staring at our feet, I feel his body towering over me, his hands trapping me in. It all feels very reminiscent of last night. Only today, I can feel the molten lava burning behind Tate's eyes instead of that healing honey from before.

"What the hell do you mean we can't see each other?" Tate's words are terse. I can feel his body pulsing with anger. Mine is too, but I can't be bothered to explain it to him. Mainly because he fooled me when I tried to last time, and I stupidly believed him. "I thought we talked it all out last night, and we were good? Hell, I had my hands down your panties this morning."

Urgh. Did he have to remind me of his nimble fingers waking me up in the most glorious way? "I had a change of heart," I say when he flicks my chin to look at him. I was expecting to see anger, but all that was there was hurt and confusion.

"When?"

"This morning." More specifically, when he went to take a shower and his phone wouldn't stop flashing. I flipped it over to turn the ringer off, only to see 16 missed calls and at least four messages from Sam. He hadn't spoken to her in a year, my butt. That's when my brain finally took over, and my heart was forced to take a backseat. I liked Tate. I *really* liked Tate, but I decided I wasn't prepared to get hauled into his messy love life. Office romances were way too messy, and even if it isn't against the rules, I would have to leave if anyone else found out Tate was the one who donated the money. I'd be waving goodbye to my dream job for a baller that would probably drop me just like he did Sam. Well, actually, I don't fully understand what happened in their messy breakup. All I know is I don't want anything like that playing out in front of the world.

"Unbelievable," he mutters, hanging his head low. "What made you change your mind?" With a tight jaw, I can almost feel the tension radiating off him, vibrating against the exposed skin on my arm.

I bend my knees and slide further down the wall, trying to get away from his touch. "I think we've both got a lot going on right now. There are another five months of the season, I need to make a good impression at my job, and I think we're both at different points in our lives," I speak almost automatically, having rehearsed that spiel in my head all morning. In a way, it's all true; five months of constant travel for him and my work *would* make it hard to build a relationship. He's also a few years older and way more in the settling down mindset than I am. But, on the other hand, I've only just started my career, and I don't want anyone or anything holding me back, even if he's everything I've ever wanted.

His eyes slowly rise from the floor to meet mine, and he stares at me, dumbfounded. "Are you actually serious?" I nod, chewing my bottom lip, hating that I'm holding back on what was really irking me. He lied about paying the money and being in contact with Sam. If he lied about those facts, what else would he lie about? I don't want to bring it up because he'll probably cover it up with more lies. It's a web I don't want to weave. Tate shakes his head in regret. "I don't believe you, Cali." His firm voice makes it hard to know what to do next.

My body seizes to work; it's like I have rigor mortis for a second. "There's something else going on with you. I know because you've been biting your bottom lip since I asked, and your left eye won't stop twitching. Are you still feeling weird about the donation?" He probes.

Blood flows back through my veins; he's given me an out without realizing it. "Yes," I yelp. It's the perfect excuse. Of course, I'm still annoyed that he did it. It felt great when I thought the team recognized my hard work, but it sucked when I realized the guy I was dating was the one paying for it. I considered rejecting the salary, but I'd have no way of knowing how to do that. Plus, I could use the money, and he knows it. "It makes me feel cheap. Like you were paying me for my affection."

"I didn't pay for you." His face is close to mine. It's like he knows that I bend to his will when he does that.

"No, you didn't *just* pay for me. You paid for all of the interns."

"So that you would get the money you deserved." He points out, almost making me forget about how much the whole Sam thing annoyed me. Now that he's mentioned it, and we're talking about it, I'm riled up. "You're ridiculous."

"No." I poke his chest, pushing him back so I can get some air. "You were the ridiculous one for donating the money in the first place." Our voices are loud, and this parking lot is like an echo chamber. Gosh, I hope it's only still us down here. I search the parking lot for flashing, just in case.

"Fine. Will it make you feel better if I ask for it back?" He says quietly. I wish he wouldn't make this so difficult.

"You can't do that. The other interns are expecting to be paid now."

He straightens his mouth, probably as annoyed as I am. I get it, he thinks he was doing something nice, and here I am berating him about it. But I can't keep doing this back and forth with him. Too many things aren't adding up, and I'm not feeling good about this. I can't hate my favorite player after all. I just can't.

"Tell me what you want me to do, Cali. I'll do it," he asks, exasperated. Why is he fighting for us so much? It's not like I'm anything special. I'm goofy and weird, and he could easily have any runway model he wants. I think Mila Donovan even mentioned how hot he was the other day. He could date her instead, or Sam. There was always Sam.

"Look, there's nothing you can do." I shrug. "Things change, and sometimes they aren't right." His hands drop, freeing me from his hold, and for the first time since he came over last night, I finally felt like I could breathe again.

Tate drops his head in silence, and after standing there for a good five minutes, I make my way to the elevator. He doesn't stop me when I walk away or protest when I press the amber button and the doors open. He says nothing when the doors shut around me, taking me to the tunnel that connects the parking lot to the office side of the stadium.

All that's left is myself and four metal walls, contemplating whether I'm really okay with that being it between the two of us.

When the game starts later that day, I don't watch it, too engrossed in a piece I was working on for the all-star weekend. At least, that's what I was telling myself. In truth, I didn't want to see Tate because I knew that the minute I saw him, my heart would finally break, and my brain was refusing my yearning heart any relief. It barely registered a skipped beat when I heard Tate scored a homer, leading the team straight to victory.

My brain barely let the thought that my lucky boxers were the reason why.

It was only when I was back home from work, lying in my bed, staring at the four walls surrounding me, that I bothered to look at my phone. Tate's name was sitting on the screen over my new Catfish background. I didn't want to open the message, but the notification would keep coming back without doing so.

Closing my eyes, I let my thumb graze over the glass of my screen; I press, knowing full well that it will be opening the message. One eye pops open, just to confirm Tate hasn't sent me another nude or something salacious, and I instantly feel myself blush, remembering the other times he had sent me some of those.

> **Tate:** I'm sorry for upsetting you but I'm not giving up on you, Cali. I like you too much. I'm going to prove to you how much I want you. I know you want this. You're just scared.

It takes about four reads to fully comprehend the message.

Great. I think I've just set off Scorchin' Sorenson. Now I've got to figure out how to keep him away, a feat I already know will be challenging because I've seen how hard he works on the field. Not to mention the fact that I turn into a pile of goo every time I'm around him too.

What have I done?

CHAPTER 24

TATE

Fireworks explode in the night sky as the band play on the field below. Standing on the balcony, I crouch down to get in view of the camera as a set of twins wrap their arms around me, pressing their chests against each of my biceps. "Thanks for this, Tate." One of them winks as she flicks her hair over her shoulder and smiles. "Alright, get ready. Three, two…" Their friend counts down, and without warning, the two girls kiss each of my cheeks. "One." I close my eyes, laughing in surprise as the flash goes off. That's going to be a terrible shot, but the girl taking the picture seemed happy enough.

"It's perfect." The girl taking the photo licks her bottom lip, smiling at her twin friends.

The other two girls giggle, still stroking my arms. This feels awkward, but I'm sure they'll be gone soon enough. I feel one of their palms snaking up my thigh until it reaches my front pocket. She quickly stuffs something in there. "Thanks, Tate," the one on the left coos as she slowly backs away from me. Turning to their friend almost simultaneously, the white of their 'Sorenson' jerseys glows like neon under the fading light as they inspect the photo.

"I love it," the one standing on the right says excitedly to her friend and flashes me another smile as they walk away with a sway in their step.

Grayson saddles up next to me, watching the bounce of their very high cut-off shorts, no doubt. He lets out some kind of approving noise. "Man. Did you get their numbers?" He asks, sinking his teeth into his fist. I roll my eyes, take the piece of paper out of my pocket and shove it into his chest.

"Here you go. I'm not interested." Grayson doesn't flinch at my aggressive move; instead, chooses to smile at the fans, or at least I should say, trying to smile. Unfortunately for him, he always seems to look permanently constipated or like someone stuck a pine needle in his pants.

Without looking, he uncrumples the paper. "Don't you want it?"

"Why would I get their numbers?" His gaze trails to the crowd to where I can just about see the twins' hair.

Chortling, he shakes his head. "Twins? In cut-offs? Do I need to say anything more?" When I look at him, he studies my face before laughing. Pointing at my cheeks, he says, "You might want to get rid of the lipstick marks before any kids come over. Not exactly a child-friendly look."

I wipe my cheeks, seeing bright red stains coating my palms. It's not the kids I'm worried about; it's Cali. I want to see her tonight, and I doubt she'd be that impressed if I had lipstick everywhere, especially since she accused me of cheating the last time I saw her. "If you're so interested, why don't you go for it?" I offer. He grumbles, shifting his weight without a response, very unlike Grayson. I knock his shoulder with my own. Something's different about him today, but I can't quite put my finger on it. "You're pushing me to get laid, but you aren't doing it yourself? What is up with you? Is Charlotte not putting out?"

He scoffs, "please, Charlotte Two and Charlotte Three are ready and waiting for me."

"Then why do you look like your balls are in a vice?"

"No reason." Anyone who didn't know Grayson would have only heard a grumble. Spending so much time with him, I can understand his angry mutterings. It's the same mutterings he uses when he loses. When I don't stop staring, he continues. "My balls aren't in a vice; I just seemed to have left them in Atlanta," he grouses, offering me no further explanation.

"What? Did one of your girls find a loophole in your contract?" I muse. Before he can answer, a fan comes up to us, asking for a signature. I sign the baseball card with a smile.

When Grayson finishes signing his photo, he leans in a little closer and says through tight lips, "something along those lines." If we weren't at the Fourth of July party after our game, I would force my friend to explain what he means, but we can't exactly get into a heart-to-heart here. Also, I don't have time. It's nearly the end of the night, and I still haven't seen Cali. I thought tonight would be the perfect opportunity to find her with all my planning. She's been avoiding me at every opportunity, but she can't avoid me here, not in front of everyone. Running away isn't a good enough answer for why she wants to end things with me. If she doesn't want to see me, that's fine, but I want to have an actual conversation with her, not one that everyone could hear in the parking lot. It almost felt like she was trying to push me back into Sam's arms and forget about her.

Yeah, that's never going to happen.

I want her to stop stressing about work and the best way to do that is to get rid of that idiot boss if hers. Instead of trying to find that tiny terrier of a man, I went straight to his boss Jonah and casually mentioned seeing Josh being overly demanding to a few of his staff members. Nothing major, but enough that someone might start watching his treatment of his staff. He'll be lucky if he keeps his job after his behavior is investigated.

Fans walk past us, and I'm being pulled in every direction, but I haven't stopped looking for Cali since the minute I stepped foot in this party. She has to be here tonight; the marketing team are the ones running this event. I may have subtly asked Jonah if his team were coming tonight, and he said yes, so I know she's got to be here somewhere.

"Mr. Sorenson. Would you be able to sign this?" A little boy asks as his mom scoots him forward while he holds up a ball proudly from today's game. "I caught it when you hit it out of bounds." He smiles, baring his missing front teeth. I crouch to his level, inspecting the scuffs on the ball and pretending I remember when it was. It wasn't my best game, and I hit a lot of foul balls.

"Wow, you caught this by yourself?" He nods with pride. "You'll be a great outfielder one day." I watch as his smile grows, and he looks to his mom to see if she heard me. He was pulsing with pride, and I loved that just a few simple words did that to him. "The Catfish could use you in a couple of years." Getting the black sharpie out of my pocket, I sign the ball and blow on it, letting the ink dry before handing it back to him.

The little boy's excitement permeates through me when I hand the ball back. He jumps with joy, skipping over to his mother, proudly displaying the ball. "Wow, look at that," she says to him in awe before looking up at me and mouthing 'thank you.'

I just smile back as I stand, adjusting my baseball cap, hoping I still look alright. I didn't have time to style my hair after my shower, and stupidly I wanted to look good when Cali saw me. I wanted to watch her eyes roam my chest like they did when she thought I wasn't looking and make her admit everything she's been trying to avoid - that she wants me just as much as I want her.

I think she's concocted some crazy story in her head about Sam. Those stories in the tabloids obviously haven't helped her already slightly neurotic tendencies. But now, all I want to do is reassure her and confirm that I only want *her,* but she won't let me. I'm not going to make walking away and forgetting me that easy.

"Catty!" The little boy yells with excitement as our mascot skates towards him. "Can I get a picture with Catty and Tate, Mom?" His mother looks over at me with apologetic eyes. I just give her a smile, striding over to join our mascot. I move as close as Catty will allow, which isn't that close since his head is a foot long on each side. I can't help but notice he shuffles a little further away. Maybe he's making space for the little boy, so I pick him up, and we all pose for the photo.

"Thank you." the little boy beams, running over to his mom for a hug.

"Thanks, Catty." I slap him on the back, noticing his back straighten when I touch it. Maybe I hit him a little too hard. "Thanks for standing on the dugout during the game today." I thought that might soften his back pain. "You're the sole reason I got that run in the 6th inning. I'm sure of it." Catty turns to look at me, almost mechanically. He seems stiffer than usual today. Then, with a hard nod, he stalks off to another crowd of kids. I don't have time to wonder for long if I've said something to offend him because I was inundated with fans asking for photos and autographs.

Finally, thirty minutes after the band finished and the crowd is filtering out, I've managed to get a moment to myself. Pathetically, I search the venue, looking for the hot, tall blonde that I can't get off my mind. I'm hellbent on speaking to Cali before the night ends.

I walk through the throngs of people with my ballcap pulled down, hoping no one will notice me. It's ridiculous to think I can hide at a baseball party held at the tank; I'm wearing my own jersey after all, but I'm so focused on Cali that I'll believe anything.

Just as I'm about to give up all hope, I notice familiar flaming red hair in the distance. *Penn. Yes.* My opportunity has finally come. He'll know where she is. I walk over, slowing my pace, when I notice frustration etched across his face. He's arguing with someone; his cheeks are nearly as red as his hair. I can't see who he's talking to with so many people around, though. I*s he annoyed at Cali?*

Taking slower steps, she finally comes into view.

Not Cali, but Mary.

She's so small that Penn has to bend his entire torso to talk to her. His hand grazes the side of her arm like he's pleading with her. Her face says it all; she's unimpressed and annoyed at something he did.

"You shouldn't have done that," Mary snipes and my ears prick with interest. I shouldn't listen in, but they're talking so loudly it's hard not to.

Penn doesn't notice me approaching because he's looking up to the sky in exasperation. "What was I supposed to do? Nothing?" He says, frustrated.

I'm close enough now that I need to make my presence known;

otherwise, I might say something I can't unhear. "Hey guys," I say loud enough so it will jolt them out of their conversation. They both whip their heads, looking at me in shock. I play innocent, pretending I don't know I'm interrupting something, and point between the two of them. "Were you two busy?" I ask. The tension makes me sweat, and this is starting to feel awkward. I should have kept walking, but my need to speak to Cali overrode anything else.

"No."

"Yes."

They answer at the same time. Mary spins on her heels, eyeing Penn with the same look Cali gave me the other night after accusing me of proposing to Sam. Speaking of, I need to change my phone number. After blocking Sam the other day, she's now using burner phones to call me. It's pathetic and strange, but I'm not curious enough to answer the phone to see what she wants. "You didn't interrupt *anything*," Mary stresses. Believable. "What is it that I can help you with, Tate?" Her sugary voice takes over, and the PR manager in her was out in full force, completely ignoring Penn.

I scratch the stubble on my chin. "I was just, uh, wondering if either of you have seen Cali?" Yes, I sound like a desperate teenager, but I don't care at this point. I need to see her. I must look as desperate as I feel because the look on Mary's face is nothing short of sympathetic and slightly pathetic.

She opens her mouth, probably trying to let me down gently. But Penn interrupts, shaking his head. "Cali's busy tonight; she's dressed – Ouch! What'd you do that for?" He scolds Mary, who just elbowed him on the side with an angry glare. "I've got to pitch tomorrow. If you've screwed up my flow, I'll kill you," he says, rubbing his side.

He hardly notices when Mary pushes him, rolling her eyes before looking back at me. She points to Penn with her thumb, huffing, "Athletes. So sensitive to any injury. Last month, Penn cried because he had a blister."

"It was on my throwing hand," he defends himself, glaring at

Mary. "I was off the rotation for two weeks until it healed. That's two weeks with no scouting potential." He turns to me but is obviously still talking to Mary. "Since you're in such a sharing mood. Why not tell Tate how I got this injury in the first place?" He flashes her a cheeky grin, and as much as Mary tries to keep a stony face, a blush creeps up her cheeks. I just walked into something I hadn't intended.

I think they might have been having a lover's tiff.

Mary closes her eyes, pinching the bridge of her nose as she takes a deep, calming breath. "Cali's busy working tonight, so you won't find her down here," she says. Penn snorts, looking up to the sky in disbelief. *Was I missing something?* Jonah said everyone would be down here. I will kill Josh if he's forcing her to miss the party because he's given her some ridiculous deadline.

"Is she at her desk?"

Mary's eyes widen, and she flails her arms around like a headless chicken. "No. No. Don't go up there to see her. She's really busy, and you'll just stress her out." Penn watches Mary almost as intently as I am. She mutters something inaudible under her breath before focusing back on me. "Look, I know you mean well, and you want to talk to her, but I think she needs a little time. She's got a lot going on with work; she'll come to her senses soon. This whole situation is just a lot for her. She's not used to being with someone like you."

"Someone like me?" I exasperate, watching Mary walk away with no further explanation. Why did women always do this to me? They don't fully explain things and seem to think I'm smart enough to figure it out myself. I'm a baseball player for crying out loud. I'm not a brain surgeon. "Why is she upset?" I call one more time, hoping Mary will take pity on me. She doesn't.

"You really like my sister a lot, don't you?" Penn asks behind me after a few moments of silence. See, he just proved my point. Baseball players aren't the smartest.

"Don't sound too surprised," I mutter.

He chuckles, glancing around the venue. "I'm not surprised at all. My sister is amazing, and any guy would be lucky to have her," he says with conviction. "She's smart, beautiful, and sweet. It's just she has this terrible tendency to not see blaringly obvious things that are right in front of her." His gaze moves to Catty, who is currently posing and dancing with some fans. "Cali doesn't date much. Only five guys were taller than her in high school, and she was awkward. She didn't think anyone would be interested in her, which was a lie." He flicks his eyes back to me. "Then, in Senior year, a few guys started to show interest. They were popular and stopped by the house a few times, asking to speak with her. She completely ignored them because she didn't believe they'd be interested in her over the short cheerleaders." He shakes his head in disbelief. "From what I've heard from Mary, these guys had it bad, and they tried really hard to get her attention, but she didn't seem interested." He glances at me, noting my reaction before bowing his head. "Sorry. I'm going off on a tangent. Basically, it was undeniable that these guys liked Cali, and she decided that she wanted nothing to do with them for no apparent reason except her own stubbornness. Once they gave up and started dating said cheerleaders, she used it as verification that she was right all along."

"They sound like idiots if they gave up that easily." I tense my jaw, concerned that I'll break my teeth if I don't let up. I hated the idea of other guys going anywhere near Cali but giving up on her and moving on seemed criminal. "But what does that have to do with me?"

Penn shrugs. "Not much. Just that she sees what she wants to see sometimes instead of what's actually there. Anyone with two brain cells can see how obsessed you are with her and would ignore those magazines. Cali seems to be the only one reading them and taking them seriously, which is funny because, with the amount of hours she's working at the moment, I didn't think she'd have time to read all that crap anyway."

Processing his words, I think there was a compliment for me in there somewhere. Cali is stubborn, and from what I can surmise, she has decided I'm like these other guys, and I'm not *that* interested in her. Well, if she thinks those guys showed her indifference, I'm going to have to show her obsession. "Hey, Penn." I clamp my hand on his shoulder. "Do you remember I mentioned a pitching session with Grayson?" He nods. "Well, I think I might have an idea, but I'll need your help."

"Sure," he replies, and I hold back on smiling too broadly. I may have the perfect plan, but I've got to make sure it comes together.

CHAPTER 25

CALI

Blood pumps through my body as my heart beats faster, watching the scene unfold before me. You'd think I'd be used to the feeling of sweat trickling down the back of my neck since I'm usually drenched in my mascot costume. Nope. I still hate it. Rolling my shoulders back, I adjust the bill of my North Davidson High baseball cap, doing my best to ignore Dad's viciously loud hot dog chewing and focus on the field. With all this adrenaline pumping through my veins, you'd think I was the one out there pitching. I'm not. I'm just in the stands, watching.

Penn lifts his right leg, expertly throwing the ball. The batter, number two in their lineup, thinks it's a fastball and hits as hard as possible, only to spin on his heel, completely missing the sinker.

Strike two.

"Yes!" I clap, punching the air and cheering at the fans around me. Half of them look bored or disinterested. We may be three hours in, but I'm just as excited at Penn's high school games as I am when I'm watching the Catfish play. Admittedly, there hasn't been a homer or a run scored by either side to get people excited, but that's what the Mascots are here for. Colonel Clucker, Penn's team mascot, sits next to Clayton's Bacon mascot, and they're boring as heck. Only the occasional cluck was leaving Clucker's beak every now and again, and the bacon was hardly sizzling. It's not the team spirit or hyping up I'd expect from my feathered friend and packaged food foe. I'm considering going down there and helping them out, albeit I'm too engrossed with Penn right now to focus on much else.

Using my hands as a megaphone, I yell, "come on, Penn!" He ignores it if he can hear me, solely focused on getting this batter out. Bending forward, he glares at the hitter with tight lips. If he gets this strike, he only needs to get one more batter out to finish the inning. I don't know if it's the potential scouts or that this is his last game before the playoffs, but he's playing like a beast. Penn sets himself up for another throw, and I hold my breath, closing my eyes.

Strike three. You're out.

I cheer so loudly; I have to apologize to the old lady in front because she dropped her phone on some teenager's head in surprise. Penn throws his fist in the air, looking pumped. He walks around the mound, doing that angry pitcher strut while the batter kicks up dust, twirling his bat, and sulks to the dugout. "Go, Penn!" I'm ecstatic. What a great outing for my brother.

My mom claws at the bottom of my jersey, tugging me down to her level. "Cali. Sit down already. You're making a scene." I nearly laugh at her unnecessary embarrassment. She rarely came to baseball games with dad because she's usually too busy running her hot yoga classes. She certainly doesn't fit in with her long, dangly jewelry and headband, that's for sure. Since it was Penn's last game, she wanted to make an effort, and it's endearing that she's wearing his jersey over her paisley dress, even if everyone else thinks she looks a little odd.

She watches Penn do his pitcher mound walk and points. "See! You're distracting him," she says, adjusting her blonde hair.

Rubbing her shoulder reassuringly, I say, "Relax, mom. Pitchers do that all the time. Besides, he's got to get used to adoring fans if he's going to be a starting pitcher in the MLB." I holler Penn's name again as he pitches to the next batter.

My mom growls, bringing her hands to her ears. "All the noise you're making is messing with my energy and flow. I don't know how Penn is dealing with it down there. He's already riled up; I think you're making it worse."

My Dad lets out a pandering laugh as he drinks a soda because

Penn just got another strike with a fastball. "I don't think it's Cali's behavior that has him riled up, dear. I think it's more to do with the fact that half of the Carolina Catfish are over there watching him." He points with his eyebrow, and I spin my head around to see what on earth he was talking about.

I drop my cheering arms as my brain tries to figure out what I'm looking at.

What the…

Players, almost all the Carolina Catfish players, are occupying an entire stand worth of seats. Their wives and kids are here too, laughing and having a good time. Didn't they have something better to do than come to a high school baseball game on their day off? *How did I miss them before?* Clearly I was too focused on the game to care about the audience. My eyes roam the seats, knowing exactly who I'm looking for but refusing to admit it to myself.

Then they stop.

Sitting right in the center of the stands while everyone else is watching the game, Tate's hazel eyes are solely focused on me. "Aw sweetie," my mom coos, still trying to forcefully make me sit. "Did you arrange this for Penn through work?" She asks.

A slow smirk grows on Tate's face when he notices me looking at him. I can't move, too scared that my parents might realize that Tate's waving at me if I do. I may have forgotten to mention that I'd been dating him, too worried they would think it was inappropriate. I kind of wish I told them now. Maybe it would have fizzled out before really starting, and it wouldn't feel like poison ivy is growing around my heart now - lethal to keep and too dangerous to remove.

I slump onto the bench, trying my best to think of an escape plan that doesn't involve seeing Tate. As if he doesn't play enough baseball, he has to come here and infiltrate my time with my family to prove a point. Yes, of course, I melt whenever I'm in his presence, but that doesn't mean we should be together, especially with all the press he's been getting recently.

Yesterday, when Mary caught me reading one of those

magazines at my desk, she yelled at me. I know I shouldn't read that stuff, but I couldn't help it because there's no sign of that stupid story about Tate and Sam dying down. I also may have wanted to see if there was any more mention of the mysterious blonde in the parking lot. But there was nothing. As far as they were concerned, I was a rebound, and we were finished.

"Yeah," I say faintly because my mind is still trying to catch up with everything that's going on. Penn had thrown another three pitches when my brain decided to focus back on the game; he had a full count. This pitch needs to be a strike; otherwise, the guy is walking to first. I clasp my hands together, doing my best to zone out and only focus on my brother.

Strike three. Out.

I punch the air when he gets that final out, so proud of Penn's performance. "Go, Penn!" A familiar voice shrieks from behind, and I slowly drop my arms in confusion.

What's she doing here?

I glance over my shoulder and see my redheaded best friend in the bleachers. "Mary?" I say in confusion, scanning the bleachers for her.

"Mary's here?" My mom perks up, following my gaze. "I haven't seen her in months. How is the little thing?"

My brows cross, searching the bleachers, trying to prove myself wrong. "No. She's not here. That wouldn't make any sense." Still, I can't stop looking. That's when a springy movement stops me. She *is* here. Jumping on the spot, her hair bouncing in the wind while she smiles at Penn like he hung the damn moon.

Did I miss something? Or is this all just a terrible dream? Maybe I'm in Penn's dream. He is playing better than I've ever seen him, and Mary's looking at him like he's her boyfriend.

"Mom, can you pinch me?"

"Why?"

"Don't ask." Mary hasn't noticed me; she's angled so that if I weren't looking, I wouldn't have been able to see her. "Ouch!" I grab my arm from the sudden shock of pain, looking down at my mom.

"You told me to pinch you." Well, at least I know I'm not dreaming.

"I'll be back in a minute," I say with no further explanation. Then, shuffling past my dad and the other parents, I make my way towards my petite pal.

The closer I get, the easier it is to see just how bright her smile is. Her gaze is glittering as she watches my brother. She's too focused on him to even notice me coming.

"Mary." She jumps at my voice, and her mouth opens in surprise.

"Cali?" It's like she's shocked to see me at my own brother's final game of the year.

"What are you doing here?" I ask skeptically, watching every part of her face, looking for a tic.

Her eyes dart around the stadium, avoiding eye contact or she's trying to come up with an excuse. "Um. Tate invited me." Her voice rose with every word, a tell of her lie.

I cock an eyebrow, watching her eye twitch and her foot tap. "So, you knew Tate was coming, and you didn't think warning me would have been a good idea?" I almost want to believe her because the alternative is too weird and creepy to comprehend.

"No," she says without thinking. "Crap." Closing her eyes, she takes a deep breath. "I mean, yeah, I did know, but -"

Raising my hand, I stop her from continuing. "Save it. I know you're lying. So why are you actually here?" I wait for her to answer, hoping she'll say it's because she felt guilty about knowing Tate was here and wanted to tell me in person, but knowing that's a long shot.

All she does is twist her lips, knotting her hands together as she dances on the spot. Last time I saw her this nervous was when she was hoping Jimmy Greer would ask her on a date. Sadly, it never happened. "Mary," I say softly, albeit I'm fuming inside. You need to treat her like a timid mouse when you want her to admit something. "Are you here to see Penn?" I ask the question even though I don't want to know the answer.

A blush blares across her cheeks, and I can feel my eyes growing. "You are?!" No answer. "Is there something going on between you and my brother?" I ask, staring down at her nervous form. But, again, she says nothing, just watches me with a guilty look smacked across her face.

This can't be happening? My mind can't process it.

Tate's here, along with the entire Carolina Catfish team. It's Penn's last regular season game ever. Mary, my twenty-three-year-old BFF, has been secretly dating my brother. What the actual hell has been going on in my life? I know I've lived in a Tate hole the last few months, but how did I miss this? I'm replaying every look, every conversation they've ever had, and keep coming up empty.

"When did it happen?" Silence. I wait for her to say something, anything that will help me figure this whole thing out, but she's still silent. Finally, she lets out a hesitant breath as her eyes flick over my head.

"Hey, Cali." The voice glides into my body, soothing the poison ivy growing around my heart, and I roll my eyes. Tate appears at the worst times, I swear.

Mary skips over to Tate, happy she has an out. "Hey Tate," she squeals, hugging him. She looks down at my shoes and then back to Tate. "I guess I'll leave you guys to talk," she says sheepishly. "I've got to go talk to someone else anyway."

"If you're referring to my brother, we're going to need to have a serious conversation," I say sternly, watching her disappear into the crowd of fans, completely ignoring my last sentence.

When I turn back to Tate, I have steel behind my eyes, already angry about this new development with my best friend and brother. It meant I had no time to remember that Tate could make me melt with just one look. When his eyes met mine, it felt like someone was poking tiny needles into a pincushion. He pierces my soul with a single look, and I don't like it. It feels too intimate. Too familiar. "What are you doing here?" I ask, bored with how much I've had to ask that today. Why couldn't this have just been a simple Collins Family outing?

His eyes bathe my body with warmth. "Missed you too." He winks. My jaw tenses because he thinks he's funny, and I find it hard to remain nonchalant. "I came because I promised Penn a session with Grayson. Remember?" He stands there with that glorious smirk plastered on his face. "And I thought it would be better to do it now, *before* his playoff games, than after."

It made sense, and it annoyed me that I didn't think of it before. That's why Penn's doing so well today. He wanted to show Grayson what he could do. I raise my eyebrows, refusing to give in to that charming smile. "Is that it? There's no other reason why you could possibly be here?" With one eyebrow cocked, I tap my foot, getting impatient with all the lies I've been fed today. It's like no one wanted to be honest with me.

He pops his bottom lip out, looking to the sky in thought before shaking his head. "No? Should there be?"

I'm not taking his bait. He's trying to rile me up and admit that his presence here affects me, but I won't give him that satisfaction. "No, definitely not," I quip, clasping his shoulder and immediately regretting it because a zing of electricity courses through my body, making me wonder why I'm resisting this gorgeous man.

Because you're not going to be a rebound, Cali. You will keep your stable job and not throw the chance away on a guy who might be two-timing you.

The internal reminder is all I need to build up the courage to say, "thanks so much for helping Penn." Ignoring everything between us, I gave him the most casual tone I could muster and flicked my hair for good measure. My nonchalance makes him falter; I can tell. Something I've learned is that Tate likes to fight. It's the athlete in him. Always competing. Always trying to win. Well, he isn't going to win with me that easily. "Nice to see you again, Tate. Now, if you excuse me, I need to head back to my seat." He frowns, and I almost feel bad, but I have to keep my cool. No matter how much I liked him, he lied about Sam, and that was enough to seep doubt in my mind.

"Do you want some company?" He asks, gesturing towards the stands.

I shake my head, looking back at him. He stuffs his hands in his pockets, looking gorgeous and somewhat shy at the same time. He'd be my perfect downfall if I let it happen. "I've got company. My parents are here."

He bares his perfect smile. "It's a little early to be meeting the parents, but I'm game," he says, and I lock my wobbling knees, too nervous they will swoon in front of him. I'm supposed to be angry.

"What would Sam think if she saw you with my family in the news?" I bite out, more to remind myself why I'm so annoyed. The tone of my voice makes me panic, and I glance around the ballpark, looking for anyone who might be watching us. Tate's front-page news at the moment, and there's no doubt someone's following him. When I turn back, the anger in his eyes is unmistakable. Maybe if he thinks I'm hard work, he'll move on to his second biggest fan instead of focusing so much of his attention on me. Although I'm pretty sure that's Larry. Maybe his third-biggest fan.

Tate rolls his eyes, clenching his fists so tightly they turn white. Amongst all of that, he's trying his hardest to look calm. "I already told you; *nothing* is going on between Sam and me." He gives me the once over, moving closer to me. "For some stupid reason, your stubborn butt is the only one I'm interested in."

Did he just say that?

He's so persistent and manly, and he's making this difficult. I try to act like it didn't affect me, gnawing at my lip to stop myself mid-laugh. But unfortunately, it doesn't work, and I end up sounding like I'm hyperventilating.

Tate rests his hand on my back, fully ready to go full-on Heimlich if I gave him the go-ahead. "Are you okay? I know first aid." Of course he does.

"I'm fine." I keep my focus on his shoes, too embarrassed to look up. He had a nice new pair of Nike's on, the team's sponsor. I wonder how many shoes they've given him this season? I shake the stupid thoughts out of my head, knowing that I need to get out of here before embarrassing myself further. "I've got to go. My parents are waiting on me." With that, I take off faster than a rocket engineered by Elon Musk and don't look back.

"I'll see you after the game." He calls after me, and I close my eyes, wincing. How the hell am I supposed to survive this whole day. And wait, did he just say he would see me *after* the game?

I can't deal with this.

CHAPTER 26

TATE

Rounding the bat behind my shoulder, I watch Penn give me his best stare down. As much as I'd consider missing the ball on purpose to make him feel good, I don't. He needs to learn how hard it will be to get someone like me out someday. Might as well be now. The ball hurtles towards me, and I whack it hard, watching it fly straight out of the park, just past the linked fence. Penn and the parents watch in awe as it disappears into the settling evening dusk.

I glance over my shoulder to the only person I wanted to impress today. Cali sits in the dugout with her arms crossed over her body to keep warm. With pursed lips, it looks like she's smelled some seriously stinky fish as she stares at the patch in the sky where my ball was last seen.

"Good hit," she says loud enough so I can hear. There's a subtle change when she looks down at Penn. Her face is more relaxed, with the hint of a smile on the edges of her lips. Why does seeing that slight curve make me so happy? I've dated women in the past, none of which have kept me on my toes quite like Cali. She's unpredictable. A little crazy and doesn't care that I'm a baseball player. In fact, I can only surmise that's the main reason she's staying away from me. She doesn't like the attention she might get, and doesn't believe that I could be faithful to her as a ballplayer. That, and she thinks it will affect her job, which it won't. She wants nothing from me, but I want everything from her.

I drag my eyes back to the field; players from the Catfish and Penn's team are scattered around, waiting for the next pitch. We've been out here playing a semi-serious game since Penn's team won about an hour ago. The light's drawing in, and the air is getting colder, but everyone wanted to stay.

Grayson stalks towards the mound, his presence immediately felt by everyone. "That was a good pitch, but if you change your grip, you should be able to get this idiot out in a heartbeat." He points his thumb back to me. I roll my eyes, kicking up dirt with my shoe and playing with my bat while I wait for Grayson to finish his lesson. I did everything possible not to look back at the beautiful sour-faced girl sitting on the bleachers.

Penn blows a breath, getting his placement on the mound before looking at me. Swinging my bat over my shoulder, I stare him down, waiting for him to throw the ball. He's harder to read this time. Less nervous, I suspect. As the ball leaves his hand, I guess it's a fastball and swing, spinning myself around because I put so much momentum into it. I miss the ball gloriously.

My eyes dart to Cali, her smile wider as she claps with excitement for Penn. Well, if her smile is the only thing to come from my bruised ego, I can't complain. Dust billows around me, covering my baseball pants as Grayson laughs hysterically in the dugout. "That's exactly it. Good job, Penn." I was surprised at how well Grayson took to mentoring. He's always been more of a lone wolf, using mathematics and his own critiques to improve. He rarely shared with others, but sharing with Penn seemed natural. It's that, or maybe he's getting softer in his old age.

I wipe my sweaty palms on the back of my pants, nodding. "He's right. You got me good," I admit, trying to avoid looking too tarnished by the miss. Seven years in the league and a high schooler can still catch me out. He pitched to me a few more times, and each one, I miss just as spectacularly as the first.

Wiping my bat down, I notice Austin standing by the dugout. "You know what, I think I need a break from the ass whopping. You can take over, A." I hand the bat to Austin, who stares at it with wide eyes. "Show them what a rookie can do," I whisper. He nods with determination like we were in the bottom of the ninth, one hit away from winning the world series.

As I walk over to the bleachers, I pat down my thighs, doing my best to get the dust off. I want Cali to find me sexy, not to choke on the cloud of sand I leave behind. By the time I get to the bleachers, though, she's gone. My eyes dart around; I know she's here somewhere. She wouldn't leave without saying goodbye to Penn.

The flash of her blonde hair waves in my periphery as she walks briskly through the bleachers heading towards the parking lot. I don't know where she's going, but I'm about to find out.

I call out her name when I'm close enough, noting her back visibly straightening at my voice. It looked like someone had poked her in the butt with a hot spike. Something irked my mind because that sudden movement looks familiar, but I can't quite place where I've seen it before. She slowly turns, her eyes watching every step as I advance towards her.

"Hi Tate," she squeals, her hands clenching at her sides and her jaw set.

"Are you okay?" I ask with a tilted head and a smirk.

She stares straight into my eyes, her cheeks reddening. "Yup. I'm absolutely fine." Still staring at me intently, it's like she doesn't want to look down. She rocks her head from side to side like she's trying to rid her mind of all that nervous energy, which is weird because she was fine with me earlier. Cali's eyes refused to look anywhere but my face.

"Are you sure?" She bites her bottom lip, her cheeks flaming. It looks like she's trying to stop herself from spontaneously combusting. Her eyes flick down for a fraction of a second, and that's when it clicks.

She has a thing for me in my worn baseball gear. How could I forget?

I slap my hands against my thighs, letting the dust waft between us, and notice her eye twitch. Damn, I shouldn't have wiped myself down. I stroll into her space, just enough to mess with her. She can say she doesn't want to date me all she wants, but I can see how much she wants me in that lusty gaze of hers. "Did you enjoy the show?"

She visibly swallows, her eyes darting from side to side. She's doing her best to look anywhere but directly at me. "Yeah." It was haughty and wistful all at the same time. "Thanks for arranging this for Penn. I can tell he loves this." She watches her brother striking out Austin with pride. I purposely move into her field of view, and her eyes finally connect with mine again. They soften like her body, but she remains quiet.

So, I decided to help her out. "At the risk of sounding like a nineties boyband, I'd do anything for you." Hushed laughter leaves her mouth as she shakes her head.

"Tate, you've got to stop saying stuff like that." She puts her palm out to push my chest, but I grab her hand before she can take it away, using my thumb to stroke the back of it. That little connection alone sent tingles through my chest, and I know what this feeling is. I just needed to convince her what it is too.

"Why?" I ask in barely a whisper.

She scuffs her shoes against the metal of the bleachers. "Because we aren't dating." It sounded so lackluster. She doesn't feel that way; she's just trying to convince herself she does.

I try my hardest not to crack a smile. "Say that to my face instead of your shoes; maybe then I'd believe you."

That's when she does it. She looks me directly in the eyes, and her mouth starts slacking over the words I know she can't say. She's being irrational, and she knows it, punishing me over the tabloids and an ex that I have no interest in. Did she not see I arranged all of this *for her?*

Kneeling to look directly into her worried eyes, I say, "the tabloids are paid to make up stories. I care more about the gum stuck on the bottom of my shoe than Sam. The only girl I'm looking at is you, and once the tabloids realize that, they'll get bored and stop reporting on it. They want drama which we won't give them." I reiterate for what feels like the thousandth time. Her brows pinch into a knot, no doubt trying to figure out how I knew about that. "You will not get fired, and a relationship with me won't be frowned upon. Three girls in accounting are dating or are married to players. I checked."

She stares back at me, processing all the information. I'm sure she's shocked, but she shouldn't be. These are all things I've said before.

"Hot Dog?" A man with scruffy red stubble holds out the meat-filled bun to Cali. Closing her eyes, she presses her lips together as her face reddens again. He completely ruined the moment without realizing it. She lets out a giant, exaggerated huff before looking at him sardonically.

"I'm okay, dad." She eyes the hot dog suspiciously. "Where did you even get one of those this late?"

He studies it, licking his lips. "Daryl decided to stay open when he saw the guys kept playing. So if you don't want it, I'll take it." I swear he's salivating just looking at it. "This is the only piece of actual meat I'll be able to eat this week."

She waves her hand. "Go ahead, Dad. I'll come to find you in a minute. I just need to finish up here." She points at me as though I'm a bank transaction she needs to fix.

He chuckles. "Yeah, with your *favorite* ballplayer," he stresses the favorite as though I didn't already know that. "I thought I'd come over and introduce myself." He smiles in my direction. "I'm John." He adjusts the hot dog awkwardly, giving him just enough space to hold his hand out in my direction. For all intents and purposes, he looked like your stereotypical baseball Dad. Slightly protruding belly with a baseball hat and jersey proudly displaying 'Collins' on the back. Absolutely nothing about him would suggest that he would be hipster enough to consider naming his children after a couple of states.

I shake his hand firmly because I have a strong sense that I will be spending a lot of time with him, and I wanted to make a good first impression. "It's nice to meet you, Sir."

"Has Cali told you about the signed jersey of yours she has hanging above her bed yet?" He laughs, finding no problem embarrassing his daughter.

"D-ad!" Cali stresses. "Stop it." She's squirming, and I love it.

He laughs innocently. "It's not my fault you worship the man like he's your own personal Buddha." That sentence had my mind trailing places it shouldn't, especially when talking to her father. Judging by that comment, though, I'm assuming she hasn't mentioned that we've been dating the last couple of months.

I cock a brow, studying Cali's pointed features until she meets my gaze. "No. She didn't mention that." I also know that currently, it's not hanging above her bed. Maybe it was the first thing she removed when she cleansed her room of me the first time I came over.

Her ears and nose pinken as she stares at the ground. "It's nothing," she answers flippantly. "Besides, it's not up there anymore because Austin is my new favorite player." She looks over my shoulder to the field, where no doubt Austin was most likely standing, sounding more desperate by the second.

"But he's not a shortstop." Her dad adds, taking a large bite out of the hot dog. "Shortstops are your jam." He smirks, seemingly enjoying her strained and frustrated face.

"They *were*."

"Uh oh. I know that tone when I hear it. What did you do, Tate?" He looks over to me, and I freeze. *Oh, nothing really. I just ate your daughter out on her desk, fingered her in bed, then banged her in my bed. Only for her to decide that I apparently want my ex-girlfriend more than her.* Yeah, I might keep that little tidbit to myself.

"Nothing," she quips, grabbing her dad's shoulder and turning him in the opposite direction. "I think Mom's looking for you." She searches the venue, tiptoeing to get a better view. For a second, I wondered what her mom might look like. Penn took after his dad, but did Cali? I wasn't sure.

"I'm not looking for him. I'm right here." A woman says from behind me. When I see her, everything falls into place. *She's* the reason that Cali and her brother were named after states. Her long flowery dress, wavy blonde hair, and huge dangly earrings tell me everything I need to know.

"Mrs. Collins," I breathe out at the spitting image of Cali, only older. "It's lovely to meet you. I'm Tate Sorenson." I felt nervous, knowing that I needed to impress her if I wanted to convince Cali to give us a chance.

She takes my hand, throwing me a blissed-out smile. "It's nice to meet you, Tate. Although, the way my children talk about you, I feel like I've known you for years."

Cali grumbles behind, "oh my God."

"Watch your language, Cali," her mother says pointedly. She then looked over my shoulder at Cali's Dad. "John, I hope that's vegan?" He shoves the last bite of the hot dog in his mouth before she can inspect it.

When he finished chewing, he ignored his wife and smiled at me. "Thanks for coming and helping Penn out today," John says, swiftly changing the subject. "The team loved it."

"Ah, it was nothing. Anything to help Cali." I elbow her, inadvertently pushing her forward. She seemed surprised that I'd have the confidence to touch her in front of her parents.

"And you did all of this for her?" Cali's dad asks suspiciously with a cocked brow. He can see through me that much is obvious.

I nod with a shrug. "She's a great girl. When I met her in the first aid room, she was limping and wide-eyed; I couldn't say no to her."

John turns to look at his daughter. "First aid room? What did you do this time?" His exasperated tone answered the question I had from the other night since I learned how prone to getting hurt she was. She hangs out with Phil a lot.

Cali shakes her head. "Nothing. Just a stupid accident," she babbles. "Anyway, I'm just going to finish up with Tate. I will see you guys in the car." She tries her best to move them along, and after the final push, they finally get the hint.

"Tate, we would love it if you would come to our house for dinner." Cali's mom says. No one could unhear the desperate squeal from Cali. "You know, as a thank you for organizing all of this." She looks at Cali in disappointment and then eyes up the used hot dog wrapper residing in John's hands. "We're having mushroom tacos," she smiles eagerly.

Just as I was about to accept her gracious offer, Cali spoke for me, "He can't tonight, mom. He's already got plans." I can take a hint… Sometimes.

"Yes, I'm sorry, I've got a few things to do before I travel with the team tomorrow. Maybe I could take you up on those tacos another day, though?" I say only to placate Cali. She keeps her mouth shut as her parents say their goodbyes and trot towards the car. I stifle a laugh when I hear Cali's mom yell at her dad about the hotdogs. They seemed like a cute, loving family.

"Are you a vegan?" I ask, still watching her parents walk off. Her brows were bunched when she looked at me. "Did I offend you when I cooked Lasagna the first time you came over? Is that what all this is about?" I'm only half-joking, more curious why she hadn't told me this vital piece of information.

She stops herself from laughing, a habit I've noticed she's started to do in front of me. "No. My mom only became a vegan a few years ago; I was already a hard-grained meat fan and living in the college dorms at that point." She fiddles with her fingers, chewing her lips. "Look, Tate. Thank you for doing this today, but it doesn't change anything." I try my hardest not to show annoyance, which is getting really tough because I know she's holding back. "We already talked about this," she adds, noticing the tension radiating off me.

"Did we?" I ask sarcastically, trying to add some humor back into the conversation. "Because I remember you were talking a lot. Babbling is actually how I'd describe it." I grin at her shocked expression. "You also gave me very little room to defend myself."

I graze my fingers against hers; she doesn't stop it. In fact, she leans closer towards me. As much as she wants to deny it, I know she can feel the zing between us. The tension fills the air whenever we are in the same vicinity. "I know Tate; it's just I -" I'm hanging on her every word, wanting so badly to understand her better.

"Thanks for arranging this, Tate," Penn says. Cali and I both jump out of the little world we've created, and I offer a smile, moving a comfortable distance away from his sister. I was disappointed that I didn't get to hear what she was going to say.

"Not a problem, man." Hugging him, I pat him on the back. "Mr. Howard was the agent that scouted me. He watched from the bleachers today, and Grayson told me he put in a good word for you. Of course, mine wouldn't have mattered much, being a shortstop and all." I wink, coming out of the hold. "You're a great pitcher, and I'm sure I'll see you on the field one day soon. I can only hope it's on *my* team instead of against me."

He smiles with tight lips, too nervous to get excited by my praise. "I appreciate it."

Cali's hand wraps around her brother's arm, dragging him. "Come on, Penn. Mom and Dad are waiting in the car, and I'm starving."

"Like vegan tacos is going to satisfy you," he snorts. She groans, using all her weight to pull him along the concrete and he barely moves. For a skinny guy, he seems to have hidden strength. Cali gave me a small, forced smile.

"Thanks again for everything today, Tate. Good luck with your next few games, and I'll see you when you get back." She had her professional voice switched on. It was kind of hot. Who am I kidding? She could slather herself with mayonnaise, and I'd still think she was hot. Penn mumbled out another thank you, looking down at his sister like she'd lost her mind.

As they walked off, I heard him say, "Is that any way to talk to your boyfriend?" He glances back over his shoulder, giving me a wink as he smirks.

"He's not my boyfriend." She defends herself adamantly.

Throwing his head back in a laugh, he says, "And I don't have red hair." I could hear grumbling from Cali from here, but not her response. "You're just chicken," Penn taunts. "You're too afraid the tabloids will find out about your deep dark fishy secret?"

Secret? Interesting. Cali ignores Penn, shaking her head as she drags him through the cars.

Is Cali hiding something? Something…Fishy?

I need to find out.

Chapter 27

CALI

Tate: Did you get my gift today?

I put my phone down, ignoring Tate's message, and stare at the bright blue Catfish cupcakes resting on my desk. I already gave away half of them to curb the urge of licking the icing off in public and showing my true self to my colleagues. In short, I know I'd willingly eat myself into a sugar coma if left with too many sweets.

My fingers twitch in desperate need to respond to Tate's message, but I force myself not to. I can't fall desperately in love with someone just because of a few nice things. Okay, what he did for Penn wasn't just nice, it was incredible, and I would never be able to thank him enough for all he did. After the game, Penn practically peed his pants when he got a call from one of the scouts. Next month he's been invited to train with Charlotte's minor league team, the Minnows. My baby brother's dreams are coming true, and it's all because of Tate.

Beautiful, perfect Tate.

Obviously, I had to text Tate the good news - it would be rude not to, but in doing so, I knew it was opening something up. However, I didn't think Tate would view it as an open invitation to text me every spare moment he had. Not that I minded too much. I still didn't let him know that, though. He had the week off since the All-Star game is tomorrow, so he had more time to think about me than I could handle. I'm too busy working my butt off to make sure all the pieces come together. We are the hosts, after all.

Buzz. Buzz. Buzz.

Another message from Tate, no doubt. I wish I had more time to spare. We need to talk; I've finally admitted that much to myself. I've found it hard to admit that I like Tate's persistence this whole time.

It's especially hard to admit when I drag my eyes across to the other gifts he's left for me the last few days. A helmet from the game where he hit a cycle, a signed baseball with all the current player's signatures, and a bat he used last week. As if I couldn't look any more obsessed with baseball, Tate somehow found a way to do it, and that stupidly brought a giant smile to my face. He knows me. He knows what would make me happy, and the more I thought about it, the more I thought about how happy I was with Tate. Of course, every couple has their obstacles, maybe ours weren't that bad, and I was overreacting.

I can't hold back any longer. I reach for my phone, about to respond, when a reminder flashes across my screen. *'All-Star Game Catch up.'* My body deflates. The mere mention of spending time with Josh has that effect on me. Yes, he's been better with me recently, but that doesn't mean I enjoy his company. I know he's only playing nice with me because Tate said something to him; he told me as much a couple of weeks ago. Suffice it to say, it didn't make me feel any less of a fraud when he mentioned it in passing.

Plucking a cupcake from my leftover stash, I make my way to his office, papers in hand, fully prepared to show him I deserve the praise I get because of all the hard work I put in. It has nothing to do with the highest player on the team doing my bidding. "Morning Josh," I hum with a little extra pep. I stop in my tracks when I see Jonah sitting next to him. "Morning, Jonah," I add, looking down at the lonely cupcake in my hand. My pulse spikes. Should I go out and get Jonah one too? Or can they split this one?

"Hi Cali, it's nice to formally meet you," Jonah smiles; my legs turn to jelly. Not the kind of jelly they go when Tate's wearing his worn uniform, the kind that makes me worried about my job and my future here. What if Josh told him about my player fraternization? After Tate mentioned a few girls from accounting were dating players, I didn't think it was much of a problem. Maybe it's the Mascot part of my job making it all difficult. Was this Josh's plan all along? To get me fired for dating Tate even though it's allowed.

I look over to Josh to gauge his reaction, but I get nothing. He's too busy staring at his shoes and hasn't even attempted a hello. The saddest thing is, it's probably the nicest greeting the guy has ever given me.

I smile at the two men, knowing it looked awkward, but what else am I supposed to do? The big Kahuna is watching me; I need to play it cool and pretend being fired won't hurt like a bitch. "Nice to meet you too, Jonah. I brought cake." I gesture to the little cake in my hand. "There's more outside," I mutter politely, gently placing the cupcake on the desk and then sit on one of the chairs.

I grin nervously and start adjusting my skirt for something to do as I face them. Jonah gives me a small smile in return, but Josh is still staring at his shoes with his arms folded.

"Do you know why you're here today?" Jonah asks.

I nod, opening up my notepad and placing it on my lap. I play with the pages of the notepad as I say, "yes, Josh mentioned last week that he wanted to go through all the work I've been given for the All-Star game to make sure everything's on track." I held my grimace, embarrassed that my voice was pitching with every extra word. Why are they putting me through this torture? If they're going to fire me, can't they just get it over with?

Jonah looks to his side. "Yes, I saw your workload. It's extensive, to say the least." I don't want to admit this, but Jonah kind of sounds amused. I can hear Josh's shoes kicking together, still completely ignoring this meeting. Jonah glances back at me and then down to the paper in front of him. "I'll take you through the list if that's okay?"

I nod fervently, feeling like one of my Tate bobbleheads. Jonah holds a pen to paper as he starts reading from the list. "Have you arranged the printing and installation of the all-star banners around the stadium?"

"Yes, the banners are being printed today, and they will be installed tomorrow evening." Thankfully, that's the first thing on my list, so it's fresh in my mind.

"Good. What about the press passes?"

"Those have all been sent off with a few freebies to each press office. Maps and instructions were also included, so they already know the timings for the day."

Jonah's brows cross. "What about the promotional t-shirts for the t-shirt gun?" He asks, almost like it's a challenge.

"They've been screen printed and delivered. I'll be able to brief the team on them the day before I get into the Catty costume."

"Have you sorted out Catty's dance routine?" He asks, flicking through his notebook. It feels like I'm in an exam room for an exam I forgot I was taking. Is he trying to catch me out or something?

"Sorted, and the audience interactions have also been planned."

He's silent for a beat, and I wait to see if he has any other burning questions. "Is that all?"

Jonah chuckles. "You've done a lot in the last couple of weeks, haven't you?" I purse my lips, not sure if the question was rhetorical. He blows out a breath when I don't respond. "Well done," he says quickly. I blink at him a few times, processing his words. "I'm impressed you got all of this done so far ahead of the game."

"Um, thanks." I wasn't sure what else to say because this was not how I thought my meeting would go today. Heck, I was fully expecting to come in here and have Josh take out all his frustrations on me like normal. "If that's all, I'll just be heading back to my desk as I've got a few more things to do." I stand, ready to scurry out the room and leave as fast as I can – you know, to give them as little opportunity as possible for them to fire me.

I scurry towards the door, almost home free, "Cali, wait," Jonah says just as I'm about to leave. "That's not all." My body sags; here's the *but.* Here's where he's going to say I've done a great job, *but* I shouldn't be in a relationship with Tate.

"I'm sorry." My face is burning red as I rush back to my seat.

"Did your paycheck come through?" Again, not expected. I swallow, processing the words and doing my best to feel less awkward that he asked me about it. I hated talking about money, especially in front of my boss and my boss's boss.

"Uh huh," I quip.

Jonah relaxes back into his seat. "Great. It was well deserved. We really appreciate all the hard work you've been doing."

What is going on? Am I in the *Twilight Zone* or something?

The back office's head is throwing compliments about me like a priest at church handing out communion. Under my notebook, I attempt to subtly pinch my leg to check that I'm not dreaming. "Ouch." Well, that hurt.

"Are you okay?" Damn it, he probably just saw me pinch myself, and now he thinks I'm crazy.

"I'm fine."

"I also wanted to let you know that we've decided to change a few things around here." My eyes grow wide, my blood pumps. Here's the kicker. They're going to tell me I'm paid for a month, and then, after I've done all the Catty work, they're going to fire me. "It's not what you think," Jonah grins.

Josh lets out a loud sigh, looking out of his window onto the field. I can't believe how rude he's being with our boss in the room. "Looking at the intern's workload, I've decided to shuffle a few things around. So you no longer need to speak to Josh about your assignments. Instead, you'll just go straight to Mary as per the original plan from when you arrived." My eyes flitter over to Josh. His mouth was screwed up while his hands were clenched tight.

Then it hits me.

Is Josh the one in trouble?

"Um, okay,"

"We also don't expect you to be Catty anymore. Tim will be back in action in a couple of weeks, and we are more than happy to say Catty is having a vacation if you'd prefer not to do it until then."

The idea of letting Catty go felt funny. As much as I've hated wearing that stupid costume day in day out, I kind of feel connected to him in a way. I can't just suddenly stop wearing him. I need to say a proper goodbye before that. "I'm more than happy to do it until Tim is fit and well," I blurt out, surprising myself.

Jonah grins. "Well, that's great news. We really appreciate all the overtime you've spent wearing that costume. I know it couldn't have been easy managing your heavy workload and mascot duties." There was a pointed silence. "We'll also make sure you get the acknowledgment you deserve."

Acknowledgment? Would that mean outing me as Catty and Tate finding out that I've been under there the whole time? He'll find out that all those secret conversations he's been having about me were actually *with* me. I wave Jonah off, "No. No. I'm happy for Tim to get all the credit. I enjoy being anonymous. But really, it would make my life a lot easier."

Jonah's lip straightens with that comment, and I notice his jaw tick slightly. "Mhm, well, in this department, we like to make sure the correct people are getting the credit for all the work they're putting in." His eyes drift to Josh for a second, and something passes between them, but I can't figure out what.

Chewing on my bottom lip, I decide it's time for me to leave; they clearly need to talk about something. "Um, okay. Well, I've got a few more loose ends to tie up before the game, so I'm just going to finish those off."

"That's fine. Thank you for all the work you've done for us. You've made a bigger difference than you've been given credit for."

I hate all the praise; it feels weird and makes me uncomfortable. "Thank you for the opportunity. I'll always work hard for the Fish," I say while leaving the room. When I shut the door, I hear Jonah say something to Josh loudly. I would have stayed to listen, but the walls are made of glass, so they'll be able to see me standing there, gawking like a bubbling fish.

Something's going on; I'm not entirely sure what, but I can tell Josh is in trouble. That much's for sure. I need to know what's happened, but the only one who can tell me is the one person I've been avoiding for the last few days. My new boss. Mary.

It takes me the whole day to garner up the courage to go to Mary's desk. She'd sent me a few work emails throughout the day, all pleasant and transactional, like normal, but things weren't normal. Now she was officially my boss and officially dating my younger brother, and because of that last awkward fact, I hadn't spoken to her since Penn's game. It was childish of me, but I needed some time and space to digest everything that happened that day. Having Tate there making my brother's dream come true was already enough of a shock to the system.

Mary bops to the beat in her headphones as I walk to her desk. She doesn't notice me immediately, so I tap her shoulder, making her jump. Her shoulders relax when she realizes it's me. As she pulls out her earbuds, we both say simultaneously, "we need to talk."

I chew my bottom lip because it's a discussion I don't want to have, but we have to have it. She's been my best friend for the better part of ten years, and we can't fall out over this. Silently, she motions for me to follow her to one of the meeting rooms with a large window overlooking the field. I'm still admiring the view when she shuts the door and starts to ramble like she's going to die in the next ten seconds and needs to get this all out before she does. "I'm sorry I didn't tell you about Penn earlier. I wasn't trying to hide anything from you." She fiddles with her hands, and I'm about to say something, but she continues before I can. "That day when I went to meet Penn to watch the game while you were working. He started flirting with me." She chuckles lightly. "Not that he didn't always flirt with me, but something about it this time felt… Different. Something about it made my heart beat faster. It was so loud; I could hear the thumping in my ears." She has this blissed-out smile adorning her face as she talks about my *brother*. It's at this point I'm happy I didn't gorge on those cupcakes; otherwise, Larry might be cleaning up my vomit.

Mary looks out onto the field, sighing wistfully. "Then the next day, he came to my apartment with roses and kissed me. Just like that. It felt right like that's how it was always meant to be between us. It was like I was finally seeing through the fog and seeing him for who he was instead of just your awkward little brother."

I wanted to yell at her and tell her my brother was off-limits because he's only just turned eighteen, but all I could see was hope in her eyes. Who am I to ruin anything going on between them? Plus, Mary's why I got this job in the first place. She's been my sidekick for so long; I can't break her heart like that. As I'm about to open my mouth to say as much, she stops me, seemingly anticipating my next words. "I know. I know. I shouldn't have let it go this far, especially without talking with you first. It hasn't gone that far really, anyway. I mean, we've only been on a couple of dates. After each one, I told him I wouldn't go on another one until he told you, but he's been putting it off at every opportunity."

"Sounds like Penn," I mutter. "But why didn't you tell me?"

She finally breathes in, which is good because I was worried she was going to faint. "You were so busy with work." Her voice trails off as she watches me. "And with all that stuff going on with Tate, I didn't want to add on any more stress."

I know she wasn't trying to blame me, but I couldn't help but think if I'd been a little more perceptive, maybe I would have seen this coming. "So, you and my brother?" I ask, tasting the words as I say them.

Her cheeks flush, and feet shuffle forward. "I like Penn a lot. But we haven't had the boyfriend/girlfriend discussion because I wanted him to talk to you first. So that didn't exactly work out." She huffs out an annoyed breath.

I was silent for a beat, taking all this in. "Okay," I say calmly. Penn's always liked Mary, and if she wants to forget my brother's acne-ridden, fart-popping days, then she can have him. There's no reason I should really push them apart.

"Okay?" Her voice was thick with hesitancy.

I shrug. "Well, you're both adults. I can't stop you from seeing my brother, no matter how gross I think it is." She suppresses the smile from growing on her lips, keeping it to a tiny twitch at the edges. I know on the inside she's dancing. It's sweet, if not a little creepy.

"Really?" She asks again, and when I nod, she squeals so loudly that a few people on the office floor turn to look.

While still in her hold, I say, "do you remember the time I accidently spat my bubblegum into Daisy Lance's hair, and she had to get it all chopped off into that ugly bob that lasted over a year?"

"Yes…"

"Hurt my brother, and that will happen to you, except it won't be an accident this time." She hugs me; it feels weird and kind of gross that my boss and BFF is dating my brother, but what can I do?

"We should go out tonight and celebrate." Her eyes dart across the room as she plans the celebration in her head. All the potential weirdness that I thought might linger disappeared with her last squeal. I'm happy for her, and I suppose I'm pleased for Penn, even if it did make me feel slightly queasy.

"You want us to go out and celebrate the fact that you're dating my brother?" I ask with a raised eyebrow.

She whacks me playfully on the arm. "No, silly, that you got Josh fired," she says the statement so casually, as though she hasn't just blown my mind with that comment.

"What? Josh hasn't been fired." I shut my eyes, replaying the entire conversation with Jonah and Josh in my head again.

She chuckles. "Then what do you call that?" She points across the floor to Josh's see-through office, the one I walked out of not long ago. Sure enough, he's packing his stuff away in boxes. He holds up a baseball, studying the signature on it before shaking his head and tossing it into one of the boxes.

"I didn't do that," I say under my breath.

She rolls her eyes, patting me on the back. "Well, no, you're right. He did it to himself, but someone tipped Jonah off about Josh's behavior towards you and a couple of the other interns. Word around the office is that he was looked into, and he was taking credit for all your Catty appearances," she whispers like she's afraid someone will hear us even though we're in a soundproof glass box.

My jaw slacks; I can't keep my eyes off Josh while he angrily packs away his belongings. "You're kidding? He took credit for Catty?"

Her eyebrows rise as she nods profusely. "It wasn't the only thing he took credit for. Basically, everything you did, he claimed was him. But you haven't even heard the worst part."

"It gets worse. For who? Him or me?"

She chuckles. "Kind of both, except yours has a happy ending. His doesn't. So get this. While you weren't getting paid anything for doing your job *and* being Catty, Josh was taking home a hefty bonus because they thought he was the mascot."

My brain nearly fries. I knew Josh wasn't a nice guy, but I didn't think he was inherently evil. "Did Tate tip Jonah off?" It's the only rational explanation. He had enough clout in the franchise to get it looked into. He was the one to donate the money so I could get paid; he was also the one with a friendly relationship with Jonah. There he is again, taking on one of my battles when I didn't even ask him to.

She tilts her head. "I mean, he might have mentioned something, but I do know someone may have left an anonymous letter on Jonah's desk, informing him of Josh's behavior." The way she said someone, I knew who she was referring to.

My eyebrows shot up in disbelief. "You did that for me?" Her smirk says it all.

She shrugs. "It was the least I could do considering I started seeing your brother without your permission and all."

"Well, I certainly can't say no to you dating him now, can I?" I joke, pulling her in for another hug. "Thank you." I smile into her hair, feeling lighter than I ever have before.

"No, thank you. Are we still BFFs?" She asks as we come out of our embrace.

I raise my fists. "BFFs and the best marketing team here." She bumps her fist with mine, and an unspoken appreciation passes between us.

Buzz. Buzz. Buzz.

"Is that Tate?" Mary asks brightly, looking down at my phone sitting on the table.

"Probably." I pick up the phone, eyeing the message.

Tate: I have a bet with Grayson that you've already eaten all the cupcakes I got you. Let me know. I've got 50 bucks riding on this.

A small smile plays on my lips as I turn and look at Mary, whose broad grin nearly startles me. "Are you and Tate back together now?" Tate never thought we weren't together. She gasps at my facial expression, jumping from foot to foot in excitement. "Oh! What did your parents think of him?"

I lean my knee on the seat of my chair, spinning around to check my emails. My parents love him. Even my mom, who has no understanding or idea of Baseball, couldn't stop talking about him and his positive energy. She wouldn't stop talking about how much our auras complimented each other after Penn mentioned Tate likes me. "I think they thought he was a very nice baseball player," I say calmly.

Her body deflates. "That's it? Nothing else?"

"I didn't introduce him as anything else." I ignore the fact that some of the stuff Penn told my parents could have only come from Mary.

"God, you're annoying sometimes." I feign hurt. "Why can't you just admit what everyone else sees? That you're crazy about him, and he's crazy about you. Why can't you two just run off into the sunset and be crazy Catfish lovers?"

I tilt my head, giving her a pandering look to hide my smile. "You know why." I pause because I don't want to go into it.

"Because of Sam."

She rolls her eyes. "This isn't about Sam, and we both know it. You're too afraid to jump into something with him because you don't want to be the one that cares too much. If you really stopped and thought about your logic, you'd see you're already wrong. Tate has put more effort into getting your attention than his batting average this year. He wouldn't be going through all this effort with you if he didn't care."

Chewing my bottom lip, I'm about to argue, but she drops a few magazines on my keyboard instead. "I put these on your desk this morning, but I guess you were too busy with work to notice them."

Right there on the front page is Sam's big perfect, and maybe slightly plastic face staring at me with a ring on her hand. Theo Leitch is right behind her, and the headline reads. *'Finally Engaged!'*

Mary makes a little smug noise as I study the paper. "Skip to page eighteen, paragraph three."

I take my time reading the words, surprised at Tate's statement to the magazine. He congratulated the happy couple and said he was delighted that they *both* could move on from their relationship.

It was nearly midnight when I got home because the subway took longer than usual since someone inadvertently pulled the alarm. The person thought it could just stop at any point and get off with no issues. It took thirty minutes for the guard to explain the button should only be used in emergencies, adding another thirty minutes to my never-ending journey home.

Exhausted, I clamber up the steps, cursing myself for not putting Tate's gifts in my locker because they were so bulky and heavy.

The long and grueling journey motivated me to save up all the unexpected paychecks and buy myself a nice used car. Driving to the stadium would be more affordable than renting somewhere closer.

Plus, I liked my place. I didn't want to move. It might be meager and nowhere near as grand as Tate's, but it's mine. My little corner of the world.

Emphasis on little.

As the rickety elevator dings onto my floor and the door opens, I look up, thanking the elevator gods, something I always did when I got into this thing. After the first time, I got stuck in it for an hour with one of my neighbors who had sushi, which would have been fine if it weren't seventy degrees outside and we had air conditioning. Spoiler alert, we had neither. When I look ahead, I stop in my tracks.

My door.

What the hell has happened to my door?

I shuffle forward, dragging the gifts and my bag down the hall. I tilt my head, inspecting the door as I stand in front of it. The peeling green paint with red underneath is gone, replaced with a beautiful shiny blue. Perfectly painted. I lift my hand to the middle of the door, where a silver catfish knocker has been installed. I play with the tail, lightly knocking against the wood. *Tate.* I haven't responded to his messages today because I've been too busy. Little did I know that he's been spending one of his days off sanding down and painting my front door.

A scurrying noise startles me, and a mouse squeaks across the floor. I'll admire the door in the morning when I feel a little safer. When I open it, there's a lone envelope sitting on the floor. I know it's from Tate before opening it.

Cali,

I hope you like your door. From the first moment I came here, I knew I wanted it to reflect your personality. Bold. Passionate… and slightly unhinged. I hope you like it.

Tate.

P.S. Don't worry. I fixed your hinges too.

I laugh out loud at his stupid letter, still in disbelief that he would take the time to do this for me. I wonder how long it took him and why he would spend an entire off day during the season just to paint my door. Those days are precious and few and far between. Then Mary's words ricochet through my mind. *This isn't a game to him. If he didn't want you, he wouldn't be trying this hard.*

It left me to wonder why I've been trying just as hard to prove to him and myself that he means nothing to me. Was it because I didn't want to get hurt, or was I too afraid to admit how much I liked him? Since he came into my life as more than just a player I admired, it's been like I'm on a rollercoaster, never knowing what will happen next, but I liked it. No one has ever gone to such an effort, and maybe it was about time I started appreciating it.

I rummage through my bag, looking for my phone. Tate stopped texting me after I thanked him for the cupcakes; I'm assuming it's because he was busy here.

Cali: The door. What can I say? It's fantastic. I love it. Thank you.

It didn't take long for Tate to respond, and his message was waiting for me after I'd put my PJs on and brushed my teeth.

Tate: You're welcome. I'm guessing this means you haven't tried the bed yet…

The bed? I glanced at my usual seersucker sheets, and nothing looked particularly different from when I left it this morning.

Tate: Sorry if it crossed a line, but a girl like you deserves to sleep on clouds, not on spears.

Spreading my hand, I flatten it onto the bed, pushing down and groaning when I feel the soft, supportive cushion. The killer spike I used to avoid is gone, replaced with more memory foam than I know what to do with. Carefully, I edge onto the bed, worried I might break it or that I'm still on the train on the way home, and this is all a dream.

As my body sags into the bed, the mattress holds firm around me. It feels like I'm melding into it. That somehow, I'm becoming one with the firm cushioning around me. With every move my body makes, my aching muscles relax, and that tension headache slowly starts to melt away. Being massaged by memory foam, the only other time I've felt this good was when I woke up in Tate's bed, and that mattress was expensive. If he bought me the same one, it's potentially the most expensive thing I now own.

Buzz. Buzz.

My eyes fling open in surprise. I completely forgot about Tate, too busy deliriously enjoying how the bed soothed my muscles. It's so deep; it takes me a few seconds to roll over and reach my phone to check his message.

Tate: Can I assume you're not responding because you're enjoying the mattress?

Tate: Hold that thought. Enjoying the mattress…I'm getting some pretty good images in my head right now.

Snorting, I pull the sheet over myself and nestle further into the bed. His playful tone makes me want to be playful back. Daring even. I type and re-type the message out to him countless times, second-guessing myself, wondering if I should do it. He may be trying to win me over, but would that be going too far? Finally, I type out a message and then delete it quickly. *Should I do it?* I bite my lip, lift the sheet, and look down at myself. Before I can send anything, Tate messages me first.

Tate: I got you the mattress with the extra layer of memory foam and may have upgraded your pillows too.

I giggle, snuggling down into the pillows. This really is a dream. Everything is so comfortable and perfect; it doesn't seem real.

Another buzz from my phone.

Tate: Please tell me I haven't offended you.

The poor guy. I need to respond before he comes over to check I'm okay. I chew my bottom lip one last time before building up enough courage to lift the sheet up and take a picture of myself in bed. He sent me one from a similar angle before. All he'll be able to see is my catfish tank and silky blue shorts to match.

Attaching the picture to my message, I write:

Cali: Now you've done it. I'm never leaving the bed.

Tate: [Fistbiting Gif]

Tate: As long as you let me join you sometime.

Cali: I'll think about it.

Tate: Oh yeah? What will you think about?

I pinch my brows.

Cali: What do you mean?

Tate: When you think about letting me stay over again. Will you think about the first time I was in bed with you? When I nudged your tiny panties to the side and put my fingers knuckle-deep inside you? I loved watching the way you squirmed and how your pussy glistened.

It's my fault he's sending me these messages. But sending that photo, I initiated the potential sext session, but I didn't realize Tate would talk quite so openly or quickly about the subject. I can feel myself heating at his words, and it's not from embarrassment. He just had to go and remind me of that, didn't he? Pressure builds between my legs, and I start to subtly rub my thighs together to try and ease some of the tension.

Tate: Your pussy tastes delicious, by the way. Strawberry champagne. I first realized that's what you tasted like when you were dripping on your office notes. Do you remember that?
Cali: That's not something I could forget.
Tate: Good because that's something we'll need to do again and again. Your pussy is too delectable not to eat out daily.
Cali: You're so bad, Tate.
Tate: You're not stopping me. Is it because you're thinking about the time you were in my bed, and I was inside you, playing with your clit while your pussy squeezed me tight? That was a good day too.

I need air. It seems now even when Tate's not around, I have difficulty breathing. The pressure feels more intense, and a tingly feeling grows in my core. My fingers itch because I want to touch myself to relieve it, but it feels strange. Not the touching myself part, but doing it while Tate texts me and knowing it's him I'm thinking about.

Tate: Right now, I'm thinking about the time my cock was in your mouth, and your tongue was skating across it before you popped it out to lick up all the precum from the tip. I swear I nearly fainted when you flicked the underside and refused to put me back in your mouth until I begged for it.

I wanted to write something back. Something that would turn him on as equally as he was turning me on, but I didn't know what to say. My brain was a little fuzzy because the throbbing between my thighs made it hard to focus.

Cali: I was actually thinking about when you took me from behind when I was on all fours in nothing but your catfish socks. I loved the feeling of you pulling at my hair as you thrust inside me.

I press send, cringing at my own words, hoping I didn't embarrass myself too much. I'm still so hot, contemplating what I should do about it.
Another message comes through.

Tate: God, Cali, you make me so hot. I want to touch you so badly, to tease your clit, then roll it around on my tongue until you scream my name, so your whole apartment block hears. Then once you've come, I want to do it all over again.

Then he sends a picture through, one that nearly makes me drop my phone in surprise. There, in my messages, is a picture of Tate's hand stuffed in his boxers, holding his clearly rock-hard erection. My mouth waters, and my body aches. I want to touch him just as badly, but tonight, I'd have to settle with touching myself.

Tate: Send me another one, gorgeous. Let me know I'm not the only one getting hot over here.

My hand is already dangerously low, dancing around my thighs. I'm hot and burning up looking at the picture he sent me. I shimmy the boxers down to my midthigh, then place my palm over my mound. My body jerks at the touch, already feeling on edge. I take the picture quickly because I want more relief than just the palm of my hand can provide.

He can't see much in the picture; my thighs are bare, and my hand covers my center, but the placement of my fingers hints at exactly what I'm doing. Once I send the message, I drop the phone and close my eyes, letting my imagination take over. I think about Tate touching me like he did the first time he invited himself up. I mimicked the way his fingers danced across my slit as he entered me slowly, only to pull out and rub soft circles around my clit. Moaning out his name, I wish he was here with me, touching me.

As I rub my clit faster, I think about how his tongue flicked against me. Then I slow, the same way he did.

With every motion of my fingers, I'm closer to the edge. Tate's bringing me there with just his memories. I need it to feel more like him, though, so I add an extra finger, stroking myself from the inside. That extra thickness is just what I need; my body vibrating now. My hips jerk towards my touch, and I know I'm close.

I want to come.

I need it.

I move my fingers quicker, biting down on my bottom lip, waiting for the crash of pleasure because I'm on the edge. Just a little more.

My orgasm takes over when I imagine Tate's tongue skating across my sensitive nub again. My body slacks against the bed, my breathing ragged as I try to gain some composure from the most intense orgasm I've ever given myself.

With shaky hands and a spent body, I lay on the bed, staring up at the ceiling.

Buzz. Buzz. Buzz.

Tate: Oh man. That picture. Your fingers. Are you touching yourself?

There's a time delay from that first message to the next one.

Tate: You there? Because I may have just had a little too much fun imagining what you were doing while you weren't responding.

Cali: Sorry. I was a little busy. I may have had a little too much fun too.

Tate: Glad to hear it. Must admit, I didn't expect our text exchange to go that way.

Cali: Me either.

Tate: It was hot.

Cali: It was. We should do it again sometime.

Tate: Nah, next time I'm over, just show me what you did. Then I'll show you.

Cali: Sounds good.

Tate: Well, California. You've exhausted me. I feel so used and spent that I'm not sure I'll be able to wake up for the All-Star Game tomorrow.

Cali: Hey! You can't do that. I never would have sent you that photo if I knew it would affect your focus.

Tate: Typical. All about the baseball.

Tate: And orgasms.

Cali: Very funny. On that note, we both need to get some sleep for the big day tomorrow. I already know I will have trouble getting myself out of this cloud of a bed tomorrow. Thank you again, Tate. I love it.

Tate: Anytime, Cali. Goodnight gorgeous.

Cali: Night

I toss my phone on the nightstand, feeling slightly giddy as I sink further into the bed. That little encounter was unexpected but much needed. The mattress soothes my aching muscles as I close my eyes and drift off to sleep.

Thinking of Tate, of course.

CHAPTER 28

TATE

Holding onto the lapels of my tux, I stretch my neck, trying to get comfortable. I may only be in this for a couple of hours, but I already miss my usual sweats. I tug at the cufflinks, so the white of my shirt peeks out, just below my jacket sleeve. The last time I had to dress this fancy was when Sam dragged me to some stupid movie premiere. I already felt awkward and out of place with all those Hollywood celebrities, but she made it ten times worse when she asked me to talk to one of the producers for her. She wanted me to convince him they should create a show called *Baseball Wives* since when she tried before, they weren't interested. That should have been a serious red flag, especially since we weren't married, and I'd never proposed; but it was easier to go with her than deal with the wrath if I didn't. What a stupid waste of time that whole thing was.

Grayson slides up next to me, already smiling and waving at the crowd of fans that have shown up for the red-carpet event. This is the third time we've walked this red carpet together - the first time as each other's dates, though. Grayson usually flies solo because no woman can stand to be with him for longer than thirty seconds, and for me, it's because it's the first time I've been able to come without Sam. She'd never miss an All-Star game and would spend two months prior getting our outfits coordinated. At that point, I wouldn't know if I was in the game or not, but she'd buy them just in case. "I'll never get tired of the all-star games," he says proudly.

We wave at the cheering fans as we stroll down the expansive walkway. The setup for this game is incredible; with the red carpet and cameras everywhere, it doesn't even look like a stadium. "Don't get too used to them, old man. Max could take your place in a heartbeat," I say through a tight mega-watt smile.

He throws his head back, howling in laughter. "Old man? Firstly, I'm a few months older than you. Secondly, as if Max is anywhere near my level of greatness." I suppress an eye roll, knowing a camera would pick up on it. "How many times have I won the Cy Young award now?" He raises a finger to his chin in thought. "Oh, that's right. *Three times.* How many times have you been MVP?" He knocks on my shoulder, still laughing. I shake my head, not bothering to answer. He can be an ass when he wants to be, like when he told the batters what he would throw just to put them off. Someone will knock him down a peg or two one of these days.

The place is littered with players from both sides of the league, their wives, and families in tow for the photos. But, my eyes were only searching for one person. Cali. After finding her door 'catfished,' she thanked me. When she saw the mattress, I got more than a text. I got a hot picture of her in some Catfish pajamas I didn't even know we sold. All I knew was that I wanted to buy as many pairs of them as possible.

I admit I got carried away, and we may have had a little sext exchange. One that made painting that door all the more worth it and helped relieve a little stress before the game today. This morning, she sent me a picture of herself licking the catfish knocker. I know I've said before that anything she does can make me hard, but that was off the scales hot. She was definitely teasing me.

All the gifts and our little text exchanges have given me hope that maybe she's willing to give us a chance instead of running away. I've made it clear to the press that I'm not interested in Sam, and the stories have died down since the All-Star hype increased. Therefore, it feels like things are moving in the right direction, and I can't help but think that maybe Cali's finally coming around.

My eyes flick around the venue, hoping to get a hint of her. Every time I see a flash of blonde in my periphery, my eyes immediately whip in that direction, but I'm always disappointed. "Come on; we promised we'd talk to Sienna before the other reporters." Grayson reminds me.

The reporters were lined up on one side of the carpet, and our newest on field reporter, Sienna, was standing to the side. She had a small smile on her face when she noticed us coming. The bright red of her lips perfectly contrasted her impeccably coiffed brown hair and cat eyeglasses, a little too glamorous for my taste, but she was gorgeous nonetheless. "Do you think she'd be up for a contract date?" Grayson whispers in my ear. We're close, but not close enough for her to hear that.

"Nah, I heard something is going on between her and - " I can't finish the sentence because my brain can only focus on one thing. Cali taps Sienna on the shoulder, telling her to move further down the line. The black dress she's wearing hugs every ounce of her curves perfectly. I'd never seen her in something so fancy. It made me want to accept some of those movie premiere invites again. Just so I could peel her out of a dress like that at the end of the night. It was the first time I wanted this game to end so I could pick her up and take her home. So focused on Sienna, she hadn't noticed me yet.

Talking into the miniature microphone that was balancing by her cheek, she's utterly oblivious to my stare, which is probably for the best. "Dude, you're drooling so hard right now; we might need to get a mop." Grayson laughs when he realizes who I'm looking at. "You've got it so bad. She must have a gold plated pu-"

I hold my hand to his mouth, nodding to a couple of Brody Winterlite's kids skipping past. "Hey, Brody, looking forward to playing with you today." I smile, pretending my friend wasn't about to defile his children with the filthiest mouth on the planet.

Brody waves, but his wife pulls him in another direction, giving Grayson an annoyed glare. He really doesn't work well with the fairer sex. "Your voice carries, G. Don't say crap like that in front of kids." He shrugs, tilting his head in Sienna's direction.

"She's waiting for us." He was referring to Sienna, but all I could think about was Cali, who was still standing close by, talking to some other reporters. Grayson pulls me to the camera and hugs Sienna. I hugged her, too, watching Cali scurry around behind her. She still hadn't noticed me, and if last night hadn't happened, I'd think she was purposely avoiding me.

"Grayson, Tate. You both look fantastic. Who are you wearing?" She specifically admires Grayson's dapper pinstriped three-piece Gray suit. He went all out tonight like he does for these things.

"Brioni." Grayson flashes a smile and the lining of his jacket simultaneously. His number peeks out underneath, and I groan audibly, knowing the camera might pick it up. "Do you like it, 'Enna?"

Oh God, he's given the new girl a pet name already.

Sienna pushes the microphone into my face, prompting me to answer. I was so busy watching Cali flip her hair over her shoulder, I hadn't noticed she and Grayson had finished their conversation. "I have no idea who I'm wearing," I admit to the disappointment of Grayson while I play with my black lapels. At least, I think they're black. They could be navy, for all I know. "Chrissy picked it out."

"Uh oh, did you just break all the Tater Tot fans' hearts?" She keeps that well-trained smile on her face as I look at her with a hint of confusion. I never get asked about my love life. I have a strict rule after the whole Sam debacle went viral. Sienna wears a tight smile, urging me to continue with her eyes. Then it hits me; my publicist must have talked to her because they've wanted me to clear this whole Sam mess up for a while now.

"Chrissy isn't my girlfriend." I chuckle lightly, thinking of the 67-year-old grandmother who has better taste in men's clothes than me. "She's my stylist, and her husband is an ex-marine."

Sienna squints. "That's a good way to dodge the question, Tate." She laughs lightly in that fake reporter way. I take my eyes off Sienna for a second, noticing Cali is watching me. When our eyes meet, it's like a bolt of electricity sweeps through my bloodstream. She offers me a half-hearted wave as her eyes drag down my body, taking my suit in. Her eyes widen and a small smile curves on her lips. Oh yeah, she likes what she sees. I'll need to give Chrissy a bonus at this rate. Cali breaks out of her trance when someone calls her name, and she turns to talk to them. I can't hear what she's saying from here, but I imagine her honey-toned voice, and it makes me a little hard.

"Tate?" Sienna pushes the mic further, and Grayson elbows me, eyeing me with an annoyed glare. "If you want to know if there is someone special in my life, then you're just going to have to wait to find out." I can feel the evil grin growing on my face as I think about everything I have in store for Cali. She has no idea what's coming her way. Let's just say the marketing department can't wait for our baseball love story to unfold.

"Well, we all can't wait to see what you mean by that." Sienna winks at the camera and then looks towards us. "Are you both enjoying yet another appearance on the All-Star team?"

Since the mic is still on me, I decide to respond first. "It's incredible. You just have to love every moment of it because you never know when it's going to be your last one, so I try to soak it all in."

Sienna giggles. "Ah, don't say that. We're hoping you'll be here for the next twenty years."

Grayson throws his head back, howling in laughter. "If old man Tate is still here in twenty years, the Fish have major problems they need to sort out."

"What about you, Grayson? Starting pitcher for the National League must be an honor." He looks her up and down, a wolfish grin growing on his face. "Oh, I'm extremely blessed to be standing right here, 'Enna." He coos her name, and I'm impressed because she seems to have an uncanny ability to ignore him. I wish I could do that.

The crowd starts chanting as my face appears on the big screen above. "Do you hear that? They're chanting MVT." Sienna says. My new nickname – MVTee, as they like to say. "If we go back to the regular season for just a second, Tate, you just hit your 34th home run last week. That ties with your career-high at this point in the season, and you're six homers ahead of Brody. Do you think you'll be able to maintain these numbers to get MVP?"

Grayson pushes me out of the way. "It is 100% about time Tate won that. Stats don't lie. He's going to be MVP this year. I would put my house on it." Coming from anyone else, I'd be flattered, but Grayson doesn't own a house, just a bunch of apartments.

"Big words. We can't wait to watch you guys play today," she says, wrapping up the interview. Before we start with the next reporter, I take my time looking around at our pimped-up stadium proudly. Cali told me about how Larry nearly fell from the ladder while hanging the banners, how a green carpet arrived instead of a red one, and how she was the one who arranged the seating plan for the photographers. Today marks the first day seeing her since Penn's game because she was putting all of her efforts into making this amazing.

As much as I enjoy this game, I can't wait for it to be over so I can finally see her.

I know I've got it bad when I watch her walk away from the reporters and back into the stadium. She said she'd only be out front and visible for the first hour, then she had some back office admin tasks to do, so she would have to watch the game from the TV inside. I had an inkling she might be doing something else, but I didn't want to push her by asking about it.

Not just yet because I have another plan on the cards.

My helmet lands on the floor with a thud. We didn't win. We weren't even close.

"You played well." Brody Winterlite offers me a high-five, positivity radiating off him. The dude was too preppy for words with his bright white smile and perfect features.

I slap his hand because I don't want to leave him hanging, not because I feel like we deserve it. "We all played well. It's just the American league played better." And that was the scariest fact of all because we'll have to play one of them again if we make it to the World Series. At least all the best players aren't on one team.

Brody shrugs. "They're a little too competitive sometimes, don't you think?" I nod, picking up my scuffed helmet from the floor. There were too many instances to count of their arrogance. One of their pitchers thought pitching with one eye closed would be fun; another batter danced and did a 'selfie' as he walked the bases after scoring a three-run homer. I wished we'd beaten them.

"Baseball is about having fun. Remembering the times you watched it with your dad and playing with a group of guys, not trying to act like a gassed up asshole." He's right, even if he does sound like a sappy Hallmark movie. It's just easy to forget when you're so caught up in stats and MVP candidacy.

"Yeah, you're right." I wipe my helmet down before hanging it in my locker. I wasn't about to admit it to Brody, but I was stressed about maintaining my streak of homers. Expectation was pounding down on me in all directions. This could be my last chance as MVP with all these younger players coming up.

"You know what I like to do when I'm stressed?" He asks, seemingly reading my mind. "I like to look up at the mascots and see what kind of stupidity they're up to. It makes me laugh but also reminds me to have a good time and give the fans something to talk about."

My mind floats to Catty and how much fun he had today, trying to get the most paid players to sign their money over to him and then pretending to play a virtual reality version of the game in front of him. Stupid stunts, but the crowd loved it, and I loved Catty. "Your Salamander is the living breathing embodiment of that," Brody says.

"It's not a salamander… It's a catfish." I correct, but he doesn't notice because the rest of the team walks in. While we congratulate each other on the game, my mind is focused on one thing. How quickly I can get this over with and get to Cali. Now that this game is over, she'll want to put her feet up and relax. After our sexting session last night, I texted her this morning, inviting her back to mine tonight. I'd planned dinner and thought she might like a soak in my giant bathtub with all the work she's done. Maybe I'd offer her a massage to help her sore muscles while she's in the tub. Obviously, I'd have to be in there with her if I wanted to give her a full body massage. All kinds of thoughts ran through my mind, and not one of them was decent.

It was another 45 minutes before I could leave the locker room. After showering and getting dressed, I lost track of time because I talked to the other players about their families and the rest of the season. It's not often that we get to chat in a non-competitive environment, and I enjoyed it.

I stroll out of the locker room, ready to make my way to Cali's desk. Hauling the bag over my shoulder, I ran a hand through my still wet hair, ready to see my girl and claim all that was rightfully mine.

Clicks of heels moved behind me, but I ignored them, solely focused on my very own little Carolina Catfish (AKA Cali). For dinner, I wanted to surprise her and take her up to my private rooftop terrace since she hadn't seen it yet. It's the perfect temperature for her to look at the pretty lights while I look at her pretty pus-.

"Tate."

I stop.

That voice.

My heart sinks.

The one person that's been getting in my way of making Cali mine this entire time is now here, cockblocking me again.

CHAPTER 29

CALI

Trudging down the hall, my legs feel like trees trying to root into the ground, and my shoulders ache from the weight of the mascot costume. I can't wait to get this thing off. After a full day of setting up, I had to take the fish reigns again and work my butt off in the Catty costume for over six hours. When the game was through, I thought I'd finally be able to relax, but Mary forgot to mention that Catty had a photo session set up with some of the younger fans, and it's not like I can reasonably say no to a child.

All I wanted to do was take a hot shower and let the warm liquid ease my tired bones, but even that still felt miles away. Walking towards the ladies' locker room, I was about to turn a corner, but then I stop. Two distinct voices were arguing very loudly.

"I told you not to come here." That familiar voice sneers and my heart beats wildly. Tate's angry at someone, but who? I wanted to walk away, pretend I hadn't heard or interrupted anything, but something about his tone stopped me.

"Did you really think I'd miss your big game?" Her voice is light and way too flirty to be Tate's mom. Sweat prickles over my forehead because he's arguing with a woman.

I need to walk away and let them have a private conversation, but as my feet start moving, Tate's words stop me. "You weren't invited." I have to know what's happening for my own sanity's sake. So I slither to the side, resting my back against the wall, and try my best to bend down and hide behind the water fountain. I know a giant human fish hiding behind a tiny fountain isn't very inconspicuous, but there's no one else around, so it will work for now. "How did you get in the building?" He asks.

The woman lets out a sharp gasp. My mind is working overtime, trying to figure out who he's talking to. "What do you mean I wasn't invited?" She asks incredulously, her nasal accent peaking with annoyance.

I lean over the top of the fountain because there's sudden silence between them. Have they moved further down the hallway? Did they leave to go have this conversation somewhere private?

"Look." Her voice is smoother and calmer than before. "I know we've had some difficulties in the past, but I didn't think this was over between us." *Over between them?*

"You're engaged!" Tate yells, annoyed to the point it almost sounds like he's pulling his hair out. "I thought we'd moved on." My back slides down the wall until my butt hits the floor. This can't really be happening, can it? I must be dreaming. I was supposed to be going to his tonight for dinner, not listening to his ex trying to finagle her way back into his heart.

"It was all a lie. You know how it works. The papers were reporting false stories." I close my eyes. This definitely isn't happening. My tired and confused brain is just playing out my worst nightmare.

"What do you want, Sam?" He grinds out, and I try to bring my hand to my mouth so they won't hear my heavy breathing, but the stupid costume gets in my way. The lack of clean air and darkness is getting to me, the dark, cold feeling of claustrophobia settling in my bones. Any doubt that I was holding onto is gone because he said her name. He's talking to his ex-fiancee, or ex, whatever; the important thing is that she's here for him.

"I want to know why you stopped calling me all of a sudden.

I've missed you. And then when I try and call you, you don't answer." My toes curl, wondering what her definition of recently is because Tate promised me they ended over a year ago.

Wait a minute. That day I told him I didn't want to see him anymore; he had missed calls from Sam on his phone. Is that what she's referring to?

I can't hear Tate's response over my heavy breathing, and color starts to blotch my vision. I need to get out of this costume soon to get some air; otherwise, I might faint. I consider removing Catty's head, so I can hear the rest of their conversation, but the embarrassment of getting caught eavesdropping is too great. I keep it on.

"What?" Sam's shrill cry echoes down the hall. Any privacy they thought they had was well and truly out of the window now. I'm sure Pam heard that all the way in accounting. "Are you *cheating* on me?" Why did I stay here to listen to this? I should have turned around and kept walking like a good little mascot. Instead, I'm hiding behind a dinky water fountain, trying my hardest not to faint while the neon green blotches in my vision get bigger.

"I can't cheat on you if I'm not dating you." I perk up from his response.

"Are we really going to go over this?" I'm hanging off every word, wanting to get more of the story, when someone taps me on the shoulder. I have to whip my head around to get the tapper in view of my tunnel vision. "You dumped me in the heat of the moment…" is all I hear coming from Sam's mouth because a parrot and a kangaroo are looking down at me in confusion.

Can panic attacks cause visions or mirages?

"Are you okay?" The parrot squawks. "I can hear your breathing from in here." It is pretty loud, isn't it?

I try to slow it down while I stand, simultaneously doing my best to listen to Tate and Sam. "I've only ever wanted you, Tate." I can't unhear that, my breath laboring now. The kangaroo tries his best to take my head off; his arms are a little too short to reach my shoulders, thankfully. No one wants to see the hot mess express going on under here. "I've been waiting for you to come to your senses and take me back. I love you, Tate." I can hear the subtle patter of their footsteps as they walk away while the Kangaroo and Parrot stare at me. The air is too thin, and the words too much. I can't handle it, so I let the green flying blobs take over.

That's all I remember before everything goes black.

"Cali?" The voice is distant; a white light makes it hard to see. Is that the good Lord calling me home? Is this what death feels like? Soothing, disorientating, and slightly damp? Wait a minute. If this is death, why is my head pounding like someone drove over it with a scooter? "Cali, I can see your lips move. Are you awake?" The light dims, and I frown. Am I that accident prone that I had to bring *him* to heaven with me?

"Phil?" I try my best to pull myself up with my eyes still closed. "What are you doing in heaven?" I grumble. Don't get me wrong. I like the guy, but not enough to spend eternity with him.

His hands rest on my shoulder, pushing me to lie down again, and he chuckles. "This might be where dreams are made, but you're not in heaven." One eye scrunches open, the colors blurry, but as my senses come back, I know exactly where I am.

Not heaven, but the first-aid room.

"What am I doing here?" I ask and gasp when I touch my forehead. "What the hell happened?" Fabric bandages are wrapped tightly around my head. When I can finally see, I stare at Phil, waiting for an answer, but get sidetracked by his clothes. I'd never seen him in jeans and a t-shirt before. *Does Phil work out?* My hands start twitching, wanting to squeeze his muscles, but I stop myself. I think I'm delusional.

"I wasn't there." He turns around to get some tool out of his drawer. "But according to the Plano Parrot and Kansas Kangaroo, you had a panic attack in your costume and fainted." So, they weren't just in my mind. They were actually there with me.

"How does fainting equate to the giant bandage on my head?" He flashes the light in my eyes again, looking between them. I have no idea what he's doing, but the bright light isn't helping my throbbing brain.

"No, that's to do with the water fountain you whacked on the way down. Do you remember anything that happened before you fell? The mascots said they found you cowering next to the water fountain, and when they tried to help you, it was already too late."

I moan, the memory of everything coming back, and I wished for just a second that I was still concussed so I wouldn't have to remember all the things I heard. Tate was talking to Sam. She wants him back, and I didn't hear him argue against it. Instead, he walked away with her and out of my life. I should have trusted those magazines. He was always in love with her, waiting for her to make the grand gesture. Well, I guess she finally made it.

"Yeah, I remember. I was boiling hot, trying to get the head off so I could get a drink and calm down." Of course, I lie because it's far less embarrassing than the truth.

"You were in there a long time today, weren't you?" He hands me a glass of cold water and gestures for me to open the other hand, dropping two white pills in my palm. "For your headache. You've suffered a mild concussion and will need to rest the next two days. Your parents were listed as your emergency contact, so I called them."

After swallowing the pills, I hang my head in shame. *Why am I so embarrassing and pathetic? And hopelessly in love with my favorite ballplayer?* "Thanks. What time is it?"

He checks his watch. "Nearly half-past ten. You're lucky I was still here when this happened. I was just about to leave. I might have had to cancel a date to tend to you." He laughed.

"Make me feel worse why don't you."

He shrugs. "It's okay. I rearranged it for tomorrow night. No game means no injury for you." His laugh is infectious, but it doesn't seep down to my toes like Tate's laugh. He places another glass of water next to me while I close my eyes, rehashing the conversation I overheard again and again in my mind.

Tate and I never really became an official item. Even though he was willing to fight for me, I kept pushing him away. I came up with every excuse in the book on why we couldn't work. Slowly, he removed every obstacle and made me realize I was scared. Scared of being hurt and falling just as hard in love with my favorite player as the team he plays for. I didn't tell him that I was having a change of heart yet. I planned on doing that tonight at his place. I chew my bottom lip. What if he took my nonchalance as my answer? I thought getting dirty via text would have told him all he needed to know about where my head was at. But even after that, I was coy. I also didn't give him a definitive answer about having dinner with him tonight. Perhaps I made it easy for Sam to walk right in and take what I thought was mine.

"Cali?" My brother's voice breaks through the loudness of my thoughts, and he dashes over to help me sit up.

A whirlwind of red hair comes rushing into the room. "Are you okay, Cali?" Mary asks, pushing Penn out of the way and she studies my bruises. Those pills better work soon because, with every move, my whole body screams in pain.

"She'll be fine," Phil interrupts Mary's freak out. "She just needs a couple of days to rest, and the swelling should go down." *Swelling?* How big is that bump? "I'd keep the bandages on, though. Just in case." Now I'm curious to know what the heck happened to my forehead.

I feel for the bump under my bandage, only succeeding in making the pain worse. Then, turning my attention to Penn, I ask, "where's mom?"

"She asked me if I could pick you up because she was making dinner for Dad."

I look over at Mary, "And what are you doing here?" Her cheeks pinken as her eyes dart between Penn and me. My head throbs more with the implication.

"Penn was at mine when he found out you were hurt. So I offered to drive him." My mouth shuts instantly, and I try to think of anything except what they were doing. "You can stay at mine until you're better if you want? I've got a spare room."

My upper lip curls at the thought, and I have to force it to straighten into a smile. "Thanks for the offer, but I think I'll just stay with my parents." Sleeping in the same house as Penn and Mary. No thanks.

Penn drapes my arm over his shoulder and helps me walk out of the room. Each step and movement hurt. I suspect I have more than a bumped head and bruised ego. My broken heart is radiating pain all over my body. "Did you want me to call Tate?" Mary asks, shuffling behind us.

"No," I say shortly.

She raises her hands. "Woah, okay. I was only asking."

I mumble out a half-hearted apology, which I know she'll accept. Right now, I need things that make my brain hurt less, not more. "Can we just get home? I'm tired and need to forget this day."

"At least this time, your accident wasn't recorded and isn't being replayed on TV." Like I need a reminder of that right now.

"Uh huh," I half-ass.

"Have you got everything you need?" I thought about my phone sitting in my locker and Tate's lone message that I had yet to respond to. I really don't want to deal with that right now.

"Yup. I've got everything." With that, I let Penn lead me to his car and take me home. I do my best to ignore the internet, just in case Tate and Sam got secretly hitched in Vegas, and they're reporting it. It's a long shot, I know, but my little broken heart and bumped head wouldn't be able to handle anything about Tate and Sam.

Chapter 30

TATE

2 hours earlier

"Are we really going to go over this?" Sam stares at me in disbelief. I don't know who's angrier, her or me. "You dumped me in the heat of the moment…" My jaw is tense, and I'm gripping the strap of my bag so tight, my knuckles are going white. "I was waiting for you to come to your senses and come back to me."

She's insane. It's the only explanation for her reasoning. I can see a parrot and kangaroo mascot in my periphery walking down the hall, so I grab Sam's shoulder, pulling her away. "We can't talk here." I gesture my head to the exit, and she follows me. I can't trust her anymore, and I have a sneaky suspicion that she's set something up to record our conversation. Tabloids would love a baseball meltdown.

I drag her to the parking lot and look around, checking it for people. It's late, and players and staff are the only people left in the stadium, none of whom are in here. Now I can finally have a private conversation with her.

She chews her overly plumped lip. It's at least two times bigger than when I last saw her. "Why did you bring me out here?" She asks, toying with the buttons of my shirt. Oh, God, this woman is terrible at reading signals.

I clasp her hands and move them down to her sides. "I brought you out here because I didn't want to humiliate you in front of a couple of mascots when I rejected you." She gasps in surprise. Honestly, she's a terrible actress, but she did seem somewhat surprised, probably more at my tone than anything else. Usually, I'm the sweet-tempered Southern boy, but I've had enough of her today, though, and all I want to do is see Cali. Naked if she'll let me.

Sam's eyes pool; the little game she's playing isn't going to fool me this time. "I missed you." The wistfulness in her voice is almost believable. If I hadn't heard it a million times before, I might think she was actually remorseful.

I shake my head, knowing little wisps of water from my just showered hair will hit her face and not caring one bit. She's the one that invaded my space without asking. "Cut the crap. There are no reporters out here. This conversation is only between you and me. Be honest, or I'll leave."

Her shoulders slump, and upper lip curls, completely changing her facial expression. Her façade has faded. "You spoke to the press," she says flatly, annoyed.

Chuckling, I knew I did something to inadvertently get her attention. "No, I didn't say a word to them. My publicist did because I was tired of you using me to get your face on magazines." And inadvertently cock-blocking me with Cali. Not that I would mention that. Sam would love that side-effect, I'm sure. My eyes narrow, studying her. "Why are you messing with me anyway? Aren't you engaged to Theo?" Surely, she's his problem now, not mine.

Her lips thin, and her left eye starts twitching, reminding me a little of Cali when she's been caught out in a lie. "Not exactly."

I wish I hadn't asked. This is too much information from an ex I don't care for. "Sorry to hear that. Are we done?" I point between us and turn on my heel to walk around the car.

Her pointy nails dig into the side of my arm, and I wince at the pain. "Tate." She pulls tighter. "Come on. Don't be like this."

"Be like what?"

"Like this!" She raises her voice, hoping it will get some kind of rise out of me and is disappointed when she gets nothing. "You're acting like we meant nothing." She hangs her head, the curled blonde locks looking fried on the ends, and a couple of her nails are chipped, a reminder that no matter how hard she tries, she's never going to be as perfect as she believes she is.

"You cheated on me with a football player. We *didn't* mean anything." I keep my voice and face stern. It's amazing how much easier it is to see through their games when you're not around someone. Thank God she cheated on me; otherwise, I never would have met Cali.

With her head still bowed, she wipes her heavily lined lashes and sniffles. How did I not see how manipulative she was before? "You don't mean that."

"Yes, I do." I shake my arm free of her claws, staring down at her. "Now, if you could let me know what the hell it is you want so I can leave." When her eyes meet mine, I can't help but compare them to Cali's. Both were blue, Cali's were full of depth and warmth, but Sam's were piercing and ice cold.

"I want you." I stare at her blankly, waiting for a few beats for her to finish that sentence so it makes any kind of sense. *I want you to mow my lawn. I want you to be my maid of honor. I want you to let me borrow your yacht for the weekend, so I can get drunk and fall overboard, only to ultimately meet my demise by gaters.* All of these would have been more plausible options than leaving that statement wide open.

I stifle my laughter, looking up to the ceiling. I'll never forgive myself for agreeing to go on a date with her. Damn my horny 18-year-old self. I scrub my hand across my face before looking at her again. "If you wanted me, why were you going to the press making up false stories about us?"

"You were ignoring my calls. So I figured the more flagrant the stories, the more likely you'd be to contact me."

Her face shows no signs of any emotion except nonchalance. It's like she thinks this is the normal way to act. "Sam, I don't say this often, but I think you need help. Help that Theo can pay for."

"But Tater Tot." I grimace at the use of that stupid nickname. What kind of man wants to be named after tiny, deep-fried balls? The other players loved it when they found out. "It was always supposed to be you and me."

She drapes her body across my car; I should have thought about this before dragging her out here. I need to try a different tactic to get rid of her. "Sam, I think it's time we moved on. Theo's crazy about you, and he can take care of you just as comfortably as I could." I leave out that I'm making five million more than him a year since I got my new deal because that's just petty, and I'm not bitter. Her only response is sputterings of a whimper. "I think it's best for all of our future relationships if we didn't talk anymore."

Her head whips up while her eyes scrutinize my face. It reminded me of the time I bought her Birkenstocks for Christmas. Apparently, there is a considerable difference between Birkin and Birkenstock. She wasn't happy, to say the least. "Are you seeing someone? Is that why you've been avoiding me."

"Even if I were, it's not any of your business." She's off my car in an instant, close to me now, and looking up at me from chest height. Those six-inch heels made little difference to my towering frame. It's one of the reasons I liked Cali so much. I didn't get neck strain while talking to her, or kissing her, or fu-.

"You are." She gasps, wide-eyed. Her demeanor changes when she sees the truth behind my eyes. Sam looks around the parking lot and huffs out an agitated breath. "Who is she, and how did you meet her?" She makes it sound like she's going to put a hit on Cali.

"It's none of your business anymore, Sam."

"It is if she's taken you away from me."

"That was all your own doing. *You* took yourself away from me, or don't you remember? You couldn't stand having to wait for my big-league contract. One million a year wasn't enough for you, so you cheated on me with Theo." I hated reminding her because it ultimately made it sound like I cared. But, looking back on it now, it was probably the best thing that ever happened to me. Besides meeting Cali, of course.

"Tater –."

I raise my hand. "Stop. That is the worst nickname I've ever heard. Please forget it and forget me. Nothing is ever going to happen between us again." Bluntness is my last resort, and watching her face fall makes me think it's finally worked.

Her chest is heaving, her lips clamped tight. Fury burns behind her eyes, but there's nothing she can do about it. Not now. The magazines stopped calling after I gave them my statement wishing her and Theo well, I changed my number, and after today, I'll block her from entering the stadium again. There's no way she can get in contact with me after this. "Well, she better be worth losing the best thing you ever had." She flicks her hair, shoving my body as she stomps past me on those tiny points. She was teetering on the edges but refused to slow down.

"Good luck with Theo," I call out, only to be met with her middle finger.

I watch her walk away, rapidly pressing the elevator button and kicking the door when it doesn't come fast enough. She nearly trips, and even though hitting metal with your Louboutin's (the only present I ever got right) looks painful, she tries not to show it. The subtle hop from side to side is the only hint that she might be in a little agony. Finally, when the elevator dings open, she limps in and turns to stare me down. Her sour face watches me as I flash her my widest grin and wave goodbye.

As the doors shut, she leaves me with one final parting gift. Her middle finger and the word "dick."

When the doors close, all I'm left with is silence, and I feel a strange peace wash over me. Like the monkey on my back is finally gone. That woman had been in my life harassing me for the better part of seven years, and I let her because I had no time and no one else to pique my interest. Now that I have Cali, I have someone I want to make happy and not just appease.

Slipping into the car, I check my phone and am slightly

disappointed that Cali hasn't responded to my invite, but I figure it's because she's probably exhausted from all the work she did today. I'll just have to treat her to that bubble bath another day. When *she's* convinced, she's the one for me. It's been a struggle showing her how much I like her, but I've enjoyed the chase more than I thought. Most of the time, I've undeservingly had girls falling all over me, and I never know if it's because of my money or if they actually like me. Cali has never once let me think she's easy, and I've had to prove at every point in this cat and mouse game that it's her I want.

I know she's slowly starting to see me for what I am, and a smile spreads across my face when I think about the final surprise I have in store for her. The gifts and door make-over were just the start. When she finds out what I've done, what I know, she'll freak out. I'll have to make sure I'm there to catch her, just in case she falls, which she's apparently so prone to doing. Of course, when the guys find out what I'm planning, they won't let me live it down either, but I don't care. If it shows Cali just how much I want her, then it will all have been worth it.

CHAPTER 31

CALI

"Are you sure you're okay to do this?" Mary zips up the back of my costume with hesitancy. "Tim said he should be able to take over as Catty from Saturday. I'm sure everyone would understand if you wanted to take a break from it."

I'm impressed; she's doing her best to look at anything but the giant lump on my head as she talks. Unfortunately, it's so large that even after a week of icing it, it still looks like my forehead is nine months pregnant. The only good news is that the double black eyes I was sporting (and no one bothered to tell me about) have faded. Only a slight yellow tinge is left around the bridge of my nose and under my eyes.

"I want to do it," I assure her, putting the Chicken vest on over the costume because the game is being sponsored by the local chicken shop, and they thought it would be cute if Catty wore their uniform. So it means that today I'm going to be a half catfish, half-man hybrid dressed as a chicken. Try and figure that one out. "It could be one of my last outings, and I want to make it count." She seems to buy it even though I actually just wanted to do something to occupy my already throbbing mind with anything other than Tate.

Ever since he found out I hurt my head, he's been doing his best to see me, and I've been doing my best to make sure he doesn't see my face. The first few days were the worst; Penn (that traitor) told him where our parents lived, and he came over with a vegan lasagna.

My mom loved it; she went on and on about his beautiful spirit. Then, they spent a wonderful evening with Tate. All the while, I did my best to eavesdrop and feign a fever.

He didn't mention Sam during the entire dinner, but then again, would he? If I'm his side piece and he wanted to ensure that keeps going, then I doubt he would bring up his potential impending nuptials. There was one point when Tate tried to sneak into my room. I knew it was him when the door jangled, and I thanked my fifteen-year-old self for having the foresight to install a lock. I pretended to be asleep when he gently cooed my name, too embarrassed about my pulped face and his impending nuptials to move.

Thankfully, since that night, he's been out of town, playing away games which has made it a lot easier for me to avoid him. Missed phone calls are much easier to ignore than his all-consuming presence lingering behind the door.

I came back to work a week earlier than anticipated to everyone's surprise. Josh was already gone, which meant Mary was there waiting for me with a much lighter workload. So I had to ask for more work which was a first for me. Jonah also gave me a fat check on top of the Catty bonus when he found out all the hours I'd been working. At least, that's what he dressed it up as. I think he was worried I might sue after my incident with the water fountain. Like I'd ever betray the Fish like that.

My head's still a little fuzzy, and every now and again, a sharp pain pierces my brain, but I'd rather be here than sitting at home with my mom any longer. The idea of eating one more vegan hot dog makes me feel sick, and I don't care what the commercials say; they don't taste the same. That, and I also don't want to get any more surprise mail from my mom either. While I was sleeping one morning, she thought she'd be nice and drop off a few magazines for me to read. It was a sweet gesture, and I thanked her for it because it wasn't her fault that the topics on the cover sucked. I can remember the last time I woke up to Tate's face. It was when I was in bed next to him; my fingers were dancing across his abs, contemplating whether they'd make a good tic tac toe board. It was a memory that I wanted to keep because it was the last time I thought I'd see them that close again. He had muscles on top of muscle, I swear. Unfortunately, waking up to his face wasn't nearly as pleasant this time. Yet again, it was plastered all over those stupid magazines with Sam's stupid smiling face next to it.

I flicked to the story, hoping it was just clickbait in paper form. I didn't bother reading the article because the pictures told me everything I needed to know. They were from the all-star game; I recognized Tate's shirt. Sam was leaning her back against the door of Tate's car, toying with one of the buttons on his shirt. It must have been after I heard their conversation. He brought her to his car, and knowing my luck, probably took her home. As if my brain didn't hurt enough from the fall, it was searing with pain after seeing that.

At that point, I made a deal with myself that no matter what happened between Tate and me, I would at least hear him out before confirming our breakup. I know Tate cares about me, the last few weeks have shown me as much, but I just don't think it's as much as he cares for Sam.

I remember that Tate was silent when Sam told him that the engagement rumors weren't true. I couldn't see his face or hear his reaction, which irked me. It made me realize that maybe things aren't going anywhere between us. I needed him to confirm that for my own sanity, but I just wanted to look a little less battered and bruised when we had that discussion.

He's been so persistent to come over and nurse me back to health, I wasn't sure if it was because he wanted to tell me he got back together with Sam in person or if he missed me. So, of course, I lied about how I got the injury. Falling face-first onto one of his bobbleheads sounds just as believable as being dressed up as a fish and fainting on a fountain while a parrot and kangaroo looked on.

What has my life become?

"I can't believe Jonah is letting you do this." Mary shakes her head as she pats down the chicken feathers on the vest. "It's ridiculous. You should still be in bed."

"I'm fine. Stop worrying and hand me my head." I point a fishy fin at Catty's face. His eyes stare at me longingly, waiting for me to bring him to life. When I found out Tim was going to take over next week, I've got to admit it hurt a little, and I nearly offered to be Catty for the rest of the season. But then, a second later, I shut my mouth, remembering that I'd never installed that air conditioning system, and we were heading into August. *Hello, humidity. Goodbye Catty.* Mary chews her lip, looking over at Catty's head reluctantly.

"Do you want me to follow you around? I want to be there in case you fall over again. You don't want to scare the kids." Her eyes are flaring. "Oh, my goodness, imagine the kids if you fell and hurt yourself?" She's being worse than my mom, who was so worried I'd get frostbite from icing my forehead so much, she hid the icepack.

"I'm fine," I stress. "No kid is going to see me keel over today. I promise."

"Are you sure? I read that some concussions can take months to heal. You've only been out a week."

I snatch Catty's head because she's so reluctant to give it to me. "Come on; this is no worse than the time I fell out of the window running away from those cows. I survived that, and I'll survive this."

Mary shudders at the memory. "Who knew cows could run. I didn't know they had knees until that day." She was the lucky one. Being so small, she could fit through the dog door of the barn. I was the one that had to climb through the window to get out. I've never felt closer to death than that day.

"Have you at least got your phone in there? In case you need to call me?" I shuffle my hips to the edge of the costume, feeling the hardness of the phone against it.

"Yes, I do." I don't bother asking her how she expects me to use it without stripping out of the costume. Now that would be a scary sight for the kids. Catty shedding his skin and birthing a fully grown woman. "Okay, the second inning is starting soon. I need to go."

She looks at me one last time, worry etched across her face. "Are you sure you're okay to do this?"

"I'm fine," I say before shoving the fish head over my shoulders and securing it in place.

I rest my back against the concrete wishing the coldness could permeate through to my back. Unfortunately, the sweltering heat is getting to me, and this outing is more challenging than I anticipated. I'm getting dizzier quicker and have to take constant breaks to drink water.

Mary followed me around for the first inning, fussing around me like a stage mom who'd missed her true calling. The only way I could convince her to leave was to tell her that Penn was sitting in the stands today, and he'd watch out for me. It's a lie that I know she'll figure out soon, but I should be out of the Catty costume by then.

The stale air isn't enough to satiate my woozy mind. I need to take this head off, so I place the fin mittens to the side and place both my hands on the fish's cheeks. I lift it halfway off my neck before I hear a voice infiltrate through the mask.

"Hey, Catty." I immediately force the head back on. I still haven't told Tate it's me under here. I figured I wouldn't have to once Tim returned and my face was healed and then we could just go on pretending it never happened. "What's up?" He slaps my shoulder and asks the question like we're old buddies shooting the shit or something. I can't put my finger on it, but something about his tone sounded… Different.

Since my hands are free, I give him a thumbs up. "I heard you had a nasty fall the other day." I sigh; the Parrot and Kangaroo mascots posted about it on their social media accounts, so, unfortunately, it was yet another airing of my clumsiness. Catty had to respond. Obviously, when the Carolina players found out, they were amiss, sending lots of get-well-soon messages to Catty and posting pictures of better times. I was surprised Tate hadn't asked me about Tim's fall when he texted about my own. He was probably too busy scoring a record number of homers since he was still leading both leagues, after all. "Are you okay?"

My back straightens off the wall, and I nod with so much intensity that I make myself dizzy. I really need hydration, but the need to protect my identity is more important. He won't be here long; we're only in the fourth inning, and he'll be up to bat soon, or the next inning will start. So I just need to wait it out, that's all.

Tate leans against the wall, shunting his shoulder and making himself comfortable. I wanted to ask him why he was back here, but I couldn't. He's never back here during the games. Instead, he prefers to hang out in the dugout during games, supporting his team. He blows out a heavy breath and rolls his neck, looking at me. "Do you remember that girl I told you about?"

I wanted to sarcastically ask *which one?* I always thought he was talking about me when he and Catty had their heart to hearts. Now, I'm not so sure. He could have been talking about Sam. Heck, it could have been someone else entirely too. I don't know. I let out an involuntary low grumble, doing my best to turn it into a Tim impression. When I look back to Tate, his eyebrow is cocked, and he's staring at me with a questioning glare. I nod in response because what else was I supposed to do?

"Something happened the other night, and it made me realize just how much I didn't want to give her up." His wording confuses me. Did he mean he gave her up once already? Because he never gave me up. He did give up Sam, though.

"She's got concerns," he continues. "I know she does, but I've got a surprise planned that will show her just how committed I am to her." If my head wasn't throbbing before, it's undoubtedly throbbing now. I want to tell him to speak in English and tell me specifically who and what he's talking about, but the fabric mask is stopping me.

I join my thumb and forefinger in an 'okay' sign because I need to talk to Tate when he knows it's me. Not when he thinks he's spilling his guts to Tim. That would be a crappy way to find out he's interested in someone else.

"Hey Tate, you're on deck next," Austin calls over, hanging from the entrance to the dugout.

He smiles in acknowledgment, whacking my shoulder hard again. Thank goodness for the padding; otherwise, I might have another bruise. "Okay, dude. I've got to go. But thanks again for always being there for me. When I get the girl, you'll be the first to know." He winks and then swaggers off with more confidence than I've seen in him in a while. Obviously, I watch his butt sway for a second or two longer than necessary. It's just so thick and juicy.

By the time he's gone, and I've had enough water to make me feel better, I'm left wondering what the hell just happened between us.

CHAPTER 32

CALI

My brows furrow as I inspect the white fabric hanging over the usual shiny blue Catfish skin. I look around the room, wondering if I'm being pranked. Catty seems the same. Only different. The newly added lips and eyelashes give him a more feminine edge. Add the white sailor-style dress to that, and you'd almost think this was a different character. *Who did this?* "Mary," I call, keeping my eyes glued to the outfit.

I hear her footsteps as she shuffles into the ladies' locker room. "Yeah?" She stops in her tracks when she sees me standing there still wearing my office clothes. "Why aren't you dressed yet? You need to be out on the field in five minutes; otherwise, the music cues will be all wrong." She's in too much of a rush to take notice of the changes and instead pushes past me and grabs the costume off the hanger.

As she pushes the outfit into my chest, I hold onto her shoulders. "Woah, hold on a sec. Was Catty supposed to be dressing up today?" She tilts her head in confusion.

"No? Why does that matter right now? We've got to get you in this and outside as soon as possible."

"I know, I know. But, have a look at Catty." I watch her slowly hold the costume at arms-length, inspecting it.

She gasps when she finally takes stock of what she's looking at.

"Catty in a dress? That's not on the rotation."

On my tiptoes, I grab Catty's head sitting above the lockers and show it to her. "It's not just a dress. Catty's a girl." I point to the pink bow and long blonde hair added to the mascot head. If this weren't so ridiculous, I'd be laughing. Instead, I pull at the ribbon to emphasize my point. "It's been sewn on."

"When did anyone have the time to do this?" She holds the outfit up, and just as she does, a small piece of paper flutters out.

I pick it up, reading the calligraphy writing scrawled across it, "*Catalina*." My eyes widen in realization. "Mary, this isn't Catty at all. This must be his girlfriend." I gasp. "Does this mean I've going to have to keep playing her?"

Mary looks at me with sympathetic eyes. She knows how I feel about this whole thing and how happy I am to put my mascotary days behind me. Continuing on this path is not in my plans. Anxiety builds in my stomach, curling the bile that resides there.

"Maybe it's a one-off," she offers. "Tim's not supposed to start until tomorrow. Maybe he offered to start a day earlier so we could do a cute little sketch?" I take some deep breaths and immediately regret pinching my nose. The bruises there are still tender and hurt to touch. "Jonah would have to ask you to agree to that first, and he would have to run it by me."

My phone's buzzing because I'm late, and I know Barry, the sound guy, will be on my case if I don't get my butt in gear. "Whatever it is, you can speak to Jonah about this later. I should get out there. I don't want to let the team down." Mary looks hesitant before handing me the costume. I ignore her looks, getting dressed as fast as I can.

Under the Sea roars as I stand at the entrance of the dugout, bouncing from foot to foot. With the first beat of the chorus, I run out with an extra skip in my step. I figure trying to be a little more feminine won't hurt the look.

I wave as seductively as one can with a fish hand on towards the players, who in turn play along, pretending to check out my butt. At least, I hope it's pretending. While some of New York's players warm up by throwing a ball, I run between them, trying to catch it, but failing miserably, obviously. Show me a fish with fins that can catch, and I'll eat my shoes.

After a couple of minutes playing on the field, the fans start chanting, "*Cat-ty, Cat-ty, Cat-ty.*" It draws my attention to the crowd, and I smile when I see Tim dressed as Catty standing on top of the dugout. He's pointing at different audience members while pulling out some dance moves that Tim never threw down in rehearsal. Did that broken leg somehow give him rhythm? I swear he was about to attempt the worm.

When Catty whips his head and sees me on the field, the music stops; that lovestruck song you hear in those kids' cartoons takes over. Then, fins on his heart, he drops to his knees, hyping the crowd to no end. This love story must have been what they planned all along. However, I wonder who did this in marketing because usually, I'm part of the meetings.

Catty points his fin, motioning me to join him in the dugout. With an invitation like that, how can I say no? The players and fans cheer me on when I curtsy and skip to the dugout. Weirdly, Grayson is grinning as I walk through the gate he's eagerly holding open for me, watching me walk through. He looks different without his usual scowl, and he normally hates getting involved in my shenanigans. I give him a high-five as I walk past. "Go get him, Catalina," he says my name seductively and winks.

Max and Austin had an arm on either side waiting for me, and I decided to take advantage. I slip a fin through each of their offered arms and let them lead me to Catty. I would have preferred this were choreographed, even if the audience loves it just so I knew what was coming.

Catty is still on his knees, standing on the plastic roof,

pretending to sweat as he watches me make my way towards him. His fin is clutched to his heart as he crawls over, then he jumps to his feet, taking my fin in his. I can see flashes of his skin showing at the edges of his costume, almost like it's a little too small for him. Maybe it shrunk when we washed it.

Catty's thumb grazes across mine, the only visible part of our hands touching, and that in itself made the whole thing feel weirdly intimate. I didn't know Tim was so handsy. There's a callous running along the top of his thumb, which seems odd because I've only ever seen him typing behind his desk for the last six weeks. He must be really hitting the keys hard to get a callous that big.

The kids giggle when Catty lifts my arm up, twirling me around, only for him to dip me down and stare his googly eyes into mine. We're putting on quite the show, and I have no doubt if this does well, they're going to ask me to keep making appearances which is not what I want. I want to retire gracefully, so I'll have to do my best to convince Jonah to tailor this costume to Mary's measurements instead. That can be her comeuppance for dating my brother. Yes, I may have given them my blessing, but it still freaks me the hell out.

It felt like hours of dancing in these costumes under the July heat, but it seemed like there was nowhere else Catty wanted to be. He backs away and points at the big screen above the outfield.

'Catalina' is written across it in bold white lettering, the black background making it easier to see. My name fades away, and another set of words appear in its place.

'When I first saw you, it was love at first sight.'

Catty clutches his heart and points at me. This is a cute idea; he must be confessing his love to me, or, I should say, Catalina, and he wants all the fans to witness the start of our love story.

Catty wraps his arm around my shoulder, pulling me as close to him as the costumes allow. I wrap my fin around his waist, kicking one leg up so my skirt flares to give the audience a show. There are coos and aws alongside the cheering this time.

'Did you know that catfish mate for life?'

He's looking at me, expecting an answer, and I shake my head. I wonder who approved that wording. Is that appropriate for kids? Catty backs away and drops onto one knee. He feels his pockets searching for something but comes up empty. The crowd roar, thinking he's about to propose to me. Dancing on my toes, I bring my fins to my mouth in excitement, waiting for the proposal to happen. This is going to be so cute. Except, I only have a fin and thumb visible. Where on earth is he going to put a ring?

Catty points at the screen again, drawing my attention to the final words because I'm too busy watching him.

'There is no other fish out there for me.'

'Will you please be my girlfriend?'

The crowd is chanting now. "Yes! Yes! Yes!" He hands me a rose that Austin was holding. At least we won't have to deal with where to put the ring. I nod my head enthusiastically and jump up and down, clapping my fins together in excitement. He, in turn, jumps up from his kneeling position and hugs me. I'm laughing inside the costume because I can't think of a better way to end my time as Catty.

He hugs me tightly, soaking in the audience's cheers. It startles me when he suddenly moves away. His fins grab his head, and I can tell he's about to out himself as Tim instead of Catty, which would be a crime against Mascots. Tim exposes his neck, which seems to be a lot thicker than I remember. Anger boils over. I want to kill him. All the hard work I've put into playing Catty, and he's going to ruin it on his first outing. What an idiot. I might just break his leg all over again.

I shake my head, trying to grab him with my fins, but it's no use. He's going to reveal himself, and all I can imagine are the children's screams and cries in my head when they find out Tim decapitated Catty. That is not how this love story should end, but what more can I do? My life moves in slow motion as he lifts the head further up.

Realization over what's happening sinks in when I see the stubble on his chin…

CHAPTER 33

TATE

I throw the Catty head to the floor, ignoring the children's cries and screams as I unmask their favorite mascot. The only person I can see is the half-fish, half-girl standing in front of me. Sweat drenches my hair, and I'll need a shower before the game, which is in fifteen minutes, so I'm glad I convinced *Chally Sports* to push back the starting time a little. I don't know how she stays in that hot suit for so long, but it makes me admire her that much more and gives me a whole new appreciation for what she does for the team. I should have donated more money to pay for this kind of sweat and determination. At least I know Jonah gave her a fat bonus for all this work.

I flick my hair to the side; the only thing I can do without the use of my hands, and draw my attention back to the crowd, who have been quiet since I 'killed' Catty. When I wave to the masses, I flash them a smile, which makes them roar in appreciation. I guess finding out your favorite mascot is also your favorite player isn't such a bad thing.

I turn back to Catalina, or should I say Cali, and laugh. She stands there frozen on the spot, the only movement coming from the twill of her skirt in the wind. Too shocked to move, her back straightens like I've seen her do so many times - in and out of the Catty costume. Now that I know it's her under there, I can't believe it took me so long to figure it out. The way Catty's arm's flail and the hop in his step has always been Cali. Not to mention how much she clams up and gets all flustered at the mere mention of his name. It's like she's been cheating on me with the mascot or something.

I pull my fins off, throwing them down into the dugout where Catty's head ended up, and stalk over to Cali, who's quaking at the end of the dugout. I can see Grayson in my periphery, smiling and hollering. If the only thing our friendship ever fosters is his help in this moment, I'll be forever grateful. Catalina's costume is perfect, and I only have Grayson to thank. He got his tailor to make a bespoke outfit in three days for this, and it's perfect. Before reaching Cali, I give him a thumbs up and a wink. I'm doing it. I'm finally getting my girl and making those damn magazines shut up about Sam.

Gently placing my hands on either side of Catalina's cheeks, I try to look into her eyes, asking permission to unmask her. It's hard because I can only see little black dots as holes. She doesn't stop me when I lift it slightly, so I keep going. In fact, she hasn't moved since I took my head off – stunned into paralysis. I want to get her head out of the way just to make sure she's okay under there.

When I pluck the head off, Austin catches it in the dugout, and I'm finally able to see Cali. The girl I haven't been able to stop thinking about since I first saw her. The girl who is the perfect mix of neurotic and sexy. She's staring at me with wide eyes, her mouth gaped open in confusion. Wisps of blonde hair are stuck to the sides of her face, neck, and forehead with sweat. Tinges of yellow and purple surround her eyes and nose from that fall against the fountain. My heart constricts because she's still the most breathtaking woman I've ever seen. Nothing is ever going to change that.

I bring my hand up, and she jumps in surprise when I place my palm on her cheek. Her glassy and confused eyes focus on me, waiting for an explanation. I grin, leaning my forehead against hers. "You said yes to being my girlfriend, Cali. You can't take it back now."

My smile grows wider, barely acknowledging my words. "What the... Huh. How did you know it was me under here?" She rattles out, confusion and hesitation running thick through her voice.

I chuckle, shaking my head. "I've known it was you under there for a while now." She looks down, her fins visibly shaking, her eyes darting from side to side. No doubt trying to remember all the times I've talked to Catty and figure out when I realized. I've had an inkling since she was in my apartment, acting all jittery like she needed her next hit at the mere mention of the mascot. It all came together when I saw Catty straighten his back one day. It was so familiar and distinct. After that, I went rooting around the marketing department and got Josh to confess who was under there to Jonah. Apparently, the asshole told Jonah it was him to get a bonus. That little tidbit and his behavior towards Cali all led to his firing.

Once I knew it was Cali, everything made sense. It wasn't Catty that was my lucky charm. Whenever Catty was standing on the dugout, and I'd batted in a run or scored a homer, it was her bringing the luck. It's always been her. She's the reason and the motivation behind doing so well this season. If I get MVP, it will be because of her, and she doesn't even realize it.

She's still quiet, so I use the tip of my finger to draw her eyes back to mine. Her perfect blue orbs stare at me. I want to kiss her so badly, but first, I need to make sure she wants this. "What do you say, Cali? Will you be my girlfriend? No pressure or anything." Only Cali could hear me over the chants. I laugh when the crowd chants *MVT* again. She nods slowly, huffing a breath out and nearly falling.

I break out in a grin, pulling her tighter into my arms, so happy we can finally admit to everyone that we're together.

Kiss.

Kiss.

Kiss.

Grayson starts, and the chant catches on. The big screen has a blue heart around us, and *Kiss Me* plays in the stadium. This moment is perfect. I look back down at her still shocked form. "Is that a yes? You'll be my girlfriend?" I needed to hear her say it. A nod wasn't enough.

"Yeah," she wisps out. That's enough for me; I can't wait any longer. Raising my hand to her chin, I bend down and seal my lips against hers. A buzz of energy ricochets through me the minute our lips touch. It's been too long since I've kissed her and really felt at home. We're both sweaty, flustered, and tentative with the cameras on us, but it's a kiss I'll never forget.

When I pull away, she grins manically, and I smile back. She nuzzles into my neck, embarrassed by all the attention. I lift her up into my arms in a bridal carry and walk her back to the field where Tim waits in a Catfish-themed golf cart. Apparently, health and safety forced them to sell the ATV after it dented the dugout. Since it was the one that nearly offed me, they auctioned it off and got a considerable sum to donate to the children's charities of Charlotte.

Cali's holding her skirt, trying to cover the Catfish's modesty, mumbling and grunting with every step. I had difficulty hearing her complaints because she's snuggled so far into my neck. Finally, I gently place her onto the golf cart. She's still just as flustered as when I took Catalina's head off. "Are you okay?"

She bites her bottom lip while grinning and nods fervently. "Well then, wave to your fans," I say, half-joking as I do exactly that. The crowd is going wild for it.

When I sit next to her, I grab her hand, rubbing soft circles around her palm. "I can't believe you did all this," she says, still in disbelief.

I stop waving at the crowd for a brief moment and look at her. "Why? I already told you, I always get what I want. And I want you." I wink cheekily, and she laughs. Then, Cali's face turns serious for a second. "You good?"

She answers by placing her palms against my cheeks and gently kissing me. "You know this is going to be all over the internet, right?" She says when our lips part.

I laugh at her flustered cheeks. "It's better than the last time you went viral, I suppose. You remember, right? When you humped my leg." I chuckle as Tim starts driving the golf cart across the field to one of the exits.

She pushes me gently. "Did you have to remind me?"

Wrapping my arm over her shoulders, I kiss her temple. "I will always remind you because it was the first day we met. So, therefore, it was the best day of my life."

I can see the hint of a smile below as she draws her arm around my torso, hugging me tightly. "Plus, if I had known it was you, I wouldn't have stopped it." She giggles at that. "Wave to the crowd, Beautiful," I whisper, kissing her forehead before raising my hand and waving to the fans myself as we ride off into a tunnel.

Today has been perfect.

Just like her.

Epilogue

TATE

A Couple of Months Later

Panting, I lock the entrance to the locker room, thread a bat through the handles, and roll a metal crate full of bats in front of the door. *That should do it.* I pause for a beat, fold my arms, and proudly admire my handiwork. They aren't going to be able to get through that quickly.

I wipe the sweat from my brow, still feeling the prickle of perspiration from all the hard work on the field. Luckily, I got out of there before they could throw a bucket of water over me and ruin what I had planned.

The crowd is so loud; I can hear the cheers reverberating off the walls in here. Celebrations are high, and my adrenaline is still pumping, knowing that we've made it through to the playoffs and that I've played the best year of baseball in my career. This is my MVP year; I can feel it in my bones. And see it in my stats.

Walking further down the tunnel to the changing portion of the locker room, my eyes soften when I see Cali sitting there. Back straight, playing with her fingers, waiting for me. She's in that damn pencil skirt again. It makes me rock hard every time I see her in it because it reminds me of the time I ate her out on the desk. Something we've done several times since. With a few variations, of course.

She looks up when she hears my footsteps. "Tate," she breathes out, running towards me and jumping into my arms. "You did it!" I catch her with ease, pecking her on the lips while walking her towards my locker. "I'm so proud of you." Her husky, whispered tones turn me on more than I care to admit.

"I know." I can feel the grin slowly growing on my face because I know what we're about to do. When I get to my locker, I lean her back against it and plant a final longing kiss on her lips. When I finally pull away, she looks a little delirious. We haven't even started yet.

She slowly opens her eyes, a small smile brushing the edges of her mouth in satisfaction. "Why did you want me to meet you down here?" She asks with pinched brows. "You should be out there celebrating with your team." I stifle a laugh.

"I can celebrate with them any time." I balance my arms against the locker, so my hands are on either side of her face, surrounding her. "I'm perfectly fine in here," I husk out, studying her features; the soft point of her nose perfectly frames the arch of her lips. I can study her face for hours and still not feel prepared enough to take an exam on it. "Celebrating." I continue, kissing that sweet spot behind her ears, and she gasps, clasping my wrists. "With you." My lips travel down her neck. If she didn't already know what I wanted, I make it perfectly clear when I push myself against her core so she can feel just how hard I am.

A moan erupts in her throat before she forces my gaze up. Her eyes are dancing with trepidation as she glances down at my used uniform and then over my shoulder. "We can't do *that* in *here*," she says, aghast.

Ignoring her, I go back down to bite her neck. "Mhm, why not? We've done it before." I remind her with a tongue swipe across her collar bone. "We've played in your office. Now it's time to play in mine." Little bites across her skin have her almost forgetting. Her legs loosen their grip against my hips, and the rest of her body relaxes as she gives in to me.

"What if they come in?" She asks half-heartedly while moving her neck to give me better access.

Chuckling into her skin, I say, "the guys will be out there celebrating for a while with the fans. We have enough time before we're disturbed." Her hands grip my shoulders, enjoying the way my tongue and lips work against her neck. "I may have also blocked their entry."

"What?" She asks, pulling away to force me to look at her. When I give her a grin in return, she smacks me on the shoulder. "You're so bad, Tate." Her eyes sparkle with mischief. She isn't stopping me, which is a good sign.

"You're the one who told me that you wanted me after a sweaty game." Her eyes track down to my sweaty, dirty uniform. I may have played rougher today just to ensure I got enough sand on it for her. She lets out a little flustered mewl while she bites her lip and looks at me bashfully. "What better game than the one that secured us a playoff spot?"

My hands dance across her hips, down to the hem of her skirt, just above her knees. Her breath catches when I scrunch the fabric, pushing it above her hips. I waste no time because we don't have much. My fingers skate to her core, flicking across her lacy panties and tickling her gently. She closes her eyes when I dip my finger underneath and start softly stroking her smooth flesh, feeling just how aroused she is by this scenario.

"Mhmm," she moans out in approval while I move my fingers across her pussy and slide my middle finger into her warm, slick heat.

"You feel so good." I lower my head, nipping at her neck and letting her body balk against mine. She wants more friction, and I want to give that to her. Cali throws her head back in pleasure when I lightly graze my thumb across her clit. Her head bangs against my locker loudly. I hope it leaves a mark so I can look at it day in, day out and be reminded of her.

"Wait." Her groan fills the room, and I release the warm skin of her neck from my mouth. "This isn't how it's supposed to go." Cali's fingers clasp my shoulders, pushing me away. "If upstairs was your fantasy, then down here is mine." The disappointment from our disconnection is short-lived. I grin because today is one of those days when she wants to take control, and I'm not about to deny her. I never do.

"What's your fantasy, Cali?" I ask, a wicked smile tainting my face. She smiles back; her eyes focus on me as she slides down my locker. She doesn't stop until she's on her knees, directly in front of my crotch.

Her eyes are locked with mine as she unbuckles my belt, shoving the bulky material down just enough to get my cock out. I purposely took off my jockstrap between innings, playing a dangerous game when I went to bat, but looking down at my girlfriend on her knees, drooling at my cock made it all worth it. Her hand wraps around it as she places the smallest of kisses on the tip.

I groan, rolling my head back in pleasure. I'm already losing my mind, and she's barely touching me. Then, when I've gained enough composure to look back down at her, she's licking her lips, enjoying the taste of my precum. I can't deal with the relentless teasing. Partly because I know we don't have much time, partly because I know just how good her mouth feels.

I shift my hips in her direction, urging her on and hoping she takes the hint. I lose all sense when she takes the tip into her mouth, letting her tongue skate across the skin there. Her lips curve into a smile as she watches the torture she's entailing on me. I didn't think it was possible to get any harder. I'm already feeling faint due to how horny I am, But that move alone, with that devilish glint in her eye, has my dick straining for her to lavish it with more attention.

Cali traces her lips around the head. Tickling her tongue all the way down the shaft to my balls, palming them when she gets there. She knows how much that move drives me wild and tortures me on purpose. I watch as she stretches her mouth over my length, letting her tongue tease my cock as she moves her head up and down. Pathetically, I already know I'm close. Cali on her knees, next to my locker, combined with adrenaline from winning, is already proving too much for me. A few more strokes, and that will be it.

She pops my dick out of her mouth, pumping languidly while she gently sucks at the tip. When Cali makes that move, I know I'm in it for the long haul, but we don't have time for such a lavish display on my cock. There's no time for indulgence because the guys can come back here any minute.

I needed to be inside her before that happened.

"Cali," I grit, unhappy that I have to pull her mouth away from me. Then, clutching at her waist, I pull her up, pushing her back against my locker. "I want you," I ground out, lifting her already ruffled skirt up and out of the way. She yelps when I grasp at the edges of her panties, ripping them off and stuffing them in my back pocket.

I give her no time to take in what I've done because in one full motion, I wrap her legs around me and thrust into her. She cries out in pleasure as I feel her heat gripping around me. This is exactly where I belong - with hands on either side of the locker and her legs wrapped around my hips. Pleasure unfurls between us as I thrust into her faster.

With every thrust, I know we're one thrust closer to getting caught. We don't have much time, and I want her to come before this ends. Snaking a hand between us, I play with her clit, rubbing quick circles while I continue to pulse in and out of her. Cali's breath is hitching, her body getting more rigid with every move. All signs she's about to come.

I grin, nipping at her neck, enjoying the fact that Cali loves this so much. It's her fantasy, after all. I toy with her nub faster, and she starts to clench around me. We are both on the edge. Then, just as she starts to moan out her orgasm, I feel a wave of pleasure take over and my body rigidly moves against her as I come inside of her.

As I open my eyes, I take in ragged breaths, trying to calm down. I swear this girl's a better dopamine hit than a world series win.

Her breath is fast as she clings to me. Evidence of what we just did, drips between us, and the air is thick with the smell of sex. Her eyes are closed, and a peaceful expression plays across her face as she comes down from her high. When her breathing calms, I kiss her on the lips. A quiet moment after a hasty session between us. "That was amazing," I whisper. "I'm not going to be able to come in here without getting hard anymore."

A light laugh escapes her lips. She's still a little delirious in her post-orgasmic haze.

"What's going on?!" A loud voice shouts from outside, banging the doors and jolting both of us back to reality as I go soft inside her.

"Shit. They're coming," I say, pulling out and unclasping her legs from around me. When she's safely on the floor, I push her skirt down. It's a crinkled mess, a clear sign we'd been up to something, but at least she's decent. Then, I pull my pants up quickly.

She fiddles with her messed-up blonde bun nervously. "They can't see me like this. It will be obvious we've just had sex." Her crumpled skirt and less than modest unbuttoned shirt would most certainly give it away.

Sounds of wood breaking mean we don't have much time. The minute that bat gives way, my teammates are in here whether I like it or not. "You need to hide," I whisper, looking around the room to find her the best spot.

Footsteps echo down the hall, getting closer, so I have to take matters into my own hands. I open my locker, pointing inside. I ignore the surprised look on her face because we don't have time and shuffle her inside. It looks uncomfortable in there. What with her bent knees and lowered head. We have no choice, though, and she'll be fine in there for the next few minutes.

I shut the door just as the guys starts to walk in, laughing and pushing through. "What's up with the door?" Max asks, walking to his locker and throwing his mitt inside. "Why was it barricaded?"

My brows furrow in mock confusion, and I walk over to where he came from, pretending to investigate. "I have no idea what you're talking about. I came in through the back of the field to get a drink ten minutes ago. I wasn't here for whatever happened." After the first sentence, I should have stopped talking, but I was still a little hazy after my orgasm and worried they would find my folded-up girlfriend in the locker.

Max shrugs it off, seemingly too blissfully happy with our win to care much about my jittery explanation. The rest of the team bound in, singing at the top of their lungs. Too busy celebrating to acknowledge me, they push past and head out the door. When I look over to Max curiously, he answers, "we're going downstairs for the Champagne shower celebration." How could I forget that celebration? I'll need to go down there once I get Cali out of her cramped metal prison.

He throws a black shirt at me, which I catch with ease. Opening it up, I smile at the postseason slogan Cali helped come up with stares back at me. I love it. "You coming?" He asks while everyone else stumbles past us, excited to celebrate.

I ball the shirt up in my hands. "Yeah, I'll be there in just a second. I've got to see Cali first."

Max grins. "Don't take too long. I want to give you the champagne shower you deserve, MVP." He follows behind the team's furor, and I casually lean against my locker, waiting for the rest of them to pass. There's no noise from Cali in the locker; the holes in the metal were the only thing that made me sure she didn't run out of oxygen in there. I can only hope my socks aren't gassing her from the inside.

It takes five minutes for the room to clear out, and I can finally open the door to my beautiful but slightly flustered girlfriend. "Finally," she gripes, clutching the sides and clambering out as fast as she can. "What is this?!" She shrieks, shoving a little black velvet box in my face, her eyes filled with worry and confusion.

I smirk, looking at her outstretched hand. Then, placing my palm over the box and take it from her. "Did you go through my bag to find that?" I ask with amusement. This wasn't how it was supposed to go, but things were never straightforward with Cali.

"What else did you expect me to do while I was in there?!" Her arms flail everywhere. She starts pacing back and forth in front of me, her whole body in a state of panic while she thinks through the ramifications of this little black box. "We've talked about this before, and I'm not ready for marriage. I'm only twenty-three. I can't have babies just yet. What are they going to learn from me? We haven't even been together that long. Are you sure you want Catfish obsessed children?" I let her babble on for a few more seconds.

She's flustered and panicking; it's kind of cute. I hold her hand, stopping her in her tracks. Silently, she stares at me, waiting for my response. All I do is put the box back in her hand. "Just open it," I say with an encouraging smile.

Cali slowly dips her head down to look at the box in question. She watches it cautiously like it's going to bite her. Then, before she opens it, she swiftly closes her eyes. The silver glints across her face, but she doesn't see it because she still has her eyes squeezed shut. "Open your eyes, Cali," I say gently.

She takes in a deep breath, then slowly opens one eye. When she sees what it is, her other eye springs open, and she glares at me with surprise. "It's a key to my apartment," I explain as the light reflects between us.

"Your apartment?" Her head tilts in confusion. "Is this a joke?"

I shake my head. "No. We've been together for a few months now; I thought since you're over there most nights and it's closer to the stadium that you might want a key." What I really want to say is, *'I know you're it for me. Move in with me and make me the happiest guy in the world.'* But that will scare her away, so I keep it brief and logical. "It also means I'd be able to see you more during the off-season."

She rocks on her feet from side to side, plucking the key from the box and studies it. "You want me to live with you?" The confusion in her voice is sweet and so misplaced.

"It could mean that if you want it to. Or it could just be a key so you can crash there when you've had a late night at work." She purses her lips. "You could even use it to surprise me naked in bed if you were that so inclined." I wink, trying to ease any tension she might have from the offer. Commitment seems to be something Little Miss Collins is afraid of.

She shows me the key. "You really want me to have this?" The hope in her voice makes my chest constrict.

There's nothing I want more than to share everything I have with you, I think, but again keep it to myself.

"I wouldn't have emptied half of my closet for you if I didn't." There's a soft twinkle in her eye when she smiles at me, surprised. "What do you say? Do you want the key?"

Chewing her lip, she studies it one more time, leaving me sweating while she thinks through the offer. "Yeah, I want the key."

I drop a kiss on her lips, sealing the deal. "Good." When I lightly whack her on the ass, she squeals. "Now let's go celebrate this win… and you accepting my key."

As we walk out of the locker room, I hold her hand, feeling lighter and happier than I've ever been in my life because not only have I just secured a place for the team in the playoffs, but I have the girl I've always wanted by my side. She isn't just accepting a key to my apartment, but the rightful place in my heart too. "Can we install the Catfish knocker on your door?" She asks playfully.

I kiss her palm. "Of course." Whether she was ready to hear it or not, I couldn't wait to spend the rest of my life making her happy, even if it meant installing a front door to my penthouse apartment so she could have that damn Catfish knocker.

THE END

Next in Carolina Catfish Series: *The Balk (Grayson Hawk's Story)*

KEEP IN TOUCH

Join Ana Shay's Newsletter: bit.ly/3aoS59z

Follow her Instagram: @AuthorAnaShay

Made in the USA
Middletown, DE
31 October 2024